"This is amazing," Lense said.

"Sonya, can you turn about ninety degrees to your left?"

Gomez turned slowly, taking small steps, until she faced the outside wall of the ring. About three meters ahead of her was a large reddish lump, about the size of a shuttlepod. It differed from its surroundings because some of its surfaces were curved panels, relatively smooth and unmarked compared to most of the rest of the ship.

She stepped toward it. Her extended foot seemed to twist to the right, pulling her off balance.

"The IDF doesn't entirely compensate for the corolis effect. We need to be careful moving at right angles to the direction of spin. Take baby steps."

Heeding her own advice, she shuffled toward the object, but she still felt dizzy.

"These suits still need a little work, Tev," she muttered, reaching out and leaning against the object of Lense's interest. A large, tree-trunk-like projection emerged from the object, made a right angle turn, and met up with the floor. It made a convenient seat.

"Okay Elizabeth, what's so interesting?"

"The crew never left. There are bodies on the ship. I'm picking up twenty-three, and there may be more around the ring out of tricorder range. Their construction is silicon-based, but the metabolism isn't entirely chemically-based. I'm still figuring it out."

Gomez looked around. She didn't see anything that looked like a sentient being. "Are any of these bodies close to us?"

"I think," said the doctor, *"that you're sitting on one."*

STAR TREK®
CORPS OF ENGINEERS

CREATIVE COUPLINGS

John S. Drew, Glenn Greenberg,
Glenn Hauman & Aaron Rosenberg, David Mack,
Dayton Ward & Kevin Dilmore, and
J. Steven York & Christina F. York

Based upon STAR TREK® and STAR TREK: THE NEXT GENERATION® created by Gene Roddenberry and STAR TREK: DEEP SPACE NINE® created by Rick Berman & Michael Piller

POCKET BOOKS
New York   London   Toronto   Sydney   Risa

Pocket Books
A Division of Simon & Schuster, Inc.
1230 Avenue of the Americas
New York, NY 10020

This book is a work of fiction. Names, characters, places, and incidents either are products of the authors' imagination or are used fictitiously. Any resemblance to actual events or locales or persons, living or dead, is entirely coincidental.

Star Trek® S.C.E.: *Paradise Interrupted* copyright © 2004 by CBS Studios Inc. All rights reserved.
Star Trek® S.C.E.: *Where Time Stands Still* copyright © 2004 by CBS Studios Inc. All rights reserved.
Star Trek® S.C.E.: *The Art of the Deal* copyright © 2004 by CBS Studios Inc. All rights reserved.
Star Trek® S.C.E.: *Spin* copyright © 2004 by CBS Studios Inc. All rights reserved.
Star Trek® S.C.E.: *Creative Couplings* copyright © 2004 by CBS Studios Inc. All rights reserved.
Star Trek® S.C.E.: *Small World* copyright © 2005 by CBS Studios Inc. All rights reserved.

STAR TREK and related marks are trademarks of CBS Studios Inc.

CBS and the CBS EYE logo are trademarks of CBS Broadcasting Inc. All Rights Reserved.

This book is published by Pocket Books, a division of Simon & Schuster, Inc., under exclusive license from CBS Studios Inc.

All rights reserved, including the right to reproduce this book or portions thereof in any form whatsoever. For information address Pocket Books Subsidiary Rights Department, 1230 Avenue of the Americas, New York, NY 10020

First Pocket Books trade paperback edition December 2007

POCKET and colophon are registered trademarks of Simon & Schuster, Inc.

For information about special discounts for bulk purchases, please contact Simon & Schuster Special Sales at 1-800-456-6798 or business@simonandschuster.com

Manufactured in the United States of America

10 9 8 7 6 5 4 3 2 1

ISBN-13: 978-1-4165-4898-0
ISBN-10:   1-4165-4898-X

These titles were previously published individually in eBook format by Pocket Books.

CONTENTS

PARADISE INTERRUPTED
by John S. Drew
1

WHERE TIME STANDS STILL
by Dayton Ward & Kevin Dilmore
97

THE ART OF THE DEAL
by Glenn Greenberg
181

SPIN
by J. Steven York & Christina F. York
277

CREATIVE COUPLINGS
by Glenn Hauman & Aaron Rosenberg
337

SMALL WORLD
by David Mack
465

ABOUT THE AUTHORS
529

Dedicated to the memory of
Rabbi David M. Honigsberg, 1958–2007

PARADISE INTERRUPTED

John S. Drew

For Raymond Hoblock Sr.
For a man who worried about everything,
you never once questioned my dreams
and schemes, no matter how crazy they may have
seemed. Thank you for being my friend as well as
my father-in-law. We all miss you.

ACKNOWLEDGMENTS

It's short but sweet, folks:

First and foremost, to Keith R.A. DeCandido. We've been through a lot together, from being "loquacious" in English class in high school, to the Wednesday Night of Cheesy Movies, to *The Chronic Rift*, to this. Thanks for always thinking of me and for giving me this opportunity. It's been fun.

Next comes Susan Drew, my better half and my editor. Like Jean-Luc Picard, I spell knife with an "n," and this piece looks as good as it does thanks to this woman.

To my son, Edward Declan, I say thanks for letting Daddy use the computer for a while. You can get back to playing with Elmo and Clay.

To my family, Mom, Dad, Denis, Anna, and Bridget—I know you don't always understand me, but I hope you enjoy reading this.

To my friends, the Geek Patrol, of which Keith (Edit Boy) is a founding member: Orenthal Vance Hawkins (Hawkman), Marina Frants (Tall Cool One), and Andrea Kristin Lipinski

(Lipchick), thanks for being understanding when I missed out on Wednesday nights.

To those who inspired me: Gene Roddenberry, David Gerrold, Robert Heinlein, Kenneth Johnson, Ben Bova, and Alan Dean Foster. It's your fault I enjoy writing as much as I do.

CHAPTER 1

"Please hang on, sir. We'll have someone out there as soon as we've reestablished power in that region." Shira, a senior technician for the Risan Operations Unit, pulled her earpiece away as the sharp squawk emanating from it became too much for her sensitive ears. She quickly lowered the volume and made another attempt. "I am sorry for the inconvenience, sir, but—"

She was cut off by an even louder tirade of expletives that would have made even a Nausicaan blush. "Please try to be patient, we—" The signal suddenly stopped. Shira wasn't sure if it was the guest's doing or another fault in the system. She hoped for the latter as the guest and two of his companions were hanging from the side of Catona Bluff, a popular rock-climbing formation on Risa. Their antigravity belts had been rendered useless as their power, along with all energy circulating in the region, had mysteriously vanished. The drain was so intense that Shira couldn't even get one of Operations' flyers in the air to rescue the three.

Shira tapped in a request from her keypad for a ground team to make their way on foot to the bluff. Unfortunately, it would take at least an hour to get there. She sighed and looked around the circular control room at her fellow technicians, their faces looking as tired and frustrated as her own. Their consoles were all lit up a bright red, indicating technical problems throughout the Monagas Peninsula, one of the most popular regions on the planet.

"I realize it's not supposed to rain, ma'am, but I'm afraid it's out of our control at the moment," she heard Milan, who was sitting next to her, say a little too wearily for her liking. Despite the troubles they were facing, it was important they maintain a positive attitude. Risa was the number-one destination resort planet in the Alpha Quadrant. It got that reputation because of its constant, stable climate, its attractive landscapes, and most of all, its very friendly staff.

But at the moment, the first two attributes were being threatened. The weather control system appeared to be breaking down. As a result, several popular areas in the region were literally being washed away by developing, heavy storms.

Shira turned back to her own console and groaned as she watched another five complaint calls line up in the queue of forty on her viewscreen. She closed her eyes and thought about how nice it would be to sit out on the white sands of Monagas Lagoon. The only problem was that most of the beach had been wrecked by a freak rainsquall that ripped through the area earlier that day. This had been the third power loss in as many days.

The swishing of the doors to the control area and the shrill voice of Tonais, director of the Monagas Lagoon resort, drew her from her thoughts. Shira said a quiet prayer, asking for strength to get through the moments to come.

"And I'm still waiting for an explanation for all this." Tonais was speaking to his assistant, a mousy little individual with his nose buried in a large data pad. He stopped short, his assistant nearly colliding with him. "Technician Shira, correct?"

Shira turned around in her seat to face the two, not attempting to rise. "Senior Technician, yes," she responded, making every effort to keep her tone even. The director had been a general pain in the neck since the crisis had begun. Granted, a great many of the complaints from the guests had fallen on his plate, but his hourly visits to the Operations Unit just seemed to add to their problems.

"Have you come to any conclusions, *Senior* Technician?" His tone dripped with sarcasm as he uttered Shira's title. He was decked out in a long flowing robe that didn't cover enough of his girth for Shira's satisfaction. He wore no shoes, and he tracked sand into the room. It was clear that the director had no respect or concern for anyone but himself.

"None, sir." Shira hated admitting it. She rose from her chair and gestured toward a map of the southern hemisphere projected on a large viewscreen overhead. Pulsing maroon indicators winked on and off in one particular area. "All we have so far is that this wave of freak—" She held up a hand to halt the oncoming protest she saw brewing in the director's eyes. "I'm categorizing them as 'freak,' since I can offer no cause for these problems—freak power outages that began in the Monagas Peninsula and are now spreading to other resorts in the region."

"There is no such thing as a freak occurrence, Senior Technician," Tonais responded. "At least, not when it comes to a magnificent system such as ours. There are fail-safes, backup systems. Why are they not engaged?"

"They have been, Director, and in some cases they are working normally."

"In some cases?" he repeated slowly.

"Whatever is affecting our systems is affecting them too."

"But those are independent arrangements, Senior Technician. You cannot tell me this is a freak occurrence too?"

"I really don't know what to tell you, sir," Shira replied, wincing as she brought her shoulders up in a shrug. She didn't like appearing so incompetent, especially in front of Tonais, but the answers were eluding her.

"Excuse me, Director," the assistant squeaked, not looking up from his notepad. He had a deep nasal tonality to his voice. "But we're getting a report from the resort. There are three rock climbers trapped on the side of the bluff."

Shira winced again. She was hoping to deal with this situation on her own.

"Well," Tonais snapped, "take care of it."

"I'm afraid it's not that simple, sir." The assistant looked up for a brief moment. Although his head was completely bald, he sported a thick mustache that curled on the ends. Shira thought the two were an odd pair. If the situation wasn't so desperate at the moment, she might have almost allowed herself to laugh aloud.

"You see, the transporters have no power to their systems and we can't seem to get our flyers off the ground. The climbers were equipped with antigravity belts, but they won't function."

Tonais's eyes flashed with anger. "You call this a freak occurrence too? I want more than a pat answer to all this!" He tapped his assistant on the shoulder. "Have a rescue team organized to ascend the bluff and get those people down!"

"I already—" Shira started to explain, but was cut off.

Tonais whirled toward Milan. "You! Contact Starfleet Command!"

Shira followed the director. "Starfleet Command? Don't you mean the nearest Federation representative, sir? Ambassador Li—"

"No, I want Starfleet Command. They're the only ones who can handle this situation now."

"The only ones?" Shira's voice began to rise in anger. "With all due respect, Director—"

"No," he cut her off, "don't say another word." He leaned over to Milan. "When you have Starfleet, get me Captain Montgomery Scott of the S.C.E. division."

"S.C.E.?" Shira was confused.

"Starfleet Corps of Engineers," Tonais explained, nodding his head and adding with a note of hopeful confidence. "They'll get to the bottom of this."

"But sir—" Shira tried desperately to regain control of the situation.

Tonais turned to face her. His facial expression had changed, softened somewhat. "Please understand. We cannot afford to have this kind of interruption in services for any lengthy period of time. At the moment, we are preparing to receive a group of scientists from throughout the Federation for a symposium. Some of the guests are already here. If word gets out that we are not capable of accommodating their desires..."

He didn't need to finish the sentence. Every person in the room, indeed, every Risan knew of the importance of total guest satisfaction.

"I have Starfleet, Director," Milan called out. "Captain Scott is waiting for you."

Suddenly, the lights in the room dimmed. Monitors began to wink out one by one around them. The large overhead viewscreen faded to black.

"This is intolerable," Tonais muttered. Aloud, he said, "Captain Scott, this is Director Tonais of the Monagas Peninsula on Risa."

The only response was static that faded away as the lights in the room continued to ebb.

"Get them back!" Tonais barked.

"I can't, sir." Milan moaned as he tried to comply with the order. "We're losing power to our systems."

Tonais turned his questioning gaze to Shira, who could only answer him with a confused stare.

"Now what are we going to do?" the assistant blurted out as the darkness engulfed them.

CHAPTER 2

"We'll take the north and you take the south end," Commander Eddie Johnson gestured toward the map that lay in front of him. "Any questions?"

Silence was the only reply. He couldn't help but smile. This was good. His people knew their jobs.

"All right, then," he said, giving his traditional thumbs-up. "Let's move out."

Eddie crouched into a squat position and moved with precision toward his goal. With each step he glanced around and brandished his phaser rifle. He was pretty sure they weren't prepared to deal with any heavy resistance and hoped that they would make it to their target without being seen.

As they neared their goal, Eddie felt both excited and nervous. He could make out the imposing target. The large monolith hung over the entrance to the temple. It seemed to look down on Johnson's team with a mixture of amusement and boredom. The team slowed their pace and waited as Eddie looked over their objective with a careful eye.

They say it's an exact representation of their god, Eddie thought, giving the one-eyed statue a defiant glare. *He's about to meet his match in Commander Eddie Johnson of Starfleet Command.*

Eddie gestured to the others to prepare to move out. With silent precision, Eddie and his team advanced on the temple, rotating the point as they moved forward. It didn't take long before they reached the entrance. Eddie stepped up to the dull gray metallic door and examined the keypad on its left-hand side. It seemed a simple enough device—almost too simple—which was why Eddie was going to handle cracking its code rather than having his science officer attempt it. Commander Eddie Johnson was not about to risk any of his crew on such a dangerous task.

Eddie noted the ten-digit entry system and closed his eyes as he tried to figure out the exact sequence to open the door. His team waited in silence; an air of tenseness around them caused Eddie to break into a sweat. If he failed to open the door on the first try, heaven only knew what fate would befall them.

He reached out with a shaky finger and began to tap in the code. The keypad buttons lit a bright green with each successful entry. Eddie worked his way through the first three numbers of the code without any interruption. He stopped for a moment and exhaled nervously.

The final number.

It had long eluded a number of people who had made the attempt to break into the temple. There were tales of the consequences of failure, but Eddie refused to be swayed by such rhetoric.

He could make out the reflection of his crew behind him in the door. They had seen him through a number of tough situations and he in turn had not failed them yet. He hoped he wouldn't now. Saying a silent prayer, Eddie ran his hand through his strawberry blond hair as he tapped the final number in the sequence.

The lights on the keypad blinked out.

A low whine filled the area.

"Get out!" Eddie barked to his crew as he started to back away from the door.

"Eddie!" an angry voice stopped him dead in his tracks. He

turned around slowly to see his father standing in the doorway opposite him. With his hands folded across his chest, his father had a look in his eyes that Eddie was all too familiar with—exasperation.

"What do you think you're doing?" His father said each word slowly and with great effort as if to keep from shouting.

Eddie looked futilely around the room, hoping that a member of his crew would appear to help bail him out. He wasn't getting such aid now.

"Well, it's like this, Dad. Starfleet contacted me and—"

"Stop right there, young man." His father, Ray Johnson, cut him off in midfantasy. "I've told you to stay away from that room, haven't I?"

"Yes, sir." Eddie looked down at his feet. "It's just that—"

"You're bored. I know. But I don't understand it, Eddie." The senior Johnson gestured out a window at the tropical paradise before them. "This is one of the most popular planets in the entire galaxy. You have access to almost any area to enjoy yourself, within reason of course, yet you choose to waste your time playing Starfleet Command and trying to break into my study."

The eleven-year-old felt the heat build up in his cheeks. He never considered his activities as "play." He tried to gain control of his emotions as he saw his father's demeanor change.

"Eddie." Ray's tone softened as he let out a sigh. "I know this hasn't been easy for you."

Here it came, the apologetic speech. Eddie heard it at least once a week. Ray Johnson ran a gentle hand through Eddie's hair.

"I miss your mother too. But it's just the two of us now and we have to rely on each other. We also have to respect each other's needs. I know I haven't been doing that lately, what with the extra work I've been putting into the modified warp coils for my presentation at the symposium, but this is important to me." He paused before continuing. "And you're important to me." Ray looked up at the ceiling as though he were making some mental notes about something completely unrelated to the conversation. "Look, how about we do a little exploring of those caves by the lagoon that you were talking about?"

Eddie's face lit up. "Really?"

"Sure. I'll tell you what, I've got some work to finish up here. Why don't you start down to the lagoon and do a reconnoiter of the area."

"What?" Eddie's face fell.

"Yeah." His father placed his hands on Eddie's shoulders and guided him toward the front door. "There are several caves there. Pick a system that interests you the most and we'll explore it together. The symposium doesn't start for another two days. We can spend some of the time together."

"Some?" Eddie repeated softly.

"Well, I've also got to finish copying my notes and putting them in some coherent order for my presentation, don't I?" They passed through their bungalow entrance and Ray gave Eddie a gentle push forward. "But I promise you we'll spend time together. Now, why don't you run along and I'll catch up with you." He backed up into the doorway. "Oh, be careful down there. Don't go too far into the caves. With the odd power fluctuations that have been happening, you might not be able to contact me if you need me. Have a good time."

He slammed the door shut as Eddie stood in the courtyard, stunned.

He just blew me off. He didn't even finish his speech. Where was the part about how it's been rough on him as I remind him so much of Mom? Where was the part about how proud she would be that I have remained so strong during such a difficult time? I feel cheated.

Eddie drew himself from his thoughts, determined not to let it get him down. He turned toward the lagoon and watched as his imaginary crew emerged from the shadows.

"Where were you guys when I needed you?" he asked aloud. He knew he wasn't going to get any answers. He shrugged. "Right then, we have a new mission. We're going to explore the caves in the lagoon. We've been getting some unusual reports from Starfleet Command. I'll explain on the way there."

Eddie trudged off toward the lagoon, developing his next adventure in his mind.

CHAPTER 3

Commander Sonya Gomez gestured to Soloman to enter the conference room first as the two converged on the door at the same time.

"Thank you, Commander," the Bynar replied as he stepped through. Sonya couldn't help but smile at the small alien. The two had been through quite a lot since she first boarded the ship. They had both watched as someone they cared greatly for had been lost in the line of duty. For Soloman, the loss had been his Bynar partner. In Bynar culture, partnership was essential for proper functioning. And yet, rather than return to his home world to recouple, Soloman elected to stay and serve on board the *da Vinci*. It took some time, but Soloman was adapting to life without his other half.

Sonya's bond with the late Kieran Duffy wasn't anywhere near as total as the one Soloman had shared, but her own recovery seemed just as slow. Her near-death experience on Teneb had been a wake-up call for her to move on with her life, but there were days when she still felt like she was walking through mud.

Captain David Gold's voice drew her from her thoughts. "Any time you'd like to join us, Gomez."

"Sorry, sir." She felt the blood gathering in her cheeks as she took her place at the conference room table. The usual crew was gathered in their traditional places. Sonya quickly acknowledged each and every one with a nod and a smile as she settled into her chair. She felt the odd stare from Mor glasch Tev, second officer aboard the *da Vinci*. She tried to meet his stare in the hope of unnerving him, but his face remained impassive.

"Commander," he said curtly with a slight snort. Sonya wasn't sure if his tone was sarcastic.

The communicator chimed as Anthony Shabalala's voice filled the room. *"Bridge to Captain Gold."*

"Go ahead," Gold replied.

"We're on course for Risa, Captain," Shabalala announced. *"I have Captain Scott standing by."*

That surprised Sonya. Risa was usually one's destination for shore leave, not a mission assignment.

"Patch him through."

The S.C.E. team turned their attention to the viewscreen over Gold's shoulder. The Starfleet emblem winked on momentarily and was replaced by the warm, smiling image of Captain Montgomery Scott.

"Captain." Gold nodded in greeting.

"Good morning, people. As I'm sure you're all aware, you're currently on course for Risa."

"What happened?" Fabian Stevens had a hint of mischievousness in his voice. "Is there a broken blender that needs repair?"

Bart Faulwell chuckled. "The entire Risan economy is on the brink of collapse because they can't make the piña coladas fast enough."

This brought a laugh from Scotty. *"'Tis a wee bit more serious than that. The entire future of Risa is in jeopardy. As I'm sure you know, Risa relies on mostly automated systems to make the stay of their guests as simple and as pleasurable as possible. Unfortunately, those systems are breakin' down. We're getting reports of random power drains from certain locales in the Monagas area. It's affecting everything from the sonic toothbrushes to the sky vehicles to the weather control network. And the power disruptions are spreading."*

"Is it a mechanical or natural phenomenon?" Gomez asked.

"That's for you lot to determine," Scott replied. *"We haven't been able to contact Risa for nearly twelve hours now. The energy problems are affecting communications. Our most recent report came from an Andorian freighter. The crew was on leave and left after one day. The heavy rains caused by the lack of control of the weather system made it unbearable for them to stay."*

Fabian grinned. "Well, they could make themselves the number-one destination spot for the Ferengi. A home away from home."

"I think they'd like to continue serving a broader client base." Gold turned to his first officer. "Your thoughts, Gomez?"

Gomez felt the eyes of everyone on her. "I would assume the Risan authorities would like this handled as quickly and as quietly as possible. So we don't want to attract much attention. We'll keep the initial team small as we assess the situation, then bring in team members as is necessary."

"Sounds good." Gold smiled thinly.

Scott nodded his consent as well. *"I'll leave you to your work then. Contact me when you arrive at Risa. Good luck."*

The image of Scott faded from the viewscreen. Gold folded his hands in front of him. "And who will make up this team?"

"Myself, Soloman, and Pattie," she replied.

Tev let out a snort of surprise. "Commander?"

"Yes?" She turned toward the Tellarite, steeling herself for the challenge.

"I understand your desire to keep the group small. In fact, I wholeheartedly endorse it, but I feel you will need my expertise on this matter."

"As I stated, Commander," Sonya began to explain, keeping her tone as even and pleasant as possible, "I will be bringing in personnel as the situation warrants. Soloman will determine if the fault relates to the computer systems. Pattie will determine if the problem is mechanical."

"It would make more sense to bring a generalist down to determine the cause, then summon specialists as needed."

"Maybe, but I think this away team configuration is what's best for the mission," Gomez said, giving Tev a sharp look.

Tev looked as though he was about to pursue the argument

further, but instead settled back in his seat and folded his arms in defeat.

Domenica Corsi spoke up. "I think you should have someone from security with you."

"Why?" Gomez asked, looking forward to hearing the expected answer.

"What if the nature of these energy drainings is hostile?"

"Then I'll call a security detachment down. Domenica, this is *Risa*. This is where you go to get away from your troubles. Even the bad guys lower their weapons there. If we run into trouble, I'll call you."

"And what if communications are out?" Gomez noted Gold's "leave her alone" look being directed at Corsi, but the security chief was ignoring it.

"Then I'll simply scream at the top of my lungs until you hear me," Gomez replied with an impish smile that drew a frustrated sigh from both Corsi and Tev simultaneously.

"It's settled then," Gold said. "We'll arrive at Risa in thirteen hours. Unless there are any other questions or comments, you're dismissed."

The staff rose from their chairs and slowly filed out of the room. Gomez and Gold watched as they departed.

As the door closed with a whispering hiss, Gold gave his first officer a look. "Gomez, you know that you've got final say over any away team you lead."

Gomez heard the implied word at the end of that, and provided it. "But?"

"Tev had a point."

"Yes, sir, he did. And honestly, with a different second officer—" Her voice caught, but she recovered. "—I would probably have him or her along. But as good as Tev is—and I admit, he's *very* good—he's still adjusting to working with the team. Until he does, I want to remind him that there are other people on the ship." She smiled. "Besides, this *is* Risa. These are friendly people, and I trust Soloman and Pattie to interact more pleasantly with the staff."

Gold grinned. "Good point."

CHAPTER 4

Commander Eddie Johnson stopped short in his hurried tracks as he approached the cave system looking out over the lagoon. He felt a heavy heart as he knew he would be exploring the area alone, even though he had the rest of his crew along in spirit. He turned to face them, holding out a hand to halt their advance.

"I haven't been completely honest with you," he said to his crew with regret. "There isn't any trouble in these caves. For a long time, you have been faithfully following my orders without question. I appreciate that. It's nice to have such a loyal crew. But I think you should know that there has been an ulterior motive to all this."

Eddie sighed. This wasn't going to be easy. "A few years ago, I lost my father. He disappeared from my life at a time when I needed him most. Every mission we have been on, while they have served the best interests of Starfleet and the Federation, has also been about finding my father.

"My father is Ray Johnson, the noted warp field specialist. He's been working on a top-secret project to produce a more efficient warp coil generator. I believe he may have been on the verge of something critical when he disappeared. I don't know if he met with foul play or if he has simply gone into hiding, but every mission we have been on in the last six months has allowed me to follow up on clues and rumors I've heard regarding his whereabouts."

Eddie pointed toward the entrance. "I have every reason to believe he is in there. So, while officially we will be exploring the caves and creating a detailed map of the region for Starfleet records, unofficially, we will be looking for my father." Eddie paused to allow everyone to ponder what he had just said. "I will understand if anyone wishes to return to the ship."

Silence was once again the reply. Eddie broke out into a big smile. He had a good crew.

"Then why are we waiting? Let's move out!"

The crew moved quietly through the caves for the better part of an hour. The only sound that could be heard was the echoing of Eddie's heavy bootsteps. The journey inward had been uneventful for the most part, save for Lieutenant McGuiness nearly falling into a chasm. Some quick thinking on Eddie's part saved her from a sad ending.

Eddie stopped for a moment and took in a deep breath. The much cooler, damper air of the caves filled his lungs and caused him to cough. He settled down on a large boulder and looked around at the craggy features of the ceiling and walls surrounding him.

A glance at his watch confirmed his worst fear. He had been in the caves for nearly two hours now.

His father wasn't joining him.

He stood up, determined not to let his crew see the mixture of disappointment and anger in his face. He cleared his throat and prepared to make the announcement when something shining out of the corner of his eye caught his attention.

Eddie stepped slowly toward the glow, which seemed to pulse and emanate a low hum. It was coming from just around the corner, where Ensign Tomkins had reported as "uninteresting" just moments before. Eddie made a note to have a word later with Tomkins about the accuracy of his investigations.

Eddie stepped cautiously forward, wishing he had thought to bring his tricorder with him. As he moved into the next chamber, he caught the first sight of its occupant—a glowing orange-yellow ball of pulsing light that illuminated the chamber.

To Eddie's surprise, it appeared to retreat slightly as he entered. Eddie stopped and watched for a moment, waiting to see if it would make a move.

Make a move? You should be the one making a move, Eddie Johnson, right out of the cave.

And yet he remained perfectly still, watching as the glowing light maintained an equal distance away from the boy. As Eddie took a step forward, it would move the same distance back and move forward as the boy retreated. Eddie wiped away a trickle of sweat that ran down the side of his cheek. The heat emanating from the creature, for lack of a better term, was sweltering.

"I'm not going to hurt you," he said, surprising himself as he said it. This thing looked powerful enough to take out most of the continent. Realization dawned on the boy. "Say, you're not what's causing all these energy problems on Risa, are you?"

As if in response to his question, the creature shuddered and Eddie's torch suddenly winked out.

"Wow," he whispered as he slowly put the torch down on the ground. "My name's Eddie."

The creature offered no acknowledgment.

"I come from a planet called Earth. We have a lot of energy there." *Nice move, Eddie. Come visit Earth, we're ripe for the taking.*

"Do you have a name?"

Again, the creature just pulsed in silence.

Eddie took another step forward. This time, the creature did not move.

"Starting to trust me?"

Eddie ran his arm across his forehead, which was producing rivulets of sweat that ran into his eyes, stinging them. He took another step.

"All right. You won't tell me your name, how about where you come from?"

Another step. The creature's glow began to increase. Eddie placed a hand in front of his eyes to shield the glare. It didn't help much.

"Can you talk at all? How are we going to communicate?"

Every instinct in Eddie told him to leave quickly, but his curiosity and the serenity of the creature kept his guard in check. He stepped forward again.

The creature suddenly shifted forward, growing somewhat larger as it did. Eddie took a fearful step back and stumbled to the ground.

He fumbled with the combadge his father had given him. "D-d-dad! This is-is E-e-eddie! Come in!"

There was no response. He looked up at the creature. It was hovering close to him. "Drained the energy from that too, huh?"

The creature continued to advance on Eddie.

"Now, look, just remember. I came here in peace. I want to go that way!"

It was less than half a meter away from Eddie now. The heat was becoming unbearable. Eddie thought he might pass out.

"I won't even tell anyone that you're here. I promise!"

The creature made one sweeping move forward, engulfing Eddie. He felt a momentary searing flash of heat touch every part of his body as the creature washed over him, but the heat quickly subsided as consciousness began to slip away from him.

Despite all that was happening and how dangerous the situation seemed, Eddie's final thought before succumbing to the darkness was *Wow!*

CHAPTER 5

"Now entering standard orbit of Risa," Songmin Wong announced to the bridge crew of the *da Vinci*. He tapped a further command into his console and smiled with satisfaction. They had arrived at Risa without incident, which made a nice change for the conn officer. After the navigational nightmare of the so-called "Sargasso sector," a simple flight to Risa was a welcome change.

Wong, like most in Starfleet, looked forward to the challenges of exploring strange new life-forms and new civilizations, but he never expected ferrying a bunch of techs across the galaxy to be so dangerous. He glanced down at his left hand and said another silent prayer of thanks that he managed to retain it after an explosion of his console hurled debris at him at Galvan VI.

"Very good, Wong."

Wong turned to look up at Captain Gold as he rose from his chair. The captain hadn't been so lucky. His hand was lost as nearly the entire ceiling had come crashing down upon him. But the captain was luckier than tactical officer David McAllan. Gold lost his left hand due to the pinning debris.

McAllan lost his life as he leapt forward and pushed the captain to safety, taking the brunt of the wreckage himself.

Wong wondered for some time after if he should have requested reassignment, the way the alpha-shift ops officer, Ina Mar, did. He still sometimes wrestled with the thought, especially after a reoccurring vivid nightmare in which he was the one trapped beneath the wreckage of the bridge as the crew lay dead around him. In the dream, the only sounds he heard were his own heavy breathing and the groaning of the hull as the badly damaged ship gave in to the pressures of Galvan VI's turbulent atmosphere.

Wong repressed a shudder and turned his thoughts to more pleasant pursuits. Despite the fact that Gold warned everyone that the trip to Risa was purely business, Wong hoped to convince the captain to allow him some time to take his pleasure yacht out for a spin.

Wong recently obtained the craft after investing inherited strips of latinum in the Ferengi market. He was fairly successful and that gave Wong further reason to think about where his life was going. He could still see much of the universe as an investor. And he wouldn't have to be placed in such hazardous situations.

The viewscreen showed the green-blue hue of Risa below them. Wong caught sight of his yacht in the lower corner of the screen.

"Permission to magnify the lower quadrant, Captain?" he asked.

Gold squinted at the viewer and smiled in recognition. "Granted."

The young lieutenant tapped in the command and the screen adjusted to the required setting. A long, sleek, light gray pleasure yacht hung just over the Olobon continent. Mooring lights faded in and out.

Gold whistled appreciatively. "She's a beauty."

"You should see her when she's all lit up and in flight," Wong replied, suddenly imagining himself in the observation lounge of his ship, entertaining potential investors. It seemed a pleasant way to live.

Tev grunted as he leaned over the railing to get a better look. "It is a practical design. What have you named it?"

Wong's face flushed slightly. "I haven't been able to come up with one yet, sir."

"You've taken her out and she doesn't have a name?" Gold asked with a grin. "What kind of a shipmaster are you?"

"I haven't really thought about it, I guess," Wong admitted.

"Well, we're going to be in orbit for a while, Wong," Gold said. "I suggest you use that time to think about it. Maybe we can take a moment to put the lettering on her. A fine craft like that needs to have an identity."

"Yes, sir," Wong replied, turning back toward his console. "Thank you, sir."

The intercom beeped overhead.

"Bridge, this is Gomez. We're assembled and ready to beam down."

"Good luck, Gomez. Try to avoid the tourist traps," Gold answered.

"Yes, sir." She chuckled.

"Captain," Shabalala called out. "I think you should take a look at this."

Gold and Tev stepped up to the tactical station where Shabalala was staring intently at his monitor.

"What is it?" Tev asked.

"I've completed a thorough scan of the entire Risan system. Risa has a lot of traffic. Each vessel's engine gives off a particular energy signature."

"And your point is?" Tev asked with a tone of annoyance.

"I'm reading no recent energy signatures, sir," Shabalala replied. "Take a look at this." He tapped a command into his console and a small freighter came into view on the monitor. "That's an Antedean freighter."

"I'm familiar with the design," Gold said.

"Yes, sir," Shabalala continued. "It features a modified version of the millicochrane warp engines in our shuttlecraft. It gives off a distinct energy signature that remains for some seventy-two hours. But as you can see with this sensor overlay . . ."

Shabalala touched a corner of his console and a grid appeared on the screen. "This freighter arrived two days ago. We're not getting anything from it. In fact, all recently arrived craft have no proper energy signature. It's as though they were all cloaked."

"Which is pretty unlikely," Gold said.

"Exactly," Shabalala said. "So what happened?"

Tev furrowed his thick eyebrows. "Whatever it is that is causing the power failures on Risa has extended its influence beyond the surface."

Gold put a hand on the tactical officer's shoulder. "Good work, Shabalala. Contact the away team with this information as soon as they arrive on planet."

"Aye, sir."

Gomez's first sight as Risa materialized around her was of a large man, dressed in what looked like a toga, moving toward her. There may have been another individual behind him; it was hard to tell with the size of the man.

"Commander Gomez, is it?" The man offered a meaty hand to her. She took it cautiously, noting the moisture in his palm. She tried not to show her revulsion, but failed. He quickly pulled his hand away. "I'm sorry, Commander. With the weather system out of control, we're being assaulted by a heat wave that doesn't agree with a man of my stature. I'm Tonais, director of the Monagas resort."

Gomez ran a finger through her collar, noting the heat was oppressive. "Quite all right, Director. That's why we're here."

"And I'm glad you are," Tonais said as he backed up into a much smaller man. He whirled on him in frustration. "Bander! Must you always be so close to me?"

The bald-headed man looked pained at the rebuke. "How else am I to serve you, Director?"

"I don't know." He turned to Gomez and smiled with a smarminess that made her flesh dimple. "He's very good at what he does, but he can be a little troublesome sometimes."

Gomez's combadge chirped, saving her from having to reply. "Da Vinci *to Gomez*."

"Excuse me a moment, Director," Gomez nodded, turning slightly away. "Go ahead."

As Shabalala relayed the information from his scans to her, Gomez took a moment to glance over her surroundings. The concourse they had materialized in featured a number of high supporting pillars similar to the architectural styles of ancient Rome on Earth. The white marble columns supported a domed ceiling featuring a collage of tropical plants. Several small water fountains dotted the large area, not activated at the moment. She also noted the lack of tourists.

After acknowledging Shabalala's report, she turned back to the director. "There aren't many of your guests here."

"No. With the weather control network not working properly, we've experienced high temperatures and wild rainstorms. It washed out our lagoon, one of the most popular attractions of this resort."

"That's terrible," Pattie said.

"Director, this is P8 Blue, who will handle the structural analysis of your affected systems." Gomez gestured to Pattie and then to the Bynar. "And this is Soloman, who will determine if it's a programming fault."

"That's the problem, Commander Gomez. I think you will find that it is neither a structural nor a programming problem. The systems being affected are widespread and, for the most part, independent of each other."

"I'd like to see a log of your most recent power failures and have my people look over the systems just to be sure."

"Of course." Tonais nodded quickly, gesturing toward the concourse entrance. "If you'll come this way." They proceeded toward the archway. "I'm afraid I cannot offer you any comfortable accommodations as none of the air coolers in any of the rooms work. But then, neither do the lights or the waste disposal systems or—"

Before the director could go on with his litany of problems, he was stopped short by a large, muscular figure.

"Excuse me, sir!" Tonais started, but his voice dipped into a squeak as he looked upward at the individual.

The seven-foot reptilian alien stood imposingly over the director. He was decked out in heavy leather that covered his entire body. An energy weapon hung from a holster to his side, while a jeweled blade featured prominently in a scabbard on his chest. His jewel green eyes flashed angrily at the sight of the director.

"Out of the way!" the imposing Gorn hissed. The reptilian alien tilted his head and glanced at Gomez and her party. "Federation!" He gestured to the other two Gorn accompanying him and they circled around the group, keeping an eye on Gomez the entire time. She turned and watched them walk across and exit the concourse without ever looking back.

"Do you know them, Director?" she asked, turning to face Tonais.

"No," he said, shaking his head. "Bander?"

Before Tonais could ask the question, the little man had the information on his data pad. "A Gorn ship entered orbit some thirty-three hours ago, sir. They have been beaming back and forth to their ship since then. They are not staying planetside, nor are they utilizing any of the facilities." He paused and then lifted his head and wiped the sweat from his nose. "Not that they could anyway. Most of the facilities are nonfunctional at the moment."

"Yes, thank you, Bander," the director snapped.

"Beaming back and forth, eh?" Gomez tapped her combadge. "Gomez to *da Vinci*."

"Go ahead," Captain Gold's voice echoed in the chamber.

"Captain, please beam down a security detachment. We may have trouble with some Gorn who appear to not be here for a holiday."

"We detected their ship a short while ago. I'll have that detachment down shortly. Keep us apprised of your situation. Da Vinci out."

"Is that necessary, Commander?" Tonais asked worriedly.

"I'm hoping not, Director," she replied. "Just look at it as a precaution."

"Well," Tonais said, the worry in his voice apparent, "just make sure they don't get in the way of the guests."

Gomez smiled. "Don't worry, Director. You won't even know they're here."

CHAPTER 6

Eddie was aware of every single nerve point in his body. He felt a continuous buzz of electricity similar to a slight static shock coursing through him and found it to be invigorating. His senses, something he had taken for granted for so long, were intensified by the experience. He could smell the dampness of the cave, make out every rock and crag that jutted from the cave walls, and at the same time admired the congruity they projected where once it had seemed chaotic. He could hear the music created by the echoing condensation falling off the cave ceiling.

"Fantastic," Eddie said, but he wasn't sure if he was saying it or thinking it. His "voice" had an almost electronic edge to it.

He looked down at his arm and marveled at the way he could see the thin hairs on the back of his limb standing up, moving back and forth like a field of grain on a windy day. He lifted his hand and intensified his stare. He squawked in surprise as he was able to see beyond his skin to the blood pulsing through his veins beneath.

FANTASTIC.

Eddie looked around the cave nervously. He could make no one out. "Who said that?"

THAT.

Eddie could hear his heart pounding, could feel it beating against his chest.

"Who are you?"

Eddie felt a ripple of electricity course through him. His body stiffened slightly as electrical blue sparks arched across the top of his head.

"Stop!" Eddie said excitedly. "Please."

PLEASE. STOP. WHO ARE YOU?

The surge diminished and Eddie felt his limbs under his control again. He took in a deep breath.

WHO ARE YOU?

"I'm not imagining it." He looked at the glow surrounding him. "You're alive. You exist."

WHO????

"Take it easy," Eddie said, feeling the voice in his head getting louder and more insistent. A mild headache began to form. "My name is Eddie Johnson. I'm from Earth."

EARTH?

"Yeah, Earth. It's a planet like this one."

PLANET?

"Is this all you can do?" Eddie asked. "Are you just going to keep parroting me?" His only answer was silence. "All right, how about we try this. What's your name?"

NO NAME. NO PLANET. NOBODY TO CARE.

"Care? Are you plucking words from my mind?"

MIND FULL OF IMAGES. FULL OF IDEAS. FULL OF THOUGHTS. LEARNING. BECOMING . . .

"Becoming? What are you talking about? Who are you? Where are you from?"

NEED TO EXAMINE DATA. ESSENTIAL. It paused for a moment. **THERE IS SOMETHING ELSE.**

Eddie felt a rumble in his stomach. He was getting hungry. He wasn't sure how long he had been in the cave, but he knew he had to get something to eat.

HUNGER.

"You're hungry too?" Eddie asked.

The being pulsed and Eddie felt his senses expand again. This time he was seeing beyond the walls of the cave. The skies were beginning to grow dark as evening was approaching.

"Uh-oh," Eddie said. "My dad's going to kill me."

DAD? KILL?

"My father. He's not *really* going to kill me. But he's going to be upset that I've been away so long. But this wouldn't have happened if he had come to the caves with me like he said he would."

The being appeared to rumble as it pondered what Eddie was saying.

FATHER. MOTHER. PROGENITORS. It said each word slowly. **UNDERSTAND. MOTHER ABANDONED. FATHER ABANDONED.**

"Well, I wouldn't say my mother abandoned me. She died a few years ago."

MEMORY IS STRONG. THERE IS SOMETHING ELSE THERE. CANNOT UNDERSTAND IT.

Eddie felt a tear falling from his cheek. "You're reading me wrong! I'm not mad at my mother!" Eddie tried to change the subject. "Look, you said you were hungry. How about getting something to eat?"

Eddie's vision spotted several flyers flitting about in the skies above. With his enhanced senses, he could make out the energy that surged through the crafts.

YES. HUNGER.

"Uh-oh," Eddie said as the realization of what the creature was about to do dawned on him.

CHAPTER 7

Sonya ran a hand along the surface of the sky flyer sitting in the landing bay of the Monagas Peninsula. She smiled at the thought of taking it out and guiding it through the deep blue skies above. But her smile faded as she glanced out a nearby window and watched the clouds outside quickly darken as a late afternoon thunderstorm was developing.

Normally, the weather control system would be able to deter the storm, allowing visitors to the peninsula to enjoy their evening. But after a sweltering hot day trapped inside, the tourists would find themselves remaining indoors to avoid getting soaked.

Soloman poked his head out of the top of the flyer. "This is definitely not a systems problem. In fact, this flyer is ready to take off." And so saying, he activated the flyer, bringing a low hum to the surrounding area.

Pattie stepped out from behind the craft. "Structurally, it's a sound vessel. In fact, all the flyers in this bay are fine."

"Then why couldn't they launch them when they needed to rescue those climbers the other day?" Gomez asked.

Soloman shook his head. "This is clearly an external influence, Commander. While I would like to take a look at the launch bay control room to see if I can determine anything else, I feel we need to shift the focus of our investigation."

"I agree," Gomez nodded.

The doors to the launch bay entrance parted and a couple of Risans entered the area. The female of the duo approached Gomez, her gaze less than friendly.

"Commander Gomez, I'm Shira from Risa Operations. How are your investigations proceeding?" Her tone was not the usual congenial, friendliness that Gomez was used to from a Risan. In fact, it seemed downright hostile.

"I don't think there is anything wrong with any of your systems, Shira." Gomez tried to keep a smile on her face, hoping that the Risan would pick up on it. "We have been through your communications systems, aircraft, and the weather control station. We can find no systemic reason for this power loss. Our current hypothesis is that an outside force is responsible."

"Outside force?" Shira repeated. "You mean alien?"

"Possibly," Gomez admitted a little reluctantly. "We don't want to rule anything out. It could be some natural phenomenon we haven't accounted for yet."

A chime from a communicator interrupted them. The Risan male stepped forward. "Shira, it's the weather control station."

"Thank you, Milan," she replied, taking the small device from him. She looked at Gomez. "Will you excuse me?" She turned away without waiting for a reply.

Pattie stepped up behind Gomez and leaned into her ear. "What happened to the famous Risan warmth? You could take the chill from that woman alone and reduce the temperature of the entire peninsula."

"She's got her feelings hurt by our involvement in this," Gomez said simply. "How would you feel if we couldn't handle a certain engineering situation and they brought in another S.C.E. team to assist?"

"Something I'll never have to worry about," Pattie replied, clicking one of her mandibles with a flourish, the equivalent of a human wink. "We never need anyone's help."

I only hope that's always the case, Gomez thought.

The approach of the *da Vinci*'s security chief changed the

commander's mood. A smile broke out on her lips. She always got a kick out of watching Corsi in "full security mode," as Gomez liked to think of it. She was like a cat, tensed, ready to spring into action on a nanosecond's notice.

Corsi stopped just short of Gomez. "We found our Gorn friends. They appear to be searching the beach areas around the lagoon. I've got Hawkins and Angelopoulos following them."

"We don't want to draw attention, Domenica."

"They're dressed as tourists. I also issued them Ferengi disruptors, which won't connect them with Starfleet. I did a check with Risan orbital control. The Gorn never stated a reason for coming to Risa. They don't have to, when contacted by the Risans, but most vessels do answer the question."

Shira turned back to face the S.C.E. team. "I am being informed that the weather control grid is back online." As she said this, the lights in the landing bay winked on. A hum filled the chamber. "As is this landing area. The portable generators you provided are working nicely." Shira looked from Gomez to Corsi and muttered, "Thank you."

"You're welcome," Gomez replied. "They should do the trick until we determine the source of the energy drain."

The lights, as quickly as they winked on, flashed off. Gomez looked at Soloman. The Bynar pulled a tricorder out and began a scan. The device gave off the usual whine for several seconds before it too began to die out.

"Not the tricorder too," Corsi said.

"It is worse than we feared," Soloman replied. He pointed toward a large window looking out into the sky. "I managed to detect an approaching aircraft." Moving rapidly toward the landing area was a small flyer.

"We've got to warn them off," Gomez said.

Milan shook his head. "From the looks of it, it's out of control."

Gomez tapped her communicator, but wasn't greeted with its familiar chirp of activation. "Gomez to *da Vinci*." There was no response.

"Quick!" Gomez ran toward the landing bay control room. "We've got to open those bay doors. Domenica, Pattie, I want you two to clear everyone in the surrounding area. Let's minimize the potential for casualties."

"Right," Corsi replied as she moved off with the Nasat.

Shira and Milan followed after Gomez and Soloman.

"You should leave the area too," Gomez said as they climbed the circular stairs to the control room, a glass-enclosed structure that rested just above the landing bay.

"This is my responsibility," Shira said coolly, "as much as it has been made yours."

"Fine." Gomez didn't have time to argue.

They entered the control room and Gomez settled herself into a chair facing the main operations panel. Soloman settled to her right, activating the scanners and getting a lock on the craft.

"Thank goodness this is still working," Gomez said, wincing as the lights began to dim. "Why did I have to jinx us?"

"Open the bay doors!" Shira shouted. "Quickly!"

Milan leaned over Gomez and tapped in the command. The four looked out as the huge metallic barriers began to part with a loud groan. They parted about five meters before coming to an abrupt halt.

"We've lost all power," Gomez said.

"We've got to stop them from landing!" Shira's voice was becoming hysterical.

Gomez watched as the flyer drew near, not exactly sure how they could accomplish that in time.

CHAPTER 8

Vance Hawkins stopped and grumbled quietly as he removed his shoe and dumped out what seemed to be the entire contents of the beach he was treading on. He looked up at his partner, Andrew Angelopoulos. The young man chuckled and ran his hand through his thick, dark mane of hair. Angelopoulos was one of seven new transfers to security after Galvan VI, and since reporting, he had turned many a female and a few male heads with his striking good looks.

"Chief, why didn't you wear sandals?" Angelopoulos asked.

Hawkins looked up at him, shaking his head. "These shoes are comfortable."

"Practical, was the term I think you used." Andrew smiled. "There's no such thing as a practical shoe on a beach."

Hawkins gestured toward a series of nearby caves. "Don't lose sight of our friends."

"As if I could." The young man looked up at the sky and placed a hand to his forehead to block out the glare. "They stick out like a sore thumb and look just about as miserable on the beach as you do."

"I'm not a beach person," Hawkins said. "Simple as that."

Angelopoulos looked down at Hawkins and smiled. The two were quite the contrast in study. Where Hawkins was dark-skinned, with a head as smooth as a marble table surface, Angelopoulos was pale with a big thatch of black hair.

"So what do you think of life on the *da Vinci* so far?" Hawkins asked, standing up and giving each foot a final shake. "I'll bet you'd never have thought you'd be following a group of Gorn on the beaches of Risa, dressed"—Hawkins flailed his arms about—"in this getup." Both he and Angelopoulos were sporting a more colorful array of clothing than either was used to wearing. Their shirts were a combination of bright primary colors mixed together in what was to Hawkins, an appalling fashion.

"It helps us to blend in, sir."

"Risan fashion leaves a lot to be desired," Hawkins grumbled. "And don't call me sir."

"Yes, sir," Angelopoulos said with a cheeky grin. Then he gestured toward their quarry. "They're moving out. Whatever it was that interested them didn't hold their attention long."

"They're looking for something. Make a quick scan of the area they were standing in as we pass."

"Right."

As they trudged through the sand, Angelopoulos kept the conversation going. Hawkins quietly approved; better not to draw suspicion from the Gorn, make them think they're tourists. "I'm enjoying it, sir. I like working with you."

"And Commander Corsi?" Hawkins asked, looking forward to hearing the awkward reply.

"She takes some getting used to, sir," Andrew said without hesitation, which surprised Hawkins. "She certainly knows what she's doing, but I don't know anyone who has such a brusque style."

Hawkins's face darkened slightly. "That's your commanding officer you're talking about, mister."

"Yes, sir. You asked me my opinion and I gave it." He stopped and then smiled. "You thought I was going to come up with some nervous reply or maybe lie to you. I'm sorry, sir. I can't do that. I respect the commander, it's part of the reason why I requested the transfer, but I feel she needn't be such a hard character."

Hawkins grinned. "No, I was making sure you *didn't* come up with some nervous reply or lie to me. A unit like this depends on trust and honesty, especially one with as many new recruits as we've got now." Hawkins stopped as the Gorn reached the entrance to a cave. "Wait a minute. They're scanning the area."

Andrew pulled out his tricorder and tapped a series of commands. "Hang on. I'm trying to lock into their scanning unit."

"Be careful not to let them detect you."

"Not a problem, sir. This was how I always knew where my fellow classmates were during field exercises when I was in training. I would develop a map of the entire area and then lock on to each person's tricorder as they scanned the immediate area."

"Very smart," Hawkins noted with some admiration. "They would only be scanning the immediate area as they didn't want to be detected."

"Yeah, but I would just link up to their tricorder and read their findings. This takes a little more finesse, but I think I can—" The tricorder chirped an alarm. "Uh-oh."

"Uh-oh?" Hawkins repeated. "What the hell does that mean?" He watched as the Gorn looked in their direction. For such large creatures, they had quickly pulled out their weapons.

"It means we've been spotted." Andrew gave Hawkins a rough shove that knocked him to the ground before diving himself. Twin streams of phased energy whizzed past them, striking a tree nearby. A shower of wood chips fell upon the two. Hawkins pulled out his own weapon and made a quick scan of the area, looking for weaknesses in the Gorn's position to exploit.

"Humans!" The Gorn's voice trailed off in a hiss. "Surrender now and we can save you the trouble of dying in defeat!"

"Listen to him," Hawkins muttered. "You'd think they had this in the bag."

"Don't they?" Angelopoulos sounded nervous.

Hawkins snorted. "Kid, after what I went through on Teneb, a couple of pissed-off Gorn are a walk in the park."

Angelopoulos did have a point, though: The Gorn's position was pretty solid. They had the cover of a number of large boulders that lined the cave's entrance and the cave itself to retreat into if necessary. A thin smile broke Hawkins's stern look.

"What are you thinking?" Angelopoulos asked worriedly as he saw the smile turn devious.

"I want you to lay down some rapid weapons fire, scattered, but centered around them." Another volley of shots whizzed past them. "We'll draw them toward the cave. When they're in position, fire at the roof of the entrance. Got it?"

Angelopoulos nodded.

"We will not fire another warning shot, humans," the Gorn announced. "Enter the clearing."

"Go!" Hawkins said.

With his best attempt at a primal scream, Angelopoulos launched himself from his crouched position and began a rapid-fire stream at the Gorn. Hawkins took the more secure route, moving from tree to tree, getting off a series of bursts each time.

Angelopoulos's disruptor was set for wide dispersal, which caused more area damage, but with less physical results. But the strategy appeared to be working as the Gorn began to back up toward the cave.

Hawkins lined up his shot of the entrance, allowing Angelopoulos to finish the herding. Hawkins never saw the shot that struck him in the shoulder, which lifted him off the ground slightly and deposited him on his rear end with a loud thud.

"Chief!" Angelopoulos shouted, stopping his barrage. He turned and ran toward Hawkins.

"No!" Hawkins shouted a warning as one of the Gorn stepped out and drew a bead on Angelopoulos.

Hawkins fumbled to lift his disruptor, but wasn't fast enough. He could see the trigger finger of the Gorn twitch on the weapon.

Nothing happened.

Angelopoulos dropped to the ground and took aim with his weapon.

Hawkins tried to return fire but met with the same result as the Gorn. He looked at his disruptor and saw that the power cell was drained.

"Angelopoulos?" Hawkins looked over at the guard, who shook his head.

"I'm out, too."

"And so are they," Hawkins said. The three Gorn lumbered toward the two. "We've got to get out of here. Give me a hand up." He tapped his combadge. "Hawkins to *da Vinci.*"

Angelopoulos tried his combadge as well and found it useless.

"Come on, move. We can outrun them."

"But, sir," Angelopoulos said, pointing toward their adversaries. The three Gorn had turned and were now moving in the opposite direction. One stopped at the mouth of the cave and stood guard there, while the other two continued along the path leading down and away. "What's going on?"

"I don't know. But we've got to get word to Commander Gomez. Look, I'll slow you down right now. This shoulder stings like a son of a bitch."

"You have to have it looked at," Angelopoulos said.

Hawkins shook his head. "It's all right. The shot grazed me, but it hurts to move. I'll stay here and keep an eye on our friends. You get to Commander Gomez and report on the situation. I want a team here to investigate whatever has the Gorn's attention."

"Aye, sir," Angelopoulos said with a reassuring smile. "I'll get back here as quickly as possible." He turned and jogged off without another word.

Hawkins settled onto a nearby rock and gently touched the throbbing wound. It was still warm to the touch. He shook his head in frustration and looked upward. "Why me?"

A low rumble filled the air and the skies above thickened with dark clouds.

"Now what?" Hawkins asked as a gust of wind began to pick up. "Great. Just great."

CHAPTER 9

P8 Blue watched as the humans wiped away the sweat from their foreheads. She understood why humans had sweat glands, but right at the moment, she was grateful that Nasats didn't have them. Then again, this sweltering heat and humidity felt just like home to her.

Pattie and the other members of the S.C.E. away team had been attempting to open the large landing bay doors by force, with no success. The lack of proper ventilation and air-conditioning made the task all the more difficult and frustrating.

"Not like I'm trying to be all doom and gloom," Corsi said, "but why hasn't that thing crashed yet?"

"The craft is light enough that it can glide on air currents for a short period of time," Shira said. "Thankfully, the pilot has determined that the doors are not open and its communications systems are most likely rendered useless, so it's entered a holding pattern."

"And with the winds picking up the way they are," Gomez added, "I can't imagine it can stay in such a pattern for long."

"So why not just land somewhere else?" Corsi asked.

"There isn't anywhere safe to land," Shira said. "This is a heavily populated area. Besides, it won't be able to land, it will crash."

"So it'll crash in here?"

Shira nodded solemnly. "But at least we can minimize the damage."

"We can do more than that," Gomez said. Corsi smiled at Gomez's confident words.

"Not possible," Milan said. "The emergency landing systems won't engage without power."

"What kind of systems are there?" Gomez asked.

Shira gestured upward to a series of pipes that ran along the walls and ceilings. "The foam in these pipes serves two purposes. It acts as a flame retardant in case of fire and as a cushion if released into the chamber."

"Are there any manual releases?" Gomez asked.

"Yes, but they're all on the main piping. We can't reach them because we have no antigravity units working."

"Leave that to me," Pattie said as she glanced up and studied the latticework of pipes. "I think I can climb up there." She walked over to the wall and began to feel around the surface.

"Be careful," Gomez said.

Pattie turned and began her ascent of the wall, using a number of nooks and crags on the surface to aid her climb. She looked down at the others watching her from below. The ceiling of the landing bay was a good thirty feet high. Pattie felt a wave of dizziness as she took a moment to catch her breath.

On her homeworld, making such climbs through the densely populated towering trees would be second nature to her. But then there was the netting that covered the lower regions to catch her should she fall.

There was no net here.

From the ground, Corsi rubbed the base of her neck and tilted her head to either side, producing a soft cracking sound. Gomez looked at her with a grin. Corsi returned it. "What can I tell you? I get a stiff neck very easily."

"Some might say you're always stiff-necked," Gomez deadpanned.

Corsi closed her eyes and tilted her head back and forth even farther, producing a louder crack this time. Gomez shuddered slightly but continued to smile. She was glad to see herself and Corsi falling back into old patterns. The wounds from Galvan VI still left scars, but they were healing and not hurting as much anymore. Like any scar, they still itched now and then, but life was going on.

Shira interrupted Gomez's thoughts. "Commander, we're going to need to leave the area when the foam is released. It will retard the atmosphere."

"Yes, of course—the foam you use removes the air so the fire can die out."

"Exactly."

"But what about the door? We've got to get it open," Corsi said.

As if in answer to her question or unspoken prayer, two Gorn entered the landing bay. Corsi's first response was to reach for her phaser, but she hesitated, no doubt realizing that whatever killed the power in the bay must surely have drained the weapon. She took a defensive step forward in front of the two, creating a human barrier.

The Gorn stopped their advance some ten feet away from the others. One of them looked upward and watched as Pattie made her way to the roof.

"I am Kazar," the lead Gorn said simply. "Why is that insect climbing the walls?"

Gomez stepped in front of Corsi. She could feel the security officer stiffen at the move, but Gomez knew she had to make it clear to the Gorn she was the leader. "I am Commander Gomez of the Starfleet Corps of Engineers. Why are you here?"

"You did not answer my question, Commander Gomez," Kazar hissed. "We do not have time to waste with trivial inquiries on your part. This landing area has suffered a power loss. According to our sources, the energy drain stretches from the lagoon and stops here. How long ago did this occur?"

Gomez sized up the large reptilian alien. He stood at least a foot and a half over her. Despite the distance between the two, she could feel his heated breath as he spoke. Along with his energy weapon, he carried a jeweled dagger, which remained sheathed.

"I'm afraid we're not in a position to discuss this situation with you at the moment," Gomez replied evenly. With effort, she met the stare of the Gorn.

"More Starfleet secrecy." Kazar let out a growl, which surprised even Corsi. "We do not care for your secrets, Starfleet! We want answers and we want them now!"

Gomez placed a hand on Corsi's wrist as she felt the security chief step forward. When Corsi settled, Gomez continued. "I didn't say we wouldn't tell you. I said we're not in a position to tell you. You see, I think we can help each other out here."

Kazar's eyes squinted in suspicion. "How?"

She pointed toward the landing bay doors. "Those doors need to be opened. We can't open them. I know of the strength of the Gorn people. With the two of you, it should be easy to pull them open."

"And you will share your information with us?" Kazar asked slowly.

"Yes. But you have to hurry."

The Gorn turned to his comrade. They didn't speak a word, but rather offered each other silent nods. Kazar turned back to Gomez. "We accept your proposal."

Gomez clapped her hands. "Great. Now, when you've managed to open the door, you'll need to find cover. We've got a flyer making an emergency landing. This entire chamber is going to be filled with flame retardant foam. It's going to make breathing very difficult."

"Wait a minute!" Milan cried out. He turned and ran toward a collection of crates in one corner of the bay. After a few moments of searching, he returned with what appeared to be a small projectile weapon. He stopped for a second and eyed the Gorn cautiously before handing it over to them.

"This is a flare gun," he explained. "Signal the flyer with it. They'll be able to see the open bay doors and can make their landing from there."

The Gorn took the gun and for a moment Corsi tensed on

the off chance that Kazar might try something devious. The Gorn examined the weapon a moment before cradling it in the sash that hung across his chest.

Gomez glanced up at the Nasat. "How's it hanging, Pattie?"

"I've been in worse spots," she replied. "But do you think we can speed it up a little?"

"You're going to be all right when the foam is released, right?" Gomez asked.

Pattie made a tinkling noise of amusement. "I can survive in a vacuum, remember? I can handle a little oxygen deprivation."

"Good—because you're the only one who can retrieve the passengers, in case they aren't in any shape to exit the craft themselves."

"Will do, Commander."

"All right, let's get to cover." Gomez looked at Kazar. "Good luck."

The Gorn didn't say a word as he and his comrade turned to the task before them.

Gomez entered the cramped control room last and closed the door behind her. She allowed the two Risan technicians to take their places at the control stations. She didn't bother to point out that they couldn't do anything while the systems were inoperative. Corsi and Soloman stood in the background, neither wanting to get in the way of the operation.

The Gorn took up positions on either side of the doors. They braced themselves, arching their backs for support. Large, clawed hands dug into the metallic surface, latching on and getting a strong grip.

Gomez glanced upward and saw Pattie hanging from the pipes, waiting for the cue to release the foam.

"Commander, if they are going to open the doors, they will need to do so now," Soloman reported. Gomez looked toward the sky from one of the windows and saw the flyer making a sharp banking turn toward the landing bay.

"They know they can't land anywhere else." Shira's voice trembled, ghostlike.

Below, the Gorn had managed to part the doors, but by less than a meter. They had stopped their work and appeared to be looking for a new way to attack the situation.

"We don't have time for this!" Corsi snapped. "They need to pull open those doors now!"

"If they do not possess the strength," Soloman said, "it is impossible."

Gomez watched as the Gorn repositioned themselves and made another attempt. This time the doors opened a bit farther. Gomez could make out the flyer as it neared the landing bay.

Kazar stepped into the opening and braced himself diagonally against both door surfaces, while his comrade reached out with both claws and gripped either side. Gomez could see Kazar's body trembling with the struggle.

The doors began to give some more.

"They're doing it!" Shira exclaimed. "We're going to make it!"

"It's not enough," Corsi said.

"No, but there is a chance," Gomez replied. "Let's stay positive. Have we got an emergency medical kit here?"

"Yes," Milan replied as he reached under the console and pulled out a small white box. "It doesn't have much."

Gomez opened the box and examined its contents. "As long as we can stabilize any shock conditions the passengers may have and prepare them to be moved to proper facilities, it's perfect."

"They're doing it," Soloman said, pointing downward.

Below, the Gorn were now in the opening doorway, pushing against the doors with their feet dug into the ground.

"Their backs are going to be a mess in the morning," Milan said.

"Maybe you can offer them a free massage," Corsi suggested with a smile.

"Estimating less than thirty meters to go," Shira said. Gomez gave the thumbs-up signal to Pattie. The Nasat scurried along the network of piping, twisting open the valves and releasing the foam. The large landing bay quickly filled up with the white substance.

"Here we go," Milan announced.

The flyer rumbled as it passed through the opening of the landing bay. The small control room shuddered as the craft struck the foam. Everyone grabbed hold of a piece of furniture or equipment to keep themselves steady. The flyer swerved and skidded toward a back wall.

"It's going to crash!" Shira shouted.

"Get down!" Gomez ordered everyone.

They ducked under the console. Gomez closed her eyes and waited for the inevitable.

It never came.

She opened her eyes and slowly rose from her crouched position.

The flyer had managed to halt its skid. A thin stream of smoke wisped from the rear of the craft.

Gomez looked to see that Pattie was already scurrying across the wall toward the craft to provide assistance.

Pattie stepped out into the landing bay and threaded her way through the foam that covered the area. She could feel the heat coming from the flyer. While the foam had done the job of taking the brunt of the crash and making it difficult for a fire to erupt, the billowing smoke pouring from the front of the craft was a warning of a possible explosion.

The Nasat stepped up to the large dome-shaped transparent aluminum covering and ran a pincer along the surface. She snapped her pincer away at the very intense heat. Inside, she could make out the two passengers, a male and female, both human. They were both unconscious. The female, who was the pilot, sported a large gash on her forehead, a thin river of blood flowing freely from the wound.

Pattie positioned herself to remove the covering, but found it impossible to do because the couplings that held it in place were fused due to the heat. She looked up at Gomez and shook her head. Gomez, in turn, pointed to several metal poles that leaned against a nearby wall.

Pattie retrieved one and proceeded to prop it against one of the couplings. She felt it give somewhat, but was startled by a loud moan from inside the flyer. The female began to convulse. Pattie dug the pole in deeper, frantically trying to pry it off.

She looked up at the sound of several more poles striking the couplings. The Gorn had returned and picked up the remaining poles. Pattie could hear the couplings begin to give. With a few more tugs, several ripped away, clattering on the floor behind her. She was still working on hers.

Kazar stepped up to her and shoved her aside without a word. He leaned over and gripped the edge of the covering and, with a low growl, tore it off. As soon as he did, the two inside began gasping for air. Kazar and his comrade grabbed the two, a little too roughly for Pattie's taste, and carried them quickly across the landing bay.

Gomez waited just outside the lower level entrance with Corsi. The Gorn released the two, dropping them roughly. Gomez ran her hand under the female's neck, while Corsi began to apply pressure to her head wound to stanch the bleeding.

Kazar stepped out into the corridor. "Commander, I have done what you have asked. The craft has landed safely and I have even aided in rescuing these two. You will now tell me what I want to know."

Gomez waved the Gorn commander off. "In a moment, Kazar. I want to stabilize these two first."

"Now Commander. You made an agreement and my time is limited."

"Now wait just a minute," Corsi began to rise from her position, but stopped at the gentle restraining hand of Gomez.

"Kazar's right," Gomez said. "I want you and Pattie to finish up here. I'm no doctor, but I think they're more in shock than anything else. Milan should be right back with the medical team." She gave Kazar her best steely stare. "Commander, if you'll walk with me."

She turned and started off without waiting for an answer. Kazar and his comrade followed, having to take a few larger steps to catch up with the seething female.

Corsi stifled a laugh. "I think they may have been better off dealing with me."

Pattie only nodded as she ran her mandible along the human male's limbs. "This one has a fracture in his left leg. I don't know if it was the crash or that Gorn's rough handling that did it."

"He's lucky to be alive," Corsi said as she pulled her blood-soaked cloth away from the female. "This one's going to need some attention, though. Hopefully, the hospitals are functioning. It's not like we can contact the ship and ask for help."

"I know," Pattie replied. "It's very frustrating."

CHAPTER 10

Surprisingly, Eddie's own hunger pains seemed to disappear as he watched the glowing entity absorb the energy around it. The walls of the cave they occupied reflected the light emanating from the two, giving an eerie glow around the cavern.

The entity hadn't spoken for some time, apparently preferring to concentrate on the task of taking in its sustenance. Eddie was starting to become antsy.

"So, what do you do for fun?" he asked aloud.

The entity shuddered slightly as contact with the energy feed was broken. It remained silent for a moment.

FUN? WHAT IS THAT?

"Fun. Fun is . . ." Eddie had to think about that one. "It's something you do. It's something you enjoy. It's . . . fun." Eddie shrugged.

Eddie felt a slight burning on his forehead. Suddenly, his mind's eye was flooded with a whirl of memories, mostly of himself and his mother engaged in a number of happy activities: playing a game on a rainy afternoon, running through a field where the cornstalks were as tall as the boy, eating ice cream and trying to catch the runoff before it hit the ground.

Tears began to well up in his eyes.

THERE IS TROUBLE? THIS FUN DOES NOT SEEM PLEASURABLE.

Eddie ran his hand across his eyes, wiping away the tears. He shook his head. "It is fun," he explained, "but they are what we call bittersweet memories."

WHY?

"My mother died over a year ago. It hurts to think about her now."

UNDERSTOOD. STUDIED YOUR MENTAL PROCESSES SUFFICIENTLY NOW. CONFIDENCE IN REMOVING THE OFFENDING MEMORIES.

"What?" Eddie asked, shocked. "No! No! That's all right. I . . ." Eddie smirked, changing the subject. "You know, I don't know what to call you. What's your name?"

NAME?

"Yeah, name." Eddie saw this meant nothing to his new friend. He searched his memory for something that might make more sense. "How about designation? What is your designation?"

NO DESIGNATION, EDDIE JOHNSON. IDENTIFIED BY RESONANCE.

"Well, I might not be able to recognize you in a crowd of your people. I gotta give you a name."

ACCEPTABLE. IDENTIFIED AS AN INDIVIDUAL.

"It isn't easy being you, right?" Eddie asked. "I know how you feel." Eddie looked down at his hands and watched as the swirling energy that was the entity sparked and snapped with loud crackles.

"I know," he said, looking up. "I'll call you Sparky!"

CHAPTER 11

On board the *da Vinci,* Captain Gold paced the length of the rear of the bridge back and forth in such a way you would have thought he had worn a hole in the floor. There had been no word from the away team in some time.

"Sir, I think you should take a look at this." Tev interrupted his routine in midstep.

Tev had been spending a great deal of time with Shabalala at tactical, poring over the various readouts from his scans.

"What do you have, Tev?" Stepping up to the station, Gold could see from the look on Shabalala's face that the Tellarite officer had been putting the young lieutenant through the paces. He appeared grateful to see his captain approach.

"I think we may have the source of the energy drain, sir," Tev said matter-of-factly.

"You do? Where?"

"Well, based on how the surges took place and the concentration of—"

Gold held out a hand to halt the lecture. "Tev, I'm sure this is fascinating and I look forward to reading it in your report, but all I need to know right now is *where.*"

Tev appeared somewhat taken aback for just a brief second. He then turned and pointed at the monitor in front of him. "Based on our scans, we believe it is occurring here, in the lagoon area. We have not been able to pinpoint the exact location as of yet."

"Very good. Nice work, the two of you. Any word yet from the away team?"

Shabalala shook his head. "No, sir. There was another surge just a short while ago and the region experienced a power loss."

"Sir, there is something else," Tev said. "The peninsula region cannot handle much more of this strain. Based on models I've been developing, I predict that another shutdown of the weather grid system in that area will be catastrophic."

Steeling himself for one of Tev's long-winded lectures, but suspecting that this time he'd need to hear the whole thing, Gold prompted, "How do you mean?"

"In order to maintain such consistent weather year-round, the control grid creates a constant low pressure system, thus essentially warding off any climactic disturbances. Now that the grid has been shut on and off, it's been allowing those disturbances to build in intensity. The higher-pressure systems that cause these storms are becoming stronger than the grid can defend against. Eventually, the grid will become useless, especially in its weakened state."

Gold let out a low whistle. "All right, Tev, I want you to take a couple of tricorders and combadges and beam down to the away team's last known position. I would imagine their equipment has been rendered useless."

Tev straightened himself. "Yes, sir."

"Give Commander Gomez the information regarding the weather situation as well."

"Aye, sir."

Tev stood there for a moment, as if waiting for something else.

"Well, go, Tev. Timing is important here." Gold made a little shooing motion with his hands.

Tev left the bridge quietly. Gold sighed and gave Shabalala a look as if to say, "No, you may not comment on Tev." The tactical officer returned to his scans, hiding a smile.

The captain turned away and walked back to his chair. He settled and wondered how centuries ago, when humanity first set out to explore the stars, all they had was one another on board those cramped vessels.

In the present day, commanding officers were always playing a juggling act, between accepting the cold logic of a Vulcan to the warrior mentality of a Klingon to the in-your-face directness of a Tellarite.

"Captain." Shabalala drew his attention to the matter at hand once again. "I'm picking up a large energy reading approaching Risa."

"Large?" Gold repeated.

Shabalala nodded. "Yes, sir. And it appears to be similar to the energy readings I'm detecting from the lagoon below."

Gold rubbed his temples and frowned. "Great, more feeders to join the party."

"This won't be a party, sir," Shabalala said. "This reading measures forty AU's in diameter, enough to envelop the entire planet and drain it completely."

Gold closed his eyes. "It just keeps getting better and better." He opened them again. "Shabalala, I want to alert Director Tonais of the situation, have him prepare for a possible evacuation. Then contact Starfleet Command and have them send us anything that can help."

"Sir, the energy masses will be in the system in less than two hours. There aren't any Starfleet ships in the area."

"Well, there are a number of ships in orbit right now. They'll just have to do their part. Tev should be planetside by now. Contact his away team and have them beamed directly to the lagoon."

"Aye, sir."

Gold rose from his seat and stepped up behind the conn officer. "Wong, plot an intercept course with those energy masses. Prepare to break orbit and take her to warp five."

"Aye, sir. Course plotted and laid in," Wong said as he tapped the commands into his console.

Gold stepped back and settled into his chair. "I hope you

have a name ready for your yacht, Wong. We're going to need it to help in the rescue operations."

Wong smiled. "Well, if they have to go, some of them will go in style."

"The away team has been transported to the lagoon, Captain," Shabalala called out. "Chief Hawkins has returned with a slight phaser wound."

Won't he ever learn to duck? Gold mused to himself. Aloud, he said, "Engage, Wong."

CHAPTER 12

If one were to watch the *da Vinci* away team materialize on the beach of the Monagas Lagoon, they would observe an interesting case study of differential behaviors of a multitude of species.

Gomez and Tev both immediately reached for their tricorders and began scanning the area, each trying to discover their quarry first. Soloman's face was a mix of wonder and fear. All his life he had been used to the sterile simplicity of his homeworld. Yet even though he had been to many a planet, the look of raw nature always filled him with a mix of emotions. Pattie always gave a slight shudder whenever she first materialized on solid ground. Even though she didn't visit her homeworld often, she still had her tree legs and was much more used to clambering about from limb to limb.

Corsi reached for her phaser and turned with a scowl to Angelopoulos who immediately drew both his phaser and tricorder. She didn't say a word to him, waiting for him to complete his task.

"There's nobody in the area for about one hundred meters. I'm picking up the unusual energy reading in that direction,"

Angelopoulos said, pointing to the caves. "That's where our Gorn friends were looking before."

"Me, too," Gomez said even as Tev said simultaneously, "As am I." They looked at each other for a moment, waiting for the other to say something. Their staring contest was cut short by a clap of thunder overhead.

"All right," Gomez broke the silence. "We're moving into the caves. I want security scanning ahead; I'll follow with Soloman and Pattie in the middle and Tev covering the rear." She brushed away a lock of her hair blown in front of her by a developing wind.

Tev was about to object when a streak of lightning sizzled across the sky. Everyone suddenly realized just how humid it was becoming.

"It looks like we're in for a storm," Gomez said. "Let's move out, people, and let's be careful. We don't know where that third Gorn is or if Kazar has joined him."

They began their trek across the sand, moving toward the cave entrance. The wind picked up its pace, staggering some of the crew with its buffeting force. Pattie reached out and steadied Soloman, who looked as though he was going to be lifted off the ground.

As they advanced, Corsi stepped up to Gomez and whispered, "I'm impressed. Tev didn't put up a fight or anything."

"He's learning. Sometimes he forgets that he's *second* in command—and I didn't help matters on our first mission when I dropped the command ball. But I think I've earned a grudging respect from him."

"That says a lot." Corsi let a grin slip out.

"Exactly," Gomez replied. "But by the same token, I can't let his brusqueness take command of any situation I'm in charge of handling. I've still got to sometimes remind him that I'm in charge."

"Heavy is the head that wears the crown," Corsi sighed.

"Speaking of crowns, how about you?" Gomez looked at Angelopoulos. "How are the new recruits adjusting?"

Corsi shrugged. "All right, I guess. I haven't heard any complaints."

"Do you ever?"

"From the recruits? No—but I trust Hawk to let me know if something's up. I've been trying to keep a looser hand, anyhow. Most of these people know their stuff—Lauoc, Krotine, even Konya."

"What about him?" Gomez asked, indicating Angelopoulos.

"Pretty straightforward and clever, based on his record. And he asked to transfer here."

"I'm impressed, Domenica—you've mellowed in your old age."

"I wouldn't go *that* far," Corsi said with a smile. "I just think that, especially after everything that's happened to us in the past few months, there are some really important things in life you have to appreciate in the here and now."

Gomez knew exactly what the security chief was talking about, especially in regards to a certain Fabian Stevens, who was waiting for her back at the ship. Gomez was of two minds about their slowly developing relationship. On the one hand, Fabian and Domenica were a good match.

On the other hand, Gomez harbored a thin, green streak of envy. Watching the two always reminded Gomez of what she and Kieran had and she wanted it again. How many times had she been the one who cooled down Duffy's advances, even hesitating when he proposed to her just before the Galvan VI mission began? Despite her words, hadn't Corsi learned anything from Gomez and Duffy?

The area around the away team began to darken, and a call from Angelopoulos ahead of them drew Gomez from her morose thoughts.

"I've pinpointed the source of the energy pattern," he reported. He held up his tricorder and tapped a command into the small unit. "I've also mapped out the interior of the cave system. I'm sending it to your tricorders. There are two entrances into the cavern."

Gomez turned to Corsi. "Well?"

"We keep it simple to start, Commander," Corsi replied quickly. "You and I and Blue will enter from one side while Tev, Soloman, and Angelopoulos will enter from the other."

Gomez nodded appreciatively. "Good. I like it. Let's make no sudden moves here. Wait for my signal to move in." She was looking at Tev as she said this. The Tellarite grunted his acknowledgment.

Sparky had been silent for some time. Eddie didn't bother his new friend as he was still getting used to the sensation of the absorbed energy washing over him. There was that little part of Eddie that wondered if he was causing any harm to himself being joined to Sparky.

Physically, he looked the same, save for the hairs on his hands and arms standing up. He reached up and felt his hair swaying about in an upright position. Other than his odd hairstyle and the tingling sensation coursing throughout his body, Eddie felt fine.

DANGER.

"What?" Eddie still wasn't used to hearing Sparky's voice in his mind.

DANGER. OTHERS OF YOUR KIND APPROACHING.

"My kind?" Eddie repeated. "Humans?"

SOLID MATTER. ENERGY DEVICES. Sparky paused. **WEAPONS. MAY HARM EDDIE JOHNSON.**

"Me? How do you know they're going to hurt us? They might be here to help us."

TRUST NO ONE.

"You trusted me," Eddie argued.

FRIEND.

"And these people could turn out to be friends too." Eddie continued to press his point. "My father could be among them."

ANGER AT FATHER. HE HURT EDDIE JOHNSON. FATHER HURT SPARKY.

"I was mad at my father, yes, but I wouldn't want to hurt him."

NOT HURT. INCAPACITATE.

Sparky began to glow again, preparing itself for an assault. Eddie tried to call out, but found that his voice wasn't echoing off the cavern walls.

CANNOT ALERT THEM. INCAPACITATE AND THEN INVESTIGATE.

"No!" Eddie cried out. "You don't know if you'll hurt them! Stop!"

The young boy, now a part of the energy being, struggled to stop the surge. He willed himself to halt the process.

STOP. EDDIE JOHNSON CANNOT CONTROL THIS.

"I have to try," Eddie said, gritting his teeth as he tried to maintain his concentration.

In the large outer cavern, Corsi and Angelopoulos checked the setting on their phasers.

"Somehow, I don't think that's going to have any effect on something that can suck the energy from an entire peninsula," Gomez said.

Corsi tapped at her phaser. "It makes me feel more secure." She lifted the weapon and examined it. "Anyway, it doesn't matter now. It's been drained."

"As has my tricorder," Soloman reported.

"I've still got my phaser," Angelopoulos said, lifting his weapon.

"As do I," Tev added. "Interesting. Some of our equipment is being affected this time, while others are not."

"Yes." Gomez was interrupted from continuing her thoughts by a cry from Soloman. He dropped to the ground, writhing in agony. Gomez was quickly to his side, pulling out her tricorder.

"Whatever is causing this drain is affecting Soloman. It's feeding on his neural impulses. He's slipping into a coma."

"That does it," Corsi said, taking Angelopoulos's weapon from his hands. "Let's take this thing out."

Before she could take another step, she was knocked off her feet by a concussive force, brought about by a phased explosion nearby.

"Well," Angelopoulos said, pointing toward the entrance to the cavern. "And I thought things couldn't get worse."

The three Gorn had entered the cavern, their weapons raised. They advanced slowly, making sure they had the entire away team covered.

"Do not move," Kazar hissed.

CHAPTER 13

"Get down!" Corsi ordered as she jumped behind a large boulder. She drew a bead on the lead Gorn and fired Angelopoulos's weapon.

Kazar stumbled back and toppled over like a great pine tree, crashing with a heavy thud. The two remaining Gorn strafed the area with their weapons fire.

Gomez ducked behind the boulder, settling beside Corsi.

"Isn't anything ever easy?" she asked.

Corsi's only reply was a shrug as she took another shot.

The chamber reverberated with the loud echo of crashing thunder and sizzling lightning from just outside the cave.

"That storm's getting worse," Gomez said, trying to look over the shoulders of the Gorn to the cave entrance beyond. The sky had darkened considerably and the wind was whipping up the sand into little tornadoes.

Gomez spotted Pattie standing close to the opening featuring the energy reading. She signaled Pattie to go in. The Nasat nodded her head in acknowledgment.

"I need some cover for Pattie," Gomez said.

"Got it," Corsi replied. She began to fire wildly above the

heads of the Gorn, sending a shower of debris upon the two. The Gorn ceased their fire for a moment as they tried to protect themselves.

"Go!" Gomez shouted.

Tonais tried to wend his way through the crowds of panicked guests who had gathered in the lobby of the Sheltered Arms resort, one of the largest in the region. He allowed himself only a moment to appreciate the effort it had taken on his part to organize the evacuation.

That was the easy part.

Now he had to make sure that the people made it off-planet safely. That was the difficult part.

Many of the guests had arrived on transports that would not return for days. What ships were currently in orbit were not enough to transport the entire planet. According to his people, the weather instability would not affect the entire planet right away. Thankfully, he would be able to get himself and the guests on Monagas Lagoon off-planet in less than twenty-four hours.

Bander, never far away from Tonais's side, had spent the better part of the afternoon coordinating the evacuation effort. He entered the spacious courtyard area, clutching his padd. Rivers of sweat poured down his balding head.

"Bander!" Tonais snapped, belying the gratitude he was feeling at seeing his assistant. "What news do you have?"

"All is ready, Director," Bander reported. He raised his data padd and began ticking off items with his fingers, rapidly playing across the screen like an accomplished pianist. "The *Daniella* is the first vessel, which will take approximately sixty-five people."

Tonais looked out at the people gathered and made a quick count. "They could take everyone here. Contact them with the coordinates."

Bander nodded. "Yes, sir."

The room erupted in a panicked scream as a lightning bolt struck a streetlamp just outside, causing it to explode in a shower of sparks. Tonais stepped forward, placing his arms out in a placating gesture.

"Ladies and gentlemen, please settle down. We're ready to begin transport. If you'll all gather your belongings and place yourselves in groups of six, we'll start the process." He turned to Bander. "Calm these people down and get them organized."

Bander looked at the growing panic and gulped. "Yes, sir." The little man moved slowly out into the crowd. "Excuse me." He turned his gaze upward as most of the guests towered over him and spoke a little louder. "Uh, excuse me."

He stopped short at the sight of a Nausicaan. The alien looked down at Bander with a scowl.

"I am going first."

Bander nodded. "Of course you are, sir." Bander struggled to keep from fainting.

Tonais walked off in the opposite direction, leaving the chaos to Bander for a moment. He tried to recall when such a disaster had occurred on Risa and could only think of the time the food synthesizers were distributing only prune danish. It was fine for breakfast, but by lunchtime the guests were getting ugly.

There was also that time when a group of subversives took control of the weather control station. If not for the intervention of two Starfleet officers, they might have succeeded in doing great harm to Risa.

But this was different. This was appearing to become something they could not rectify, not even with the aid of the S.C.E. Tonais looked out the window at the gathering storm. In the distance, he could make out a number of complexes buckling under the intense winds that were whipping up wildly. Several of the roofs of these structures had already been torn off and the destruction of the rest appeared imminent.

"Excuse me."

Tonais was drawn from his thoughts by a human, an Earther from the looks of him. His clothes looked as though they had been slept in for some time and his face was in need of a shave. But what most stood out for Tonais were the man's eyes. They were bloodshot as if the man had been crying for hours.

Tonais smiled with the warmth he usually saved for either visiting dignitaries or wealthy socialites. "Friend, you have nothing to fear. If you'll just stay with the group, you will be beamed off-planet shortly."

The man shook his head. "No, you don't understand. My name is Ray Johnson. I'm missing my son."

Tonais looked around the concourse. "I'm sure he must be here somewhere."

"You don't understand," Johnson said, his voice becoming panicked, his eyes welling up with tears again. "He's not here. He was exploring some caves by the lagoon and never came home. And now the storm's getting worse! You've got to help me!"

Tonais saw this was not something that simple public relations was going to resolve. He looked over toward Bander, who was stuck between a Nausicaan and an Andorian who appeared to be jostling the little man back and forth.

"Very well, Mr. Johnson," Tonais said reassuringly. "Now why don't you tell me again what happened to your son, from the beginning?"

CHAPTER 14

Captain David Gold watched the forward monitor as the warped star field re-formed into normal space. He focused his vision on two pinpricks of light, moving forward at a rapid speed. He looked toward Shabalala, not asking the question.

The tactical officer magnified the screen, bringing the energy waves into view. "Confirmed, sir. I'm reading just under forty AU in diameter with a power output of . . ." he adjusted his console and leaned back with a slight whistle. "You don't want to know, sir. Shall I raise shields?"

Gold thought about it for a moment. "No. Not yet, anyway. Let's try the hand of friendship. Open hailing frequencies."

"Frequencies open," Shabalala said.

The only sound the bridge crew heard for the next several moments was that of the various instruments at work. Shabalala broke the silence with an exhalation of panicked breath. "I'm reading fluctuations in the energy output. The two masses are slowing down."

"Let's do the same. Take us to half impulse, Wong."

"Aye, sir," Wong replied.

"Any response?" Gold asked Shabalala.

The tactical officer shook his head. "No, sir. Just a minute." He tapped on his console. "We're getting some sort of emission, sir."

"A weapon?"

Shabalala shook his head. "I don't think so."

"Let's not take a chance. Shields; go to yellow alert."

Personnel scattered about, moving themselves into position, ready to play their part in the situation.

"Impact in ten seconds," Shabalala said. "It's not a weapon, sir."

The bridge shuddered slightly with the impact. The bridge lights winked out for a moment, but immediately snapped back on. Several monitors began to display schematics of the ship.

"It's a scan of some sort, Captain," Shabalala said. "It's reading everything in our data banks." He tried to cut off the flow of information but was not successful. Shabalala looked to Gold and shook his head. "And we've lost shields."

The lights flickered again, to be replaced by emergency lighting. It cast disturbing shadows throughout the room.

Shabalala softly pounded his console in frustration as he watched the information from their records flow. The final image on the monitor was of the warp core chamber. It slowly faded away.

"Uh-oh," Shabalala said softly.

Pattie, having curled herself into a near-perfect sphere, rolled toward the chamber entrance. One of the Gorn, ignoring the fact that he was being pelted by large chunks of falling debris, focused his weapons fire on the Nasat. Luckily, her shell provided protection.

Gomez yelled above the whine of the firefight, "Keep them back!" She turned and made her own dash for the cavern. Bits of the cavern wall exploded on her with each impact of the Gorn's weapons.

Pattie was the first to make it through the opening, with

Gomez following. As Pattie emerged from her rolled-up position, she let out a series of chime-like noises that Gomez recognized as her being startled.

"Commander," Pattie said, "I believe we've found our energy disruption."

Gomez took a cautious step forward toward the glowing ball of light. She placed a hand before her eyes, trying to block out the glare, but it was no use. Her hand appeared translucent in the being's presence.

Tears began to stream down Gomez's eyes as she struggled to take in the image before her. She blinked several times, unsure if she saw something in the middle of the pulsing orb.

"Hello?" she asked tentatively.

HELLO. The voice appeared to be that of two people speaking at the same time. There was a stereophonic tone to the slightly reverberating speech.

Gomez took in a breath. "All right, you can understand me. My name is Commander Sonya Gomez."

ARE YOU WITH STARFLEET COMMAND? The voice was now only one and very excited. **I WANT TO BE IN STARFLEET WHEN I GROW UP.**

Gomez stopped for a moment to think about how to answer. There were many alien races among Starfleet's personnel, but she wasn't sure how such a being would fit in the organization.

Pattie, who had been slowly making her way around the pulsing orb, examining it as best she could without her instrumentation, said, "Commander, there is a humanoid being within the pulse."

Gomez turned and took another look, despite the slight headache she was developing. She managed to make out the form. "Who are you?"

The pulse shuddered slightly for several seconds before replying. **MY NAME IS EDDIE JOHNSON AND THIS IS MY FRIEND, SPARKY.**

"Then there are two of you?" Gomez asked.

YES, MA'AM. The voice was singular once again. **MY FATHER IS RAY JOHNSON. WE'RE HERE FOR A CONFERENCE.**

"Eddie," Gomez said slowly, trying to make sure she didn't lose control of the situation, "where is your father now?"

PROBABLY AT SOME BORING LECTURE OR SYMPOSIUM. I'LL BET HE DOESN'T EVEN KNOW THAT I'M GONE.

"I'm not so sure of that," Gomez replied. "Eddie, are you aware that you're disrupting many of the services on Risa?"

I KNOW. ISN'T IT FANTASTIC?

"Yes, it is," Gomez said, "but, it's also dangerous. The weather control station has been shut down and a storm is brewing that could destroy this entire region."

The being pulsed another moment. *Probably discussing this with each other,* Gomez thought.

WE ARE SORRY FOR THE PROBLEMS WE ARE CAUSING. The voice was once again plural.

"We appreciate that, Eddie, but you have to do more than that. You have to stop feeding on the planet's energy."

WE MUST FEED TO SURVIVE.

"And you can survive," Gomez continued. "We can help you. We can take you to a world where you can feed all you want. There are countless stars full of energy orbiting dead planets. But you have to stop here."

The being pulsed somewhat brighter as the argument between the two began to become more intense.

NO. The vocal tone was singular again, but different in its pitch. **NO HELP FOR SPARKY. HURT SPARKY.**

"Eddie! Please listen!"

EDDIE IS NOT SPEAKING NOW.

The pulse erupted into a bright light strobe, causing Gomez to fall back and cry out in pain. Pattie dropped quickly to her side.

"The light!" Gomez said with tears falling down her cheeks. "It's blinded me!"

THERE IS FIGHTING. WHO WILL TAKE SPARKY? NOBODY! I . . . WILL NOT BE TAKEN! WE WILL NOT BE TAKEN!

CHAPTER 15

The bridge crew of the *da Vinci* sat in tense silence as they watched the growing masses quickly approaching on the main viewscreen.

"Captain, I can give you shields again. It's limited, though," Conlon reported from engineering.

Gold rose from his chair and approached the tactical station. Shabalala looked up at his commanding officer and asked, "Shields, sir?"

Gold nodded. "Modulate frequencies so we make it difficult for them to get through. Weapons on standby."

"Aye, sir."

Gold turned toward the viewscreen. The twin energy fields slowed their pace.

"I think they're aware of what we're doing, sir," Wong said.

"*Thank* you, Wong," Gold said with a wry grin. "Let's look sharp, people. Stand ready."

Shabalala's station suddenly lit up and a low beeping sound filled the bridge. "Sir, we're getting a signal. It's coming from the energy masses."

"Can we make it out?"

"It appears to be . . ." Shabalala shook his head. "No, wait a minute. It's in Standard."

Gold raised an eyebrow in surprise. "Let's hear it."

An electronic tinged voice echoed from the ship's speakers. **GREETINGS, WE WISH TO INITIATE CONTACT WITH YOU AND YOUR SHIP.**

"I am Captain Da—" Gold began.

DAVID GOLD, CAPTAIN OF THE *U.S.S. DA VINCI*. WIFE IS RACHEL GILMAN. FIRST OFFICER IS COMMANDER SONYA GOMEZ.

"You have me at a disadvantage," Gold replied. "You know who I am. Who are you?"

WE HAVE NO NAME AS YOU WOULD BE ABLE TO IDENTIFY US. WE ARE WHO WE ARE. WE WISH TO SPEAK WITH YOU. MAY WE ENTER YOUR SHIP?

Gold looked about the bridge. The crew waited to see what move he would make next. *They did ask,* he thought. Aloud, he said, "Drop shields. We look forward to meeting you."

Shabalala cut off communication at a gesture from Gold. "Sir—"

"I know, son, but you see the power they're generating. They asked if they could come aboard when they could just as easily barge in. Let's see what they want."

"Captain!" the voice of Laura Poynter, the transporter chief, called from the speakers. *"My console just came alive—something's beaming aboard."*

"Don't touch anything, I'm on my way. Security to the transporter room. Wong, you have the conn."

Gold raced for the turbolift as it opened to admit him. As the doors closed, Wong rose from his station and settled slowly into the captain's chair. He looked around the bridge at his fellow crew members.

Susan Haznedl turned in her seat at ops and looked up at him. "How does the chair feel?"

Wong shifted slightly. "It's not very comfortable."

Haznedl shook her head. "I don't think it's ever supposed to be."

Wong stopped moving and leaned forward in the chair with a sigh. "I guess so."

*   *   *

The doors to the transporter room parted and Gold reached up to cover his eyes. The intense glow from the transporter platform reflected off some of the surfaces in the room, making vision next to impossible.

"Any way to tone down the light?" Gold asked.

There was a moment as some consideration on the matter was given.

YOU MAY REMOVE YOUR HAND NOW, CAPTAIN GOLD.

Gold slowly lowered his hand, surprised at how the lighting was now near normal. A soft glow emanated from the platform. Gold was even more surprised as his eyes adjusted. He noticed that Lauoc and Krotine from security were already present, phasers at the ready, flanking Poynter at the transporter console.

The two energy beings now assumed humanoid form.

"Lower your weapons," Gold said to the guards.

Krotine placed her weapon back in her holster. Lauoc did the same, but his hand remained poised over the weapon.

AH! THIS IS A PERSONAL VERSION OF YOUR SHIP'S ARMAMENTS. INTERESTING.

"Yes," Gold said slowly.

One of the figures stepped forward and extended a hand to the captain. Gold wasn't sure what to do. It withdrew its hand slowly.

I MERELY WISH TO GREET YOU IN A MANNER YOU ARE FAMILIAR WITH, CAPTAIN. IT WILL NOT HARM YOU.

What the hell, Gold thought, and accepted the handshake. A tingle went up his arm, but that was all. "Would you care to follow me? I would like to give you a tour of the ship, give us a chance to get to know each other a little more."

THANK YOU, CAPTAIN, BUT THAT IS UNNECESSARY. WE ARE MORE THAN FAMILIAR WITH YOUR SHIP. WE WISH TO DISCUSS OUR CURRENT SITUATION WITH YOU AND TO SEE HOW YOU MAY BE ABLE TO HELP US.

"To be honest, I'm not going to be much help at the moment as you have incapacitated my ship."

The being nodded its head and turned to its partner. A low hum filled the transporter room as the instrumentation panel came to life.

"Captain, this is engineering," Chief Engineer Conlon's voice sounded quite relieved. *"We have full power again."*

"Thank you," Gold replied. He turned to the entities. "I think I can help you." He tapped his combadge. "Bridge, set course back to Risa."

"Aye, sir," Wong replied.

Gold stepped up to the doors, which parted at a gesture from him. "If you'd care to follow me, we can discuss your problem in my conference room."

TIME IS CRITICAL, CAPTAIN.

"I'm aware of that, but I also feel that I need to know a little more about you. As I've said, you have me at a disadvantage."

The two stood silent for a moment.

They must be telepathic or something, Gold mused. *I wish I knew what they were saying.*

One being looked to the other and giving a nod, they stepped out into the corridor.

Bander winced at Tonais's shrill scream, uttered as a large chunk of the ceiling above him came crashing down. The rains had become so heavy that the roof could not hold up under the pressure.

"What was that?" Tonais asked angrily.

Bander shrugged. "I'm just thinking how remarkable our world was."

"Was?" Tonais sounded outraged. "What do you mean, was? *Is.* It is a remarkable world and it will be again."

Bander shook his head. "No, sir. I'm not speaking of Risa now, but of a time before we introduced technology to it."

Tonais rolled his eyes. "Please, don't tell me you're one of those naturalists who want to return the planet to its original state."

"No, sir," Bander repeated. "We cannot return the planet to its natural state as you can see by the view outside. There was a time when Risa was like a paradise."

"It's a paradise now, Bander."

"I'm sorry, sir, but it's not." Bander could see the anger rising in his director's eyes. But uncharacteristically, he felt the need to press on with his thoughts. "What we have now is an illusion. Risa has been unstable for centuries. Our atmospheric, meteorological, and tectonic equipment keep it from sliding over the edge." Bander pointed out the window. "This is the real Risa."

Tonais started to say something and then stopped. He folded his hands behind his back. "How many more transports remain?"

Bander only nodded before looking down at his padd again. "Five, sir."

"Good. It will be nice to be somewhere civilized again. I am tired of all this humidity."

"Yes, sir."

"What is the status of the Johnson boy?"

Bander shook his head. "The teams have returned, sir. The storms are becoming too intense. The winds have reached a sustained strength of a hundred and twenty KPH. It's impossible to maneuver people out there, especially without powered equipment."

Tonais grunted. "And nothing from the S.C.E. team either?"

"Not a word since they beamed away from the landing bay. And the *da Vinci* left orbit a short while ago."

"Left orbit?" Now Tonais sounded startled. "Why?"

"We don't know, sir. We've had no contact with them for some time."

Bander followed Tonais's gaze out at the storm. The complexes by the lagoon had been swept away. The very building they were standing in was on the verge of falling down. He turned his gaze toward Ray Johnson, trying hard not to meet his stare of expectation.

"This can't be the end," the director whispered.

* * *

Pattie gazed into Gomez's eyes trying to see if she could identify any type of damage that may have occurred.

"As far as I can tell," she said, "I can see nothing wrong with your eyes. They're not reacting to the light, but that is to be expected. How do you feel?"

Tears were still streaming down Gomez's face. "It stings a little. And I can't see anything. Otherwise, I'm fine. What's happening?"

"The entity is still just hovering there," Pattie replied. "Corsi and the others are keeping the Gorn at bay."

"Help me up," Gomez said, reaching out with a hand, which the Nasat took. She rose slowly. "Now turn me in the entity's direction." Gomez cleared her throat. "Please, if you would give me a moment. I can explain everything. You're friends with Eddie. I am sure he can tell you that you can trust us."

The entity did not reply immediately. **TRUE. BUT EDDIE IS YOUNG. EDDIE DOES NOT UNDERSTAND THE DANGER.**

"You trusted Eddie," Gomez said.

HE IS YOUNG.

"I would think compared to you, we're all young," Gomez said with a smile. "If nothing else, could you at least tell us how you came to be on Risa?"

I . . . EXISTED. I WAS CONTENT. MY PROGENITORS WERE NOT PRESENT. I THEN FOUND MYSELF RIPPED AWAY FROM EVERYTHING I KNEW, WITHOUT ANY CONTROL. I FELT MY ESSENCE BEING DRAINED AWAY. I MANAGED TO ESCAPE AND DISCOVERED THIS WORLD. I DISCOVERED EDDIE.

"And I'm sure his father is very worried about him," Gomez said.

The tone of the entity changed again. Eddie was speaking. **SOMEHOW I DOUBT THAT.**

"Eddie, does your friend have a name?"

SPARKY. I NAMED HIM THAT.

"Well, Sparky," Gomez began. *First contact with an alien named Sparky. Can't wait to write* this *report.* "I think we may be able to help you. You have been taken from what we call a nebula. If you allow us to examine you, we could determine where you came from."

POINT OF ORIGIN? THIS IS POSSIBLE?

"If that's what you want."

I DO NOT KNOW.

Within the mass of energy, Eddie squirmed excitedly. "What's there to not know? Sparky, these people are the real deal! If they say they can get you home, they mean it. Besides, I can come along with you and see the actual insides of a starship!"

BUT EDDIE, WHAT IF THEY ARE LYING? HAVE YOU EVER KNOWN A PROGENITOR TO BE ENTIRELY TRUTHFUL?

"Well, my parents did keep me in the dark about Santa until I was six," Eddie admitted. "But this is different! This is Starfleet!"

I DO NOT TRUST THEM.

"Look," Eddie said, "you scanned my mind before. Do it again. See what I mean when I speak about Starfleet and its people."

VERY WELL.

Eddie felt the slight surge tap the front of his mind once again. Images of Starfleet operations that he had viewed from newscasts began to flood his mental senses. The Dominion War. Wolf 359. Voyager Six. Captain Jonathan Archer and the launch of the first warp-five vessel called *Enterprise*. Zephram Cochrane discovering warp drive.

YOU ADMIRE THESE PEOPLE GREATLY.

"They're fantastic," Eddie said.

IS THIS A SUBSTITUTE FOR YOUR FATHER?

"What?" Eddie asked, shocked.

In the cavern outside, the phaser fire had stopped, thanks to the entity's last power surge. Every weapon had been rendered useless.

Tev was the first to throw down his phaser and lunge himself with a growl at the Gorn. He struck one of them with a balled-up fist to the jaw. The Gorn's head jerked slightly. He laughed at the Tellarite officer before backhanding him against the wall.

Corsi and Angelopoulos circled around the other Gorn, making sure they kept out of reach. At a signal from Corsi, Angelopoulos dropped to all fours. The Gorn, momentarily surprised by the odd movement, was unprepared for Corsi's dropkick to his stomach.

The alien fell down hard. Angelopoulos rolled and grabbed a large rock, bringing it crashing down on the Gorn's head. He didn't try to get up after that.

Corsi turned her attention to the remaining Gorn as it made its way slowly to the cavern entrance.

"Oh no, you don't," Corsi said as she tried to drop-kick him. The Gorn reached out and caught her foot and twisted it just enough to hear a cracking sound. He then threw her like a rag doll against the cavern wall.

Angelopoulos started to move to her side, but she held out a restraining hand. "I'm fine. Stop him."

The young security guard ran off after his target. Corsi turned and saw that Tev was coming around.

"Are you all right, Commander?" Corsi asked.

"Just tell me when the quakes have stopped. It is difficult for me to get my bearings." He looked around. "Where is Crewperson Angelopoulos?"

"Gone after the Gorn," Corsi replied.

"He stands little chance on his own without a weapon." Tev spoke in his usual dismissive tone.

Corsi snapped, "This is what he's trained for, Commander."

Tev shrugged. "If you say so."

The Gorn lurched into the chamber, leveling a device that Pattie had never seen before. It was beeping softly and a small red light flashed in time to the sound.

Pattie stepped up before the Gorn. "Stop." *What am I doing?*

The Gorn regarded the Nasat with a look of disdain. "Out of my way, insect," he hissed threateningly.

Out of the corner of her eye, Pattie spotted Angelopoulos entering the chamber and moving himself into position to attack. She took a step back, far enough away to keep her out of the Gorn's reach, but still holding her ground.

"You're not getting through me," she said, trying hard not to let her voice quiver.

"I have not killed anyone," the Gorn replied, adding, "today."

"It doesn't have to be this way," Pattie said, steeling herself for what she had to do next.

"Only if you let it happen," the Gorn growled. "We discovered the energy being first. It is ours by right! With such an energy source at our command, we will rule the quadrant as we were meant to!"

"You discovered him?" Pattie asked. "How?"

"We found it in a nebula and followed it here after it fled the nebula."

"Are you sure it fled?" Pattie asked. "Perhaps it caught on to your sensors or maybe you were using a ram scoop?" *Come on, kid. I can't keep him talking much longer.*

"It doesn't matter. The entity is ours. Stand aside and you can live another day."

Angelopoulos finally made his move. Racing forward, he launched himself at the Gorn. Pattie dropped into her spherical position and rolled away from the danger.

The young security guard struck hard, startling the Gorn into dropping his device. It clattered on the ground and rolled toward Gomez.

Angelopoulos tried a roundhouse kick that the Gorn caught. But before he could inflict the same damage he did to Corsi, Angelopoulos swung his arms out, slamming them into the sides of the Gorn's head.

The Gorn released the young man, who quickly ducked under and attempted to punch the Gorn in the stomach.

That was his mistake. The Gorn connected with an uppercut to Angelopoulos's jaw, lifting him off the ground and knocking him against the wall where he collapsed in a pile on the floor.

The Gorn turned and advanced on Gomez, who was reaching out, trying to find the dropped instrument.

"Give it to me!" the Gorn hissed.

Within the energy mass, Sparky and Eddie continued to argue.

"This is not about me!" Eddie said. "This is about you and your unwillingness to trust anyone!"

I TRUST YOU.

"Then why won't you trust me when I say to trust these people?"

Eddie felt a slight jolt run through him.

"What's wrong?"

DANGER. WE ARE IN DANGER.

"What? How?"

MUST PROTECT US. MUST PROTECT SELF.

Eddie felt an energy surge build around him.

"What are you doing?"

I WILL NOT ALLOW ANY HARM TO BEFALL US.

Eddie felt as though every nerve was on fire. Whatever Sparky was going to do was affecting him as well.

"Please! You're hurting me!"

ONLY FOR A MOMENT.

Sparky released the surge and Eddie screamed worse than the time he broke his leg in three different places and had to have it set without painkillers.

And then he blacked out.

CHAPTER 16

David Gold had sat with any number of different species in the observation lounge since taking command of the *da Vinci*, from the usual array of Nasats, humans, Bynars, Tellarites, Atreans, Vulcans, Bajorans, and so on, to the Klingons of the *Qaw'qay* to representatives from worlds all across the quadrant.

This, however, definitely qualified as one of the strangest. He was speaking to two energy masses that were currently in humanoid form only as a courtesy. They had even taken seats, in order to make the proceedings appear more normal.

But they were far from that.

Gold knew that he was conversing with two beings powerful enough to wipe out an entire star system. Despite their cordial appearance, he kept up his guard, waiting to see if the other shoe was going to drop.

Lauoc and Krotine were stationed on either side of the conference room door, ready to offer assistance should the situation warrant. But given the power the two possessed, Gold wasn't sure what kind of aid they could offer.

CAPTAIN, WE THANK YOU FOR YOUR KINDNESS AND HOSPITALITY, BUT WE COULD HAVE ARRIVED AT THIS PLANET IN MUCH FASTER TIME.

"I'm sure you could," Gold said, "but it is not that often I get to engage in a first contact situation, especially one of such importance. Now, how did you happen to lose your, well, for lack of a better word, your child?"

WE EXIST WITHIN STELLAR NURSERIES. YOU DESIGNATE THEM NEBULAE. WE HAVE OCCUPIED WHAT YOU CALL THE KELLER NEBULA FOR SOME TIME. THERE CAME A TIME WHEN IT WAS DECIDED THAT WE CREATE OFFSPRING.

"And it is your offspring that we believe is on Risa."

IT IS HIGHLY LIKELY, BASED ON WHAT YOU HAVE TOLD US OF THE SITUATION THERE. IT WILL BE IN NEED OF LARGE AMOUNTS OF ENERGY TO SUSTAIN ITSELF. THE NEBULA PROVIDED SUCH SUSTENANCE ADEQUATELY.

"And how did the child come to leave the nebula?"

THERE WAS A VESSEL, SCANNING THE NEBULA. THE CHILD WAS ATTRACTED TO THE ENERGY OF THE SCAN AND WENT TO INVESTIGATE. WE ONLY REALIZED WHAT HAPPENED WHEN THERE WAS A DISRUPTION IN THE NEBULA. WHEN IT ENDED, THE CHILD WAS GONE. IT TOOK SOME TIME TO DETERMINE ITS WHEREABOUTS.

A chime from the intercom interrupted them. *"Now entering orbit of Risa, Captain."*

"Very good, Wong," Gold said. He noted the two entities sitting straight up in their chairs. "What's the matter?"

THE OFFSPRING IS FEEDING WILDLY. THERE IS GREAT STRESS TO THE ECOSYSTEM OF THE PLANET.

Gold nodded. "It has affected the weather control station."

THERE IS MUCH MORE. THERE IS GREAT DANGER.

Before Gold could say another word, the two winked out of view.

* * *

Within the cave, the two energy beings materialized.

YOU CAME! an excited voice called out to them.

They surveyed the number of bodies about the cave. **WE HAVE BEEN SEARCHING FOR YOU FOR SOME TIME.** They stepped forward and scanned their offspring. **WHAT IS YOUR STATUS?**

WE'RE FINE.

WE?

The younger energy being made itself more translucent, revealing a young human boy inside. **THIS IS MY FRIEND, EDDIE.**

THE HUMANOID IS NOT A PET.

I KNOW THAT. EDDIE IS MY FRIEND.

DO YOU SEE WHAT DAMAGE YOU HAVE CAUSED? ARE YOU AWARE OF WHAT IS HAPPENING OUTSIDE?

The voice changed as Eddie answered. **IT WAS NECESSARY, SIR—MA'AM. SPARKY WAS FEELING THREATENED BY EVERYONE. HE WAS ONLY PROTECTING HIMSELF.**

SPARKY?

THAT'S MY NAME FOR HIM.

IT IS NOT A PET FOR YOU EITHER, EDDIE.

NO, SIR. NO, MA'AM, Eddie stuttered.

THE STARFLEET HUMANOIDS WOULD NOT HAVE HARMED YOU. THEY HELPED US FIND YOU.

THEY DID? Sparky asked, surprised.

TOLD YOU SO, Eddie said, matter-of-factly.

YES, AND NOW WE MUST REPAIR THE DAMAGE YOU HAVE CAUSED. WE WILL START BY RETURNING THESE HUMANOIDS TO THEIR SHIP FOR TREATMENT. THEN WE SHALL CORRECT THE ECOSYSTEM.

Sparky/Eddie rumbled slightly. **ARE YOU THINKING WHAT I'M THINKING?** They asked simultaneously. Without another word, Sparky/Eddie winked away.

WAIT! one of the two elder beings called out.

NO. The other realized what was happening. **LET THEM GO. THEY MUST MAKE AMENDS.**

Its companion thought over this for a moment and nodded. **VERY WELL. WE SHALL TRANSPORT THESE.**

A soft glow filled the two chambers as the energy beings, the away team, and the Gorn faded from view.

On the bridge of the *da Vinci*, Shabalala reported to Gold that a force-five gale was brewing and increasing in strength at Monagas. It was enough to wash the entire peninsula away if something wasn't done about it.

Gold twitched in his seat as he watched the viewscreen, which was filled with the image of Risa from orbit. He was startled, intent as he was on the screen, by the sound of the intercom.

"*Sickbay to bridge.*" Dr. Elizabeth Lense's voice sounded over the speakers.

"Yes, Lense, what is it?" Gold asked a little more tersely than he intended.

"*Captain, the away team has just—well, materialized here. They're being treated, but otherwise they're unharmed. Soloman appears to be worst off. He's in a self-imposed type of coma, which I'm monitoring. It appears he'll come out of it.*"

"Appears, Doctor?"

"*Well, for lack of a better explanation, Soloman is going through some kind of systems check. His vital signs are improving slowly, so I'm hesitant to administer any treatment to him. I'll keep you posted. I am going to need a couple of people from security to handle the three Gorn we have here as well.*"

"Gorn?" Gold repeated. Suddenly, a swell of cloud cover, moving rapidly into the northern region, caught his attention. "Very well, bridge out." He turned to the tactical station behind him. "Have Lauoc and Krotine report to sickbay, then get whoever's next up on the duty roster, along with Stevens and Conlon, and have them report to the transporter room."

As Shabalala moved to carry out the orders, Haznedl said from ops, "Sir, we can't transport down there. That storm is out of control. It's ionized the region, making transport impossible."

Gold frowned for a moment, before snapping his fingers

with the realization. "The energy beings. They can take us down."

Shabalala said, "Sir, I'm getting a signal from Risa."

"Put it through."

HELLO. CAN ANYONE HEAR US? IS THIS THE *DA VINCI*?

Gold frowned. "Yes, this is the *da Vinci*. Who is this? What are you doing playing on an official Starfleet channel?"

FANTASTIC. I TOLD YOU THIS WOULD WORK IF YOU CONCENTRATED HARD ENOUGH. SIR, MY NAME IS EDDIE JOHNSON AND I'M AT THE WEATHER CONTROL STATION WITH MY FRIEND, SPARKY.

As the voice spoke, the senior two energy beings faded into view before Gold.

"Do you know anything about this?" he asked the two.

OUR OFFSPRING AND ITS HUMANOID COMPANION ARE TRYING TO CORRECT THE ECOLOGICAL DAMAGE THEY HAVE CAUSED.

"They sound a little young. What can they do?"

The young voice said, **THAT'S WHY WE CONTACTED YOU, SIR. IF YOU CAN EXPLAIN TO US WHAT NEEDS TO BE DONE, WE CAN MAKE THE REPAIRS.**

Gold rolled his eyes in frustration and looked at the older beings. "Can you just help us to beam down a team that can work on the problem?"

WE COULD, CAPTAIN, BUT THEN WHAT LESSON WOULD BE LEARNED? THEY NEED TO CORRECT THE PROBLEM IN ORDER TO LEARN. HOW ELSE WILL WE AVOID THE SAME SITUATION IN THE FUTURE?

By locking them up in their rooms until they're ancient, Gold thought. He nodded, knowing full well he didn't have time to argue the point. "Very well. Shabalala, get Stevens up here."

"Aye, sir."

Sparky/Eddie walked about the small room, which was lined with banks of consoles and computers. A number of Risans lay about the floor, unconscious.

"Now do you see the damage you've caused?" Eddie asked. "These people meant you no harm."

WE DO NOT KNOW THAT.

"And you don't know that they did either. You never gave them the chance the way you did me. You never talked to them. You never . . ." Eddie stopped and chuckled. "How do you like that? I think this is what a counselor would call a breakthrough."

EXPLAIN.

"I've been so wrapped up in my own guilt and sorrow over my mom's death, I never really gave any thought to my father's. I never really talked to him. All we've been doing is talking the same talk, the same speeches, avoiding how we really feel."

DETERMINED THAT?

"Yeah, isn't that something? Now I really want to set things right here and see my dad again."

"Hello, my name is Fabian." Eddie could hear the Starfleet engineer's voice clearly through the link Sparky had established. *"Can you just give me a rough description of the consoles before you?"*

I THINK WE CAN DO BETTER THAN THAT, SIR. SPARKY, TAP INTO MY MIND AGAIN. I'VE GOT AN IDEA.

On the bridge of the *da Vinci,* the view of the northern hemisphere faded from the main screen to be replaced by a level view of the main monitors and computers of the weather station. The image was in monochrome.

"How the hell—?"

FANTASTIC. RIGHT, CAPTAIN?

"Yes, very fantastic," Gold replied. He looked to Fabian Stevens, who was now seated at one of the aft consoles.

Stevens smiled. "It works for me." All the monitors were dead. What lights lit up the consoles were all blinking a dull, dark red. Stevens's smile quickly faded. "This isn't good. This isn't just a case of repowering the system. It looks as though they may have fried a number of them as well. I need to get a look at the thing's innards."

HOW DO WE DO THAT?

"I want you to walk behind the environmental console and remove the backing. It's the large console with the silver trim."

ALL RIGHT. The image shifted slightly as Eddie/Sparky moved around to the rear. They easily removed the back panel, exposing a network of wiring and circuits. Many of the circuits were dark and burned out. The wiring appeared to be intact.

"Eddie, can you touch the larger blue wire leading into the console, please?"

A glowing hand reached out and grabbed the wire, producing a spark.

"Good. We don't need to worry about replacing that one. Can you feed a little juice into the system from there?"

There was a moment's hesitation. **IT'S ALL RIGHT, SPARKY. WE CAN DO THIS. LET'S JUST TAKE IT SLOW.**

"Yes," Fabian said quickly, "just a *little*. We don't want to damage the system any more than we already have."

The hand's luminescence increased slightly, and the bridge crew heard a sparkling sound coming from the speakers.

IS THIS GOOD?

"I really can't tell from here," Fabian replied. "Can you see any of the monitors coming back on?"

NO, BUT SOME OF THE RED LIGHTS HAVE GONE OFF.

"Primary circuitry is fried," Shabalala said softly from tactical.

"I know," Fabian said, "but why didn't secondary systems kick in?"

Shabalala shrugged. "Probably the same reason."

"Which means we're going to have to rewire the system and we don't have time for that."

AM I TO UNDERSTAND THAT YOU NEED A CONDUIT FOR THE TRANSFER OF POWER TO THIS EQUIPMENT?

"That's right," Stevens replied, trying not to think about the fact that he was talking to a glowing ball of light.

THEN WE VOLUNTEER OURSELVES AS A CONDUIT. WHERE MUST THE POWER FLOW?

"That wiring you were looking at. You must discharge a

steady flow of energy at three thousand joules." Stevens turned to Gold. "I need to get down there, sir."

One of the "parents" said, **WE CAN BE OF ASSISTANCE, CAPTAIN.**

Gold pointed to Stevens. "Take someone from security with you."

A few moments later, Stevens and Security Guard Frank Powers appeared in the center of the weather control room. Monitors were coming online as well as a number of the consoles. While power to the lighting hadn't been restored, the room was well lit thanks to the glow emanating from Sparky.

"That's it," Stevens said encouragingly. "Keep it up. I'm gonna start initiating the weather pattern program." Settling into a seat before the main console, he added, "Thank goodness nothing's burned out here." He began to tap in a series of instructions.

On the viewscreen above, a topographic image of the peninsula appeared, covered by a grid. Various areas of the grid, normally green in color, were a deep maroon.

"How are we looking?" Powers called out, sounding nervous.

"What's the matter, Frank, worried about a little rain?" Stevens asked with a smirk.

"I'm worried about the glowing balls of energy that fried the entire away team," Powers said, putting a hand to his holstered phaser.

"You security guys worry too much." Stevens chuckled. "Anyhow, the program is engaged and running. The satellites are generating the proper low-pressure system to disperse the clouds and lower the temperature."

A low rumble from beyond the station filled the room.

"Are you sure?" Powers asked.

"This isn't good." Stevens leaned over and tapped further instructions into the computer. "We can't generate a strong enough low-pressure system to combat the storm. It's out of control."

THERE IS TOO MUCH ENERGY? Sparky/Eddie asked.

"Yeah. Mother Nature's got her hold back on this planet and she won't let go. We need to reduce the temperature of the land and water, reduce the high humidity."

I CAN DO THIS. It was Sparky only speaking now. It detached itself from the console. **PLEASE BE PREPARED TO TAKE CARE OF EDDIE. HE WILL NEED TO ADJUST TO BEING OUTSIDE MY ENERGY STATE.**

With that, Eddie emerged from Sparky, dropping to his knees. Stevens placed a hand on his shoulder to steady him.

"Are you all right?"

Eddie ran a hand through his hair, which was standing on end. "I think so. It's a strange feeling being away from Sparky."

I SHALL RETURN.

Sparky reduced its size to that of a marble before winking out of sight. The viewscreen registered the new energy source as a bright yellow on its grid. The yellow expanded across the entire grid field.

Outside, the pitch-black clouds that covered the sky lit up with the expulsion of energy from Sparky. The wind began to pick up in intensity.

"What's happening?" Powers asked.

"I'm not a meteorologist," Stevens said, "but I think some of this storm will have to run its course. I should be able to control it now." Stevens sat back down in his seat and tapped on the console. "Yes! It's working. It looks like there's gonna be rain throughout the hemisphere for a while."

"The entire hemisphere?" Powers repeated.

"Just sharing the love." Stevens smirked. "It has to go somewhere or else the peninsula will get washed away." He winked at Eddie. "Nice work, kid."

A large smile crossed Eddie's face. "Thank you, sir."

Stevens rose from his chair and held out a hand to Eddie. The young man was unsteady on his feet as he tried to walk to a nearby window. A gentle rain was falling, guided by a brisk wind.

"I've always liked rainy days." Stevens smiled.

CHAPTER 17

Tonais stepped into the courtyard of the resort and let out a low moan of frustration. Parts of the ceiling had caved in due to the heavy rains. Deposits of mud, washed in by wind-swept floods, were scattered about the area. The courtyard's main feature, a large marble statue of a nude couple holding hands, was missing a couple of appendages.

"What do we do now?" Tonais asked with a groan.

Bander entered from the rear of the courtyard, his nose buried in his padd. He looked up briefly to survey the damage and let out a low whistle before returning to his padd.

"That's all you have to say about this?" Tonais struggled to keep his anger in check. He knew, although he would never admit it, that he needed Bander.

"We have a great deal of work to do, sir," Bander replied, not looking up from his padd. "I would estimate repairs to take over a month to complete."

Tonais felt his knees go weak. "A month? We can't remain out of operation for a month."

"I'm afraid we'll have to, sir. Many of the complexes in the resort are structurally unsound. We can salvage a number of them, but some will have to be torn down and rebuilt."

"You can add this courtyard to the list of buildings to tear down, Director," Commander Gomez called out as she and the Nasat entered the courtyard.

"Commander," Tonais said with only a halfhearted smile. "How are you feeling?"

"Better, thank you," Gomez said. "Dr. Lense was able to fix the damage to my eyes, and Soloman is recovering nicely as well. He should be leaving sickbay by the end of the day. Everybody else was patched up pretty quickly."

"Wonderful news." Tonais looked around the courtyard and let out a sigh. "This courtyard was one of the first structures built when the resort was designed."

"I'm sorry, sir, but it can't be salvaged. In fact, we shouldn't be standing here now."

"Yes, yes, of course. Let's step outside, Commander."

The four exited the courtyard where the view of the washed-out bay was still breathtaking on an early morning.

"So much to do," Tonais muttered.

"All good things take time, Director," Gomez said with a smile. "But when it's done, you can make this resort even better."

Tonais's eyes lit up. "Yes. We can make this better. I never liked the rugs in the main reception area or the way the lights hung and the shape of the aqua pool. This is fantastic. Bander! Come with me! We have a great deal of work ahead of us."

Tonais didn't look back or say good-bye as he walked off. Bander gave one look to the two Starfleet officers before walking off. He stopped and shrugged. *"We* have a great deal of work ahead of us? Who is he kidding?" Bander turned and walked away, muttering to himself.

"Commander." Pattie tapped Gomez on the shoulder and pointed toward the approaching Eddie and Ray Johnson.

Ray stepped up to Gomez and extended a hand. "Commander, I want to thank you for helping in rescuing my boy."

"Dad!" Eddie said, his voice tinged with warning.

"I think it's safe to say that Eddie helped rescue everyone, sir," Gomez said, winking at the young man and bringing a tinge of red to his face.

"Thank you," Eddie replied softly.

"Well, in any case, now that the conference is over, I'm going to take some time off. I've done all the work I can on the warp coil for now. I think it's time I work on my relationship with my son." Ray placed an arm around Eddie's shoulder.

"I'd like that, Dad," Eddie said, looking up at his father with a grin. "Have you seen Sparky, Commander?"

"It and its parents have been busy helping to restore power to areas of the region and by dispersing any residual storms that the weather system couldn't handle. But everything's under control now. I would imagine they're ready to return to their home."

"Oh," Eddie said quietly. He turned to walk off, but stopped at the appearance of three glowing humanoid forms. "Sparky!"

EDDIE, MY FRIEND. IT IS TIME TO RETURN.

"For me too," Eddie said. "Will I ever see you again?"

I THINK THAT IS POSSIBLE. I CAN SEND YOU MESSAGES THROUGH YOUR SUBSPACE CARRIER SYSTEM. AND SOMEDAY, YOU CAN VISIT ME WHEN YOU COMMAND YOUR STARSHIP.

"You really think I can do it?" Eddie asked.

MY FRIEND, I BELIEVE YOU CAN DO ANYTHING YOU WANT. I WILL MISS YOU.

"I'll miss you too." Eddie tried hard not to let the tears in his eyes fall.

Sparky took a step back to his parents.

"Thank you for your help," Gomez said.

WE ARE SORRY FOR THE PROBLEMS OUR OFFSPRING CAUSED.

Gomez looked about and shrugged slightly. "Boys will be boys. Have a safe trip home. And make sure you avoid any ram scoop collectors."

FAREWELL, COMMANDER GOMEZ. The three spoke in unison as they faded away.

Gomez's combadge chirped sharply.

"Commander Gomez." Shabalala's voice came from the small device. *"We're reading the departure of the three energy beings."*

"That's right, Tony," Gomez said.

"Commander, Captain Gold has requested that if you have completed your duties planetside, you are to report to the transporter room to help in one more engineering task."

"What is it?" she asked.

"He didn't say. He's already on his way to the transporter room and I'm leaving as soon as my relief gets here."

Gomez looked to Pattie, who only shook her head. "Don't look at me."

"All right," Sonya said, "alert the transporter room to beam us up."

She turned to the Johnsons. "Good-bye, Professor Johnson, Eddie."

"Good-bye," they said in unison.

She offered a friendly wave as the transporter beam gathered around them and they faded away.

Gomez materialized into darkness. She had no clue what was going on. And apparently neither did Corsi, Stevens, Wong, Shabalala, or Haznedl, who had just gathered in the transporter room several seconds earlier. Wong was the quietest of the bunch, which led Gomez to believe he might know.

"All right," she said. "Now can you tell me what's going on?"

"Lights," Wong called out.

Gomez blinked, startled by the sudden brightness around her. It took her a moment to adjust to the illumination. She let out a gasp as her vision cleared.

The crew was aboard the bridge of a luxury yacht. Gomez recognized the leather trim around the seating in the rear of the cabin. She stepped over and ran a hand along the surface of one of the seats.

"Andorian leather." Gomez smiled.

"This has to be a Starstream-line yacht," Stevens said.

Corsi looked at Stevens and chuckled. "All the engineering knowledge at your disposal and you determine that based on the type of leather on the seats."

Stevens shrugged. "Sometimes it's not about the technology. Only Starstream yachts use Andorian leather for their interiors."

"That's one of the reasons I chose this particular vessel," Wong said. "I also like the fact that she gets up to warp one-point-five."

"It's beautiful, Songmin," Haznedl said.

"Congratulations." Shabalala offered a hand to shake.

The doors to the cabin opened and Nancy Conlon entered. "Well, I've inspected the engine room. It's a bit cramped down there, but everything's in order. I also took care of that little bit of business you asked me about, Songmin."

"Thank you," he replied.

"Well, Wong," Gold said, giving a slight tap on the shoulder to the *da Vinci*'s helmsman, "what say we take your yacht out for a little spin?"

Wong grinned. "Yes, sir."

Gold held out a hand. "Oh, no. The only 'sir' here is you." He straightened himself at attention. "Permission to take her out of orbit, sir?"

Wong nodded. "Granted." He gestured to the leather seats in the rear of the cabin. "If you'd all take your seats, please, we'll get under way."

Gomez noted Corsi limping ever so slightly. The security chief's ankle had been broken in her fight with the Gorn and although Lense had healed the break neatly, it was going to be a day or two before Corsi could put her full weight on it.

So much for paradise, Gomez thought. *Quite a few of us have some scars from it. Thank goodness they're not permanent.*

Gomez stepped forward and offered a salute to Wong. "Captain, I would like to assist, er, the captain."

Wong laughed. "Take your station."

Gold and Gomez settled into the conn and ops positions. Wong stepped up behind them.

From the communications board, Stevens said, "I have Risan Control for you, sir."

"Risan Control—" Wong paused for a moment. "—this is the pleasure yacht *Nagus*, requesting permission to depart." Wong could swear he could feel the wind hitting his back from the quickly raised eyebrows of those behind him.

"Granted, Nagus. *Have a safe and pleasant trip."*

"Mr. Gold . . ." Wong said, feeling a little self-conscious as he said it.

Gold picked up on it immediately. "If you want the center seat for good someday, son, you're going to have to get used to it."

"Yes, sir," Wong replied and then caught himself. "Take us out."

David Gold tapped a series of instructions into his console. The yacht hummed to life and tilted slightly as it moved into escape orbit.

"We'll be clear and free to navigate in one minute," Gomez reported.

"Give me an image of the hull, please," Wong asked.

"Switching visual," Gomez said.

The viewscreen showed the greenish-blue color of the hull. Emblazoned across the side was the name, NAGUS.

"It looks great," Wong said with pride. "Thanks, Nancy."

"My pleasure," she said as she took a seat with the others in the rear. "This is a fine yacht you have. Although I'm curious about the name."

"I figured I should acknowledge how I obtained this craft. I won some latinum playing the Ferengi stock market."

"Be careful the nagus doesn't try to tax you for using his name," Corsi teased. "I'm sure there's some kind of Rule of Acquisition that covers it."

"Escape orbit achieved," Gold said.

"Let's get a look at Risa," Wong said.

"Aye, sir," Gomez said.

The viewscreen changed again and the main continent on Risa came into view. Its deep green landscape was charred somewhat now due to the extreme storms of recent days.

"It's such a shame," Shabalala said. "Risa is such a beautiful world."

"And it will be again," Gold replied. "It's just going to take some time. Just like everything else that's worth having." His console chirped. "Warp power at your command, sir."

"Let's take her to half impulse," Wong suggested. "We'll cruise out of the system and then take her to warp."

"Sounds like a plan," Gold said.

"So how about a tour?" Haznedl asked.

"Sure," Wong said. "Mr. Gold, take us to warp one as soon as we clear the system."

"Course, Captain?" Gold asked with a smile.

Wong looked out into space and nodded. "How about the nebula? We can check in with Sparky and his parents."

"Nice choice," Gold replied, tapping in the commands to make it so.

The *Nagus* pulled away from Risa and the orbiting *da Vinci*, gathering speed as it traveled. Wong stared out one of the viewports that lined the walls of the bridge and admired the view of the departing starship.

Haznedl stepped up behind him and tapped him on the shoulder. "This will make a nice retirement vessel someday."

"Yes, it will." Wong smiled as he took the ops officer's arm and crooked it in his. "Someday."

WHERE TIME STANDS STILL

Dayton Ward & Kevin Dilmore

ACKNOWLEDGMENTS

We would be remiss in our duties as storytellers if we didn't take the time to thank the following people:

Joyce Perry, of course, for writing "The Time Trap" for the animated *Star Trek* series.

John Ordover and Keith R.A. DeCandido, codevelopers and past and present editors of *Star Trek: S.C.E.*, who gave us the opportunity to tell the first stories about the *U.S.S. Lovell* and her crew in the *Foundations* trilogy. They trusted us to create the "secret origin" of the S.C.E. and agreed to indulge us occasionally whenever we felt the tickle to write another story featuring Commander al-Khaled and company. Thanks, guys!

Dan Abnett and Ian Edginton, writers of, among other things, the entire seventeen-issue run of Marvel Comics's *Star Trek: Early Voyages*, which chronicled the adventures of the *U.S.S. Enterprise* under the command of Kirk's predecessor, Captain Christopher Pike. In addition to several other crew members they conceived for the comic, Dan and Ian created Chief Engineer Moves-With-Burning-Grace, and they gave us their blessing to add him to the crew of the *Lovell*. We are grateful to them for the opportunity, and hope that our portrayal of Mr. Grace meets the high standards they established.

And finally, Curt Danhauser, fan and consummate guru of all things pertaining to the animated *Star Trek* series. With his assistance, we were able to tackle some of the tricky continuity challenges that have arisen since the series first aired and as the franchise has continued to evolve. His website offers an unmatched repository of information about this unique chapter in *Star Trek*'s history, as well as just being one incredibly fun stop along the information superhighway.

CHAPTER 1

Stardate 53800.9, Earth Year 2376

Sitting in the momentary quiet of the *U.S.S. da Vinci*'s conference lounge, Carol Abramowitz found herself once again captivated by the silvery object on the polished oval table before her. A four-sided obelisk not half a meter tall, the object boasted no remarkable qualities that might make it of any great value, intrinsic or otherwise, to a casual observer.

In many ways, she mused, *it's a lot like the world that produced it.*

The obelisk was composed of an ore relatively common to its native world of Valzhan, a place that never had drawn her interest and one she had judged long ago to be an unimposing, somewhat minor member of the United Federation of Planets. It was so far off her personal awareness sensors that the obelisk was the first artifact Abramowitz had ever physically encountered from the planet, an admission she made somewhat sheepishly considering her role as a cultural specialist attached to the Starfleet Corps of Engineers.

"Guardian Royano," she said, breaking what she hoped had not become a noticeably long silence, "thank you again for allowing me to study this. I've never seen anything quite like it, and I'd be lying if I said it was anything other than breathtaking."

Bowing his head formally, the Valzhan courier replied, "I am happy to be of what limited service I am able to provide. It is the least I can offer, considering how accommodating you and your captain and crew have been during this affair."

Royano had come aboard the *da Vinci* three days previously. Like the majority of his race, the Valzhan was essentially humanoid in appearance, with amber skin that contrasted sharply with his rich brown robes. His emerald-green eyes seemed to bore into anything he subjected to his gaze. Rather than an actual nose, his face featured a set of four small holes centered beneath his eyes, giving his face an oddly flat appearance broken only by the long blond hair cascading around his shoulders. Everything about Royano's comportment, from the way he spoke with a measured cadence to the dignified way he occupied his chair, worked to cultivate a scholarly air about him.

"I must admit I'm not as well versed in your culture as I'd prefer to be," Abramowitz said to the Valzhan. The words sounded like a pathetic excuse to her ears, even if Federation databanks held only scarce information on the planet. The Valzhan had long been regarded as a private people, a trait they had retained even after finally accepting Federation membership.

Her gaze again settled on the obelisk, which was supported by a circular pedestal no bigger than the palm of her hand. Each of its four faces narrowed to the object's pyramidal top and featured an intricately detailed etching. One engraving was an unknown artist's rendering of a barren, rocky plain from which a vicious reptilian beast bared its teeth and raised one clawed foot, possibly poised to strike, while another portrayed a goggle-eyed, winged fish leaping just beyond the crest of a wave within a turbulent seascape. Yet another was an intricate, labyrinthine pattern that produced a mesmerizing effect on the young woman.

It was the object's fourth side that appealed to her the most, however. Arguably the simplest in execution, it depicted a waterfall framed by a mountainside and thick with foam and rage at its base. With no superfluous detail to distract her, Abramowitz found her gaze repeatedly following the water's path from its initial plummet to the rocks below. Her imagination took over where the obelisk ended, restoring the natural, powerful flow of the water that had been stilled in the engraving. The roar of crashing falls seemed to ring in her ears even here in the restrained calm of the briefing room.

"What is the significance of these etchings here?" she asked.

"The additions to each *jelorakem* are unique to the clan that they represent," Royano said. "Most are allusions to significant events, with members of the clan choosing the representations to act as a sort of family historical chronicle." Lowering his head for a moment, he added, "I am sorry that I can offer only general information, but it is a long-standing tradition among my people that only a member of the clan to which the individual *jelorakem* belongs is permitted to explain the meaning behind its engravings. For anyone outside the clan to do so is considered a breach of ancestral privacy."

Abramowitz nodded, half expecting such an answer. Despite his willingness to share information about his own life on Valzhan, Royano had repeatedly found a polite way of deflecting her queries whenever she broached the topic of the clan *jelorakem*.

"Do you think it will be possible to meet with its rightful owners when we present it to them?" she asked. The part of her that thrived on research desperately wanted to run a tricorder scan on the obelisk, which Royano had told her was more than eleven hundred years old by Earth measurements. However, her heightened attentiveness to cultural sensibilities, to say nothing of the courtesy and respect she felt was owed to the Valzhan courier himself, swayed her from such action.

Royano replied, "I do not see why not." He reached for the obelisk, and after taking it from Abramowitz, held it in his own hands and studied it for several seconds in silence before looking up again. "Given the lengths to which Starfleet and the Federation have gone to honor our request, it seems the least that can be done. If not for your assistance, this *jelorakem* would go unclaimed and would have to be destroyed."

Simultaneously intrigued and disturbed by the notion, Abramowitz shifted in her seat. Her brow furrowing in confusion, she asked, "Is that the normal custom when there's no patriarch to take possession?"

"With Clan Briphachi having faded from existence on Valzhan," Royano replied, "their *jelorakem* no longer holds any meaning, and only a properly designated overseer is allowed to possess it. Guardians such as myself can retain them for limited periods, and then only with special dispensation granted by the Ancestral Commission for the express purpose of transporting them to their proper custodians."

"What is the Ancestral Commission?" Abramowitz asked.

Royano indicated a decorative emblem on the right sleeve of his robes. "It is charged with maintaining the records of all the *jelorakems* held by the various clans in our society, and it is they who ultimately determine the fate of the artifacts when a family can no longer do so for themselves."

"What about someone with close ties to the family?" Casting another look at the *jelorakem* the Valzhan still held in his hands, Abramowitz was nearly incredulous that such an artifact would be so easily forsaken. "Aren't they allowed to take custody of it to avoid having it destroyed?"

Shaking his head, Royano's reply was simple. "It is not our way."

It was an unusual and seemingly harsh way of handling a family's affairs, Abramowitz decided, though she of course did not articulate that opinion. Instead, she said, "Well, whatever the reason, I'm happy we're able to help you carry out your duties, though I confess I'm a bit surprised that they tasked the *da Vinci* with this assignment. I know that you specifically asked for an S.C.E. vessel, but I would have thought Starfleet might have offered to send a ship of the line for this occasion."

And you'd think some diplomat would want to grab such a plum assignment, she mused, *rather than leave it for your average, everyday cultural specialist.*

"Our leaders insisted that it be a vessel such as yours," Royano replied, sounding almost surprised that Abramowitz would even question the situation. "We owe a great deal to your Corps of Engineers, after all."

In actuality, dispatching a ship from the S.C.E. to ferry what essentially amounted to a family heirloom was anything but an ordinary use for such a vessel. However, Abramowitz and the rest of her shipmates had become accustomed to performing all manner of duties that were not in line with their primary role as a shipload of engineers. No one, not even Captain Montgomery Scott and the others who directed the S.C.E. teams to their various assignments from Starfleet Command back on Earth, was able to predict when the diverse base of knowledge and experience harbored by the crew of the *da Vinci* would prove useful in addressing a decidedly nontechnical issue.

Abramowitz had read the relevant reports from the Valzhan's last dealing with the Starfleet Corps of Engineers, which had taken place more than a century ago. It had happened at a time before the organization had evolved into the dynamic, multipurpose unit it was today, but the repercussions from the incident had been positive and long lasting, lending strength to what was now a formidable bond between the Valzhan people and the Federation. Those effects apparently were still being felt now, as evidenced by the *da Vinci*'s current mission.

Her brief reverie was interrupted by the voice of the ship's captain, David Gold, sounding over the room's intercom. "*Bridge to Abramowitz. We've arrived, and I thought you and Guardian Royano would want to be here when we establish contact.*"

"Thank you, Captain," she replied as she tapped her combadge. "We're on our way."

Even as she rose from her chair, she could feel all of the enthusiasm and anticipation she had barely succeeded in restraining throughout the voyage to this region of space beginning to force their way around the mental barriers she had erected.

This is why I joined Starfleet in the first place. The *da Vinci*'s destination, in addition to being a place she never thought she would ever have the opportunity to visit, was the very stuff from which a cultural specialist's dreams were made.

She was, however, able to rein in her growing excitement as she waited for Royano to return the *jelorakem* to its ornate yet protective carrying case and take the parcel under his arm. Abramowitz knew better than to suggest that the Valzhan courier leave the artifact here rather than carry it with him wherever he ventured aboard ship. As the guardian had explained to her upon his arrival, his duties required that the object never leave his presence, and it was a responsibility he undertook with utmost care.

All appeared normal as she directed Royano onto the bridge. She noted the *da Vinci* command center's typical muted tones as various workstations carried out their tasks, but she also observed that while personnel occupied each of the bridge stations, everyone seemed to be focused on the main viewscreen. Her own interest piqued, Abramowitz turned her attention to the viewer. Despite what she had read about this area of the galaxy, she was still surprised when the image on the main viewer depicted nothing but empty space.

"Doesn't seem like anything special, does it?" said Fabian Stevens, the S.C.E. team's tactical expert, from where he sat at one of the aft stations on the bridge's upper deck. "I was hoping for fireworks, or something."

His mild sarcasm was unmistakable and elicited a few chuckles from other members of the bridge crew. There was no doubting that everyone here, just like Abramowitz herself, was familiar with this part of space as well as the history and mystery that surrounded it.

"Just mind your station, Stevens," Captain Gold said, his tone communicating that, given their current situation, he was not in the mood to tolerate flip commentary. Abramowitz exploited the moment and shot the engineer a playful smirk, and he rewarded her with a mock glare before returning his attention to the matter at hand.

"The sensors are definitely taking a beating, Captain," said Susan Haznedl from the ops station in front of the viewscreen, "but the readings are normal for this area of space."

"What about communications?" Gold asked.

Looking up from his console, Stevens said, "The subspace beacon is functioning normally, sir." He shook his head, and

Abramowitz noted the small, appreciative smile forming on the tactical expert's face. "Over a hundred years old and still kicking like the day it was deployed. They sure knew how to build those things back then."

"What about the other one?" asked Commander Sonya Gomez, the *da Vinci*'s first officer and the leader of the ship's S.C.E. detachment. "Anything from it yet?"

Stevens did not reply at first, his attention focused on his workstation. After a moment, he nodded. "We just received the test message." Looking over to Gold, he added, "We're ready when you are, sir."

"Good," the captain replied. "Transmit the signal."

Tapping a sequence of commands to the touch-sensitive console before him, the engineer said, "Transmitting now."

Gold rose from his seat and turned to Abramowitz and Royano. "Guardian, I'm pleased to inform you that we've arrived on schedule, and if all goes well we should be receiving approval for passage anytime now."

The Valzhan bowed his head in response. "On behalf of all my people, Captain, I thank you once again for all you have done to assist us in this matter. It is indeed a great service you are providing."

Smiling, Gold replied, "The privilege and the pleasure are mine, sir, believe me." To the rest of the bridge crew, he said, "Congratulations, people. We're about to venture where no Starfleet vessel has gone for more than a hundred years." Abramowitz thought she detected an almost boyish thrill in the captain's voice. "For us, at any rate, this is likely to be a once-in-a-lifetime opportunity." Casting a look of warning toward Stevens, he added, "Let's try to behave ourselves, shall we?"

"Best behavior, sir," the engineer replied, maintaining a stern expression while placing a hand almost reverently upon his chest. A beeping sound from his station caught his attention, and he moved to check the console. "We're receiving an incoming hail, Captain."

"On-screen," Gold ordered.

After a moment, the image of empty space on the main viewer was replaced by that of a striking green-skinned woman with dark hair and exotic features, whom Abramowitz recognized as being of the Orion race. The woman said nothing at first, appearing instead to study the bridge crew with a gaze that, even to the cultural specialist, seemed to border on the hypnotic.

"*Greetings, crew of the* U.S.S. da Vinci," the woman finally said. "*I am Devna, representing the Elysian Council. Welcome to . . .*"

CHAPTER 2

Stardate 5309.3, Earth Year 2268

"... the Delta Triangle."

Even as he spoke the words, Lieutenant Commander Mahmud al-Khaled could not suppress an almost dismissive shrug. "It just doesn't seem all that mysterious, does it?" he asked, more of himself than anyone else. Studying the main viewscreen on the bridge of the *U.S.S. Lovell*, al-Khaled saw nothing about the region of space displayed before him that differentiated it from anywhere else he had traveled during his Starfleet career.

"Come now, Mahmud," said a gently teasing voice from behind him, and al-Khaled turned to regard his commanding officer, Daniel Okagawa. A wide grin brightened the captain's face. "Do I sense a certain jadedness?" Okagawa rose from his chair at the center of the *Lovell*'s circular bridge and crossed the command well to where al-Khaled stood at the forward railing. "Surely, even after all your years in Starfleet, there must be something out here that can still impress you?"

Al-Khaled nodded in conceit, offering a smile of his own. "Of course, sir." Shrugging, he added, "What I meant was that, given everything we've heard about this area over the years, I just expected to see something more dramatic, I suppose."

Shorter than the engineer, Okagawa was a stocky, barrel-chested man who looked up at al-Khaled and chuckled as he ran a meaty hand through his close-cropped black and silver hair. "Well, we've still got time. Perhaps the Triangle will honor your wishes before we leave."

Standing near the weapons and defense control station on the starboard side of the main viewscreen, Commander Araev zh'Rhun turned and cast a sarcastic frown in their direction. "You'll forgive me, Mr. al-Khaled, if I don't await that occurrence with your level of enthusiasm."

Bobbing his eyebrows with a hint of mischief as he regarded the *Lovell*'s first officer, al-Khaled replied, "I've resigned myself to the fact that I'm just not that lucky, Commander."

"Well then," the Andorian said, keeping her voice level even as her antennae twisted independently of each other to point in the engineer's direction, "may your lack of good fortune continue unchanged until we are well away from here."

Okagawa exchanged smiles with al-Khaled in response to the commander's comment. "You know how she is, Mahmud," the captain said. "She's not happy unless we're at red alert and the phasers are fully charged."

Both men resisted the urge to laugh as zh'Rhun turned her attention back to checking over each of the console's readouts without saying anything else. Contrary to Okagawa's remark and despite her heritage and the array of volatile emotions that normally characterized her species, the *Lovell*'s first officer was the very model of a Starfleet commander, with steadfast bearing and poise. Even on those occasions when the ship or its crew encountered dangerous situations, zh'Rhun had always proven unflappable. Her imposing image was enhanced by her habit of opting for the standard uniform trousers and gold tunic instead of the short skirt variation favored by many female Starfleet officers and enlisted personnel.

If that was not enough, the commander's reserved deportment also lent itself to a droll, deadpan sense of humor that she often used to her advantage when dealing with subordinates and superiors alike.

"Somehow," al-Khaled said as he turned to study the main viewer once more, "I get the feeling it's her wish that will be granted." All the available evidence certainly seemed to point to that conclusion. The *Lovell* had been navigating this area of space for nearly two weeks but had encountered nothing out of the ordinary, and certainly none of the odd occurrences that had long fueled the legends surrounding this region of the galaxy.

Ah, but that's the rub. The beauty of the Delta Triangle, as well as its inherent danger, al-Khaled reminded himself, lay in its apparent harmlessness.

The *U.S.S. Enterprise*, along with the Klingon battle cruiser *Klothos*, had barely succeeded in escaping from the mysterious triangle and the equally peculiar rift in the space-time continuum it was now known to harbor. Inside the odd stellar anomaly, the *Enterprise* had discovered a vast collection of vessels representing over a hundred spacefaring species. Ships from Earth dating back more than a century could be found there, along with those from civilizations both familiar and previously unknown. All of the ships had been stranded within the rift by an unexplained dampening field that permeated the region and drained their power systems.

This same phenomenon had nearly succeeded in disintegrating the *Enterprise*'s dilithium crystals and marooning the starship inside the Triangle along with the rift's other inhabitants. The people who had once traveled in the spaceships now ensnared within the Triangle, many of whom represented civilizations that had been and still were at odds with one another, had over time forged a joint nation within the confines of the rift. Such unity had proven a necessity for the society of Elysia, as it had been named, due to the region's other astonishing property. According to the report submitted by the *Enterprise*'s science officer, time flowed at a different pace inside the Delta Triangle, far slower than outside it. For those who lived there, a century was nothing more than the blink of an eye.

Confronted with the chance to acquire firsthand knowledge not only of Earth's first deep space exploration efforts but also the histories of dozens of races never before encountered by the Federation, Starfleet had dispatched a science vessel to study the phenomenon more closely. Arriving on site only three days earlier, the *U.S.S. T'Saura* and its dedicated team of astrophysicists had been given the assignment of understanding the region's debilitating properties while finding a way for ships to enter and exit the rift without suffering those ill effects. Al-Khaled was also certain, although it had not been stated openly, that Starfleet Intelligence was also very interested in learning if the energy-draining properties of the Triangle could be reproduced artificially.

Nodding in the direction of the main viewer and, by extension, the mysterious void that lay beyond, Captain Okagawa said, "You never know, Mahmud. Our friends on the *T'Saura* might well find a way to control passage in and out of there. If that happens, then your friend Mr. Scott will be the one who's jealous while you get a guided tour of some of those ships."

The notion elicited another smile from al-Khaled. "Well, one in particular, anyway."

He had read his friend's report on the wondrous array of space vessels the *Enterprise* had found inside the Triangle, some of which had been trapped there for more than a thousand years. Included among the more recent additions was the *U.S.S. Bonaventure*, a piece of engineering history if ever al-Khaled had read of one. The first Earth vessel equipped with the second generation of Zefram Cochrane's warp drive and assigned to the planet's budding space fleet, the ship had been reported lost early in the twenty-second century during her third patrol mission.

At the time, it was generally believed that the *Bonaventure* had fallen victim to a design flaw in its warp engine, a theory Cochrane himself would continue to dispute vehemently until his eventual disappearance only a few years later. Still, the incident seemed to amplify the man's desire to push the boundaries of the technology he had pioneered for humanity, driving him to establish the Warp Five Complex and create the foundation for interstellar travel capability that many, including al-Khaled himself, now took for granted.

"Captain," he heard a gruff voice say, and both he and Okagawa turned toward Lieutenant Xav, the *Lovell*'s science officer, seated at his station on the starboard side of the upper bridge. The stout Tellarite's heavy brow, large porcine nose, and recessed eyes gave him a perpetually sour expression, which he now directed at the two officers. "Engineering reports that the last of the navigational beacons has been deployed."

Unlike the enviable assignment given to the science crew of the *T'Saura*, the *Lovell*'s task was much less glamorous although equally necessary: establishing a network of subspace beacons to act as navigational hazard warnings for other ships traversing the area. Though two weeks spent deploying the devices had given Xav and his own small science contingent plenty of opportunities to record volumes of sensor data about the region, the mission had provided little else in the way of excitement for the rest of the *Lovell*'s crew.

Nodding to the science officer, Okagawa said, "Excellent." He waved to the viewer. "Let's have a map of the area, Mr. Xav, and see why the Delta Triangle got its name."

The image on the screen changed from a view of empty space to a computer-generated map of the region. Al-Khaled watched as a line of blue dots began to materialize, outlining a triangular area on the two-dimensional schematic anchored at two points by the stars identified in Federation stellar cartography databases as Kessik and Bellatrix. The third position was the most recent entry to the catalogue, possessing only the unflattering entry number FGC-82659. A small crimson indicator denoted the location of the *Lovell*, currently traveling within the area defined as the Triangle.

"All of the beacons are functioning normally, Captain," Xav reported from his station. "I will have my final report for Starfleet Command ready for your review by the end of my duty shift."

"Thank you, Lieutenant," Okagawa said. He continued to regard the schematic for a moment before pointing toward the upper left-hand corner of the viewer. "If my memory hasn't started to fail me, we're not all that far from the last known position of the *Courageous.*"

Al-Khaled nodded in agreement. He had recently studied Federation star charts of the area and recalled the notation about the vessel. One of the early DY-500 class of ships designed for long-duration travel within Earth's solar system and launched before the start of the third world war, the *Courageous* suffered a failure in its propulsion system that made the ship unable to decelerate or deactivate its engines. The vessel continued on its trajectory out of the Terran system, with support stations on Earth and Mars receiving periodic communications for years afterward, both from the doomed ship itself and from recorder markers left in its wake.

"Their last marker buoy was recovered twenty-six years ago," al-Khaled said. Incongruously enough, it had also been found less than fifty light-years from the *Lovell*'s current position and nowhere near the projected trajectory for the ship that had been computed by various historians, astrophysicists, and assorted "lost ship" enthusiasts. The message stored in the marker's tiny communications system was dated only thirteen months after the accident that had sent the *Courageous* on its ill-fated journey, and years before Cochrane's inaugural warp-speed flight from Earth. Most people believed that it had probably encountered a wormhole or similar stellar phenomenon, and speculation also abounded that it might in fact be yet another prisoner of the Delta Triangle. However, nothing about the vessel had appeared in any of the reports submitted by Captain Kirk following the *Enterprise*'s escape from the region.

Well, maybe we'll have a chance to find out for ourselves, al-Khaled mused, feeling his pulse quicken in anticipation of the unparalleled opportunities that this part of space offered.

"It is our proximity to the Gorn border that makes me uneasy," zh'Rhun said. "They are almost certainly aware of our presence, even if they have not yet done anything."

Starfleet's first and only encounter with the reclusive, violent reptilian race had come nearly a year previously, when a Gorn vessel attacked and destroyed a Federation outpost on

Cestus III, a planet claimed by them as being within their sovereign space. They had subsequently rejected all attempts at diplomatic overtures, instead offering repeated warnings that all future violations of their space would meet the same fate.

"We're still outside their territory," Okagawa replied, "and they've made it clear that so long as we leave them alone, they'll return the favor. With that in mind, let's see if we can't find something more immediate to concentrate on." He turned from the railing and made his way back to his chair at the center of the command well, pointing to the young Rigelian officer on duty at the communications station near the turbolift at the rear of the bridge. "Ensign Pzial, open a channel to the *T'Saura*."

To al-Khaled he said, "Now that we're done laying out street signs, maybe we can offer to help Captain Sivok and his people with their little project one more time."

"Considering his reaction the first time you asked," al-Khaled said, "somehow I doubt he'll be any more receptive this time around." The science vessel's Vulcan captain had been quite plainspoken in his belief that his people could handle their assignment without any outside assistance.

Okagawa shrugged, the corners of his mouth curling into an impish grin. "He just doesn't like the idea of getting help from anyone who travels around in an old rust bucket like ours."

It was a good-natured jab, al-Khaled knew, and one that the members of the *Lovell*'s crew only tolerated from one another. After all, they were proud of their little ship, the *Daedalus*-class vessel being one of three the Corps of Engineers had retrieved from the salvage depot at Qualor II. Removed from active service seventy years earlier, the *Daedalus* ships at one time had been Starfleet's workhorses. Their basic spherical and cylindrical hull sections had been designed with ease of manufacture and replication in mind, as the still-evolving United Federation of Planets found itself in need of large numbers of ships to secure its rapidly expanding borders in the aftermath of the Earth-Romulan War.

Now, however, the *Lovell* and her two sister ships were all that remained. Outdated and inferior in nearly every measurable sense to the more modern *Constitution*-class vessels that were the current pride of the fleet, they also suffered for the notable lack of replacement components available. The engineers assigned to the trio of craft therefore found their abilities and ingenuity constantly tested as they strived to keep their ships working at peak operational efficiency.

"Captain," he heard Pzial call out from the communications station, "we are receiving an urgent incoming message from Admiral Komack at Starfleet Command." After a moment, she added, "It's been encoded for us and the *T'Saura*."

Urgent? Given that any subspace message sent from Earth would take three weeks to reach the *Lovell*'s current position, al-Khaled had to wonder about the nature of any such communication. Besides, there was the unavoidable fact that their ship, assigned to the Corps of Engineers, was simply not in the habit of receiving priority messages from Starfleet Command, or anyone else for that matter.

"Let's have it on-screen, Ensign," Okagawa said, and the image on the main viewer shifted to show the weathered, lined face of Admiral Byron Komack, the staff officer in charge of all Starfleet operations in this sector of space. Seated behind a nondescript desk inside an equally austere office, Komack stared out at the *Lovell*'s bridge crew with the dour expression that had long been the admiral's trademark.

"Captain Okagawa, Captain Sivok," he said, *"a situation has arisen that requires your immediate attention. Effective immediately, your first priority is to work together to find a safe method of passage into the Delta Triangle."*

CHAPTER 3

"Well, so much for Captain Sivok not wanting our help," al-Khaled said, unable to suppress a grin.

"As you may or may not be aware," the recorded image of Komack continued, "the Federation recently welcomed a new member race, the Valzhan. Given their star system's proximity to the Klingon border, you can imagine the significance of having an ally in that part of space."

Al-Khaled was indeed aware of the Valzhan's admission to the Federation. According to the reports he had read, their civilization at one time had been quite advanced, having attained interplanetary travel capabilities before global war decimated their planet and the survivors spent centuries rebuilding. They had developed faster-than-light propulsion only within the last decade, but after their initial encounter with a Starfleet first-contact team, the Valzhan had shown great reluctance to accept an invitation to join the Federation.

While not strictly a pacifistic race, the Valzhan nevertheless held deep-seated convictions against violence except in defensive situations—and then only after all other conceivable options had been exhausted. Though they understood that the military portion of Starfleet's charter was not offensive in nature, they had expressed concern over being drawn into the Federation's ongoing political tensions with the Klingon and Romulan Empires, which had at times in recent years threatened to spill over into full-scale war. It had taken years of negotiations on the part of the Diplomatic Corps before Valzhan leaders would even agree to discuss the possibility of allying with the Federation, let alone convincing them of the virtues inherent in accepting an invitation to become a member world.

On the main viewscreen, Komack said, *"As part of a cultural outreach program, Federation specialists have been working with Valzhan scholars to learn more about their planet's long and quite colorful history. Here at Starfleet Command, a team of stellar cartographers began tracking the course of a generation ship the Valzhan launched more than four hundred years ago, and they're trying to ascertain where it might have ended up."* Pausing for a moment, the admiral leaned forward and rested his forearms on his desk, his craggy features staring out from the viewer. *"Based on telemetry received in the years before the Valzhan's global war caused them to shift their priorities to that of simple survival, a probable trajectory for the ship has been determined."*

"Don't tell me," Okagawa said.

As if knowing how his briefing would be received by those listening to it, Komack nodded and offered a knowing smile. *"That's right, you guessed it: the Delta Triangle. Now, the Valzhan understand that we've deemed the area a hazard to navigation and that entry to and from the rift, if it's even possible, will be highly restricted. However, a review of the* Enterprise's *sensor logs during its encounter with the rift shows the presence of a vessel that looks to be of Valzhan design, and their planetary government is requesting our assistance to confirm the ship's existence and to make contact with any Valzhan who might still be alive in the Triangle."*

Komack paused again, and this time his expression turned more serious. *"Ambassador Robert Fox, the lead diplomat who brought the Valzhan to the Federation in the first place, is very enthusiastic about this idea and has promised Starfleet's full cooperation. As you can probably imagine, a lot of eyes are on you. Good luck to you and your crews. Komack out."*

The message ended, and the image on the viewscreen reverted to that of empty space, and for several moments al-Khaled heard nothing save the chorus of background sound generated by the bridge's different workstations as well as the omnipresent thrum of the *Lovell*'s engines. Looking around, he noted the variety of expressions on the faces of the bridge crew, from the usual neutral aloofness offered by zh'Rhun to the furrowed brow of Captain Okagawa as he considered Komack's message, to the uncharacteristic enthusiasm brightening Xav's rounded features.

"How exciting," the Tellarite said as he turned from his science console, and al-Khaled noted that even his normally caustic expression had brightened at the thought of the new challenge Komack had issued. "Searching for long-lost brothers and sisters has such a romantic, adventurous appeal, does it not?"

Okagawa said, "While I can't help but share your zeal, Lieutenant, you can be sure that Ambassador Fox has no interest in romance and adventure. Considering the importance of establishing a Federation presence in the Valzhan system that close to the Klingon border, you can bet he'll be watching us like the proverbial hawk."

Of that, al-Khaled had no doubt. Fox's reputation as a no-nonsense diplomat was long renowned, as was his lack of tolerance for Starfleet, particularly when achieving his goals was made more difficult by something they did or failed to do. With that in mind, the engineer gave silent thanks to whatever cosmic forces had conspired to keep the ambassador from being on hand to watch over this mission personally. *Small favors, and all that,* he mused.

"Well," zh'Rhun said as she stepped closer to the railing separating the upper bridge deck from the command well, "at least this falls closer to the types of missions we are supposed to be assigned. A salvage operation is infinitely more desirable than deploying navigational markers."

"That's the spirit, Commander," Okagawa replied, smiling. "When I was a boy, I used to read and wonder about various ships that had gone missing over the years. *Ares IV*, the *Hawking*, the *Mariposa*. To think that any of those, and so many others, might be somewhere out here, just waiting for someone to find them." He shook his head. "Fascinating stuff."

Al-Khaled agreed, remembering a similar interest in such stories from his own childhood. Such tales were scattered throughout not only Federation history but also among that of just about any other spacefaring race that came to mind. On many of the occasions where a wayward vessel had been found, the discovery had been a grim one, with no heroic tales of survival in the face of overwhelming odds to honor the crews of the ships.

Could this time be different?

Besides, Commander zh'Rhun was right. Salvaging a lost or damaged vessel *was* more interesting than laying out a network of warning buoys. It was also right in line with the types of missions to which the Corps of Engineers typically was assigned, and when compared to tunneling through a moon or asteroid, building a colony, or repairing a remote starbase or space station, there was simply no contest.

When he realized he had allowed his mind to wander, al-Khaled looked up to see Okagawa regarding him as if he might be reading the younger man's mind.

"Yes," the captain said, "I think we might just have an interesting mission on our hands." He turned toward the communications station. "Ensign Pzial, hail the *T'Saura*. I think it's time for us to have a little chat with Captain Sivok."

Al-Khaled had met his share of Vulcans over the years, and with few exceptions all of them sported the same neutral, stoic demeanor for which the proud, almost regal race had long been known. Captain Sivok, as far as the engineer could see, fit the typical mold.

"Our sensor scans of the region support the hypothesis of the *Enterprise*'s science officer," Sivok said, "and show that an interdimensional rift does exist in this area of space, perhaps leading to an alternate universe. This rift appears to be protected by an energy barrier that is the source of the disruption in most shipboard systems reported by the *Enterprise*, notably sensors and propulsion."

Occupying the position at one end of the angled conference table that was the dominant feature of the *Lovell*'s main briefing room, the Vulcan captain sat ramrod straight in his chair, with his hands clasped together in front him, and his two forefingers extended and joined at the tips. To his right sat Lieutenant Commander Curtis Danhauser, the *T'Saura*'s science officer. Rounding out the attendees in the small room were Okagawa, Xav, and al-Khaled.

"Commander Danhauser," Okagawa said, "one of your reports also stated that you believe this barrier to be in a constant state of flux, which might explain why some ships can safely navigate the Triangle while others become trapped inside the rift."

The young man nodded. "That's correct, sir. Based on the sensor data we've collected, there are a handful of areas where the energy levels appear weaker than in the rest of the barrier. My best guess right now is that the ships that became trapped inside the rift passed through the field at one of these points."

Leaning forward in his chair and resting his forearms on the conference table, al-Khaled said, "From what I read of Commander Spock's report, the energy discharges the *Enterprise*'s sensors detected from outside the rift could have been caused by the reactions of these weak areas when they come into contact with normal space. He's also quite certain that this is the cause of the energy drain on a ship once it's trapped inside the rift."

Danhauser replied, "We think it has something to do with an incompatibility between the barrier and the energy generated by dilithium crystals in a ship's warp drive." He paused, looking up as the doors to the briefing room opened before returning his attention to al-Khaled. "Of course, it's a theory we can't really test until we find a way to pass back and forth through the barrier." Sighing in mild frustration, he added, "Bit of a vicious circle, isn't it?"

"Maybe not."

The officers at the table turned at the sound of the new

voice, its deep resonating tone instantly commanding the notice of everyone in the room.

"Captain Sivok," Okagawa said, indicating the new arrival with a wave of his hand, "allow me to introduce my chief engineer, Lieutenant Commander Moves-With-Burning-Grace. He also doubles as second-in-command to Mr. al-Khaled for our team from the Corps of Engineers."

Tall and possessing a lean yet muscled physique, smooth mahogany skin, and rugged features made even more prominent by his baldness, Grace was an imposing man, at least as far as al-Khaled was concerned. In keeping with his people's culture, swaths of red paint, their hue nearly matching that of his uniform tunic, adorned his cheeks and forehead as well as the top and sides of his hairless scalp, around which he also wore a thin blue headband.

Nodding in formal greeting to the *T'Saura*'s captain and science officer, Grace then said, "I apologize for the interruption, Captain, but I have been studying the information sent to us by Commander Danhauser, and I believe I may have a suggestion that will allow us to safely enter and exit the Triangle."

"Then your arrival is no interruption at all, Mr. Grace," Okagawa said. "What've you found?"

By way of reply, the chief engineer took the unoccupied chair to the captain's left and pressed a control on the small pad set into the table near his right arm. In response to this action, the three-sided viewscreen in the center of the table flared to life and displayed a computer schematic illustrating a *Constitution*-class starship and a Klingon D7 battle cruiser, joined together by way of their secondary hulls. "According to the reports submitted by the *Enterprise*, the breakdown in the crystalline structure of their dilithium was a cumulative effect. This meant the *Enterprise* and the Klingon ship it partnered with still possessed enough power in their respective crystals to mount a joint venture to escape the rift."

Another tap of the control pad produced what al-Khaled recognized as a technical schematic of the *Lovell*. "I believe that if we introduce a more tightly focused nutation cycle in our deflector shields, and channel power to the shield generators directly from the warp engines, we can produce sufficient energy for the shields to protect against contamination of the dilithium crystals."

"It is an intriguing notion," Sivok said. "However, given what we know of the field's effects and how rapidly it appears to drain the power systems of a wide variety of spaceships inside the Triangle, this would seem to be nothing more than a temporary solution."

Nodding in agreement, Grace said, "It's not intended as a permanent fix, but by my calculations, we should be able to protect ourselves for nearly ten hours, as long as we do not overly tax our onboard systems." Looking to Captain Okagawa, he added, "That would mean no high-speed travel while inside the rift, and only limited use of weapons."

"Well, considering what Captain Kirk reported about the people living in there," Danhauser replied, "that shouldn't be a problem. Some of the residents possess psionic powers, which they use to neutralize all weapons within the rift."

"Channeling power to the deflector shield generators directly from the warp engines is not a conventional use for either system," Captain Sivok said. "One must ask what led you to devise such a scheme, Commander Grace."

The engineer smiled. "My previous assignment was on Earth, as a member of the design team for the proposed upgrades to the *Constitution*-class ships. One of the proposals put forth by some of the civilian engineers was the idea of channeling phaser power from the warp engines in order to increase their power." Shrugging, he added, "I do not agree with the idea, mostly because I've been in enough situations where our engines were offline and yet we needed our weapons. Still, the concept struck me as having certain limited uses, such as what I'm proposing here."

"Don't let Mr. Grace's modesty fool you, Captain," Okagawa said. "Before joining us and before his stint on Earth, he served on three other ships, including a tour on the *Enterprise* under Christopher Pike. He's the latest in a long line of great engineers, and he's forgotten more about what makes a starship go than most people will ever know."

And lucky for me this is where he ended up, al-Khaled reminded himself.

"So," he said, nodding in satisfaction at Grace's proposal, "how long to get this done?"

"Engineering to bridge," the voice of the *Lovell*'s chief engineer echoed over the intercom system. *"We've completed our modifications to the shield generators, Captain. We can proceed at your discretion."*

From where he sat at the engineering station behind and to the left of the captain, al-Khaled watched as Okagawa glanced at the chronometer set into the console between the helm and navigator's stations in front of him, then shook his head and released a soft chuckle.

"Eight hours and thirty-seven minutes," the captain said. "As good as your word, Commander. Please stand by."

Grace had projected a time frame of nine hours to perform the task of realigning the ship's deflector shield systems so that they could accept power directly from the warp drive. In contrast to other engineers, who as a group tended to err on the side of caution when providing estimates for how long a task would take to accomplish, Grace instead was known for his accuracy and bluntness when offering such assessments, even if it was something his captain or anyone else might not want to hear. Still, that practice engendered a trust from Okagawa and the rest of the *Lovell*'s crew, al-Khaled included, who knew that their chief engineer's guesses were almost always more reliable than most other people's attempts at fact.

Turning his command chair toward the science station, Okagawa said, "Mr. Xav, what about communications once we're inside the rift?"

The Tellarite replied, "We are ready, Captain. I have fed the coordinates for one of the entry points plotted by Commander Danhauser to the helm. Once we maneuver into the rift, the *T'Saura* will deploy their subspace repeater beacon near the point where we pass through the barrier. Our own beacon is set to launch the moment we've made the transposition."

Though the beacons normally were used to amplify subspace communications signals over great distances, it was Commander Danhauser's opinion, based on the weeks of data collected by the *T'Saura*'s science team, that they also presented the best option for establishing communications into and out of the rift. By positioning one of the powerful devices on either side of the weak area in the energy barrier through which the *Lovell* would pass, he believed that the beacons, working in unison, would be able to overcome any disruption generated by the rift and amplify any signals transmitted through the barrier.

Sounds good in theory, al-Khaled conceded. *Here's hoping Danhauser's as good as he seems to be.* If the plan did not work, they would have no way of contacting the *T'Saura,* a smaller and less powerful ship than the *Lovell*. The chief engineers of both ships had concurred that the science vessel would not fare well traversing the energy barrier, and was instead better suited to remain outside the Triangle in a support capacity. Truth be told, it would be of little help to the *Lovell* should there be any trouble inside the rift, a proposition that did not set well with the engineer.

If Okagawa shared that apprehension, he did not show it. "Commander zh'Rhun," he said, "are we set?"

"All sections report ready, sir. Thanks to Mr. Grace's modifications, the shield generators are operating at one hundred seven percent of peak efficiency."

The captain nodded. "Excellent."

When he paused, al-Khaled turned to see Okagawa studying the main viewer, his attention seemingly focused on the field of stars it displayed, and the engineer sensed that his captain might be taking a moment to consider what else was waiting for them. It was an enthralling question, one that al-Khaled himself hoped would be answered in short order. Though he had read the reports submitted by the *Enterprise* crew following their experience here, he knew that those cold, emotionless words could not compare to a firsthand encounter with the phenomenon.

"Well," said Okagawa, the beginnings of another playful grin playing at the corners of his mouth, "unless I've missed something, I don't believe there's any reason to put this off any longer." He waved toward the main viewscreen. "Helm, take us in."

CHAPTER 4

Al-Khaled knew when they hit the barrier.

It was not due to any sensor alerts fed to his console or because an alarm klaxon blared in the confines of the bridge or even because Commander zh'Rhun or Lieutenant Xav said anything. Instead, the first indication came from his stomach, which lurched at the precise instant that the *Lovell* struck the leading edge of the odd energy field marking the true entrance to the Delta Triangle.

Then a flash of light engulfed the image on the main viewer and stars danced in al-Khaled's vision. A slight but steady vibration began in the deck plating, its intensity increasing with each passing second as it moved upward into the bulkheads, the bridge consoles, and even his teeth. Everything around him seemed to fade into a haze, the blinking indicators on his workstation's array of status monitors stretching and shifting as they smeared together into a single chaotic mass of jumbled color. He tasted bile as nausea washed over him and his stomach protested as the deck suddenly shifted beneath his feet.

"Captain," called out Lieutenant Sasha Rodriquez from the helm, "I've lost maneuvering control. Everything on my console is going haywire." Al-Khaled heard the heightened concern in her voice, which echoed his own growing anxiety as his disorientation continued to worsen.

"Sensors are offline," Xav shouted over the rising din as the ship seemed hell-bent on shaking itself apart. "I cannot tell how far we've moved through the barrier."

His hands gripping the arms of his chair to avoid being thrown to the deck, Okagawa said, "Hang on, people. This will pass."

It was several more seconds before al-Khaled sensed his dizziness waning. The blur of color began to pull apart and resume familiar shapes on the console before him, and he could already feel his queasiness ebbing. Shaking his head in an attempt to clear it, however, unleashed a sharp reminder of the abuse his body had just undergone.

"Commander zh'Rhun," he heard Okagawa say, "collect damage reports from all decks." Even the captain sounded as though he was still recovering from the effects of their transfer through the rift.

"Reports are coming in already, sir," the Andorian replied, "but no indications of any serious damage." Al-Khaled noted that her left antenna seemed to be drooping, lying almost flat atop her pale white hair in a sure sign that the commander had also been rattled by their passage. "Systems that were disrupted during the transition are returning to normal."

In front of him, Rodriquez reported, "I can confirm that, Captain. Helm control is restored."

"Sensors are clearing," Xav added. "Once we passed through the barrier, all instruments began to register and record normally."

Okagawa nodded and looked up at the main viewer. "So if everything is okay, then I guess I'd better get used to seeing this, eh?"

Feeling comfortable enough to look away from his own console, al-Khaled turned to get his first glimpse at what lay inside the Delta Triangle. Struck first by the curtain of rich red rather than the all-too-familiar black star field, he could hardly believe his eyes as he beheld the score of spacecraft now depicted on the viewscreen.

"Scotty's reports don't do this place justice," he said, rising to his feet as he regarded vessels he recognized drifting alongside those whose origins baffled him. Any imaginings of the interior of this rift he may have conjured from reading the *Enterprise*'s reports paled in comparison to this array of derelict ships, each hanging motionless in a sea of ruby-tinted light.

"A little caught up, Mahmud?" Okagawa asked.

"Oh, yes," the engineer nearly whispered in reply. Grasping for something to say that might seem appropriate to the vista displayed before him, he added, "It's like time-traveling through a history of spaceflight."

Their moment of shared awe was broken by Pzial, who, al-Khaled noted, was literally sitting on the edge of his seat, his bright red eyes wide in wonder. "That's a Rigelian border frigate," the communications officer said, pointing to a squat, boxy vessel near the top of the viewscreen. "The markings are unmistakable!"

"And that is a *Duroc*-class cargo freighter," Xav said, tugging a tuft of hair on his chin. "By Kera and Phinda, my grandsire crewed on a ship just like that."

"So much for calm, professional detachment," Okagawa said in a mock defeatist tone as he toggled the intercom control on the arm of his chair. "Bridge to engineering. Mr. Grace, we've crossed into the rift. How are things holding up down there?"

Though he knew that the *Lovell*'s chief engineer undoubtedly had his hands full monitoring and calibrating the modified deflector shields, al-Khaled was not surprised when Grace promptly replied, *"The shield generators are performing flawlessly, Captain. Everything is well within tolerance levels."*

"Keep me informed of any change, Commander. Okagawa out." He tapped the control with the bottom of his right fist, severing the connection before turning in his chair to face Pzial. "Ensign, let's test the subspace beacons. Try to raise the *T'Saura*."

"Already doing that, sir," the Rigelian replied with an obvious tone of pride at his own efficiency. "They are reporting a clear signal on their end."

"Excellent," the captain replied, clapping his hands together in satisfaction as he rose from his seat. "I suppose we should announce our arrival to our hosts. Open a channel to the Elysian Council." There was a pause as Pzial activated the frequency, which had been identified and recorded by the *Enterprise*'s communications officer during her ship's encounter with the Delta Triangle.

After getting Pzial's nod to proceed, the captain cleared his throat and said, "Elysian Council, this is Daniel Okagawa, commanding the Federation Starship *Lovell*. We have come on a mission of peace, and I request to meet with you in order to discuss a matter of some importance."

Several moments passed before Pzial turned from his console and shook his head. "No response on any channel, sir."

Al-Khaled felt a pang of disappointment at the ensign's report. Had they traveled all this way simply to be ignored? Would the people of Elysia forsake them, refusing even to acknowledge their greeting?

It was a feeling that vanished quickly, however, along with Captain Okagawa.

The bridge of the *Lovell* had dissolved into an orange burst of energy that seemed to overload Okagawa's vision as a tingling sensation played across his exposed skin that was not unlike what he experienced when being transported. Then it was gone, the strange haze of color fading to reveal the sweeping arc of a semicircular meeting table appointed with twelve high-backed chairs. Each seat was occupied by a representative of a different species—Orion, Romulan, Klingon, Andorian, Phylosian, Vulcan, Tellarite, Gorn, along with a few that Okagawa did not recognize.

"Captain Okagawa," a soft feminine voice said, and he turned to where the Orion, a woman, was seated. "Welcome to Elysia. I am Devna, interpreter of laws."

Studying the green-skinned woman, Okagawa noted her lithe form, dark hair that swept down past her shoulders, and bright eyes that seemed to bore straight into him. He was familiar with Orion females and the captivating beauty they commanded, of course, but he had encountered them in person only on infrequent occasions. It took him an extra moment to realize he was staring, and he blinked several times in an effort to refocus his attention on the matter at hand.

Eyes on the mission, Daniel, he reminded himself, *and not the host.*

"Thank you, Devna," he replied. "I appreciate your granting me this audience. As I stated before, I am here on a peaceful mission, representing the United Federation of Planets."

"We know all about your Federation, Captain," a deep male voice said. Its owner was seated near the center of the curved table, and Okagawa recognized the man's clothing as being Romulan in origin. "I am Xerius," he said. "Given the short span of time that has passed since your comrades visited us, I trust they are your reason for being here."

"After a fashion," Okagawa answered. "That ship's captain made a full report of his experiences here, but he's not the reason we've come."

Xerius nodded. "In your transmission, you mentioned discussing a matter of importance. Given that you appear to have arrived here of your own free will, are we to assume that you have found a method for successfully navigating through the barrier that surrounds the Delta Triangle?"

"That is correct, sir," the captain said. "We've made some technical modifications to our vessel's systems that will allow our departure once our business here is concluded." He watched as a wordless wave of skepticism crossed the features of the council members in response to his statement. Some of them turned to each other and nodded almost condescendingly.

Undeterred, Okagawa pressed on. "At the request of the people of Valzhan, we've come on a mission to contact and, if possible, retrieve the crew of a ship that became trapped here hundreds of our years ago. We're also willing to provide that same capability to anyone who wishes to leave Elysia."

A string of chattering noise erupted from one of the council members, a red-hued, insectlike being, which culminated in a sound that seemed to the captain as reminiscent of a human chuckling. In response to this outburst, the lone Klingon seated at the table expressed himself in a manner Okagawa had seen many times in the swarthy, aggressive race: He released a booming, hearty laugh.

"That's very presumptuous, Earther," the Klingon said. "We have built a model society for ourselves here. Why would we want to return to the life of struggle and conflict that you apparently still enjoy?"

"Please, Kelthos," said a wide-eyed woman who spoke in a thickly accented voice, "open yourself to this idea. Not everyone shares your unwavering desire to remain here, after all." Okagawa noted that the woman's head was encapsulated in a transparent dome, presumably a device that allowed her to breathe freely within the council chamber.

Seated farthest to the captain's right, the Gorn hissed and clicked something in its native language, leaning forward in its chair as it did so. The action caused its large muscles to ripple beneath thick, green-scaled skin.

"Yes, Glind," the woman said, her voice carrying what Okagawa perceived as a hint of exasperation as she turned to the Gorn, "we know you will never leave here, but as much as my people have embraced Elysia, this eternity of peace and goodwill has come at the cost of our physical freedom. Many of my people—myself included—still long for home beyond the confines of our native spacecraft, a place to feel the warmth of the sun or a fresh breeze across our faces."

Okagawa noticed the shock of surprise that seemed to grip several of her companions, most notably Kelthos, who folded his arms and sat back in his chair, his expression indicating that the Klingon was through with the current conversation.

"It seems obvious," Devna said after a moment, "that the captain's arrival and pronouncement have given us new fodder for debate." To Okagawa, she said, "Make no mistake, Captain, though we live in peace as a requirement for our survival here, we do not always agree on all matters. Many of us have been here for centuries, and as a consequence, we are unaware of what has transpired outside the Triangle. As for your offer, there are many among us who will be intrigued by the possibility of returning to normal space. Of course, anyone who wishes to go may do so, and everyone will undoubtedly be interested in learning as much as possible about the worlds we left behind. Regardless, many of us have long since come to accept that this will forever be our home."

"We are not here to impose our wills upon any of you," Okagawa replied. "We will offer safe passage out of the Triangle for anyone who wants it, or my people can teach you what you need to do to your vessels so that you can leave on your own terms. You don't *have* to stay here, not anymore."

Indicating the other eleven council members flanking her at the large table, Devna said, "As you know, several of the races represented here were bitter enemies at one time or another. It would be interesting to learn if such situations were ever resolved. Do enemies now live in peace, or do they even exist at all? These are just some of the many questions that we have."

Okagawa nodded. "I'd be lying if I said that the rest of the universe had achieved the level of collaborative spirit that you seem to share among yourselves in this place. You've demonstrated that even bitter rivals can find common ground upon which to build a lasting friendship. In fact, I have no doubt that you would have much to offer by virtue of the example you've created here." As he spoke, he found himself looking once again at the wide-eyed alien woman, her face partially obscured by a glare reflecting off the surface of her protective helmet. Still, he saw her offering what he took to be a reassuring smile, and he realized that he had made at least one convincing connection among these people.

One step at a time, he thought.

"You raise an interesting notion, Captain," Xerius replied. "However, you must remember that given the rather peculiar nature of our situation, we were forced to undertake actions, many of them very drastic, in order to forge our society rather than descend into chaos. We have long since come to believe that such success cannot, in many instances, be enjoyed outside Elysia."

Frowning at what he considered to be a near condemnation of the rest of the universe, Okagawa almost as quickly conceded that the Romulan may well have a point. For a moment, he imagined how the Elysian form of cooperation might work if employed on Nimbus III, a planet located near the Neutral

Zone where Federation, Klingon, and Romulan representatives had agreed to live together in the interests of fostering peaceful relationships between the three peoples. At last report, the so-called "Planet of Galactic Peace" was going through more than its share of growing pains, and many sociopolitical experts as well as the usual assortment of cynical naysayers were already foretelling the colony's eventual collapse.

The problems these people face are magnified exponentially compared to Nimbus, the captain mused, *and yet they made it work. What does that say about us?*

"It is a most unexpected and generous offer, Captain," Saraven said from where he stood before the expansive table of the Elysian Council. "However, it is one I must decline."

Tall and wide-shouldered, the Valzhan wore a simple arrangement of dark green robes that seemed to heighten his already bright amber complexion. His long gray hair was gathered at the nape of his thick neck, helping to frame a face lined deeply with age. Okagawa could not help but be impressed with the commanding air Saraven affected.

His eyes seeming to focus for a moment on some wistful memory, the Valzhan said, "Do not mistake me. Of course there is much about life on my homeworld that I miss. I was the patriarch of a large family at the time of my departure, but when I took command of our vessel so long ago, I made a commitment to the people traveling aboard it. That we arrived here instead of a planet we sought to colonize is not relevant, for my duty to those I lead has not changed."

"Indeed," Xerius said from where he sat near the center of the elongated conference table, "Saraven has become one of our most trusted advisers. His was among the first ships to arrive here that was designed for long duration, deep-space flight. It carried a variety of essential supplies and materials that the Valzhan graciously offered to share with the rest of Elysia. Saraven's is a voice of reason and leadership that truly helped to create the lasting community we enjoy to this day."

As he listened to the elder Romulan's words, Okagawa tried his best to ignore Kelthos, who was just visible behind Saraven and who was making no effort to hide the smile of smug satisfaction creasing his dark features. Okagawa knew that the council member was not his enemy, but he decided that even the uncounted years Kelthos had spent among the Elysian community had done little to dull the edge of his typical Klingon sense of self-importance.

Keeping his attention focused on Saraven, Okagawa said, "I understand and respect your position, sir, though I hope you will at least communicate our offer to the rest of your people."

The Valzhan nodded. "Indeed I shall, Captain, but do not be too hopeful of spiriting many of them away with you. Life on my world was not pleasant, with clashes and clan disputes that sometimes lasted for generations. Elysia has given us a different way of life."

"You'd be happy to hear that life on your planet has progressed quite well in your absence," Okagawa said. "After a prolonged war, your people have thrived, and they were recently accepted as members of our Federation. Working in cooperation with us and the many other civilizations we represent, the quality of life on Valzhan will only continue to improve."

He held out a padd that he had asked Lieutenant Xav to transport to him from the *Lovell*. "This contains a history of your family." He paused for a moment, unsure of how the next part might be received by the Valzhan captain. "I regret to inform you that several of your children, including your eldest son, were killed during the war, and your clan was among those who suffered many losses as the fighting dragged on. Those who survived have played an integral part in the progress your world has made. It's quite an exciting time for them, actually, but they very much want to know that you and your people are safe."

Saraven said nothing for several seconds, no doubt contemplating the sobering news. Even though the tragic events had occurred centuries ago, Okagawa knew that the Valzhan captain's sense of time had been skewed by his lengthy stay here in the Triangle, perhaps even to the extent that his memories of home were as fresh and vibrant as the day he had departed on his ill-fated journey.

Finally, he said, "Perhaps you would be so kind as to take word back that we too have found peace and contentment, albeit of a different sort. And there may be those who wish to go with you. In that event, we will craft a suitable presentation to convey to our homeworld."

Buoyed by the progress he was making, however small it might be, Okagawa smiled. "It would be my honor, sir." Turning to the council members, he added, "Naturally, we would do the same for anyone who requested it."

"In the spirit of cooperation that is the hallmark of Elysia," Devna replied, "we will do all we can to assist those who wish to leave. However, do not be surprised if your offer is received with less enthusiasm than you might expect."

While he respected his audience enough not to dispute out loud what the Orion woman said, Okagawa could not fathom anyone's desire to remain here. To be cut off from everything and everyone he had ever known, locked in this pocket of space that hovered outside the regular universe for all eternity, even when a means of escape was provided? The very notion was anathema to everything the captain held dear. Could life here truly be that rewarding and fulfilling?

Ask that again, he reminded himself, *after you've lived here a thousand years.*

CHAPTER 5

"The Phylosian ship is exiting the rift now, Captain," Xav reported from the science station on the *Lovell*'s bridge.

Turning from his own console, al-Khaled was in time to see a long cylindrical spacecraft waver and coalesce into existence on the main viewscreen. Though he had seen the effect repeated with half a dozen other vessels over the past two days, the sight still engrossed him. More than simply being a ship emerging from the depths of the Delta Triangle into real space, it represented a group of people freed from a prison and given the opportunity to return to the lives so cruelly taken from them.

"Outstanding," Okagawa said from where he stood next to his command chair. "Ensign Pzial, confirm that their navigator has the proper coordinates to get them home." The Phylosians had been trapped inside the rift for less than a decade, and had leapt at the chance to escape. Al-Khaled knew that their home planet had already been alerted to the discovery of the ship, and he was sure that arrangements to receive the wayward travelers were already under way.

After leading the first vessel, a Talarian battle cruiser, back to normal space, the *Lovell* had remained on station while the others followed at varying intervals over the last forty-five hours. Of the other vessels that had been helped so far, each of their crews had similar stories to tell. They had been among the more recent additions to Elysia, and as such had not yet formed the steadfast bond that seemed to join most of those who had lived in the rift for greater spans of time. Still, many of the long-term residents had also changed their minds, citing first the *Enterprise*'s miraculous escape and the *Lovell*'s demonstrated ability to enter and exit the Triangle at will. As a result, they were making their own preparations to return to normal space and the worlds they had long ago left behind.

"Given the success we seem to be having here," Okagawa said as he stepped around the helm console to take up his habitual stance of leaning against the forward bridge railing, "you can bet Starfleet won't waste any time taking advantage of the situation." Indicating the screen with a nod of his head, he added, "I wouldn't be surprised if Captain Sivok and the *T'Saura* received new mission orders that take them inside the rift."

"If that is the case," Xav said, "then I will be envious." His gruff voice harbored more than a bit of what al-Khaled recognized as jealousy, but he knew it was more in jest than anything else. Disappointed though he might be at missing out on the incredible opportunity for scientific research the Triangle represented, the Tellarite also knew his place and his obligations were on the *Lovell*, which in all likelihood would receive its own new and markedly different assignment in short order.

Standing next to him at the engineering console, Moves-With-Burning-Grace said, "I for one would not envy the *T'Saura* if they should be given such a mission. To remain stationary for any length of time is not something I would enjoy. Our vessels are designed to travel the stars, after all."

"Ready for warp eight, Grace?" al-Khaled asked, unable to keep the teasing note from his voice.

His expression neutral, the chief engineer nodded. "That would be an acceptable beginning, yes."

Al-Khaled laughed at his friend's deadpan response, knowing that there was more than a bit of truth behind the words. Descended from the Masai, an African tribe who had traveled to the desert planet Eristas during the first wave of colonization from Earth in the twenty-first century, Grace's people had long been renowned for their almost religious appreciation for velocity. The names they took often reflected this symbolism, particularly with respect to those animals that moved with utmost speed and elegance. This, more than anything else, al-Khaled knew, helped to explain why Grace had left the *Constitution* refit project on Earth and requested reassignment to a ship—any ship—rather than remain stagnant at a planet-based facility.

"Captain," he heard Xav say from the science station, "long-range sensors are detecting the approach of three vessels, all of similar configuration." After a moment, the Tellarite turned in his seat to face Okagawa. "They're Gorn."

"The Gorn?" Okagawa exclaimed. "What the hell are they doing here?"

Al-Khaled exchanged puzzled looks with the captain. "Well, we know we're not that far away from their territory. I suppose it's possible they might be interested in what's going on out here." Even as he spoke the words, he felt a twinge of anxiety grip him. It appeared that zh'Rhun's uncertainty about their proximity to the space claimed by the Gorn Hegemony had proven to be well-founded, after all.

"Their shields are raised and their weapons are powered," Xav reported.

Zh'Rhun turned to the captain. "Recommend alert status, sir."

"Do it," Okagawa replied, moving toward his chair as he gave the order. "Shields up, but let's leave the weapons on standby for the moment. There's no need to rush into this with hot heads, and all that." Waving to the viewer, he added, "Let's see what we're dealing with."

Having never seen a Gorn ship himself, it was with no small amount of curiosity that al-Khaled turned to the screen. Displayed on the screen was a trio of vessels that reminded him of old-fashioned boat anchors, with stocky primary hulls flanked by a quartet of nacelles. Stabilizer fins mounted to the rear of the ships' main hull sections implied the craft were maneuverable within a planet's atmosphere.

Could ships like these have been used for the attack on Cestus III? The question came unbidden, rattling around inside his head and vainly searching for an answer al-Khaled knew he was unlikely to receive, at least not today.

"Where's the *T'Saura*?" Okagawa asked.

"They are currently studying another portion of the rift, sir," Xav replied. "Sensors detect no other vessels in their vicinity."

Nodding at the report, the captain said, "Pzial, alert Captain Sivok to our current situation, and advise him to maintain his current position. When you've finished that, hail the Gorn."

Moments later, the image on the screen shifted from the three vessels to show what al-Khaled surmised was the bridge of one of the ships. Cloaked mostly in shadow, the chamber did not offer much in the way of detail that he could see, except for the lone figure seated in the center of the frame. Large and muscular, the Gorn regarded the *Lovell*'s bridge crew with silvery, seemingly compound eyes peering out from under horned brow ridges that echoed a third ridge dividing his skull. Al-Khaled felt himself gripped by an involuntary shiver as he noted that the creature's most intimidating feature was its mouth, with its double row of sharp-fanged teeth peeking from behind curled lips.

The Gorn was speaking in its native language, the flurry of hisses and clicks no more pleasant than the alien emitting them.

"What's he saying?" Okagawa asked.

"One moment, sir," Pzial replied, "The universal translator is deciphering and comparing it against the limited samples of Gorn dialects we have on file." Several moments passed before the Rigelian turned in his seat once again. "Switching over now."

The bridge's ambient noise was cut by a deep-throated voice. "*. . . speak to us immediately, we will be forced to take action to defend our interests.*"

Standing up, the captain raised his voice in greeting. "Gorn commander," he said in a tone that al-Khaled hoped retained its friendliness as it was washed through the translator, "I am Captain Daniel Okagawa of the Federation Starship *Lovell*. We experienced some initial trouble with your message, and ask that you repeat it."

There was a pause, perhaps while the Gorn captain received the translation of Okagawa's message, before the large reptilian being leaned forward in his massive chair. Al-Khaled caught himself leaning back in his own seat in response to the Gorn's gesture as the alien finally replied.

"*I am Lahr,*" came the computer-generated voice, "*commander of this Hegemony protector vessel. We have noted the increased traffic of vessels in this region of space, an area we have long believed to be a spatial trap for unfortunate ships. What is happening here?*"

Keeping his hands behind his back and adopting what al-Khaled hoped was a diplomatic and, more important, nonthreatening stance, Okagawa replied, "We have recently developed a means of safely traversing the Delta Triangle. In doing so, we have discovered many other ships from a large number of spacefaring races that have been trapped inside what is best described as an alternate universe. We are now using our newfound abilities to assist some of those vessels to leave this region and return to their home planets."

Lahr appeared to digest this information for several seconds. When he responded, his voice seemed to take on an added layer of menace. "*Tell me, human, is there one named Glind among them?*"

Okay, that one was out of left field, al-Khaled thought.

The captain nodded. "Yes, that's right. It may please you to know that there is a thriving community inside the rift, and that Glind plays an integral role in its government."

Though al-Khaled did not think the Gorn captain could appear any more ominous, that was exactly what happened as the alien rose from his chair, muscles rippling beneath his thick, dark skin, and stepped forward until his visage nearly filled the screen.

"He is also a wanted criminal, Captain," Lahr said, "*and we want him. Now.*"

* * *

Standing once more before the Elysian Council, Daniel Okagawa allowed himself a brief moment of contemplation. After all, navigating dicey diplomatic waters was not a specialty for which he had ever considered himself well suited.

Where the hell is Ambassador Fox when I need him?

"According to Gorn law," he said to his audience of twelve, "murder is a crime for which there is no statute of limitations or other comparable legal term of expiration. Even though Glind and his accomplices left their homeworld more than a century ago, they are still criminals in the eyes of the Hegemony."

"We are aware of this, Captain," Xerius replied from his seat at the center of the group of council members, "as we have been since their arrival." He gestured with an open palm to where Glind sat at the far end of the conference table. "It was obvious from the amount of damage their vessel had sustained prior to entering Elysia that they had been in some sort of confrontation, and it did not take long for Glind and his companions to confess to their crimes."

"The damage was inflicted during our escape from authorities," Glind said. "Only our falling into the trap that is the Delta Triangle saved us."

Nodding, the captain said, "When they lost track of you, the Hegemony closed the matter, believing you to be lost forever." Casting a downward glance toward the floor, he added, "That's changed now, however, thanks to us. With a proven ability to enter and exit the Triangle at will, they either want you extradited back to normal space, or else they want the technology given to them so that they can come in here and retrieve you themselves. Their concern is, now that a proven method of leaving the rift is available, you and your friends will use that knowledge to escape from here, and from them."

The corners of Xerius's mouth turned down in a disapproving frown. "Though we of course do not condone such actions by members of our community, it is Elysian law that citizens cannot be punished for crimes they have committed prior to being stranded here. It is a valued tenet of our society, one that must be preserved if new arrivals are to feel they have any chance of acclimating to this reality. In the case of the Gorn, Glind and his people have proven themselves over time to be valued citizens. We cannot allow them to be taken from here if they choose not to leave of their own free will."

Okagawa's attention was drawn to the sound of the doors at the near end of the council chambers parting, revealing an exotic-looking alien woman. Fair-skinned and with flaming red hair piled high atop her head, the woman's narrow facial features and her yellow, catlike eyes that possessed an almost hypnotic allure easily identified her to the *Lovell*'s captain as a native of the Omega Cygni system.

"Welcome, Magen," Devna said from where she sat next to Xerius. "Is something wrong?"

There was a look of worry in the woman's eyes as she replied, "We have seen the presence of the ships beyond the barrier. There is much anger and distrust, and it threatens our sanctity."

Sensing the mood of the council beginning to shift, Okagawa said, "Yes, we know of the psionic abilities some of your people possess. For what it's worth, I conveyed that information to Captain Lahr, and we were at least able to reach a temporary understanding. They have no immediate plans to enter the Triangle, and I've convinced him that I need time to consult with my government before we can move forward."

"It does not matter," Glind said after a moment. "We have means of protecting ourselves from outsiders, and we will not leave this place. You have our word. My people will understand."

Unable to suppress a tired smile, the captain shook his head. "Trust me when I say that, right now, your people are very skeptical. Still, Lahr is willing to report to his superiors that there may be a workable solution here. In order to secure his cooperation, I had to promise that you won't leave Elysia, at least until this matter is settled."

"That is most impressive, Captain," Glind replied. "Given my people's aggressive nature, I would not have expected such a compromise to be possible."

Nodding in agreement, Okagawa said, "From what I know

of your people, you're probably right. However, we've had some limited contact with the Gorn in the past, a fact that seems to have helped us here." In truth, Lahr had been the one to bring up Captain Kirk's encounter with another Gorn vessel at Cestus III. The honor and integrity demonstrated by the *Enterprise* commander even when locked in mortal combat had earned him, and by extension the organization he represented, a measure of respect in the eyes of the Hegemony.

But it won't last forever, Okagawa reminded himself. *We need to come up with a solution here, and fast.*

CHAPTER 6

"And considering the length of time the people of Elysia have been together and in light of the very real society they've formed here, they should be allowed to decide for themselves whether they leave, and their wishes should supersede those of any outside influence, be it ours or anyone else's."

Okagawa halted his dictation, reaching up to rub his tired eyes. "Computer, pause recording."

Seated in the only other chair flanking the small desk in the captain's quarters, Commander zh'Rhun regarded Okagawa with an expression of worry. "Are you all right, sir?"

The captain shook his head. "I'm fine. I just want to make sure I get the wording of this right. Diplomacy has never been my strong suit, but it takes on a different level of complexity when you can't even rely on real-time responses to your questions or concerns."

Leaning against the wall of Okagawa's quarters with his arms folded across his chest, al-Khaled nodded in sympathetic agreement. A subspace message transmitted from their current location would take nearly three weeks to reach Starfleet Command, leaving the captain in the unenviable position of having to anticipate wishes and decisions that might not be conveyed to him for more than a month while continuing to deal with the fluid and chaotic situation unfolding right in front of him.

"If Starfleet agrees with your line of thinking," zh'Rhun said, "and the Gorn really do intend to stay in Elysia, then it would be equivalent to their being granted asylum."

Okagawa reached for the cup of coffee near his right hand and took a sip before replying, "I'm no lawyer, but it seems to me that there'd be some kind of precedent for what I'm proposing. A colony that's declared independence from its homeworld . . . something." Shrugging, he added, "I'm sure there's a legal expert or diplomat who can find some way to justify it and back us up, but saying they support our position and their being able to help us defend it are two different things entirely."

"Somehow I don't think the Gorn are going to side with our lawyers or politicians," al-Khaled said, shaking his head. Despite the Gorn captain's agreement to allow Okagawa a chance to consult with his superiors, the engineer knew that the situation here, already tense, would likely continue to deteriorate.

"Agreed," Okagawa replied, "which is why I've already dispatched a call for any Starfleet ships in the area to get here as quickly as possible. Ensign Pzial tells me that the *Lexington* is already en route, but Commodore Wesley says he can't get here in less than eighty hours even at his ship's maximum speed." He released a tired sigh. "For better or worse, we're on our own until then."

Though no one in the room said anything further, al-Khaled figured that the thoughts running through his own mind were not all that different from those preoccupying his captain and Commander zh'Rhun. The *Lovell* and the *T'Saura* were not ships of the line, possessing only minimum armaments and defensive systems. While the *Lovell* itself had benefited from a team of engineers eager to upgrade the ship's systems far beyond their expected operational efficiency, even that would not be enough should the Gorn ships summon reinforcements.

Enough of that, he thought, chastising himself for concentrating on aspects of their current circumstances over which he had no control. As an engineer, he knew he should be focusing on ways to improve their situation in any way possible. Sooner or later, Captain Okagawa would want options, and he needed to be ready. *Focus, Mahmud.*

His thoughts were rudely interrupted by the sound of a red alert klaxon, and the captain's quarters were suddenly bathed in harsh crimson as the alarm indicator mounted over the door began flashing.

"*Bridge to Captain Okagawa,*" said the voice of Lieutenant Xav through the intercom system. "*Sir, two of the Gorn ships have broken from their formation and are maneuvering away, and sensors show that the remaining ship is launching an unoccupied craft.*"

Sharing a puzzled look with zh'Rhun and al-Khaled, Okagawa's brow knit in alarm. "What the hell are they up to now?"

The turbolift ride from deck three to the bridge was quick, but not quick enough for Okagawa's liking. If al-Khaled had not known better, he would have sworn the captain was pushing through the still-opening doors even before the car had stopped moving.

"Report," he said, bypassing his chair and instead moving around the helm console to stand near the forward bridge railing.

Turning from the science console, Xav replied, "The vessel is deploying mines, sir." He touched a control on his console, and the image on the main viewscreen shifted to a computer-generated map of the Delta Triangle region. Blue indicators marked the current positions of the *Lovell* and the *T'Saura*, while a trio of red icons symbolized the Gorn vessels as they moved away from each other. Each ship appeared to be heading toward different areas of the Triangle. It was the red marker nearest the *Lovell*'s position that drew al-Khaled's attention. Xav had programmed the schematic to represent the smaller, unmanned vessel in green, and while everyone on the bridge looked on, it began to describe its own arc across the screen.

His attention still on the viewscreen, Okagawa said, "I guess they've decided not to wait for us after all."

"The other two ships look to be heading for spots we've

identified as potential entry points into the rift," al-Khaled said, watching as the schematic continued to update with information supplied by the *Lovell*'s sensors.

From the science station, Xav said, "Assuming they are doing the same thing as the other vessel, they will be in position to begin deploying their own mines within the hour."

Acknowledging the report with a nod, Okagawa looked to al-Khaled. "What do you know about Gorn weaponry?"

The engineer shook his head. "Not a lot, sir. I've reviewed the sensor data collected during the *Enterprise*'s initial encounter with the Gorn ship at Cestus III. The ship they pursued wasn't much different from what we're facing now." He knew that the Gorn had all but retreated into their own space following that first meeting with a Starfleet vessel, and that subsequent sightings of their ships were decidedly rare.

"Then let's start learning," Okagawa said. "Get me everything you can as quickly as possible, Mr. Xav." He looked over his shoulder to the communications station. "Pzial, hail the Gorn commander."

There was a momentary delay as the Rigelian ensign established the connection, and then the computer graphic on the main viewer was replaced with the still-imposing figure of Captain Lahr.

"Captain," Okagawa said, "may I ask what you are doing?"

Seated in the oversized chair at the front of what passed for the command center on the Gorn's ship, Lahr replied, *"As your sensors have undoubtedly revealed to you, we are deploying a network of protective mines. Our superiors are concerned that the criminals will find a way to escape their prison despite your assurances. They do not believe our governments can resolve this situation in a timely manner, which only allows ample opportunity for the criminals to escape. Therefore, we are to prevent any ship from leaving the Delta Triangle until such a resolution is reached."* He paused for a moment, lowering his massive head as if contemplating what to say next. Al-Khaled tried to read the Gorn's expression, but of course that was impossible. *"I apologize for this turn of events, Captain, but I have my orders. Please do not attempt to challenge us in this matter. I would regret destroying your vessel."*

The connection was severed an instant later, returning the map of the Triangle to the screen.

"That certainly went well," Okagawa said as he turned away from the viewer, his expression of concern a mirror of al-Khaled's own.

"The minefield has been deployed in a spherical configuration," Commander zh'Rhun said as she stood next to the main viewer, which now sported a split screen. One half of the screen featured a computer rendering of the Gorn mines, while the other was an image of Captain Sivok and Commander Danhauser, standing on their own bridge aboard the *T'Saura*. "By our count, there are five hundred individual mines comprising the field. As you can see, we, along with the entrance to the rift, are at the sphere's center."

At the science station, Xav said, "The mines themselves are generating a dampening field that nullifies our attempts to scan them. We are working to find a way to counter that effect, but it will take some time due to our unfamiliarity with Gorn weapons technology."

"One other thing," zh'Rhun added. "The mines do not seem to be holding a single unchanging formation. Instead, they are repositioning themselves at irregular intervals. This suggests some kind of intricate onboard navigational system, or perhaps a centralized control scheme. We're scanning communications frequencies to see if we can find any sign of transmissions being sent to the mines, but so far we have found nothing."

Leaning forward in his chair in order to better study the screen, Okagawa shook his head. "Is there any good news?"

Zh'Rhun shrugged. "These do not appear to be gravitic mines such as those employed by the Klingons along the Neutral Zone, nor are they cloaked, as the Romulans have been known to do. We can see them, and they do not seem attracted to us as long as we remain stationary."

From the viewer, Captain Sivok said, *"We cannot be certain of anything until we learn more about the mines' internal* construction. Commander Danhauser has suggested capturing one of the devices for further study, though I confess I find the idea somewhat hazardous given our present lack of information."

Nodding, Okagawa said, "Well, I don't plan on sitting idle until Starfleet figures out what they want us to do here, and I think we can safely say that hoping the Gorn remain patient is a sucker bet." He looked to al-Khaled, who with Commander Grace was standing next to the engineering station. "Mahmud? Do you or your team have anything to add?"

"Commander Danhauser's right, sir," the engineer replied. "We're flying blind here until we get a good look at one of those things." Reaching to one of the keypads on his engineering workstation, he tapped a sequence of commands and the image of the minefield on the viewer was replaced by that of another technical schematic. "My first suggestion would be to use a polaron burst to try and disrupt the dampening field surrounding one of the mines." Al-Khaled knew that such an approach had been successful in disrupting deflector shields and tractor beams. "If we can do that, then we can give it a thorough scan before trying to bring it aboard."

"Makes sense to me," replied Danhauser from the screen. *"It's something we can do from a distance with our shields raised, and configuring one of our deflector dishes to deliver the burst shouldn't take that long."*

"Only a few minutes, I should think," Grace said. "In fact, I would submit that the deflector dish on the *T'Saura* is better suited to the task than our own."

Okagawa smiled at that. "I'll bet that hurt to say." To the screen he said, "Captain Sivok, are you agreeable to that?"

The Vulcan captain nodded. *"It is also logical that you remain on station, Captain. Your vessel's armaments are superior to ours, and would be better suited to defend against any attempt by the Gorn to enter the rift."*

"Sounds as though we have a plan," Okagawa said. "Our science and engineering staffs will be standing by to render any assistance you need."

Several minutes passed, with the *Lovell*'s bridge crew continuing to carry out their various assigned tasks, before Ensign Pzial said, "Sir, the *T'Saura* is signaling that they are ready to make the attempt."

"Excellent," the captain replied. "Keep a frequency open to them, Ensign." Looking to the science station, he said, "Let's see what they're doing, Mr. Xav."

Hearing the order, al-Khaled turned from his station to see an image of the *T'Saura* as it moved away from the *Lovell*. The stout, utilitarian hull of the *Antares*-class science vessel was comprised of the same basic components that applied to most Starfleet ships, with two main hull sections and a pair of warp nacelles. Unlike other vessels in the fleet, however, the *Antares* ships held little in the way of aesthetic design features. Their nacelles were mounted below the engineering section, and their primary hull was little more than a blunt, rounded rectangle housing four decks, including the main bridge.

No one said anything as the *T'Saura* approached one of the mines drifting alone in space. As depicted by the *Lovell*'s sensors and image-rendering software, the cylindrical device appeared inert, offering no clue that it might be an active and dangerous weapon. That made sense, al-Khaled knew, as part of a mine's effectiveness would be its ability to seem innocuous to a passing vessel until it was too late.

"We have selected one of the mines," the voice of Captain Sivok said over the bridge intercom. *"We are holding our distance at twenty-five kilometers, and Commander Danhauser is preparing to activate the deflector dish and release the polaron burst."*

"Acknowledged, Captain," Okagawa replied. "We are standing by."

As al-Khaled and the rest of the bridge crew watched, a golden beam of energy emitted from the *T'Saura*'s main deflector dish, lancing out and away from the ship until it enveloped the squat cylinder.

"Captain," Xav said, "our sensors are detecting fluctuations in the mine's dampening field. The polaron beam seems to be working."

Just as quickly as the Tellarite offered his report, however, an alarm klaxon suddenly blared, echoing in the bridge's confines. Xav returned his attention to his sensors' displays even as zh'Rhun spun to face Okagawa.

"Energy readings from the minefield, Captain. Other mines are reacting to the beam. Seven of them are moving out of position and converging on the *T'Saura*."

"Captain Sivok!" Okagawa shouted, bolting from his seat. "Deactivate that beam! Now!"

On the screen, the energy beam disappeared, and al-Khaled watched as the science vessel abruptly rotated on its axis, its helmsman no doubt responding to orders for evasive action. Eight mines, including the one originally targeted by the polaron burst, were maneuvering to surround the *T'Saura* even as the ship continued to move away from the perimeter of the minefield.

"They're still moving in," the engineer said, feeling his mouth go slack as he watched the situation unfolding on the viewer.

"Commander zh'Rhun!" Okagawa prompted.

Standing behind Lieutenant Diamond at the weapons and defense station, the Andorian first officer said, "Phasers standing by, sir." Even with the rising anxiety that was beginning to envelop the bridge, zh'Rhun continued to maintain her unruffled demeanor. To the lieutenant, zh'Rhun said, "Fire at your discretion."

Diamond wasted no time carrying out the order, her finger pressing a fire control button even before the words finished leaving the first officer's mouth. On the screen, blue phaser energy spat forward, closing the distance to the mine the lieutenant had targeted and washing over it an instant before the Gorn weapon detonated.

And then another alarm sounded.

"Captain!" Xav yelled. "Four mines are leaving the perimeter and closing on our position!"

Of course!

The words screamed in al-Khaled's mind as realization dawned. "They're swarming defensively to any threat they detect!" he shouted. "Cease fire!"

"Impact in five seconds!" Xav warned.

Al-Khaled sensed Grace moving toward his console and

saw the chief engineer stab at the intercom control. "Engineering! Divert emergency power to the shields!"

The last thing al-Khaled heard was Okagawa's warning for all hands to brace for impact before the first of the mines struck the *Lovell*'s shields. The lighting flickered, and nearly every display on the bridge went dark as a third and fourth collision came.

"Damage report!" Okagawa ordered even as the main lighting failed and was replaced by emergency illumination in the seconds following the final attack.

Zh'Rhun replied, "Shields are down seventy-nine percent, and there is some buckling on the outer hull near the shuttlebay."

Al-Khaled added, "One of the mines struck near engineering and overloaded the shield generator in that section, Captain. We've got a host of circuit burnouts and a few power relays are down. Repairs should not take long to complete."

Okagawa pointed to the viewscreen. "Get that thing back on. What's the status of the *T'Saura*?"

"I am unable to reestablish contact, sir," Pzial replied. "They are not responding on any frequency."

Al-Khaled felt the knot of dread forming in his gut even as the viewscreen chose that moment to respond to Xav's attempts to reactivate it. The engineer turned in time to see it sputter and shimmer before resolving into a picture of open space, along with an expanding cloud of debris—all that remained of the *T'Saura*.

CHAPTER 7

Somberness hung like an ominous dark cloud over the *Lovell*'s briefing room. His own mind consumed by the tragic events of the past hour, al-Khaled noted that all of the officers seated at the conference table appeared content to wallow in their own thoughts. Apparently unwilling to look at one another, each person's attention was instead focused on something, anything, else. Commander zh'Rhun studied the padd she had brought with her while Lieutenant Xav kept his gaze fixed on the table's polished surface. Engineer Grace merely sat back in his chair, his eyes closed and with his hands clasped in front of his face, adopting an almost Vulcan-like meditative posture. The sheer burden of emotion weighing on the room's occupants seemed to al-Khaled to have been here forever, despite his having arrived mere moments ago.

"Okay, people," Captain Okagawa said from where he sat at the head of the table, "we've got ourselves a situation here. We need some ideas on how to solve it, and we need them pretty damned quick." He said nothing else as he settled into his chair, instead taking the opportunity to study the faces of the other people in the room who were now looking to him for guidance. Al-Khaled watched as Okagawa's expression seemed to soften, and he nodded slowly.

"Losing a ship—any ship—is hard," he said after a moment. "Even if we didn't actually know anyone aboard the *T'Saura* personally, they were still our brothers and sisters. But I think you know we have to put our feelings aside for the time being and concentrate on our immediate situation." Turning to Commander zh'Rhun, he asked, "What's your tactical analysis of the minefield?"

Already seated ramrod straight in her chair, the first officer replied, "The mines are not simply holding station wherever they are deployed, sir." Her voice and demeanor were all business, her bearing in place and holding steady as she concentrated on answering the captain's question. "A scan of communications frequencies has revealed a steady string of encrypted burst transmissions between the individual devices and the unmanned vessel that dispersed them. We have not been able to decipher the encryption scheme yet, but our analysis shows a heavy correlation between the transmissions and the maneuvering of the mines into different spread patterns at irregular intervals."

"Interesting tactic," Okagawa said. "It lets them defend a large area with a limited number of devices by altering their dispersal pattern as needed to compensate for new threats."

Nodding, zh'Rhun replied, "Yes, sir. They also appear to have stand-alone defensive capabilities that come into play whenever an outside influence attempts to compromise the field. Each mine is apparently programmed to react to any such situation within a predefined range of distance." The Andorian paused for a moment, and al-Khaled noted the slow, deep breath she took before continuing. "That is essentially what happened to the *T'Saura*. When the ship fired its polaron beam at one mine, others within that defensive sphere reacted to the threat, homing in on the source of the beam and attacking it en masse."

Okagawa's brow furrowed as he listened to the report, and al-Khaled imagined the various scenarios playing out in the captain's mind as he considered their situation. "What if we try to disrupt this link between the mines and their control ship?"

Sitting across from zh'Rhun, Lieutenant Xav replied, "If their previous behavior is any indication, they will view such an act as aggressive and respond in similar fashion against us, sir."

"It gets worse, Captain," al-Khaled said. He had also spent the time since the destruction of the *T'Saura* performing his own sensor scans of the minefield, and his findings were no more encouraging than the information zh'Rhun had conveyed. "The control ship also has the ability to replenish the minefield. It's already replaced those lost during the attack on the *T'Saura*, and it was able to reconfigure the existing devices into patterns that minimized the gaps created by any mines that were detonated. Between that and their preprogrammed defensive schemes, the field's doing a pretty good job of hemming us in."

Okagawa said, "Commander zh'Rhun reported earlier that the mines didn't seem interested in us as long as we remained stationary. Is that still a valid assessment?"

Leaning forward in his chair, Commander Grace nodded. "They do not appear to be attracted to our propulsion system in a manner similar to devices employed by the Klingons or Romulans, sir. As long as we do not cross their defensive perimeter, or attempt to attack or disrupt them in any fashion, they seem content to ignore us. In fact, remaining in place and doing nothing seems to be the safest course of action."

"Except that I have a problem when those terms are dictated to me," Okagawa snapped. "The Gorn don't get to decide who enters and exits the Triangle, and their actions have already cost us the *T'Saura* and her crew. That's as far as they go, at least as long as I have anything to say about it. I want that minefield neutralized, and I want it done damned quick."

The expression on the captain's face appeared almost to be a challenge, daring anyone at the table to say that his demands were impossible to meet. Al-Khaled knew from past experience that offering such repudiation carried nearly the same risk as freefalling naked from orbit through a planet's atmosphere. Simply put, Daniel Okagawa would not take no for an answer, especially now.

"If we can't disrupt or disarm the mines without them turning on us," al-Khaled said, "then it seems like the only other option is to figure out a way to disable their control ship."

Shaking her head, zh'Rhun countered, "It makes sense that some form of protection scheme exists for it, as well."

"Even if we disable the ship's ability to communicate with the mines?" Xav asked.

"If I were designing a system like that one," al-Khaled said, "the first thing I'd do is build in a program that reacted to that scenario. For all we know, the second the mines detect any kind of interruption in the signal from the control ship, they could attack any enemy ship in the area."

"Well then," Okagawa replied, "let's try to avoid that, shall we?" His tone had lightened somewhat, the captain no doubt heartened by watching his people turning their energies toward the process of analyzing their current problem and devising potential solutions. "The ship is unoccupied, but the Gorn obviously have some method of retaining command of it. There has to be something there that we can imitate for seizing control of that thing."

"Perhaps the solution we need is not a technical one."

The statement was simple, delivered in a subdued voice, but even then it was enough to make everyone else at the table turn to where Grace sat, his hands still held in front of him as he maintained his familiar contemplative pose.

"Mr. Grace?" Okagawa prompted, his raised eyebrows illustrating his curiosity.

His expression neutral, the *Lovell*'s chief engineer remained silent for an additional few seconds, appearing to compose his answer before saying, "It is prudent to assume that any strategy we attempt that can be traced back to the ship will prove disastrous. Therefore, it seems that we must look beyond mere mechanics for our answer." Dropping his hands to his lap, he added, "Fortunately, we are in a position to request some rather specialized assistance."

* * *

Sitting in the copilot's seat of the Shuttlecraft *Mizuki*, al-Khaled could not ignore the knot of worry forming in his gut as the small vessel left the safety of the *Lovell*'s shuttlebay and maneuvered into the void of empty space.

"If anyone cares," he said as he studied his console and reassured himself that all systems were operating normally, "I'd like to go on record one more time as being very uncomfortable with this idea."

From where he sat in the pilot's chair, Grace did not look up from his console as he replied, "This is not altogether different from a simulation that was once offered at Starfleet Academy as part of the strategic operations curriculum. During one of the more difficult exercises, you were confronted with a ship that laid mines in random patterns, which you were required to navigate while attempting to destroy the ship itself and avoid damage to your own vessel."

"How did you do on the test?" al-Khaled asked, already feeling his stomach tighten again in anticipation of the answer.

Grace shrugged, his expression remaining neutral as he worked. "I passed the simulation two out of four times."

"And this is supposed to make me feel better?"

"As team commander, you did have the option of remaining on the *Lovell*." The words were delivered in a bantering manner, one al-Khaled recognized as the chief engineer's usual way of defusing tension.

"You know me," he said. "I'm a glutton for punishment." In truth, he could count on the fingers of one hand the number of missions assigned to his team that he had not led personally. This was not due to an inflated ego or sense of self-importance, but rather that al-Khaled preferred to think of himself as one who led first by example. He did not exempt himself from the less glamorous missions to which the *Lovell*'s team of engineers often found themselves assigned, and if his people had to face a dangerous situation, they did so while following him.

Just like now.

"*Lovell* to *Mizuki*," The voice of Captain Okagawa sounded over the shuttlecraft's intercom. "*Sensors aren't detecting any activity from the minefield. So far, your flight isn't attracting any attention.*"

Confirming Okagawa's report with the shuttle's own sensor readings, al-Khaled replied, "Acknowledged, Captain. Everything reads good to go here, as well."

"We're preparing to maneuver back into the rift, Mahmud. You'll be able to keep in contact with us via the subspace beacons, but otherwise you're on your own."

At Commander zh'Rhun's insistence, it had been decided that *Lovell* would return to Elysia before al-Khaled and Grace put their plan in motion to combat the Gorn minefield. Okagawa had initially resisted the idea, preferring instead to remain in a position to offer possible assistance to the shuttlecraft, but had finally acceded to his first officer's recommendations. If the engineers aboard the *Mizuki* did something that triggered some kind of defensive scheme and caused the mines to target any enemy vessel within range of the field, the safest place for the *Lovell* to be was inside the Delta Triangle.

"Understood, sir," al-Khaled said. "We'll keep you apprised of our progress."

"See that you do," Okagawa replied, a hint of teasing now apparent in his voice. *"Not that I'm really worried about anything happening to you, but that is a brand-new shuttlecraft you're flying there. Try to bring it back in one piece, if you don't mind.* Lovell *out."*

"Always the doting dad," al-Khaled muttered, exchanging knowing grins with Grace before turning in his seat to face the shuttlecraft's third occupant. "Magen? Are you all right?"

Seated in the chair positioned behind Grace, the alien woman nodded in reply. "Yes, Commander. Thank you." Slender and petite, Magen appeared too fragile to be able to withstand any sort of physical demands placed on her body. Like the rest of her race, however, she was ideally suited to the undertaking for which the *Lovell* crew had called upon her.

"I see the mines," she said after a moment. Seated with her arms folded across her chest, the Cygnian woman appeared to be staring off into nothingness, but al-Khaled knew she was instead focusing her considerable mental talents to the task at hand. "There are so many of them."

Grace's idea of employing the psionic abilities possessed by several of the Triangle's inhabitants had been a stroke of genius, in al-Khaled's opinion. Such individuals had been providing the eclectic community with an invaluable service for centuries, using their formidable mental powers to neutralize weapons and any other instruments that posed a threat to the peace of Elysia.

Still, even these remarkable people, including Magen, had limits. Within minutes of arriving aboard the *Lovell*, the Cygnian woman had determined that the Gorn minelayer vessel, currently positioned well outside the minefield it had created, was also beyond the range of Magen's psionic abilities. For her to exude any influence on the ship, she would have to be closer.

This, of course, meant navigating through the minefield.

"Approaching the first mine now," Grace reported. If the chief engineer was nervous, al-Khaled could detect no sign of it in the man's voice. Instead, his attention was focused on his console and the viewing ports in front of him. He manipulated the *Mizuki*'s controls with the confidence and flair befitting his well-earned status as the most accomplished shuttlecraft pilot among the *Lovell*'s crew.

"One moment," Magen said, her eyes closing and her brow wrinkling in concentration. She had been the one to suggest this course of action, maneuvering through the minefield and attempting to divert only those mines that posed a danger to the shuttlecraft during its flight. It was not an idea that al-Khaled had welcomed, but neither he nor any of the other *Lovell* engineers had been able to propose an alternative.

Al-Khaled watched her, already beginning to wonder if the woman was attempting something that exceeded her abilities, when an alert tone sounded from his console. Turning in his seat, he checked his sensor displays, a smile tugging at his lips as he saw what the readouts were reporting.

"The mine just went inoperative," he said. "I'm picking up movement in three others." He looked up from his console at Grace. "They're reacting to the first one going off-line."

"Magen?" Grace prompted, not turning from his controls.

"I see them," the Cygnian replied, her eyes still closed.

Within seconds, al-Khaled noted new sensor readings that

showed those three mines deactivating. "She's got them," he said, but any excitement he might have felt was short-lived. "I'm picking up seven more reacting to the situation."

Tapping rapid-fire strings of commands to his console, Grace called out, "Increasing speed to one-half impulse."

The acceleration was so sudden that al-Khaled actually felt himself pressed into his seat in the instant before the shuttlecraft's inertial dampeners could compensate. A proximity alert beeped, and he had just enough time to register it before his stomach detected the ship's roll to port.

"Nicely done," he offered as the alert signal terminated.

Beads of sweat were now visible on Grace's forehead. "More of the mines are reacting to our presence."

"I know," al-Khaled replied, attending to the sensors. From the looks of things, Magen was doing a superb job diverting the mines that lay in the *Mizuki*'s path, but for every one she disabled, several of its adjacent companions reacted to the strange disruption in the minefield's integrity. "Every mine within two hundred kilometers of our position is going haywire." Sparing a second to glance over his shoulder, he looked at their passenger. "Magen?"

There was no mistaking the strain that was now evident on the woman's face. "I cannot control them all," she said, her voice a tortured whisper. "I have to let some of them go."

Al-Khaled felt his pulse racing, heard the blood rushing in his ears as the shuttle's sensors told him what Magen was doing. "Okay, I see what you mean." To Grace, he said, "She's releasing control of any mines that aren't posing an immediate danger to us." According to his sensors, the first act of the reactivated mines was to assume a defensive patrolling posture, searching for whatever had disrupted their operation in the first place.

Still, it was not enough.

"The entire field seems to be reacting," he reported seconds later. "The dispersal pattern is shifting, assuming a new configuration."

"Almost there," Grace said, biting off each word through gritted teeth. "Four thousand kilometers and closing."

Then a secondary warning blared for attention, louder than

the rest, and al-Khaled nearly felt his heart burst from his chest. "Mine, port side aft!"

Grace's fingers moved as though possessed of their own will, almost too fast for al-Khaled's eyes to follow, and the *Mizuki* lurched as the chief engineer applied more speed while attempting an evasive maneuver. The stars outside the viewports seemed to stretch and streak as the shuttlecraft banked hard to starboard.

The hull shuddered around them, and al-Khaled grabbed on to the console for support as he felt the deck plates pitch beneath his feet. "What was that?"

"I managed to make the mine miss us and collide with another one that was homing in on us," Grace replied, his voice tense as he fought to keep the shuttlecraft under control.

"There's too many of them for you to keep this up," al-Khaled said. "We have to get out of here."

Grace shook his head. "Eighteen hundred kilometers and closing."

Casting a glance over his shoulder, he saw that Magen had nearly tucked herself into a ball, her entire body shaking as she struggled under the increasing demands being forced upon her. Her eyes were tightly shut and her lips moved, though she said nothing aloud.

Then the sensor board in front of al-Khaled suddenly lit up like a Christmas tree, and his attention was torn between multiple proximity warnings and more indications of mines maneuvering from their passive defensive positions than he could count. Most of them were altering their trajectories.

Toward them.

"I'm tracking twenty-seven mines heading for us!" he said, hearing his voice crack under the strain. For an insane moment, he mentally rebuked himself for his momentary loss of self-control before the alarms beckoned him once more. Between working to track the constantly shifting sensor readings and trying to keep from being thrown from his chair by any of Grace's vicious evasive maneuvering, there simply was no time left over for him to be scared. His attention was locked on the sensor display and its representation of twenty-seven red indicators closing on a single point, the small blue dot that was the *Mizuki*. Some of the red dots winked out as Magen's psionic abilities overcame individual mines, but far too many were still getting through. Not that it mattered, of course. Just one of the devices would be more than enough to obliterate the shuttlecraft.

The circle of red tightened with each heartbeat, and when his mind finally communicated to him that only a handful of those remained, al-Khaled closed his eyes.

Then the alarms ceased.

His eyes snapped open and immediately homed in on the sensor readouts, only to see that all of the red indicators were gone.

"What the hell just happened?" he asked no one in particular as he bent forward to get a better look at the sensors.

"The entire field has gone inoperative," Grace said. "Magen?"

From behind the engineers, the alien woman had sunk into her own seat, fatigue clouding her exotic features. Perspiration ran freely down the sides of her face, and dark circles had formed under her yellow eyes, but nevertheless she nodded to al-Khaled. "Commander Grace was able to maneuver us close enough for me to disable the control ship."

Releasing the pent-up breath he only now realized he was holding, al-Khaled blinked several times as he tried to comprehend what had just happened. "That's it? It's over?"

"Apparently so," Grace said, his tone also exhibiting signs of unfettered relief. "The minelayer is completely inert, along with all of the mines."

Still facing Magen, al-Khaled saw her rub her face with her hand. Her eyes fluttered, and she took several short, shallow breaths. "Are you all right?" he asked.

"The effort was more than I was prepared to cope with," the Cygnian replied. "I must rest for a time." Offering a weak smile, she added, "I will be fine."

Entering another string of commands to his console, Grace said, "There's a docking port on the top of the ship that we can link up with."

"Let's do it, then," al-Khaled said, nodding tiredly and allowing himself to slump into his seat. A moment later he felt the hull of the *Mizuki* vibrate lightly as it made contact with the exterior of the Gorn ship.

His fatigue was pushed aside, though, replaced by a new wave of worry as a sensor alert sounded from his console.

"Let me guess . . ." Grace said, letting the sentence trail away.

Al-Khaled nodded. "The Gorn are coming back."

CHAPTER 8

Red gave way to black and stars filled the viewscreen as the Delta Triangle yielded its grip on the *Lovell*, and for a second time Daniel Okagawa breathed a sigh of relief. Although he knew that Commander Grace's modifications to the deflector shields protected the ship's dilithium crystals from the region's debilitative effects, it was still comforting to be back in normal space.

Well, he reminded himself, *almost comforting*.

"Go to red alert," he ordered as he rose from his chair. "Mr. Xav, where are our friends?"

Bent over the hooded viewer at his station, the science officer did not look up as he replied, "Three vessels, sir, approaching from different directions. All of them are closing on the minelayer. Estimated time of arrival is two point four minutes."

"Rodriquez," Okagawa said as he stepped up behind the helm officer, "get us there now. I want to be ahead of the Gorn."

"Aye, sir," the lieutenant replied as she entered the necessary commands. Leaving her to her task, Okagawa looked to Xav again. "Just the three? They didn't call for backup?"

The Tellarite shook his head. "No, sir. There are no signs of other ship activity anywhere in sensor range."

"I suppose we should be thankful for small favors," Okagawa said. "They may not know what's wrong yet, except that all of their mines suddenly fell asleep." Had the Gorn somehow failed to detect the *Mizuki* as it navigated the minefield? Were their sensors more limited than those on the *Lovell*?

Too good to be true, he reminded himself.

"Let's have the phasers, Lieutenant Diamond," he said. "How are the shields holding up?"

"Functioning normally, sir," the weapons officer responded. "Now that we are out of the rift, we are no longer experiencing the strain of the Triangle's effects. We'll be ready when the Gorn get here."

It seemed obvious to Okagawa that the Gorn would not want to destroy the ship they had left to oversee the minefield, even if members of the *Lovell*'s crew were aboard. Still, they would almost certainly send a boarding party to deal with the intruders, a proposition that did not sit well with the captain.

Nodding in approval at Diamond's report, Okagawa said, "While you're at it, feel free to destroy as many of those mines as you can while we're en route." Looking to the communications station, he ordered, "Pzial, get me the *Mizuki*," he said.

A moment later the Rigelian reported that he had established contact with Commander al-Khaled, and Okagawa turned to see the image of the young engineer on the main viewscreen, standing in a room that looked nothing like the interior of a Starfleet shuttlecraft. "Mahmud, I probably don't have to tell you that we've got company on the way."

"No, sir," al-Khaled said. *"We've managed to get ourselves aboard the minelayer, and we're getting our first look at its systems now. Basically, this thing is a flying armory. There's a small control center here, presumably for maintenance workers or technicians."* Shrugging, he waved to one of several workstations lining the bulkheads of the cramped room, all of which looked to be designed for the larger physiology of the Gorn. *"It has what looks like a helm console for a living pilot, but other-*

wise it's nothing but an automated dispersal system for the mines and the computer and communications systems to oversee them once they're deployed." Holding up his tricorder for emphasis, he added, *"I've set up a link to what looks to be the weapons control system. With T'Laen's help, we might be able to gain access."*

Looking over to where the young Vulcan woman was seated at the bridge station adjacent to Diamond's, Okagawa said, "What about it, Lieutenant?" It was almost a rhetorical question, he knew, but one he still had to ask. As the resident computer expert on al-Khaled's team, T'Laen was well versed not only in the hardware and software that comprised all of Starfleet's systems, but also those of Federation allies and enemies alike.

Her long, slender fingers already moving over her console, she replied, "The system is not complex, but there is a great deal of inefficiency in its design. It will take time to negotiate some of the more cumbersome aspects of the software."

"Captain," Xav reported, "the Gorn ships will be within their weapons range in fifty seconds."

Looking to the helm, Okagawa asked, "Where are we?"

"We'll be in transporter range in less time than that, sir," Rodriquez replied, her attention focused on her console.

"Time's up, Mahmud," the captain said to al-Khaled. "I'm pulling you out of there."

On the screen, the engineer replied, *"Captain, wait. If the Gorn get back here, they'll just reactivate the minefield themselves. I don't think Magen is strong enough to repeat what she did to get us this far, at least not without some rest."*

"Can she do anything about the ships heading this way?" Okagawa asked. "Disable their weapons? Anything?"

Al-Khaled shook his head. *"Just getting here exhausted her, sir."*

The options available to them were dwindling with each passing second, the captain knew. For a moment, he considered simply transporting his people away from the minelayer and destroying it, but just as quickly discarded the notion. After all, he reasoned, such an act might trigger some sort of final defensive maneuver in any remaining mines.

"Captain," zh'Rhun suddenly called out. "The Gorn are within weapons range."

Anything else the Andorian might have said was drowned out as an alarm klaxon echoed across the bridge. An instant later something slammed into the *Lovell*.

"Return fire!" zh'Rhun shouted even as Okagawa cried, "Get me a visual!"

The image on the main viewer shifted to show one of the Gorn vessels just as it moved beyond the edge of the screen. As it disappeared, another arrived to take its place, harsh green energy spitting forth from the foremost point of its hull and hurtling through space directly at the *Lovell*.

"Firing phasers," Diamond said, and Okagawa watched as twin beams of blue energy lanced forward to strike the enemy vessel. The effects were immediate, with the Gorn ship veering up and away from its flight and maneuvering out of range of the viewer. Any sense of victory Okagawa might have felt, however, vanished as the *Lovell* once again came under fire.

"The Gorn vessels are faster and more maneuverable at sublight speeds than we are, Captain," Xav said.

"Are they firing on the minelayer?" Okagawa asked.

"No, sir," the Tellarite replied.

They don't want to damage it, the captain mused, *which means they can't control the minefield without it.* It also meant that the Gorn would almost certainly transport a boarding party to their wayward ship at the first opportunity.

"Give me a tactical view," he said. Xav entered the necessary commands, and a computer-generated graphic appeared on the main screen, showing the *Lovell* at the center of the display and a trio of red wedges moving about the ship. Okagawa tensed as he saw green indicators leap from two of the ships. The *Lovell*'s shields absorbed the double strike.

"Captain," Lieutenant T'Laen said, though she did not turn from her station, "one of the Gorn vessels is attempting to access the minelayer's onboard computer system."

"Can you keep them out?" Okagawa asked.

Her fingers still moving with incredible speed over the array of controls on her console, the Vulcan replied, "I am endeavoring to do just that, sir."

Another energy blast struck the *Lovell*'s shields, and this time Okagawa was sure the effects of the attack were more pronounced. How much more punishment could they take?

"Mines!" Xav suddenly yelled. "Sensors are registering activations throughout the field!"

Okagawa looked over to T'Laen, who only shook her head. "It is not me, Captain."

On the viewer, the tactical schematic was already updating its imagery to show dozens of the mines coming back online, represented by small crimson dots flaring into existence all across the screen.

"They are moving from their established configuration and heading in our direction," Xav reported.

"How many?" Okagawa asked.

"All of them, sir," the Tellarite replied. "Three hundred eighty-seven."

Okagawa watched the scene unfold on the viewer, the computer-generated map now showing the hundreds of mines in a spherical formation that had begun to contract in on itself. It took him an extra moment to realize that the network of weapons was adjusting its position not to the movements of the *Lovell*, but instead to the trio of Gorn ships attacking it.

And he smiled.

"It seems that al-Khaled and Grace have been busy," he said, making no effort to keep the rising excitement from his voice as, on the viewscreen, the bubble of red dots continued to tighten until the three Gorn ships were surrounded and they stopped moving altogether.

"*Al-Khaled to* Lovell," the voice of the engineer called out over the intercom. "*Captain, as you might be able to see, we've had some success with the computer systems over here.*"

Nodding in satisfaction at the now stationary formation of Gorn vessels and mines depicted on the viewer, Okagawa said, "Nicely played, Mahmud. How long can you hold them there?"

"*Now that we've figured out the system?*" al-Khaled said. "*How long did you have in mind?*"

*   *   *

Al-Khaled forced himself to remain still as Ambassador Robert Fox made his fourth circuit of the *Lovell*'s briefing room. Tall and thin, the diplomat was dressed in a muted gray suit that only served to highlight his severe, hawklike features, which at this moment seemed to be set in a permanent scowl. In keeping with his notorious reputation, the man had said little that was not related to the matter at hand since arriving aboard, his mood undoubtedly hardened not only by the nearly three-week journey out from Earth but also by the political quagmire into which he had stepped.

"The Gorn have accepted the Elysian Council's proposal," he said, his voice thick with that variety of egotism that seemed to al-Khaled to be standard issue for most Federation diplomats. "They have already withdrawn the minefield, and have agreed to take no offensive action against Elysia in exchange for the assurances they've made."

Seated at the far end of the conference table, Okagawa nodded. "They'll continue to take responsibility for those Gorn who reside there. Their laws won't permit punishment for any actions prior to their arrival in Elysia, but the council has agreed that the Gorn will never leave the Triangle."

"You can be sure the Hegemony will establish some type of observation outpost to keep an eye on things here," Commander zh'Rhun said, leaning forward in her chair, "but I don't think they'll ever venture into the rift itself." Shrugging, she added, "Not that it would matter, as the Elysians who possess psionic powers would be able to neutralize any threat that arose. It seems it will be a case of everyone leaving everyone else alone."

Sitting across from the first officer, al-Khaled said, "That'd seem to be the best we could hope for, all things considered. We can be thankful the Gorn are willing to give in to the peculiar dynamics of this situation in favor of the larger benefits it affords them with the Federation." Shaking his head, he exhaled a tired breath. "It seems that like us, they've learned a few things since our first encounter. Still, I'll be surprised if creating any kind of lasting understanding with them takes less than a century."

"You're not alone in that assessment, Commander," Fox

said as he stopped his pacing and faced the table. "To say that the unorthodox tactics you used against Captain Lahr and his ships didn't sit well would be a gross understatement. They'll be smarting over that one for quite some time. While I wouldn't normally condone what you did, I've come to learn that in some extreme situations, such aggressive actions are necessary. In this case, it did have the effect of causing everyone to step back and take a breath." To Okagawa, he said, "Nicely done, Captain."

"Thank you, Ambassador," Okagawa replied, offering a polite nod.

Resuming his stroll around the table, Fox said, "What does raise concern is Elysia's request to be declared off-limits. Naturally, the Federation will honor their wishes, but we'd be missing out on a huge opportunity to tap into the historical and scientific knowledge the Triangle represents."

Al-Khaled had to force his expression to remain neutral. Was this the same Ambassador Robert Fox who despised such issues clouding the politics of any situation? Had he been replaced by some sort of alien with a better temperament?

We should be so lucky.

"I'm sure an agreement can be reached, Ambassador," Okagawa said. "Their request is meant more as a means to further assure the security the Gorn have requested, as well as an attempt to keep their society as free from disruption as possible. As you've already pointed out, they present an unmatched allure to the curious, something they'd want to minimize as much as possible."

"So far as most of the rest of the galaxy is concerned," Fox replied, "the Delta Triangle is still a mystery of space, and we'll do our best to keep it that way. Now that the subspace beacons are in place, they'll call us if they want to talk to us." Pausing for a moment, the diplomat offered an appreciative nod to Okagawa. "As for you and your people, Captain, it seems you've got one last affair to tend to before you can call this mission complete."

Smiling in satisfaction, Okagawa said, "Indeed we do, Ambassador. We've got three very special passengers with us, and an entire world waiting to greet them."

The *Lovell* had already been assigned the enviable task of ferrying three members of the Valzhan colony ship back to their planet, so that they might tell the incredible story of the wayward vessel and its fate to the descendants of its passengers and crew. It promised to be an unprecedented homecoming, an event al-Khaled was already looking forward to witnessing. As for the other Valzhan and the rest of the people who had chosen to remain in Elysia, it was difficult for him not to be drawn to the fascinating and even awe-inspiring aspects of their reality.

Beyond the limits of the Delta Triangle, suns would be born and die out, civilizations would rise and fall, territorial boundaries would be drawn and redrawn, enemies would become allies and perhaps even adversaries yet again as the ages passed.

But for the people of Elysia? Things would continue as they always had, tucked away as the Elysians were in their small pocket of the universe where time stood still.

CHAPTER 9

Stardate 53801.1, Earth Year 2376

Standing in the reception chamber with Guardian Royano, Carol Abramowitz marveled at the size of the room. It was larger than she had expected it to be, especially considering the limited nature of the artificial constructs the people of Elysia had developed in order to sustain their existence here in the Delta Triangle. What it lacked in size, however, it more than made up for with its ornate beauty.

"This hall is magnificent," she finally said, no longer able to hold her admiration in check. "It's truly a monument to the society you've created here."

Had she not been told beforehand, Abramowitz would never have believed that this enclave had been forged from the hull sections of several vessels. Colocated with the meeting chamber used by the members of the Elysian Council, this hall was the single surrender to indulgence that she had yet seen. It was lavishly appointed with a vast collection of artwork, tapestry, and furnishings which had been donated by nearly every race represented by the ships trapped here in the Triangle and which were as varied as those who had created them.

One area of the chamber had caught her attention almost from the moment of their arrival: an anteroom of sorts that featured a gallery of portraits, rendered in a variety of styles and an equally wide variety of materials. Still, the paintings all followed a common theme, with each offering a representation of an individual being.

Devna, the Orion woman who had first contacted the *da Vinci* upon its arrival at the Delta Triangle and who was now acting as escort for Abramowitz and Guardian Royano, walked across the room to stand next to Abramowitz. "We have always felt it important to recognize each race of people who have joined us," she said, her voice almost lyrical as she spoke. "Here we honor the leaders of the vessels who were drawn to Elysia over the centuries, and who by their example showed the way for all of our people to work through our differences for the greater good of our community."

Watching and listening to Devna, Abramowitz could not help but be struck by the study in contrasts the woman represented. At first glance she appeared as feral and beguiling as Orion females were said to be, with her dark, voluminous hair and her scant dress that clung provocatively to her lithe, green-skinned body.

Abramowitz had never encountered an Orion woman in person before today, but she was more than familiar with the numerous stories and myths surrounding their sensuality and the hold they were known to have on other humanoids, particularly males. Yet everything about how Devna projected herself—her openness, her calm attitude to her surroundings, her almost passive behavior—flew in the face of what the cultural specialist had heard or read about the exotic women. She had to wonder whether Devna had always stood apart from others of her race, or whether she had merely learned over the centuries to suppress her baser instincts in this culture of strictly enforced peace in order to survive.

Either way, she mused, *there's still more to those old space* tales than some people would like to believe. Fabian will be so very disappointed to hear that.

"We appreciate the opportunity to visit your society, Devna," Abramowitz said as the Orion woman began to lead them down a short corridor toward a pair of polished silver doors. "After all, it's such a rare occurrence for a Federation vessel to enter your space."

Nodding, the Orion woman replied, "Lest you forget, a century means nothing to us. When the council notified the Valzhan delegation of your intent, they even remarked that it seemed as though your people had just left us."

"Well, in that case," Abramowitz said, smiling, "I hope we don't wear out our welcome by dropping by too often. Of course, we can still return the favor by ferrying anyone who wants to leave Elysia out of the Triangle."

Devna offered a knowing smile. "Yours is not the first such offer we have received, but my answer now is as it has always been. Though I have found myself longing to see my home planet, or even the stars of the galaxy it inhabits, this is my home now. I have made peace with that, and accepted life here along with all it offers."

Her comments were the last for several moments as the group walked down the long corridor and finally arrived at the ornate doors, which parted at their approach. Beyond the entry was another room, this one featuring furnishings that lacked the extravagance of the reception chamber and an overall reserved décor that Abramowitz recognized as being intended to host more formal ceremonial activities, such as the one they were about to begin now.

Standing in the center of the room, dressed in a regal array of cobalt-blue robes that clothed him from neck to feet, was a distinguished-looking Valzhan male. Abramowitz recognized him instantly, having seen his image in the files she had studied while en route to the Delta Triangle: Saraven, the ship captain who had volunteered to command the first Valzhan deep-space colony vessel. She also knew that while he was well over five hundred years old by Earth standards, he appeared no less affected by the passage of time than the last time he had confronted a Starfleet crew.

A wide smile spread across Saraven's face as he beheld the group before him. "I see we have visitors. This is indeed a special occasion." Looking to Devna, he asked, "Is this why I was summoned here today?"

Indicating the *da Vinci* away team with a wave of her hand, Devna replied, "Saraven, our guests have traveled a great distance to be with you this day."

"With me?" Saraven replied. "I do not understand."

Stepping forward, Royano held the protective case he had been carrying since departing the *da Vinci* in front of him with both hands before bowing formally. "Saraven, former patriarch of the Clan Briphachi, I come to you today as a duly appointed envoy of the Ancestral Commission in order to present you with this, the *jelorakem* of your family."

The last vestiges of any smile disappeared from Saraven's face even as Royano opened the case to reveal the cherished heirloom cradled within. At first he appeared awestruck at the sight of it, but that sense of wonder vanished almost as quickly, and Abramowitz saw the elder Valzhan's features darken, his brow furrowing in apparent confusion. "Why have you brought this here?" he asked. "Guardian, what has happened? What has become of my clan?"

His voice measured and solemn as he carried out the duties of his office, Royano replied, "In keeping with our customs, when one family ceases to exist as an independent clan, its *jelorakem* must be properly retired. Clan Briphachi is no more, its eldest son having married a daughter of another family. The two families are now one, and identify themselves as Clan Iggrazo." Bowing again, the Valzhan courier added, "I am told it was a joyous union."

"Joyous?" Saraven repeated, making no effort to hide his surprise at the revelation. "For generations, our families often found ourselves cast on opposite sides of numerous ideological conflicts, and faced one another in battle more than once. There was much fighting and suffering, and whenever the hostilities ended and we thought there might be a chance at peace, another conflict would arise."

He lowered his head as if momentarily lost in thought, saying nothing for a moment. Abramowitz was certain she perceived a moment of regret cross the Valzhan's features before he returned his attention to her and Royano. "I am pleased that our two families were able to leave our past behind, though I am saddened that I was not there to see them forge their new beginning together." A hint of a smile tugged at the corners of his mouth. "It is yet another example of how time can be an interesting companion to those who reside outside of Elysia."

Holding up the carrying case still in his possession, Royano said, "Saraven, as is our custom, your family's *jelorakem* would normally have been interred by the Ancestral Commission once they joined with Clan Iggrazo. However, given your unique circumstances the commission has granted an exception to established tradition so that you might look upon this *jelorakem* one final time before its retirement."

Saraven smiled knowingly. "Yes, of course." He reached for the heirloom's carrying case, taking it gently from Royano's hands to cradle it in his own. His fingers caressed the container's smooth, polished surface for a moment before looking up again.

"When I was asked to command the colony ship on its long voyage," he said, "I knew I would in all likelihood never return home. It was a difficult time for my people, and the ship was seen as a beacon of hope, a way to cast light into the darkness in which we found ourselves. I was one of a very select few people with the skills deemed necessary to make the journey a success, and so it was with great reluctance that I accepted the assignment. In doing so, I surrendered my place as head of my family and so entrusted that responsibility to my oldest son, Maltim." Holding up the case for emphasis, he added, "That meant giving him responsibility for this, as well."

Focusing his attentions on Abramowitz for the first time, Saraven said, "When the last Starfleet ship came to us and I learned that my clan had not fared well during the massive war that had plagued my planet, I was sorely tempted to leave Elysia and return home. However, I decided that I was needed here, and that my family would continue to persevere without me as they already had for so long." He shook his head. "I have often wondered if I erred in my decision, but never so strongly as I do now."

Abramowitz sensed an opportunity to lend her skills to the situation. "Saraven, like many of your people whom we have encountered since your world joined our Federation, you have repeatedly demonstrated a willingness to answer the call of a higher purpose without regard for personal sacrifice. Though I have no way to be certain, it seems that your family would have respected your decision as well as understood the reasons behind it. In fact, is it reasonable that your eldest son, and all who took up the mantle of leadership in your clan after him, would have strived to continue on in your stead, if for nothing else than to honor the commitment you made to the Valzhan people."

Having stood in respectful silence just behind Abramowitz and Royano during the past several minutes, Devna now stepped forward and placed a hand gently on Abramowitz's shoulder. "You have a wisdom about you that belies your age, my young friend." After a moment, she smiled and added, "Of course, my perception of age has changed since my arrival here in Elysia."

"It's more a simple desire to learn than any real wisdom," Abramowitz replied. "My role in Starfleet is to understand the many different cultures we come into contact with and to use that knowledge to build stronger friendships with them. I'm fortunate in that my duties are in actuality just extensions of a natural curiosity I've had all my life."

Saraven nodded in approval at that. "I have no doubt that the Valzhan appreciate all that Starfleet has done on our behalf." He held up the case and the prized family possession it contained. "It therefore seems appropriate that I ask you to remain while I carry out the final act of my clan."

Releasing the case's small latch, he pulled open the container's front cover, revealing the obelisk ensconced inside. Withdrawing the *jelorakem*, he set the case on the floor at his feet so that he could hold the object in both of his hands. He placed the palm of his right hand on the heirloom's apex, and Abramowitz heard a distinctive click as the entire crystal seemed to sink slightly into its pedestal.

Then the *jelorakem*'s four faces rose upward, opening like the petals of an exotic crystalline flower and revealing the interior of the obelisk as a mosaic of vibrant and multifaceted gemstones. Feeling her mouth drop open as she beheld the breathtaking sight before her, Abramowitz instinctively stepped closer to get a better look as the stones began to emit a soft light. It reflected off the interior faces of the obelisk itself, producing an almost holographic image that was projected outward between her and Saraven. The light coalesced into what she now saw was a scene depicting a small group of Valzhan gathered around a fire.

"Who are they?" she asked, noting as she did so that both Devna and Royano appeared to be similarly enraptured by the *jelorakem*'s effects. "Members of your family?"

Standing perfectly still as the obelisk continued to generate its remarkable imagery, Saraven replied, "The *jelorakem* carries a clan's history within itself, storing and protecting that history so that it can be passed on from generation to generation. In the case of our family, that history dates back several thousand years. Many of the stories that comprise such a chronicle are private matters and not usually shared with those who are not of the clan. Because of this, it is rare for an outsider to witness an event such as this."

Abramowitz felt an almost electric sensation in the air that played across her exposed skin, no doubt a reaction to the enormous significance represented by the elegant object in the Valzhan's hands. "I'm honored that you're allowing me to see this, Saraven. I don't know how to thank you."

"You have already done so," the Valzhan replied. "It is through your efforts that Guardian Royano was able to bring this to me. Because of that, I am granted the privilege of carrying out one last act on behalf of my family."

Closing his eyes, Saraven raised the obelisk over his head. "Our clan is no more. May those who once lived under that name find peace and prosperity in union with their new family. As a final testament to the heritage we embrace as well as the legacy we leave behind, we consign the *jelorakem* of Clan Briphachi to the ages."

As she watched, Abramowitz saw the image generated by

the cherished heirloom begin to shift and move, as the entire millennia-spanning record of Saraven's family was played out before her.

"Fate saw fit to lure me and my ship to this place where time has no meaning," he said as the *jelorakem* continued to present its chronicle of the family to which it had been entrusted for uncounted generations. "It drew us from the lives we had known, only to hold us here while our families and friends continued in our absence. Now it has conspired with the peculiar qualities of Elysia to offer me some measure of recompense."

"It's magnificent," she said, making no attempt to hide the wonder in her voice. The images passed almost too fast for her to comprehend fully, but she reminded herself that receiving a cold, straightforward history lesson was not her mission here, nor had she been tasked with devising a solution to a problem she and her shipmates faced.

Time had brought Saraven full circle in the sequence of events he himself had put into motion centuries ago, and in the process had also provided her with the unparalleled opportunity to bear witness to this extraordinary event.

Not a bad day's work for your average, everyday cultural specialist, Abramovitz decided with no small amount of pride, unable to suppress a feeling of giddiness as she reflected on the circumstances that had brought her to this wondrous place. *Not bad at all.*

THE ART OF THE DEAL

Glenn Greenberg

ACKNOWLEDGMENTS

I'd like to give special thanks to those people who contributed to the development of this story, in ways they may not even be aware of: Stan Lee, Mark Gruenwald, Ralph Macchio, Greg Plonowski, Tom Brevoort, Bob Budiansky, Mark Bernardo, Tim Tuohy, and the gang at MacAndrews and Forbes.

I must also express a great deal of gratitude and appreciation to Keith R.A. DeCandido, for reasons he probably *is* aware of.

And a lot of love and affection for my wife, Ginny, and daughter, Maddie, who were both very understanding and supportive when I got the chance to play in the *Star Trek* universe again.

CHAPTER 1

U.S.S. da Vinci, Captain's Log, Stardate 53803.6:

The da Vinci *has been assigned to the planet Vemlar in the Norvel system, where the Federation has entered into a partnership with business tycoon Rod Portlyn to transform the planet from a farm world into a major industrial complex and scientific research and development center. This partnership is expected to benefit both sides greatly. Portlyn will gain access to technology and resources normally beyond his reach, and the Federation will share exclusive proprietary interest in any and all scientific breakthroughs and inventions developed on Vemlar by some of the most brilliant minds in the galaxy. The role of the Starfleet Corps of Engineers is to assist in the construction of the new key facilities on Vemlar. I expect this to be a reasonably easy mission.*

* * *

Captain David Gold finished recording his log entry into the ship's library computer. Alone in his quarters, he leaned back in the chair situated at his work desk and sighed deeply. His ship and crew were now coming out of a relatively slow period, in between assignments. Of late, during these slower periods, Gold tended to look back on his long career and the choices he'd made.

Like any ambitious being, Gold was prone to wondering from time to time if he'd done as much as he could to go as far as he could in his career. Commanding the relatively small *Saber*-class *da Vinci*, with its crew of forty, was satisfying, to be sure, and he never felt any regrets. But of late, during his periods of downtime, Gold found himself reflecting on how things might have been different for him if he had been more ambitious, if he had tried harder, pushed harder.

If he were in command of a larger, more powerful ship, maybe a *Sovereign*-class vessel like Jean-Luc Picard's *Enterprise*, perhaps he would not have had to endure the tragic loss of half his crew, which occurred during the *da Vinci*'s fateful mission at Galvan VI. Perhaps he would not have lost his hand, now replaced by a realistic but nonetheless artificial appendage.

Gold knew that even a ship like the *Enterprise* was not invulnerable. Hell, Picard was now on his *second* ship of that name, the previous one having crash-landed on Veridian III a while back. But that knowledge did little to change how Gold was feeling.

The time that had passed since Galvan VI, served to remind the captain that while he had since come to terms with what had happened and was moving on, it would never be far from his thoughts. Losing people like Kieran Duffy and David McAllan and Stephen Drew and . . .

Enough, Gold finally told himself, shaking his head as if to wipe the slate clean in his mind. But he knew he would never completely be able to stop looking back and wondering about all the "what ifs."

Looking at the chronometer on his desk, he realized he was about to get a reprieve from his downtime. He was due in the transporter room, to beam down to Vemlar with his senior officers for a meeting that would officially get this project started. That was good; keeping busy would help him get his mind off the question that crept in and would not go away: *Is this really how things were supposed to be?*

Gold strode into the main transporter room to find the rest of his away team already there: Commander Sonya Gomez, first officer and head of the S.C.E. team; Dr. Elizabeth Lense, the ship's chief medical officer; Lieutenant Commander Domenica Corsi, the ship's security chief; Soloman, the Bynar computer specialist; and Fabian Stevens, tactical specialist and one of the most reliable and trusted engineers on board.

"So, what have you heard about this Rod Portlyn fellow we're meeting with?" Lense asked him as he came up beside the group.

"Not much more than what's in the official records," Gold replied. "Self-styled, independent entrepreneur and real estate mogul, friends in pretty high places. That includes Starfleet Command, by the way. He's known for buying up the majority of the real estate on various worlds, so that he essentially ends up owning the planets and adding them to his ever-growing business empire."

"Which the Federation is now getting involved in," Corsi chimed in with a tone that could only be interpreted as skeptical. Apparently, the blond security chief was not in complete support of this new business arrangement.

"I guess he made us an offer we couldn't refuse," Stevens said with a grin. Turning serious, he added, "On paper, it seems like a good situation for us. Who knows what kind of great stuff they'll come up with here once this place is up and running? And the Federation will own a piece of all of it."

Gomez said matter-of-factly, "It also brings the Federation into an area of space we've never really gone to before."

Soloman, apparently in agreement with Stevens, then spoke up. "It is not as if the Federation has never before involved itself in civilian projects. The late twenty-third-century

Genesis Project was partially funded by the Federation, and even involved the participation of that era's Starfleet Corps of Engineers."

Corsi responded, "It's not exactly the same situation. The Genesis scientists were Federation citizens. Portlyn is a non-aligned, independent tycoon who mostly operates outside of Federation space—like this solar system, for example. He's been pretty much a law unto himself, not having to answer to anyone—"

Gold finally cut off the conversation with a wave of his hand. "What say we stop talking *about* the man and start talking *to* him? We're due at his headquarters right about now."

The group fell silent and followed Gold up to the transporter platform, where they took their places on the pads.

Gold nodded to the transporter chief, Laura Poynter. "Energize."

Poynter activated the console, and seconds later, Gold felt a brief, familiar wave of dizziness. He knew that he and the rest of the away team had just been transformed into shimmering columns of energy. But from his point of view, the transporter chamber faded away, to be replaced by a huge indoor reception area on the surface of the planet Vemlar.

The away team materialized on the ground floor of a sprawling, partially completed, five-story building complex. This was to be Rod Portlyn's headquarters on Vemlar, and as such, it was the first structure on which work had begun. Construction workers—a hardy-looking bunch of men and women—were scattered all around the chamber, engaged in heavy lifting, laser-drilling, and energy-sawing. Some were taking breaks. All were dressed in dark blue uniforms bearing the Portlyn name in large, stylized letters emblazoned on the backs. Before long, the S.C.E. would be working with these people.

Suddenly, a thin, tall, young human man with flat dark hair, dressed in an expensive-looking business suit, approached the *da Vinci* team.

"Captain Gold?" the young man inquired. When Gold nodded, the young man continued, "I'm Wellim Belvis, Mr. Portlyn's assistant. He asked me to escort you to his office."

"After you, Mr. Belvis," Gold replied with a smile.

Belvis guided the away team to the building's sole working turbolift, which Gold noted was reserved exclusively for transport to and from Portlyn's office suite. The lift deposited them on the top floor, which looked almost totally completed. The floors were newly carpeted—that distinctive "new carpet smell" was the first thing that Gold noticed when the elevator doors slid open. The suite's waiting area was furnished with several new, comfortable-looking chairs and a matching sofa. At the far end of the room was a plain-looking metallic desk occupied by a pretty young Andorian whom Gold assumed was Rod Portlyn's secretary. She was unpacking some of her belongings and getting her cluttered desk into some semblance of order, but she paused long enough to smile at the new visitors. Behind her were two tall, massive doors, which presumably opened into Portlyn's private office.

"Mr. Portlyn is wrapping up another meeting," Belvis said. "He'll be with you shortly."

Gold and his team headed over to the sofa and chairs to sit as they waited. But the two massive doors suddenly opened, and a beautiful, regal-looking, older human woman walked out, headed directly for the elevator. She carried a briefcase and wore a somewhat conservative red dress that began at her neck and ended at her ankles, although her shoulders were exposed. Her hair, jet-black with streaks of silver, was long and lustrous, but pinned up in a manner befitting a serious, businesslike atmosphere. Gold initially gave her no more than a passing glance, until something clicked inside his head and, almost involuntarily, he blurted out, "Patrice? Patrice Bennett?"

The woman turned abruptly, searched out the source of the voice that called out to her, and settled on Gold. She narrowed her eyes, scrutinized the captain's face, locked on to his eyes, until she finally displayed a look of recognition, then surprise. This was followed by a smile that could melt the heart of a Vulcan.

"David," she said in a voice that was both soft and captivating. She walked over to Gold and met him in a fond embrace that he happily returned.

She smells exactly the same, Gold thought as he felt the decades falling away.

After a long moment, they broke from their embrace and looked each other over.

"You look wonderful," Gold told her. "Just as I remember." And it was true, she was exactly as he remembered her, despite wrinkles and silver hairs that weren't there when he last saw her. How else could he have recognized her so quickly, after all this time?

"You don't look so bad yourself, old-timer," she responded wryly. "The white hair makes you look very distinguished. And still in Starfleet, I see. What are you now, the commanding admiral or something?"

Gold was grateful for the fact that she apparently hadn't been following his career. That meant there wouldn't be any questions about things like Galvan VI, or his hand, or anything else he was trying not to dwell upon.

"No, just a humble starship captain," he told her with a grin. "Here on business, a special project with Rod Portlyn."

She chuckled. "Oh, you've got business with ol' Roddy too, huh? That's why I'm here, as you've probably guessed. I needed to go over some details of a new venture of his I'm investing in—a planetwide resort on Rando III, something he says will rival Wrigley's Pleasure Planet and even Risa. I didn't know he'd gone into business with the Federation. He sure does get around, doesn't he?"

"I guess so," Gold replied. "But the same can be said about you. You've come a long way since . . . the old days." He couldn't help but smirk at that phrase.

Turning to his crew, he said, "This is Patrice Bennett, one of the sharpest, shrewdest, most successful business leaders in the Alpha Quadrant."

"Flatterer," Patrice laughed.

"She's an . . . old friend. Patrice, these are some of the senior members of my crew." He introduced each of them.

"A pleasure to meet all of you," Patrice said. She then turned her attention back to Gold. "I wish I could stay longer and talk, David, but I have to get back to Tau Ophiucus—that's where I'm headquartered these days. Pending business meetings, contracts to read, inventory shipment arrivals to oversee—"

"In other words, the usual," Gold said with a chuckle.

"Precisely," she replied, laughing. "Oh, David, it's *so* good to see you." She hugged him again.

"You too," he told her softly, then gently kissed her cheek.

Patrice Bennett then walked toward the elevator again, but turned one last time and said to Gold, "Don't be a stranger!"

Gold nodded. "I'll get in touch with you as soon as I can. We should catch up with each other, reminisce about old times."

With a final wave, Patrice entered the elevator and was gone.

Gold was disappointed that she had to leave so soon—seeing Patrice again gave him a nice, warm feeling inside, took him to another time and place, and he could not help but smile.

The smile was still lingering on his face when he turned back to his crew, all of whom had expectant looks on their faces. But if what they were expecting was a more complete explanation of his connection to Patrice Bennett, they were going to be disappointed.

"Always nice to bump into old friends, isn't it?" was all Gold would say as he sat down.

"Especially if you don't owe them any money," Dr. Lense responded dryly.

After a few moments, Belvis reappeared to tell Gold and his crew that Rod Portlyn was ready to meet with them.

Portlyn's office was enormous, at least twice as large as the bridge of the *da Vinci*. The windows extended from ceiling to floor and provided a breathtaking view of the terrain of Vemlar and the tall, majestic Kirtko Mountains in the distance. The chairs and couches were of the highest quality, even better than what was in the waiting area outside. The office was decorated with exotic paintings and sculptures from different worlds, including Earth, Betazed, Delta IV, and Argelius II.

Portlyn came out from behind his massive desk to meet his guests. The tycoon was humanoid, albeit with pale green skin and scarlet-colored eyes. He was balding on top of his head, and his slight potbelly betrayed the fact that he could do with some more frequent physical exercise. But he was impeccably dressed, in a dark brown suit made of the finest silk from Rigel IV. And he was smoking a long, thick Yridian cigar.

Gold introduced his team to Portlyn, who happily shook their hands. The captain explained each of their roles in the project: Commander Gomez would oversee the entire operation on the S.C.E. side of things, as the senior officer in charge; Dr. Lense would consult on the construction of the medical facilities; Corsi would do the same with the security systems; Soloman would lead a team in setting up all of the computer systems; and Stevens would help to finalize and install the emergency and damage control functions of all key facilities. Other members of the S.C.E. would beam down the next day to work under these section leaders and take part in the actual building of the various structures, including the main power plant, the central transportation center, and the laboratory complex.

Portlyn seemed pleased with everything and everyone. He sat back down behind his desk, a beautiful, centuries-old antique made of rich, burgundy-colored Arcturian wood. Atop the desk sat the tycoon's state-of-the art personal computer system, which had yet to be set up. Puffing on his cigar, he waxed enthusiastic about his joint venture with the United Federation of Planets.

"I've sought this partnership for a long time. I'm looking forward to making it a success for me and for the Federation. I plan for Vemlar to be the capital of my business empire, and I couldn't be happier that the Starfleet Corps of Engineers is involved in getting things rolling. I've long had an admiration for Starfleet and its technical wizards."

Seated in the chair closest to Portlyn's desk, Gold leaned back into the profoundly comfortable cushion behind him. "So, Mr. Portlyn, have you ever done such extensive rebuilding of worlds before?"

Portlyn's face broke into a wide grin, and there was a

twinkle in his eye. "I'm glad you asked that question, Captain. But instead of just answering, how about I *show* you? Allow me to give you and your team a tour of my properties in this system. Once you see what I've accomplished, I think you'll agree that all will benefit from my purchase of Vemlar."

Gold was intrigued, and he saw from the looks on his away team's faces that they shared his curiosity.

"We'll take you up on your offer, Mr. Portlyn. Shall we beam up to the *da Vinci*?"

Portlyn waved him off with a chuckle. "No need, Captain. I'll bring all of you aboard my yacht. Let's do it in *style*. A nice little cruise around the Norvel system. Once we're done, I think you'll see why this region of space has been nicknamed 'The Corporate Corridor.'"

CHAPTER 2

Domenica Corsi had to admit it: She was impressed. Aboard Portlyn's streamlined, luxurious space yacht, Corsi and the rest of the *da Vinci* away team were treated to a guided tour of the Norvel system and the various properties owned and operated by Portlyn, hosted by the tycoon himself.

As the yacht made its way to the core of the system, the *da Vinci* crew members were shown several planetoids that, under Portlyn's guidance, were transformed from moderately developed, underdeveloped, or totally undeveloped worlds into fully operational chemical plants, computer manufacturing factories, dilithium cracking stations, and uridium processing centers. They also saw asteroids that had become mining colonies and reliable sources of various desirable minerals and metals. One of the system's larger planets, Creccus, housed Portlyn's shipbuilding facilities. Another planet, called Jemada, served as the location for a continent-size shopping mall and a family-oriented amusement park.

Seeing what Portlyn had accomplished, Corsi could not help but think of her father and his beloved freighter business on Fahleena III. She reflected on how hard he had to work even now to keep it a success, how tiny and fragile it seemed next to Portlyn's thriving empire.

Finally, the yacht turned and began making its way back to Vemlar and the *da Vinci*. The conversation turned to the S.C.E.'s role in the construction project, which would begin in earnest the next day. Gomez, Lense, Corsi, and the other team leaders would beam down first thing in the morning with their various subordinates. The *da Vinci* would remain in orbit around Vemlar until the project was completed.

Corsi noted that Captain Gold and Portlyn had established a friendly rapport in the short time they were together. It made sense—both men were in important positions of power and authority, with many people working under them who depended on their leadership abilities. And Captain Gold obviously felt comfortable among people of Portlyn's social status, given his past involvement with that woman, Patrice Bennett. Corsi briefly wondered about the exact nature of that involvement, before getting her thoughts back on track and deciding that the captain's rapport with Portlyn would certainly make the project run more smoothly. Corsi stood nearby as the captain and the tycoon, each holding a glass of Saurian brandy, engaged in conversation as they looked out at the stars through one of the yacht's large windows.

"This won't be the most glamorous or exciting assignment for you, will it, Captain?" Portlyn asked good-naturedly.

"They can't all be life-and-death missions to save the universe," Gold replied with a grin. "Besides, our voyages are usually more about investigation and problem solving anyway. But we're proud of the part we play in the grand scheme of things."

"As well you should be, Captain. I was quite happy when Admiral Adair made sure you were assigned to this project. Ian and I go way back, as you may know, and I must admit to having pulled a string or two to get the best engineering crew in Starfleet out here."

Pays to have friends in high places, Corsi thought. She heard the captain reply simply, "We appreciate your confidence in us."

The conversation turned to the subject of the yacht they

were aboard. Gold mentioned that he admired the vessel, and Portlyn replied by telling Gold how much he paid for it, and for the five others he owned.

Corsi, remaining a silent bystander and following the conversation between the two men, noticed that Portlyn had a tendency to attach a price tag to nearly everything he talked about. She found that somewhat off-putting. Corsi doubted she would ever be completely comfortable around someone like Portlyn, who had no qualms whatsoever about showing off his vast wealth, power, and influence to anyone and everyone. His aggressive capitalism and naked materialism reminded her too much of the Ferengi, and that put a bad taste in her mouth. But Corsi accepted this as her own shortcoming—it certainly wasn't Portlyn's problem. She knew she'd just have to accept that Portlyn was someone who seemed to subscribe to an old saying she'd heard over the years: "If you've got it, flaunt it."

By the time Portlyn's yacht returned to Vemlar, it was already local nighttime. Corsi was relieved that the tour was finally over. Portlyn had proved to be a gracious host, but she was anxious to get back to the *da Vinci*, devote some time to preparing for the next day's activities, and get a good night's sleep.

She knew that not all of her crewmates felt as she did. Her close friend and occasional lover, Fabian Stevens (one of these days, they'd figure out exactly what they were to each other), thoroughly enjoyed himself and was disappointed that his time aboard the luxury craft had come to an end.

"And I thought the *Nagus* was a beaut," he'd said to Corsi, referring to the luxury ship recently purchased by *da Vinci* conn officer Songmin Wong. "But the impulse engines on this baby are so state-of-the-art, they're not even available to the general public yet! And the leather on the seats—it's from Sarpeidon! You know how rare Sarpeidon leather is? Their sun went nova a hundred years ago!"

Corsi, not wishing to trample on his enthusiasm, simply

smiled and nodded as Stevens went on—and on. About the gracefulness of the vessel's overall design, the quality of the warp core, and even the wood that the bar in the main lounge was made of. She just hoped his eagerness to point out every edge that Portlyn's ship had over Wong's would give out before her patience did.

Standing together in the yacht's main lounge, Gold and his team wished Portlyn a good night as they were caught up in the *da Vinci*'s transporter beams and brought back to the starship.

"Quite an operation Mr. Portlyn has out here," Gold commented as he stepped down from the transporter platform.

"'The Corporate Corridor' is a very appropriate nickname," Gomez said.

The group exited the transporter room and walked down the corridor together toward the nearest turbolift.

"Portlyn's quite a character," Lense said with an amused tone in her voice. "Very . . . larger than life."

Gold nodded and replied, "He would have fit in very well on Earth a few hundred years ago, when 'Big Business' dominated and wealthy tycoons were the major driving forces around the world."

Corsi privately wondered if those old-time tycoons were as enamored of their own wealth and material possessions as Portlyn was of his.

"I was most intrigued by the methods by which his computers are manufactured, and how their standard systems are set up," Soloman commented, obviously enthused about his upcoming responsibilities on Vemlar. "It will be an engaging exercise, getting our systems to fully integrate with his."

They arrived at the turbolift and stepped through the open doors. As the doors closed and the lift began moving, Corsi turned to Gold and asked him point-blank, "So, what's the story between you and Patrice Bennett?"

If Gold was at all surprised or uncomfortable by being put on the spot, he didn't show it. No doubt he was used to the security chief's forthrightness by now, and maybe even expected the question to come up eventually.

He folded his arms across his chest and said, "Okay, we

dated, as you probably surmised. It was a long time ago. We were kids, really. I was in my early days at Starfleet Academy; she was attending Stamford University. It was . . . very nice." A gentle smile appeared on his face.

The smile seemed to turn wistful as he continued. "But we drifted apart. Patrice found that she had a real head for business and finance, and that took up most of her time. And I eventually came to realize that I needed to be with someone a bit more . . . *spiritual*."

"So you married a rabbi," Lense said.

Gold shrugged his shoulders and chuckled. "Hey, if you're going to aim, aim high."

With that, the doors to the lift opened and Gold stepped out. "My stop—and just in time. Good night, all. Get some rest, tomorrow's going to be a busy day."

The doors closed and the lift started moving again. The remaining occupants rode in silence. Gomez, Lense, Stevens, and Soloman cast long glances over at Corsi.

"What are you all gawking at?" the security chief finally blurted out. "You all wanted to know just as much as I did."

After a brief moment, they shrugged their shoulders, smiled sheepishly, and nodded their heads in agreement.

CHAPTER 3

From what Corsi could tell, things were going well on the S.C.E.'s first day as part of the Vemlar development team. As security chief, it was her responsibility to know the whereabouts and activities of everyone from the ship who was down on the planet, on top of her own responsibilities to the project.

She knew that first thing that morning, the S.C.E.'s structural engineering specialist, the eight-limbed Nasat named P8 Blue (informally known as "Pattie"), had a meeting with Portlyn's designers and construction team. They were discussing ways in which the building being constructed to house the main power generator could be extra-reinforced, in the unlikely event of a major systems overload.

Elsewhere, *da Vinci* cultural specialist Carol Abramowitz met with the leading citizens of the native Vemlarite population to determine what cultural barriers, if any, needed to be addressed to ensure that cooperation and harmony among all parties were maintained. Although Vemlar was being transformed from a farm world into something entirely different, its native inhabitants were still an important part of the planet and its future. The Vemlarites were all farmers who sold their land to Rod Portlyn and were now employed by the tycoon in various capacities, particularly as construction crews, food service workers, and sanitation teams.

The fact that everything seemed to be going smoothly was satisfying to Corsi, even if she wasn't overly enthusiastic about the mission itself.

Corsi didn't know exactly why she had such a prejudice against Portlyn. Clearly he had worked hard for his success, and she respected him for that. He possessed a great deal of personal charm, even if she found him to be insufferably materialistic. But there was something about him and his empire that made her uncomfortable. Perhaps it was the fact that this tycoon, who had always operated outside of the Federation and made a point of the fact that he owed allegiance to no one but himself, wielded such power and influence and had connections to certain higher-ups at Starfleet and within the Federation government. Striking a deal with the Federation allowed Portlyn, in Corsi's view, to use that power and influence to suit his own needs and involve Starfleet personnel—specifically the crew of the *da Vinci*—while he was at it.

But Corsi was nothing if not a consummate professional, and she would not let her feelings get in the way of the job.

At lunchtime, she caught up with Gomez, Abramowitz, Soloman, and P8 Blue, who were sitting at a table at a makeshift outdoor cafeteria near the site of the main headquarters. Blue, of course, was seated in a special chair designed for her insectoid body structure.

Corsi caught the tail end of Blue's status report as she plopped down on the bench next to Soloman.

"Mr. Portlyn's engineers seemed receptive to my suggestions," the Nasat was saying. "Best of all, they told me that my ideas could easily be incorporated into the plans, even though construction on the building began today. They assured me it was not too late."

"Excellent," Gomez responded. "Thank you very much, Pattie."

Blue twitched her antennae humbly.

Gomez then turned her attention to Soloman. "So how goes getting this place online?"

"It is going quite well," the Bynar answered brightly. "We had to start with Mr. Portlyn's personal system."

"Yes, he gets first dibs on *everything* around here, doesn't he?" Gomez interjected with a mischievous smirk.

"Rank has its privileges," Corsi replied as she unwrapped a baked Altairian dogfish sandwich and opened the lid of a cup containing iced coffee, which she'd brought down from the ship.

"Most of the morning was dedicated to Mr. Portlyn's system," Soloman continued, unfazed by the interruption. "Mr. Portlyn's computer connects to the main network, but it also has a separate, exclusive system, strictly for his use, and he wanted access to that as soon as possible. It took some time to get it running, but now that we have, he seems very pleased. We are now working on setting up the main network."

Gomez nodded. "How long do you think that'll take?"

"The initial stages should be done by the end of the day. The most crucial parts of the network should be accessible, at least in a limited capacity, at that point. Tomorrow, we will begin working on all the other computers and getting them to interface with our software."

"That's great! Good work," Gomez told him enthusiastically. He gave her an appreciative nod.

Corsi saw that they were being joined by a new arrival: a middle-aged, male Vemlarite, with the pale orange skin and small, round, pitch-black eyes of that species. He was dressed in dark blue construction coveralls. Abramowitz introduced him as Delfo, one of the Vemlarites' leading citizens. He sat down at the table, pulled a meat-filled sandwich out of a tan-colored paper sack, and ate with them.

"So what made you all decide to sell your land to Portlyn?" Corsi asked Delfo after several minutes of casual conversation. She was genuinely curious about how the tycoon managed to convince the Vemlarites to sell out to him. She then chuckled. "What did he do, hold your families prisoner till you signed the real estate over to him?"

She thought Delfo would understand that she was only kidding around, but his face remained impassive.

"You might want to be more careful what you say about

Rod Portlyn around here, ma'am," he told her, looking around at the various Vemlarites and Portlyn employees passing by. "He's got a lot of admirers here, including me, and comments like that could be misinterpreted."

Corsi wasn't sure what to say. She certainly did not share Delfo's high regard for Portlyn, but she immediately regretted offending the Vemlarite. She hoped Delfo was not so offended that whatever cultural bridges Abramowitz established had not just been irreparably burned.

"I'm sorry," Corsi told him. "I was just trying to make a joke."

Abramowitz then stepped in, trying to smooth things over with a smile that Corsi recognized as desperately upbeat. "Sometimes we humans forget that not every species in the galaxy shares our peculiar sense of humor."

Delfo shook his head. "No harm done. Just a little friendly advice. To answer your question about why we sold our farms—we didn't have much of a choice. Not long ago, the soil on Vemlar became infertile, totally incapable of growing any more of our crops. All of a sudden, the land was just . . . barren. You have to understand—our farms had been our lives, and our livelihoods, for . . . well, I don't know how many generations. And now they were useless. After that, we just started sinking into poverty. We became desperate."

Delfo paused for a moment, and though his face remained expressionless, Corsi could tell that he was silently reliving that dark period. Finally, he continued.

"Luckily, Mr. Portlyn came along with a very generous offer to each and every one of us, to buy our land. And he offered to keep us all on, give us jobs helping him build this place up. And once that's done, he's promised us steady work helping him to keep things running day-to-day. It was the best solution we could get, and he made it possible." Delfo then looked Corsi squarely in the eyes and told her, "Rod Portlyn's a hero and a savior in my book, and most other folks here feel the same way." He then went back to his sandwich and ate in silence.

Corsi was left with much to think about. Her skepticism about Portlyn remained—she'd learned long ago to always trust her first impressions about people and situations. But clearly there was another side to the tycoon. He personally saved the inhabitants of Vemlar and provided them with a future. In that sense, he was exactly the kind of person with whom the Federation should be doing business. Having come to that realization, Corsi felt a bit more enthusiastic about the Vemlar project and her role in it.

As night fell on Vemlar, Sonya Gomez and some other members of the S.C.E.—including Stevens, Soloman, Abramowitz, and Blue—chose to remain on the planet overnight. For Gomez, it was out of a desire to feel more connected to Vemlar and the construction project, and to get used to the environment, since she was going to be spending a lot of time there for an extended period.

In the aftermath of Galvan VI, Gomez was grateful for assignments like this and the responsibilities that came with them. She'd found that keeping as busy as possible was instrumental in getting her to move past the tragedy and the loss of Kieran Duffy, who gave his life to save the *da Vinci* on that fateful mission . . . and who had asked Gomez to marry him shortly before. Having a goal, focusing on it, working toward achieving it, helped to ease the pain and get her moving forward with her life.

Guest quarters had not yet been set up, so Gomez and her companions had to camp out in Federation-issue tents and sleeping bags. They didn't mind—they thought it could be a lot of fun "roughing it," and even had marshmallows beamed down from the *da Vinci* for toasting later in the evening. But Gomez quickly discovered that not everyone shared that enthusiasm—starting with the *da Vinci*'s security chief.

"Are you sure you don't want to stay tonight, Domenica?" Gomez asked as she stood outside of her tent with Fabian Stevens and watched Corsi gather up her gear and prepare to beam back to the *da Vinci*.

"I have some paperwork to catch up on, reports to fill out . . ." Corsi replied. That sounded like a lame excuse to

Gomez. It was more likely that the notoriously no-nonsense Corsi just didn't feel comfortable socializing with her crewmates in such a fashion.

"C'mon, Dom, it'll be fun," Stevens chimed in cheerfully. "There'll probably be a sing-along and everything."

Corsi grimaced. "Was that supposed to be an enticement?"

Suddenly, they were joined by Dr. Lense, who was carrying her own gear and looking eager to get back to the ship.

"Not you too, Elizabeth?" Gomez asked with disappointment.

"No offense, but given the choice, I'll pick the relative comfort of my bunk over a sleeping bag any day. Besides, I spent enough time 'roughing it' during those weeks I was on that Shmoam-ag ship."

"But, Doc, you haven't lived until you've heard my rendition of 'Moonlight Bay,'" said Stevens.

"Guess I'll have to stay among the nonliving, but thanks," Lense replied wryly.

Corsi tapped her combadge. "Corsi to *da Vinci*, two to beam up." A moment later, she and Lense were gone.

"Their loss, right, Commander?" Stevens asked with a lopsided grin. "I'm going to go set up my tent. See you at the campfire!"

As it got later into the night, with the campfire dying down and everyone's voices hoarse from all the songs they sang together, the Starfleet engineers finally went to sleep. Gomez had fallen into such a deep slumber that she barely heard the beep of her combadge well past local midnight. But once it registered in her mind that the device was summoning her, she suddenly bolted up in her sleeping bag, wide awake, and reached over to tap it.

"Gomez here," she said, her voice dry and rough.

"*Gomez, it's Captain Gold. Sorry to wake you.*" His voice sounded serious.

"No problem, sir. What's going on?"

"*We picked up distress calls from two of Portlyn's other prop-*

erties in this system—a planetoid named Kalibiss and an asteroid called P-12. It seems that maintenance workers at both locations discovered activated time bombs."

"When are they set to go off?" Gomez asked, surprised by this news.

"We're not sure. The maintenance workers saw the bombs and fled to safety before contacting Portlyn. I spoke to him and offered our assistance, which he's accepted."

Makes sense, Gomez thought. *If there are time bombs needing to be deactivated, why turn down help from a ship carrying some of Starfleet's best engineers?*

"What do you need from me, sir? Should I beam back up?"

"No—I'm not sure how long we'll be gone, and you're needed on Vemlar to keep the project moving along. That's why we're here in the first place. But I'm going to need Stevens, Soloman, and Blue back aboard. The *da Vinci* is heading to Kalibiss and since we can't be in two places at once, a second team will travel by shuttlecraft to P-12. Hopefully we can stop both of these things in time. I'll be in touch when there's something to report."

"Take whoever you need. And good luck, Captain."

"I hope we won't need luck, but I'll take it. Gold out."

Gomez sat in silence in her tent for half an hour before concluding there was no way she was getting back to sleep. She had too much on her mind. The *da Vinci* had already left orbit and was well under way by now. Who would plant time bombs? Why? Would the S.C.E. be able to stop them from detonating? Would her crewmates be all right? Her tent began to feel very small and cramped. It was still several hours before sunrise, but she decided to go for a short walk and get some air. Maybe that would help clear her head.

Gomez wandered aimlessly until she walked up a hill and found herself overlooking the construction site for the main laboratory complex. This would be the center of everything on Vemlar, the point around which everything else revolved, once Portlyn's operations were up and running. The lab would, for all intents and purposes, be the "heart" of Portlyn's Vemlar. Gomez remembered what Stevens had said earlier, about all the amazing things that could potentially be created at this place in the future. She silently acknowledged that this facility could one day be one of the most important places in the galaxy.

She walked down the hill to get a closer look at the building. Maybe she would see areas in which she could make suggestions for revisions and improvements once work resumed later in the morning.

As she approached the building, she tried to keep her mind off the *da Vinci*'s dangerous mission and to stay focused on her own responsibilities. She did not expect the blinding flash of light that burst forth suddenly from the site. Or the searing heat. Or the deafening, thunderous boom.

Then everything went black.

CHAPTER 4

Captain's Log, Stardate 53804.9:

The da Vinci *has arrived at Kalibiss, the location of Rod Portlyn's warp engine manufacturing company. Lieutenant Commander Corsi, P8 Blue, and Soloman have beamed down to the operations center to examine and hopefully deactivate the bomb. I have been informed by the crew of the shuttlecraft* Kwolek *that they have arrived at asteroid P-12, which houses Portlyn's robotics factory. Lieutenant Commander Tev, Fabian Stevens, and Deputy Security Chief Vance Hawkins are on site and conducting their own investigation.*

Captain Gold, seated in the captain's chair on the bridge of the *da Vinci*, did not have long to wait before he heard back from the away team on Kalibiss. Corsi contacted him seven minutes after beaming down.

"*It looks like the bomb is set to explode in two hours, twenty-three minutes, sir,*" she reported. "*It seems we had plenty of time to get here.*"

"Fortunately." Gold then thought for a moment. "Almost two and a half hours from now . . . that would be the middle of the night here. Who would be in the building at that time?"

"*No one, sir.*"

"So no one would be hurt or killed when the bomb detonated," he pondered aloud.

"*Thoughtful terrorists—go figure.*"

"Corsi, how was the bomb discovered in the first place?"

"*A maintenance worker was cleaning the ground floor of the operations center for the evening. He heard a loud beeping that lasted about ten seconds. He was able to follow the beeping to its source—it was the bomb, planted inside a supply closet.*"

"So the bomb might never have been discovered if not for the noise. Any idea what the beeping was about?"

"*So far, Soloman and Pattie don't believe it served any particular purpose. They think it might have been a minor design flaw in the bomb.*"

"A flaw that's certainly seemed to work in our favor. Are we going to be able to defuse this thing?"

Gold was answered by the voice of Soloman. "*We are already finishing up, Captain. Pattie is just about to disconnect the final wire from the explosives.*"

Gold's curiosity grew. "What kind of bomb are we dealing with here? Could it take out the whole site?"

Now P8 Blue herself answered, though her voice sounded muffled. She was apparently working on the bomb as she talked. "*It's a fairly simple device, sir, although it seems well made, and I estimate it would cause a fair amount of damage if allowed to detonate.*"

"Okay. Just be careful, all of you. And good work."

The conversation was interrupted by a transmission from Tev on asteroid P-12. Gold anxiously opened the channel to hear the report from the *da Vinci*'s Tellarite second officer and S.C.E. second-in-command.

"*It turns out there was no need for urgency, Captain,*" Tev told him. "*The bomb is not set to detonate for another seven hours.*"

A theory immediately popped into Gold's head. "At which point it would be the middle of the night cycle on the asteroid, and no one would be in the factory?"

"*Quite correct, sir. But most unusual was how the bomb was discovered. You see—*"

"Loud beeping?" Gold interrupted, his theory catching fire.

Tev hesitated before answering. "*Affirmative, Captain,*" he said in a bemused voice. "*As for the bomb itself, it is—*"

"A simple design and fairly easy to deactivate."

"*Sir, would you like to give the report to us?*" Tev was clearly frustrated and confused.

Gold chuckled. "Sorry, Tev. Needless to say, what you're telling me is not coming as a shock. Okay, you and Stevens finish deactivating the bomb. We'll set up a rendezvous point to retrieve you."

"*Aye, sir. We will contact you again once the bomb is neutralized. Tev out.*"

Gold's mind was racing. Obviously the two incidents were linked. But what was all this about? Who was behind it? Why these targets?

Before he could ponder these questions any further, the *da Vinci* received an emergency transmission, this time from Vemlar. It was Carol Abramowitz. Her image popped up on the main viewscreen, and Gold was struck by how shaken she looked. Her dark hair was a mess and her cheeks and uniform were covered with dust, dirt, and . . . was that blood?

"*Captain, we were attacked.*" Abramowitz's voice revealed her dismay, yet somehow remained controlled. "*The main lab construction site was bombed! It's completely demolished. Sir, Commander Gomez was in the vicinity when it happened.*"

"Dear God," Gold muttered. Sonya Gomez just recently had a near-death experience, on the planet Teneb, and Gold's first thought was that this time, her luck had run out. Maintaining his composure, he asked, "Is she all right? Is she . . . ?"

"*Minor burns, slight concussion, some cuts and bruises. Luckily, she was far enough away that it wasn't more serious. She's resting right now, but she needs proper medical attention— I've just about used up my knowledge of first aid. The local Vem-*"

larite physician is on his way to take over and get her to his hospital."

Gold was well aware that any Vemlarite hospital was downright primitive by Federation standards. "We're on our way," he assured Abramowitz. "Lense will take over as soon as we get there. Was anyone else hurt?"

"None of us or Portlyn's people, sir. No one else was at the site at the time of the explosion. But Portlyn's security force chased down a suspect trying to leave the planet shortly afterward. Shots were exchanged, and the suspect's craft was hit and crash-landed."

"What kind of shape is this suspect in?"

Abramowitz frowned. *"He sustained serious burns and extensive injuries, sir. He's being taken to the hospital too, of course . . . but I'm not sure he'll survive."*

"Lense will be the judge of that," Gold told her sharply. It then dawned upon him that this explosion on Vemlar happened in the middle of the night.

"Abramowitz, this bomb wasn't discovered *ahead* of time? There wasn't any kind of loud beeping from it that could have led to its discovery?"

"Not as far as I know, sir. If there was any loud beeping, I think it would have been heard by someone. *The lab site was one of the busiest areas today until work ended for the night."*

Gold nodded gravely. "Where's Mr. Portlyn right now?"

"At the construction site, assessing the damages. He's extremely agitated, sir."

"I don't doubt it." Gold then turned in his chair to Lieutenant Anthony Shabalala, stationed at the tactical console.

"Shabalala, contact the away team on Kalibiss. Tell them we need them back aboard. The second they're done with that bomb, I want them beamed up."

"Aye, sir," Shabalala replied. He began to send the call signal, but the captain was not finished.

"Then, contact our team at P-12. Tell them that when they're done there, they should head back to Vemlar on their own aboard the *Kwolek.*" Time was of the essence, and a rendezvous with the shuttlecraft would only slow the *da Vinci* down.

Gold then turned in his chair again, this time to address his conn officer. "Wong, plot a course for Vemlar. Full impulse power, as soon as we're under way." At that speed, they would be back at Vemlar in less than an hour.

"Course already plotted, Captain," Wong replied.

Gold smiled inwardly—he liked when his people showed that kind of initiative.

"Captain," Shabalala called from tactical. "The away team has just beamed aboard."

"Go, Wong," Gold told the conn officer. He then turned his attention back to the main viewscreen, where Abramowitz's face remained.

"Abramowitz, we'll be back as soon as possible. *da Vinci* out."

Gold felt the ship smoothly accelerate as it left Kalibiss behind. The situation had become very clear to him: The *da Vinci* had been lured away from Vemlar. The bombs on Kalibiss and P-12 were *intended* to be discovered, so that the *da Vinci*, the only Federation vessel in the region, would rush to deactivate them and therefore not be able to interfere when the *true* target was hit.

So much for the reasonably easy mission.

"He'll probably live, but he may end up wishing otherwise," said Dr. Lense, delivering to Captain Gold her report on the condition of the suspected terrorist. They stood side by side in the *da Vinci*'s sickbay, looking down at her patient, who was lying unconscious on a diagnostic bed within a sterile field. His burned and broken body was covered with a clear healing gel and wrapped in loose bandages.

Lense looked exhausted. Six hours of nonstop emergency surgery and two and a half hours of intense post-op examination and research will do that to the hardiest of doctors, even one who was aided by her Emergency Medical Hologram.

"Third-degree burns over eighty percent of his body," she continued. "There are more bones broken than not. His vocal cords are destroyed—he'll never speak again."

"Damn," Gold muttered. "He's our only link to the terrorists responsible for those time bombs and the explosion on Vemlar."

"Assuming he *is* a link," Lense noted pointedly. "We don't know that for sure. Innocent before proven guilty and all."

Gold nodded. "Is there any way we can determine his identity?"

Lense frowned and shook her head. "Not at present. His fingerprints are completely burned away. And so far, there are no DNA matches. Right now, I can't even be sure what species he belongs to. His blood type doesn't match anything in our database."

Gold let out a disappointed sigh. "All right, tell me about this chip you found."

Lense lifted up a small pair of tweezers that held a tiny metal square, no larger than a centimeter, in its prongs.

"This was inside him, at the base of his skull. I'm not sure if it's a computer chip, a transmitter, a receiver, a medical device, or a joy buzzer. Which is why I asked Soloman to join us. I figured with his ability to interface with computers, he could determine—"

Suddenly, the doors to sickbay opened and the Bynar entered, looking very curious about why the doctor had summoned him.

"Right on time," she said, and handed the tweezers over to Soloman. "Here. Maybe *you* can make heads or tails out of this thing."

Soloman examined the chip closely, slowly cocking his head from left to right as if looking for an entry point. Finally, he placed his index finger against the chip and closed his eyes. He remained that way, completely motionless, for five minutes. Gold and Lense waited in silence until Lense yawned, plopped down in a nearby chair, folded her arms across her chest, and closed her eyes.

"Wake me up when he opens his eyes," she murmured.

Three minutes later, Soloman did just that.

"It took some time to familiarize myself with the device and determine how to tap into it," he explained, the sound of his voice immediately waking the doctor. "However, I think I can safely say that this is a combination receiver and data storage unit."

"What kind of data is stored on it?" the captain asked.

"I don't know, sir," the Bynar answered. "The data is in some sort of complex language or code with which I am totally unfamiliar."

Gold and Lense exchanged a glance. "Language or code, hmm?" the doctor said, raising her eyebrows.

The captain nodded, knowing exactly where she was going with this. "Faulwell. Let's get him in here *now*."

Bart Faulwell liked challenges. But the *da Vinci*'s linguist and cryptography expert quickly realized that the one laid out before him by Captain Gold was the toughest thing he'd faced since he cracked Dominion codes during the war.

Soloman had downloaded the data from the chip onto the *da Vinci*'s main computer, and now this data was displayed on the computer screen in Faulwell's quarters. He had been working at it nonstop for nearly four hours, a cup of French roast coffee with half-and-half never far from his reach. But things were not progressing as quickly as he wanted, and his sense of frustration was growing.

At least he no longer had to worry about Commander Gomez. She received proper medical care as soon as the *da Vinci* returned to Vemlar, and was already back on active duty on the planet surface.

But this strange code was throwing Faulwell for a loop, and he was feeling very tense. He was about to take a short break—and a quick shower—when Captain Gold summoned him to the main conference room to give a status report. Faulwell felt a momentary flash of panic. It had been at least ninety minutes since he felt he'd made any real progress with the code, and as far as he was concerned, that progress was minimal at best. He would have preferred to give his report when he had more to say.

He arrived at the conference room to find Gold with Lense, Corsi, and Soloman.

"I'm afraid I haven't really been able to crack this code yet, sir," Faulwell began reluctantly, scratching his beard.

He activated the small viewing screen atop the table at which everyone was seated, and the code popped on the screen for all to see.

"However," he continued, a bit more brightly, "a few things show up a number of times within the code—names or phrases—which I *think* I was able to decipher. One is 'Vemlar.' That was easy enough. Another seems to be 'Taru Bolivar.' Is anyone familiar with that?"

Everyone in the room thought for a moment before shaking their heads "no."

"The other is 'Fantasixun'—I think. That's the closest I could make out so far."

No one reacted, so Faulwell assumed that the second name was as unfamiliar to everyone as the first.

Soloman accessed the ship's library computer and entered both names. Within seconds, he had results.

"No listings for 'Taru Bolivar,'" the Bynar said. "However, there is a planet named Phantas 61, located on the outskirts of this system. Perhaps this is 'Fantasixun?'"

"What's on record about it?" Gold asked.

Soloman read the information on the monitor out loud. "A somewhat isolated planet, known as a thriving, financially successful, independent mining world with an abundance of dilithium crystals and other natural resources. Purchased by Rod Portlyn ten years ago, when the inhabitants agreed to sell out to him. Portlyn kept the inhabitants on to run day-to-day operations, and he publicly vowed to 'exploit Phantas 61's equities to the fullest potential.' Under his control, Phantas 61 became more productive and more profitable than at any other time in its history. It remains part of Portlyn's business empire to this day."

Gold sat silently for several moments, mulling this over. Finally he spoke.

"Maybe we should pay a little visit to Phantas 61, try to find out what the connection is—if indeed there is one."

"Makes sense," Lense responded. "Maybe my anonymous patient is from that world."

The captain reached for the communications transmitter. "I'll contact Mr. Portlyn, let him know what we're doing."

"Sir, before you do that . . . ?" Corsi interjected, causing Gold to pull his hand away from the transmitter.

"Go ahead, Corsi," the captain said as he leaned back in his chair.

"These terrorists, whoever they are, apparently know quite a bit about Portlyn and his operations—when and where to strike. We don't know how they know so much, but it's reasonable to assume there's a leak somewhere inside Portlyn's organization. If too many people know about us heading to Phantas 61, the terrorists could find out and interfere with our investigation."

Gold nodded in agreement. "Yes . . . from this point on, maybe it's best if we kept our actions and whereabouts on a strictly need-to-know basis."

"That's what I'd suggest, sir," Corsi responded.

"All right, then," Gold said as he stood up. "Meeting adjourned. We'll get under way shortly. And Faulwell—good work."

"Thank you, sir," Faulwell replied with a smile, pleased that what little he had accomplished was apparently enough, at least for the moment.

CHAPTER 5

The frowning face of Rod Portlyn dominated the main viewscreen on the bridge of the *da Vinci*.

"*Let me get this straight, Captain—you've got a possible lead on the terrorists, but you won't give me any details?*"

"Only that we're looking into it, Mr. Portlyn," replied Gold. He added, as earnestly and reassuringly as he could, "It's really for the best. Until we learn how the terrorists know so much about your operations, releasing any details of our investigation could hamper our efforts. But we'll be in touch if we learn anything. In the meantime, Gomez, Tev, and a team of S.C.E. specialists will be staying behind to help clean up the site of the explosion and get the construction project moving again."

"*But surely you can tell me what you've learned from the suspect?*"

"In the interests of security, sir, I really think it's best to keep that on a need-to-know basis, as well."

Portlyn pursed his lips and nodded once. "*Very well, Captain Gold. Good luck.*"

THE ART OF THE DEAL

With that, Portlyn signed off and his image disappeared from the screen.

Corsi, standing behind Gold during the conversation, stepped up and stood beside the command chair.

"I get the distinct feeling he's not used to being told 'no,' sir," she said wryly.

Gold shrugged nonchalantly. "We're just doing whatever's necessary to accomplish our goal—and accomplishing our goal directly benefits him. Portlyn's a big boy, a seasoned businessman. I'm sure he understands."

Gold turned in his chair to face the helm.

"Wong, take us out of orbit."

The viewscreen showed the ship's orbital departure, with Vemlar quickly receding. "Next stop, Phantas 61," the captain said to the helmsman. "Have gravitational potentials been taken into account?"

"Yes, sir," Wong replied confidently. "We can safely go to warp speed inside the solar system."

"Very good, Wong. Warp factor two, please." At that speed, the *da Vinci* would arrive at Phantas 61, located across the Norvel system, in just two hours—an eighty-eight-hour trip at full impulse power.

The ship accelerated, approaching warp factor one and beyond. Gold settled back in his chair, expecting an uneventful journey for the next couple of hours. He watched the stars as they began to streak by on the viewscreen.

"Captain!" called Lieutenant Shabalala. "Urgent incoming transmission for you, sir, from Starfleet Command. It's Admiral Adair, sir. He, uh, wants to talk to you—*immediately*, sir. About Mr. Portlyn's grievances."

Gold rose from his chair. With a good-natured smirk, he told the young officer, "You're lucky Starfleet captains are no longer allowed to kill the bearers of bad news. I'll take it in my ready room. You have the conn, Shabalala."

Stepping off the bridge, Gold waited until the doors closed behind him before muttering to himself, "Lousy *momzer* went right over my head."

* * *

"Captain Gold, why is Rod Portlyn waking me up in the middle of the night with complaints about how he's being treated by Starfleet?" asked Admiral Ian Adair, his scowling face on the viewscreen in David Gold's ready room.

Adair was five years younger than Gold but appeared to be about ten years older, with thinning white hair, many wrinkles on a face that seemed perpetually grumpy, and a wiry frame that bordered on being frail-looking. But it was clear that there was still plenty of fire in the admiral's belly, and his piercing blue eyes remained filled with energy.

Gold took a breath before responding, and concentrated on maintaining his composure.

"Admiral, I strongly believe it's in the best interests of our investigation that the details remain classified to all but the most essential participants, at least for now."

"*Consider me one of the essential participants. So what's going on?*"

Gold knew he had no choice in the matter. He took another breath.

"We're en route to Phantas 61, Admiral," he told Adair, and then he explained why. When Gold finished, Adair remained silent as he considered everything he had just heard.

Finally, the admiral said, "*This investigation isn't the kind of assignment you and your crew normally handle, Gold. The* da Vinci *is a boatload of engineers. These are* terrorists *we're talking about here. Maybe you should wait for assistance from a ship better suited for this situation.*"

"As you're undoubtedly aware, sir, no other Starfleet vessels are currently available to take this on. And these terrorists seem able to strike anywhere, at any time. The *da Vinci* is the only ship currently in a position to act *right now*. Besides, we're already on the way."

Adair still seemed skeptical. Gold pressed on.

"Above all else, Admiral, the people aboard this ship are problem-solvers, and this is a problem that needs solving. At the moment, we have the best chance of doing that."

Gold could almost see the wheels turning inside the admiral's mind.

"What about the Vemlar project? I don't need to remind you how important it is to the Federation."

And to your close personal friend Rod Portlyn, Gold thought. But out loud, he said, "No, sir, I'm well aware. Rest assured, Commander Gomez and most of her team are hard at work back on Vemlar."

Adair finally nodded. "All right, Captain, proceed as you see fit. I'll contact Portlyn and try to soothe his bruised ego. I'm sure that's what this is all about."

"Thank you, sir," Gold said, relieved.

But on the screen, Adair pointed a warning finger at Gold. "Now, I don't want any more complaint calls, so you'd better become more of a diplomat, and I mean pronto."

"I'll work on that, sir," Gold replied with an amenable grin that disappeared as soon as Adair signed off and the screen went dark. He leaned back in his chair and shook his head.

"Mr. Portlyn," Gold said aloud, "you are a royal *putz*."

Rod Portlyn was seated in his office on Vemlar with his feet up on his desk, trying to look as calm and casual as possible, as he listened to Starfleet Admiral Ian Adair, whose image was being transmitted to the tycoon's desktop viewing screen.

"Rod, Captain Gold and his crew are among Starfleet's very best. I wouldn't have had them assigned to this project if they weren't. I understand Gold's decision for secrecy, and I believe it was made for the right reasons. It's in the best interests of all of us."

Portlyn folded his arms across his chest and sighed. Injecting a slight edge into his voice, he replied, "Look, Ian, I have no doubts about Captain Gold's abilities or his competence. I just don't understand why I, of all people, have to be left out of the loop. I mean, 'essential participants only'? Who's more essential than *me*? Who's been more affected by these terrorist activities than me? Don't I deserve to know what's going on in my own backyard?"

He sighed again, displaying his frustration and dissatisfaction.

"I'm just disappointed, Ian," Portlyn continued with a frown. "I thought there would be more trust here in this joint venture."

Adair mulled that over. Finally, he replied, *"You're right, Rod. You have been the one most adversely affected by these terrorists. All right. I'll qualify you as someone who 'needs to know.'"*

Portlyn's raised his eyebrows in surprise. "Won't Captain Gold have a problem with that?"

"I outrank him, old friend. It's my prerogative."

Adair proceeded to tell Portlyn about the microchip, "Taru Bolivar," and the *da Vinci*'s trip to Phantas 61. Once he was done, Portlyn nodded and told the admiral, "Whatever it takes to stop these terrorists once and for all. Thank you for sharing this with me, Ian."

"Just keep it to yourself for the time being, Rod. Gold was right about the need to keep a lid on this."

"Absolutely, my friend. Thanks again, and be well."

With that, Portlyn signed off. Then, he punched a numerical code into his communications console, a code he had committed to memory. A moment later, a new face appeared on his screen: a gray-skinned man with ivory hair, violet eyes, and a thick, almost square-shaped head.

"What can I do for you, Mr. Portlyn?" the man on the screen asked.

"Mr. Gerard, what is your current status?"

"I'm departing Asteroid Station P-16 now, sir. I've made sure that security at the chemical plant has been beefed up, as per your request. I guarantee, no terrorists will be infiltrating that location."

P-16, Portlyn thought. *Very good. Not far at all.*

"I have a new assignment for you, Mr. Gerard. A very important one. One that can only be assigned to my Senior High Security Agent."

"What do you need, sir?"

"I need you to go to Phantas 61. Keep a very low profile. Watch for the arrival of a Starfleet crew, find out what they're doing there, and report back to me on their activities."

"I'm not far from Phantas 61, sir. I can be there within thirty minutes."

The tycoon smiled faintly. "Yes, I know. I'll be waiting for your call, Mr. Gerard." He then cut the transmission.

Portlyn leaned back in his chair and looked out the window of his office, gazing at the stars in the evening sky.

"Phantas 61," he said softly to himself. "Very interesting."

CHAPTER 6

Captain's Log, Stardate 53812.5:

The da Vinci *is approaching Phantas 61. An away team led by Lieutenant Commander Corsi will beam down upon our arrival to investigate the planet and find out what connection, if any, it has to the terrorist activities aimed against Rod Portlyn's properties. We also hope to find out what "Taru Bolivar" means. Is it a person? A place? A weapon? Hopefully, we are not far from the answer.*

The turbolift doors on the bridge slid apart and Corsi stepped out, accompanied by P8 Blue.

"Captain," Corsi began as she approached Gold, who was seated in his command chair. "We have a volunteer for the away team." She tilted her head toward P8 Blue.

"Oh?" Gold replied, somewhat surprised. He turned to the

Nasat. "Blue, this is really a matter for security, not engineering."

"Captain, I may be able to help facilitate communication with the inhabitants of this world," Pattie said. "Or, at least *some* of them. When I heard we were going to Phantas 61, I recalled that there are a number of Nasats who settled there several decades ago. They're probably still there."

That piqued Gold's interest. "Any relatives of yours, by any chance?"

"I doubt it, sir. From what I understand, they were all Reds who decided to leave the homeworld and forge new lives for themselves. Naturally, they were viewed as 'strange' by mainstream Nasat culture—I can certainly relate to that. And I've always admired them for their fortitude."

Gold nodded. "If they know anything, they may feel more comfortable talking to you. Okay, Blue, you're on the team."

"Thank you, sir," Pattie replied with a grateful nod.

On the main viewscreen, the small yellowish planet that had come into view a short while earlier was rapidly increasing in size. The *da Vinci* entered its final approach.

"Captain, we're receiving a hail from the planet," Shabalala said as the ship achieved standard orbit.

"On screen, Lieutenant."

A moment later, a smiling male with pale yellow skin appeared on the viewscreen. He was apparently in early middle age, with long, slightly graying hair that was pulled back in a small ponytail and matched by a thick mustache. He wore a maroon jacket and slacks and a collarless white tunic.

"*Greetings,*" the man said in a smooth, easygoing voice. "*Welcome to Phantas 61.*"

"Thank you. I'm Captain Gold of the *U.S.S. da Vinci*. And you are . . . ?"

"*Ramark,*" the man replied. Then he added, with a chuckle, "*The only one here who still has an actual job—or at least a reasonable approximation.*"

"I . . . see," Gold replied. He glanced over at Corsi, who stood beside the captain's chair and looked as bemused by this introduction as he was.

"*I run the communications center,*" Ramark continued. "*Not* that anyone really contacts this mudball anymore. So, what brings you here? You get lost or something?"

"An investigation on behalf of the Federation, actually. Perhaps you can put us in touch with your local authorities?"

Ramark grinned. *"I'm about the closest thing there is to that here. I'd be glad to help you, if I can."*

"Thank you very much, Mr. Ramark. An away team will beam down momentarily, if you don't mind."

"That's fine. Have them beam down in the center of our main city—I'll send the coordinates, and I'll meet them there."

Ramark signed off, and Gold turned to Corsi with a small grin. "He seems . . . interesting."

"Hopefully he can point us in the right direction," she replied, all serious.

"We'll know soon enough. Happy hunting, Corsi."

It was midday on Phantas 61 when Corsi and her away team materialized on the surface. Standing on one side of her was her trusted deputy chief of security, Chief Petty Officer Vance Hawkins. On the other side was security guard Frank Powers, a brown-haired, capable young man from Earth, who joined the crew following Galvan VI and the ship's refitting. Bringing up the rear was P8 Blue.

"Not exactly the thriving, successful mining world I was expecting," Corsi commented.

They stood at the center of a wide avenue and gazed upon a long, pothole-filled, broken road that extended several miles in each direction and was littered with rubble and old garbage. Along both sides of the avenue stood shut-down, boarded-up businesses—a clothing shop, a hardware store, several restaurants and saloons, and a barber shop were just a few.

"Business seems to have taken a turn for the worse in this neighborhood," the dark-skinned Hawkins commented as they passed a building in disrepair that had once been a holographic entertainment theater.

In the distance, the away team could see a number of tall office buildings that at one time must have been beautiful, gleaming structures, but were now nothing more than abandoned husks. The gray, murky sky provided the perfect backdrop for this gloomy scene.

Farther down the avenue, they saw several four-story residential buildings still in use. These structures too were in disrepair, with numerous cracked windows, crumbling façades, and an overall dingy appearance. The occupants of these buildings could be seen walking into, out of, and around the structures. They included male and female humanoids of the same species as Ramark, of all ages, shapes, and sizes. And there were several Red Nasats there too huddling together. Corsi glanced over at P8 Blue, who seemed eager to approach these former inhabitants of her homeworld.

But Corsi also noticed that there was a certain . . . *aimlessness* to all of them. Some of the humanoid males sat on the front steps of one of the buildings, looking like they had all the time in the world and absolutely no idea how to spend it. Several of the older humanoid females cooked some sort of food on old, dented garbage cans that had been converted into makeshift stoves. Everyone had on outfits that were worn-out, shabby, looking about ready to be turned into rags.

Turning to her teammates, Corsi said, "They don't look like they're part of a successful mining operation. They look like . . . *this* is all that they have going on in their lives."

"Hey there!" shouted a voice from behind her.

Corsi turned to see Ramark approaching, waving and bearing a friendly smile. He was of medium height, a few inches shorter than Corsi, but he carried himself with confidence. After introductions were made, he pointed to a small, nondescript building down the avenue. "The comm center is right over there. We can go to my office and talk. I'd love to know how Phantas 61 is involved in this investigation of yours. I can't imagine its name coming up in anything other than a cautionary tale."

"What do you mean?" Corsi asked.

Ramark smirked. "Well, look around you. Things aren't exactly what they used to be around here."

"And why is that?"

"How about we talk while we walk?"
"Very well, Mr. Ramark, lead the way."

The doors to the main chamber in the communications center slid open, and Ramark led his guests in. He continued his explanation about the fate of Phantas 61.

"So when Portlyn bought the mining operation and all the real estate here, we had a really good thing going. I mean, we were *thriving*. Portlyn kept us all on as his employees, to keep things running smoothly. But pretty soon, ol' Roddy-boy needed more funds to buy up more planets and businesses. So he started giving us ridiculous, unrealistic budgets that we were supposed to meet, to generate enough revenue to support his other deals. We became his cash cow. At first, we became more successful than we'd ever been, but we couldn't sustain that forever, not at the rate he had us going. He didn't seem to understand, or care. In the end, he ended up draining Phantas 61 of its natural resources, leaving us with this sad, desiccated corpse that we proudly call home."

The walls of the chamber were lined with outmoded, but still functioning, computers and monitor screens. As Corsi and the away team walked around the room inspecting the technology, Ramark activated the main communications console, which was built into a circular desk at the center of the chamber. He sat down in the chair behind the desk and put his feet up on the console.

With a melodramatic flourish, he raised an imaginary glass and said, "So here's to Rod 'The Shaft' Portlyn, who's made the people of Phantas 61 what we are today—broke."

This guy is just lucky that Farmer Delfo isn't here listening to this, Corsi thought. Ramark's portrayal of Portlyn was in sharp contrast to the image of the tycoon that was so popular back on Vemlar. It only served to reinforce her own misgivings about him. But that was not why she was here.

"You said you might be able to help us," she reminded him.
Ramark nodded. "What do you need to know?"
"There have been several terrorist actions taken against

Portlyn-owned properties in this system. We have reason to believe there may be some sort of connection between these actions and Phantas 61. Would you know anything about it?"

"No, not at all," Ramark replied without hesitation. "I haven't even heard gossip about it on the subspace channels."

Corsi pressed on. "What about the term 'Taru Bolivar'? Have you ever heard of it? Would you know what it means?"

Ramark turned his gaze upward, apparently searching through his memories. He then looked back at Corsi and said, "No, I can't say that I have." He gave her a quizzical look. "So, are you people working for Portlyn?"

"We're here to protect Federation interests," she told him.

"I see. Well, look, let me check through the communications archives for the last month or so. If Phantas 61 *is* somehow involved, maybe there's a past transmission we picked up that can provide you with a lead."

Ramark placed a communications earpiece in his ear, adjusted various controls on his console, and started checking through his archives. As the minutes passed with no hint of success, Corsi began to think it might be more productive for her and her team to search elsewhere. She appreciated Ramark's cooperation, but now doubted that his efforts would lead to anything. If he hadn't heard anything about the terrorists before now, it was probably too much to expect for him to suddenly stumble upon a direct line to them. But she would give him at least a few more minutes before she and her team moved on.

Corsi was just about ready to thank Ramark for his efforts and depart with the away team when he perked up and said, "I found something, Commander Corsi. Some mention of . . . Kalibiss. It seems to be in a language I don't recognize, but I'm sure that's what I heard."

Corsi glanced over at the other members of her team, all of whom looked as intrigued as she felt. *Kalibiss. That's promising.*

Ramark continued adjusting the controls. "I'm feeding it through our translator. If it recognizes the language, the transmission will start showing up as text on the large monitor screen." He pointed to a unit on the far side of the room.

P8 Blue glanced over at the screen and became enthusiastic. "It looks like text is showing up now!" She rushed toward the monitor screen.

Corsi and the rest of the away team joined the Nasat at the screen. They all wanted to see what the transmission said. But Corsi noticed that Ramark remained at his console. He seemed uninterested, which was odd, considering all the effort to which he had gone. Sure enough, text scrolled across the screen. Corsi scowled.

"It's just gibberish," Hawkins said, voicing Corsi's own thoughts.

Something didn't feel right to her. She slowly reached for her phaser, just to have her hand near it, just to be on the safe side. Suddenly, on the other side of the room, one of the large computers, about seven feet in height and positioned up against the wall, popped open and swung away from the wall, revealing a secret entryway behind it. Four humanoid figures—three males and one female—burst out of the entryway, armed with crude hand weapons they immediately aimed at Corsi and her team. They were dressed in tan-colored paramilitary uniforms.

Phony computer—how clever, Corsi thought. *I should've known.* She swiftly pulled out her phaser and fired at the figure in front—a tall, burly male with straight blond hair, who went down in a stunned heap. She saw Hawkins and Powers following suit, but the ambushing figures scattered so fast that the phaser beams missed their targets and struck only the far wall.

At least the odds are pretty much even, Corsi thought. Out of the corner of her eye, she saw Ramark duck behind his communications console for shelter.

One of the ambushing figures—the female, a short, tough-looking young woman with her dark hair in a buzz-cut style—aimed her hand weapon at Corsi and fired. Corsi scrambled and managed to evade the blast of energy, but Hawkins was not so lucky. The blast hit him across the shoulder, knocking him off his feet.

Out of the corner of her eye, Corsi then saw five more armed ambushers emerge from the entryway. Three of them were Red Nasats.

P8 Blue, who had been aiming her phaser at the tough-looking woman, also noticed the new arrivals. "Wait! Stop!" she called out to them, waving six of her eight limbs. "Let me talk to you—I'm a Nasat, too!"

One of the Red Nasats fired its weapon at P8 Blue. The blast hit her phaser, knocking it out of the limb that was holding it.

"Drop your weapons and surrender!" shouted the tough-looking woman.

Corsi realized there was no way for her team to come out of this situation on top. They were outnumbered and outgunned, with an injured man. But she would not surrender to them.

She hit her combadge. "Corsi to *da Vinci*—emergency beam-out now!"

No response.

She hit the combadge again. "Corsi to *da Vinci*, come in, *da Vinci*."

Still no response.

She heard Ramark clear his throat, and glanced over at him. He was standing at the communications console, with a smug grin on his face, waving to her mockingly. Then, he pointed to the console, looking quite mischievous.

Jamming communications, she thought, stifling a particularly strong curse.

Still more armed ambushers entered the room through the secret entryway. Another Red Nasat, an Arcturian, a Betelgeusian, and several more humanoids. The group now numbered thirteen, and they closed in and surrounded Corsi and her team, hand weapons at the ready. Corsi looked over at Powers, P8 Blue, and Hawkins, who was still conscious and rubbing the shoulder that had been hit. Corsi saw no blood or even burn marks on Hawkins's shoulder—he was apparently grazed by nothing more than a stun blast. The ambushers' weapons weren't set to kill. That was interesting.

Corsi nodded at her team reluctantly, conveying silently that they didn't stand a chance. They dropped their phasers to the floor. The tough-looking woman—"Buzz-cut" was as good a name for her as any—confiscated the phasers and handed them over to a compatriot.

"You and your people, come with us," Buzz-cut told Corsi, pointing her hand weapon directly at the security chief's chest.

"Powers, Pattie, help Hawkins," Corsi said, her eyes never leaving Buzz-cut's.

Powers and P8 Blue walked over to Hawkins and helped him to his feet.

"I'm all right, I can walk," Hawkins said, waving them off. "Shoulder and arm are just numb, that's all."

Elsewhere in the room, two of the ambushers lifted up the unconscious body of the man Corsi had stunned. They shot smoldering glares at the *da Vinci* security chief as they passed by her, carrying the unconscious man over to the secret entryway. They headed inside.

Buzz-cut then motioned Corsi and her team over to the same entryway. A flight of stairs leading downward lay before them, dimly illuminated by a series of small glowing light rods attached to either side of the stairwell. With a wave of her hand weapon, Buzz-cut indicated that she wanted Corsi and her team to enter.

As she walked down the steps, Corsi could hear the large computer being put back into place so that it would once again block the secret entrance.

"I'm sorry, Commander," Hawkins told her, his voice filled with self-recrimination. "I should have been more alert. I never should have let my guard down with that weasel."

"Same here, Commander," added Powers.

Corsi waved off the apologies. "I'm as much to blame as anyone," she said.

They reached the bottom of the stairs and, at the prodding of the ambushers, moved on through a narrow corridor until they entered an underground cavern converted into a headquarters of some kind. Corsi saw a long conference table covered with various maps, charts, and graphs, fifteen chairs, and several computer consoles.

The ambushers, weapons still in hand, continued to surround her, Hawkins, Powers, and P8 Blue.

"Where are we?" Corsi demanded.

A gruff masculine voice responded. "You're where you *wanted* to be, Commander Corsi."

A fairly young-looking, yellow-skinned humanoid male with wavy brown hair and intense, piercing blue eyes stepped out from a side alcove. He moved forward to face her.

"You wanted to find the Taru Bolivar," the male told Corsi. It was his voice that had answered her. "Well, here we are."

In the communications center, Ramark was chuckling to himself about how easy it had been to defeat those Starfleet suckers, when he heard a noise behind him.

He stood up swiftly, pulling a small, laser-powered firearm out of a pocket in his trousers.

"Who's there?" he called out. No one should have been able to get into the building without the proper authorization code. And everyone with proper authorization was now down below.

Suddenly, he felt a sharp pain in the wrist of the hand holding the firearm—so much pain that he dropped the weapon. He looked down to see a large, gray-skinned hand holding his wrist. How could anyone have been able to sneak up beside him so fast? He twisted around to see who had seized him.

"Gerard?" he said in shock.

"Hello, Ramark," said Rod Portlyn's Senior High Security Agent with a malevolent grin.

Gerard, towering over Ramark, shifted his expression to a cold glare. "I need to get down to that underground hideout, and you're going to show me how."

"What underground hideout?" Ramark responded defiantly, placing his free hand on the communications console and reaching for the toggle that would sound the alert signal to warn those down below.

But Gerard pulled Ramark closer to him and squeezed harder on the wrist, causing Ramark to wince despite his best efforts to show no weakness.

"I'm dead serious, twerp. And unless you tell me what I want to know, you'll just be plain dead."

"I can't hear you, Gerard. Your head is too far up Portlyn's rear end."

"Wrong answer," the big man replied.

Continuing to hold Ramark's wrist, Gerard strode over to the wall where the seven-foot-tall computer blocked the secret entryway. He lifted Ramark, turned him in a horizontal position, and then placed the smaller man under one of his large, muscular arms.

"I figure both sides of this wall have their own control switches to open the computer. The one on this side has to be hidden around here somewhere," Gerard commented in an almost casual manner. "All I have to do is find it. And I can't think of anything better to use than your head."

Without warning, Gerard slammed Ramark's head into a section of the wall. Ramark was too shocked to even cry out in pain.

"Nope, it's not here," Ramark could hear Gerard say through the intense pounding in his ears. "Let me try this section here . . ."

Wham!

Amid his agony, Ramark was filled with anger and hatred, wanting nothing more than to tear out Gerard's eyes and wrap his fingers around his throat and squeeze the life out of him. But Portlyn's agent was too big, and too strong.

"Nope, not there either. Guess I should try a little further up. Gee, I might have to cover this whole room. This could take a while. . . ."

Ramark felt Gerard rushing him toward another section of wall. "Wait," he managed to croak out. "I'll talk." He couldn't take another blow to the head. And he hated himself for it.

"Where?" Gerard demanded.

Ramark pointed weakly to the computer itself.

"Now what?" Gerard hissed.

"Button, side of 'puter," Ramark mumbled.

Through blurred vision, Ramark saw Gerard examine the sides of the computer and find a small camouflaged stud near the top. The big man pressed the stud and watched in triumph as the front of the computer popped open, exposing the entryway and the dimly lit stairway leading downward.

"All right, Ramark. I won't be needing you anymore."

Gerard dropped Ramark onto the floor and quickly inspected the entrance. Ramark tried to get to his feet, but he was barely holding on to consciousness. He looked up to see Gerard pull out a phaser.

"It's set for stun," Gerard told him. "This way, you can live out the rest of your life knowing that you betrayed your friends down there."

That was the last thing Ramark heard before he was bathed in the light of the phaser beam and all went black.

Gerard descended the winding stairway quietly and carefully, until he entered a narrow corridor and then heard a voice echoing from up ahead. He stopped as soon as he could make out clearly what the voice was saying.

And Gerard found that he recognized the voice.

Elless, he thought.

"We intend to be a constant thorn in Portlyn's side, and prevent him from spreading his taint to other worlds," Gerard heard the voice say.

This is good stuff, he thought as he pulled a small transmitter out of his jacket, activated it, and began broadcasting to a specific location: Rod Portlyn's private office on Vemlar.

CHAPTER 7

"My name is Elless," the young man with the piercing blue eyes told Corsi.

"I take it you're the leader around here?" she replied in a cold tone.

The young man shrugged his shoulders. "More or less."

Corsi's tone remained cold. "I hope you realize this terrorist organization of yours will be stopped, one way or another."

Elless frowned. "I was hoping you and your Federation would be more reasonable."

Corsi scowled. "You don't know much about the Federation if you believe we would ever condone acts of terrorism."

Elless stood his ground. "We're *not* terrorists. I assume Ramark told you what happened to this world under Portlyn's ownership?"

"He told us. So we have one side of the story now. That doesn't mean we buy it. And even if it's true, that doesn't excuse your actions. Planting time bombs, blowing up a key facility under construction, endangering lives—"

"Oh, come on!" Elless interrupted. "We arranged everything so no one would be killed—or even hurt! We made sure of it!"

"Not as well as you think," Corsi fired back angrily, thinking of Sonya Gomez and the anonymous suspect who remained in the *da Vinci* sickbay.

At that, Elless looked as if someone had suddenly splashed ice-cold water in his face. "Someone was . . . killed?" His body seemed to deflate.

"Two people injured on Vemlar, one severely," Corsi said. "He's one of yours, I think."

Elless closed his eyes and lowered his head. "Jaxxon," he whispered. "My brother. Vemlar was his assignment."

Corsi felt a brief flash of sympathy, but was determined not to show it. Not to a terrorist. She told him flatly, "That's the danger of playing with fire—you can't always control the forces you unleash."

"You have to believe me," Elless insisted. "Bloodshed isn't what we want."

Corsi looked upon him doubtfully. "So what exactly *do* you want?"

Elless straightened up, looked her square in the eyes, set his jaw firmly, and told her with passion, "We intend to be a constant thorn in Portlyn's side, and prevent him from spreading his taint to other worlds."

"Don't you think you're overreacting a bit?" Corsi asked. "I mean, assuming everything we've heard is true, the bottom line is, his business here took a downward turn. It happens—believe me, I know. That's no reason to view him as some sort of disease."

Elless chuckled bitterly. "Let me tell you about the *real* Rod Portlyn. We've learned that he's found a way to keep profiting from Phantas 61, but it doesn't include us. He intends to turn this entire planet into a giant dumping ground. For a price, he's going to offer space to any interested governments across the galaxy, provide them with a place to drop their excess trash. All Phantasians will have to get off the planet, or else willingly live in a cosmic garbage dump."

Corsi was unmoved. "Assuming this information is true, I agree, it's an unfortunate situation for all of you. But Portlyn is well within his rights. You sold him your land. He can do whatever he wants with it."

Elless exploded. "We don't have anyplace else to go! And we're down to the barest essentials here—we don't have the means to transport our whole population to another world!" He then took a breath and spoke more calmly. "Besides, this planet is our home—has been for generations! *We* made it the success it was, not Portlyn. We have a vested interest in this place that goes beyond balance sheets and profit margins. That's why we created this group, the Taru Bolivar. That's a Phantasian term that means 'to see reality as it should be.'"

"And just what should your reality be?" Corsi asked skeptically.

"Our ultimate goal is to regain this planet's independence and make it a success again. To do that, we need to make Portlyn realize it's in his best interests to relinquish his ownership. Until then, we intend to do whatever we can to interfere with his operations, to prevent him from doing to other worlds what he's done to us. That's why we targeted Vemlar."

Corsi sighed, growing increasingly frustrated. "Look, the fact of the matter is, the soil on Vemlar became infertile. Had Portlyn not offered to buy the land from the farmers, they would've had nothing but famine and starvation. Like him or not, he saved those people."

Elless snorted. "You think you know everything, don't you? Portlyn himself oversaw a top-secret bioengineering project conducted on Vemlar, well *before* he bought it up. That project involved reorganizing the molecular structure of Vemlar's soil, using a newly developed viral agent. One that rendered itself undetectable after it was used."

"What are you saying? That Portlyn—"

"Portlyn secretly ruined the soil on Vemlar, to intentionally create the famine and ultimately manipulate the farmers into selling their land to him."

Corsi rolled her eyes. "This is getting ridiculous."

"What, you think I'm some paranoid conspiracy nut making wild accusations?"

"I have to admit, Elless, the thought is crossing my mind. I'm supposed to just believe a gang of terrorists over a respected businessman with no criminal history?"

"We're not terrorists!"

THE ART OF THE DEAL 237

"Terrorists rarely see themselves as such. They usually call themselves, what? Freedom fighters? Revolutionaries? Heroes?"

"What I've told you is true."

"If it is, we'll need solid proof."

Elless turned away from her and walked over to one of the computer consoles. He held up a small computer file that was sitting atop the console.

"This is a highly classified data file that details everything about the Vemlar project," he explained. "I read it myself, and then managed to extract it directly from Portlyn's home office."

"Fine, let's take a look at it."

Elless grimaced and sighed heavily. "Once I brought the file back here, I tried to show the data to the rest of the Taru Bolivar. But it wouldn't open. We discovered that it was encoded so intricately that it'll only open on Portlyn's personal computer." He shook the file and sighed. "The proof is right here, but I can't get to it!"

Elless then angrily shoved the file into a side pocket of his uniform.

He seems sincere enough, Corsi thought. *But it's also mighty convenient that the one piece of evidence he has is unreachable. If I could get it to the* da Vinci, *have it checked up there . . .*

"It doesn't matter, though," Elless continued. "We, the Taru Bolivar, know the truth. And we intend to prevent Portlyn from completing his project on Vemlar—regardless of whether you stand in our way. Don't you see, Commander? We're the only ones who can stand against him—with Portlyn's businesses located in nonaligned space, he doesn't have to answer to anybody but himself."

Now where have I heard that *before?* Corsi thought, with more than a hint of irony.

On Vemlar, Rod Portlyn stood in front of one of the huge windows in his office, alone, holding a half-full glass of Romulan ale. He stared out at the night-shrouded sky and the distant stars as he listened to the conversation being broadcast over the receiver unit in his desk.

"We, the Taru Bolivar, know the truth. And we intend to prevent Portlyn from completing his project on Vemlar..."

Portlyn turned off the receiver. He'd heard enough. He'd already set in motion his response.

Ah, Elless, Portlyn thought. He focused his gaze on one particular tiny spot of light in the sky: Phantas 61. *Thanks to your antics, I've had to take harsh steps to solve this insurgency problem.*

He glanced at the chronometer on the far wall and did a quick mental calculation.

The Orion mercenary ships should be arriving at Phantas 61 shortly. As should the robot freighter from Creccus. All in all, I would say I responded quite efficiently to this turn of events.

He then looked back at the sky, and that tiny spot of light. *I knew you had to be involved in this, Elless. As soon as Adair told me that Phantas 61 was somehow connected.*

Portlyn took a sip from the glass and closed his eyes as the ale went down his throat. He savored its powerful kick.

I told you time and time again, Elless, back when you were my right-hand man—never take business personally. But apparently, you never learned that lesson. A shame, really.

Elless ordered his operatives to holster their weapons and back off. But they remained in possession of the Federation team's phasers.

"You're in league with our enemy," Elless told Corsi. "But you're not our prisoners. Nor are you hostages. We've no intention of harming you in any way. Would that be the case if we were the terrorists you think we are?"

Corsi considered that, and the fact that their hand weapons had been set on stun, not kill.

"I'll grant that your efforts to preserve life do seem genuine," she replied. "And incidentally, we're not 'in league' with Portlyn. We have a business arrangement with him that doesn't extend beyond Vemlar."

Elless nodded. "Understood. Maybe we can talk this out under less tense circumstances, perhaps open a real dialogue to understand each other better?"

"I'll need to contact my ship and consult with my captain. He'll decide how to proceed from here."

"Absolutely," Elless told her solemnly. "I've already signaled Ramark to stop jamming communications. You can contact your ship."

Corsi nodded and slapped the combadge on her chest. "Corsi to *da Vinci*."

There was no response. She slapped the badge again.

"Corsi to *da Vinci*, come in. Captain Gold, do you copy?"

Still no response. She looked over at the away team. They all started slapping their combadges and calling to the ship, but were met with silence.

Corsi immediately turned to Elless and glared at him.

In response, Elless strode over to one of the computer consoles in the room and flipped a switch.

"Elless to Ramark. I told you to stop jamming outgoing transmissions."

No response.

"Ramark, respond."

Still no response. Elless turned to Buzz-cut.

"Vazga, check on Ramark, find out what's going on with him."

As Buzz-cut—Vazga—headed out of the chamber, Elless started adjusting the controls on the console. He became increasingly agitated as he studied the monitor screen while fiddling around with the knobs and dials.

"According to these readings," he began, "our equipment up top is no longer jamming outgoing communications."

"So what's the problem?" Corsi replied with an annoyed scowl.

Elless pointed to an undulating energy pattern on the monitor. "All communications in this entire region of space are now being jammed by an *outside* source."

CHAPTER 8

Captain Gold paced the bridge of the *da Vinci*, wondering what was happening on Phantas 61. Corsi was supposed to report in an hour after beaming down, and those sixty minutes had come and gone ten minutes ago. She was a highly competent officer, and Gold trusted her completely, but she was also punctual to a fault, so missing her check-in deadline was not something he took lightly.

He decided that he'd waited long enough and turned to the tactical console.

"Shabalala, open a channel to Commander Corsi."

A moment later, Shabalala looked up from the console, concerned.

"Sir, I can't reach Commander Corsi—or any other member of the away team. Something is jamming all transmissions."

Gold scowled as he headed back to the captain's chair. Given the circumstances they were in, he could guess where this was headed.

Sure enough, Ensign Susan Haznedl, stationed at the operations console, suddenly said, "Captain, sensors detect ten vessels closing in on us. They just appeared out of nowhere, sir—they may have been cloaked."

"What do you make of them?"

"They're more than twice the size of one of our shuttlecraft, sir, and heavily armed—each ship has a torpedo bay, phaser banks, and disruptor cannons. They're essentially arsenals with warp drives."

"Any idea who they are?"

"Unable to ascertain, sir. The ships seem to be . . . cobbled together, from various alien technologies."

"Shields up," Gold ordered. "Shabalala, stand by on defensive maneuvers."

Soon, the ten vessels were close enough to be seen on the bridge viewscreen. They approached in a V-formation.

"Magnify, maximum setting," Gold ordered.

Instantly, the image on the viewscreen increased in size. Gold had never seen vessels like these before. As Haznedl surmised, they indeed appeared to be cobbled together from different technologies. From what Gold could tell, the warp engines were Ferengi in design. The disruptor cannons mounted to either side of the cockpits were most likely Klingon in origin. The torpedo bays were located on the underbellies of the vessels, but each one seemed to be of a different alien technology—there was no consistency from ship to ship.

"The terrorists, I presume," the captain said aloud.

"Shall I fire a warning shot, sir?" Shabalala asked.

But before Gold could reply, the lead ship on the viewscreen pulled ahead of the pack and opened fire with its disruptor cannons.

The *da Vinci* shuddered slightly under the barrage, which was deflected by the Starfleet vessel's shields.

"Lock phasers on target and return fire," Gold snapped. "No warnings about it!"

Gold watched the main viewscreen as twin phaser beams erupted from the *da Vinci*. But the lead attacking ship swiftly banked to the side, completely evading the beams and pulling away.

Haznedl, eyes glued to her console, reported, "The other

ships have broken off from the V-formation, sir. They're moving to surround us."

And as the attackers surrounded the *da Vinci*, they opened fire, their disruptors alternating with their phasers.

"Maintain phaser fire!" Gold ordered.

Shabalala targeted another attacker and fired. The phaser beams struck the small ship, but were deflected by its shields. The attacker fired back with disruptors that struck at the upper hull of the *da Vinci*'s forward section, right near the bridge.

"Our shields are holding." Haznedl then looked up from her console. "Captain, another ship is arriving!"

"Another attacker?"

"A freighter of some kind, sir. It's heading away from us and toward the planet."

"Then we can't worry about it right now—our hands are full enough as it is."

As if to emphasize that point, three of the attacking vessels swooped in closer.

"Photon torpedoes one, two, and three—fire!" Gold shouted.

Shabalala complied, and the *da Vinci* launched three torpedoes, each aimed at one of the three attackers. Two of the attackers evaded the torpedoes, but one was hit directly on its side.

"No damage to enemy ship, Captain," Shabalala reported. "Its shields deflected the torpedo with a minimal loss of power."

Another attacker closed in, on a direct course for the front of the *da Vinci*. It became bigger and bigger on the viewscreen as it got closer and closer. Then, it began spitting disruptor bolts at the bridge, trying to continue the work of its sister ship.

"Quantum torpedoes one and two—fire!" Gold ordered in response.

The *da Vinci* unleashed two of the more powerful quantum torpedoes, both of which hit their target head-on. The small attacker seemed to stop in midstream, and then started tilting to its side.

"Its shields are down, Captain!" Shabalala exclaimed.

"Quantum torpedo three—fire," Gold told the tactical officer.

Shabalala fired the additional torpedo, which hit the now drifting attacker dead center. The small ship exploded like a miniature supernova.

But there was no time to celebrate. The two other attackers closed in again, taking up positions on either side of the *da Vinci*, and fired photon torpedoes.

Gold noted that the attackers held off on firing their torpedoes until they were at point-blank range, presumably because torpedoes were in short supply aboard the fairly small vessels and the pilots wanted to make sure that every shot counted.

"Our shields are down by twelve percent, Captain," Haznedl announced.

The attackers' strategy was starting to work.

Gold glanced at the viewscreen. Beyond the nine remaining attackers that streaked in and out of view, he could see the freighter entering low orbit around Phantas 61, completely ignoring the battle. But Gold had no time to even wonder what it was up to.

"We're surrounded, sir," Haznedl reported.

And then all the attackers opened fire.

Vazga returned to the Taru Bolivar underground headquarters, carrying the limp body of Ramark.

"Unconscious," she reported as she placed him gently on the conference table. Two of the Taru Bolivar—one of the Nasats and the Arcturian—went over to examine him.

"Some kind of head injury," Vazga continued. "Looks like somebody beat him up and then stun-blasted him."

"Who?" Elless demanded.

"No idea," Vazga replied. "There was nobody else up there—but I found the entryway open when I got upstairs."

Suddenly, an alarm signal blared out. Corsi swiftly turned toward the large piece of machinery that was the source of the noise. Elless rushed over and started flipping switches. A large, flat-panel monitor rose up from inside and a schematic representation popped on, of a planet and the region of space surrounding it.

There were eleven blinking dots on the screen, in high orbit above the planet, clustered around one another. A twelfth blinking dot was off on its own, slowly getting closer to the planet.

"Is that supposed to be *this* planet?" Corsi asked, pointing to the schematic.

"Yes," Elless replied. "This is our sensor device. It's been monitoring local space. Those dots are all spaceships—there's a lot of traffic above us all of a sudden."

"One of those ships is ours," Corsi noted. "Who are the others?"

Elless took a closer look at the sensor readings. "I've identified your ship, but I can't seem to identify the ten circling it—they defy standard classification. But this *other* one seems to be a freighter of some kind."

He then noticed something new, and grimaced. "There's fighting going on. Looks like your ship is under attack."

"But who would attack us?" P8 Blue asked. "And why?"

"There's only one possibility," Elless said, turning back to face Corsi and her team. "Portlyn."

"How did I know you were going to say that?" Corsi responded with a sigh. "Now he's behind an attack on a Starfleet vessel? I suppose he beat up your friend Ramark, too?"

"Well, if *he* didn't, I'm sure it was someone connected to him. Look, it's the only logical explanation. As for why he'd have your ship attacked . . . my guess is, he somehow connected the time bombs and the explosion on Vemlar to us. And he found out that you came here."

"You're making him out to be pretty damned omniscient," Corsi told him.

"With all of his connections, and all the operatives he has running around spying for him, he might as well be."

Elless then paused. He looked as if he had bitten into the sourest of fruits. Finally, as if spitting out the words, he said in a voice dripping with bitterness, "Look, I know Rod Portlyn. I know how he thinks. I was his right-hand man here. I helped him build this place up . . . and watched helplessly as he ran it into the ground." He glanced back at the schematic. "My guess is that the attackers are Orion mercenaries. Portlyn often uses them on a freelance basis." He turned back to Corsi, his intense eyes boring into hers. "Portlyn can't take the chance of Starfleet finding out the truth about him, not if he wants to keep the Federation as his partner on Vemlar. Those mercs are here to blow your ship out of the stars."

Vazga abruptly called out to Elless. She directed his attention back to the monitor, and the twelfth blinking dot that was closest to the planet.

"The freighter just launched something," she informed him.

Elless swiftly adjusted the controls and studied the sensor readings. "A missile of some kind. I'll see if I can augment the readings so we can determine exactly what it—"

"What?" Corsi prompted.

Elless's voice sounded hollow when he finally answered. "The sensors say the missile is loaded with contagion—the same kind that Portlyn used on Vemlar. But much more powerful. In this form, it'll wipe out all life on Phantas 61." He turned away from the screen and looked at everyone in the room. "It all makes sense—he wants the galaxy to believe the *da Vinci* was destroyed by the Taru Bolivar. And to make sure no one can say anything different, everyone on this planet will be exterminated."

"What about his investment in this world?" Corsi asked, hoping against hope that Elless was somehow wrong. "He's going to just write it off?"

"Not at all," Elless replied. "Phantas 61 doesn't have to support life to be used as a dumping ground for space garbage."

Corsi couldn't argue with that. She had to face the very real possibility that Portlyn was far worse than even she had believed.

"Look, Elless," she began. "We have to work together if we—everyone on Phantas 61 and the *da Vinci*—are going to have any chance of surviving this."

"What do you have in mind?"

"Do you have ground-to-air defenses?"

"No, we're not *that* well-equipped."

"If I may point out," P8 Blue stepped in, "blowing the missile out of the sky would be most inadvisable. That would only release the contagion into the air."

Okay, Corsi thought. *That rules out all of my other ideas.*

But then she had a flash of inspiration. "Elless, what kind of spaceship capability do you have?"

"We have a small fleet of ships that we've modified to act as escape vehicles and fighters."

She nodded quickly. "Do they have tractor beams?"

"Yes, but not very powerful ones. They can only handle objects not much larger than a standard cargo container."

"That'll have to do." Corsi turned to her team. "Hawkins, how's your shoulder?"

"Uh, much better, Commander. I can do whatever you need."

"Hawkins," Corsi said to her deputy in a tone filled with skepticism.

The dark-skinned security officer frowned and sighed. "Okay, it's still numb. And I can't feel my fingers—yet. But I'm sure I can—"

Corsi cut him off. "Can't risk it. You'll have to stay here—no arguments, I don't have the time. Powers, Pattie—you're coming with me."

She then turned to Elless. "Have a couple of your people stay here and try to find a way around the communications jamming. If they can, they should make contact with the *da Vinci*—our captain must be informed about what's really going on here."

Elless summoned over one of the Red Nasats and a small, middle-aged, humanoid woman with yellowish skin and frizzy, blue-tinted hair. "R1, Fila—I need you two working on this. Use smoke signals, if you have to."

Corsi, stifling a smirk, turned back to Hawkins. "If they do make contact, I'll want *you* to do the talking, Vance—the captain will need to hear this from someone he knows and trusts." Hawkins nodded.

"Now let's get to those ships of yours," Corsi told Elless. "And you'd better bring your best pilots—we'll need them for what I have planned."

* * *

THE ART OF THE DEAL 247

Captain Gold felt both gratified and frustrated watching another attacker explode on the viewscreen after a bombardment of quantum torpedoes and a barrage of phasers at full power.

That's two down . . . and eight more to go.

The attackers continued their hit-and-run maneuvers, zooming in close to the *da Vinci* to fire their weapons and then swiftly peeling away to avoid the Starfleet vessel's retaliatory fire. The *da Vinci* managed to break out of orbit to gain more maneuvering room and hopefully turn the tables on the attackers. But the smaller ships managed to keep pace and surround the *da Vinci*, pounding at its shields.

"Our shields are now at forty-two percent efficiency, Captain," Haznedl reported.

Didn't take us long to lose that fifty-eight percent, Gold thought grimly. The *da Vinci* endured several hits from all sides. He could almost feel the shields of his vessel weakening even further.

For this *I argued to come to this planet?*

"Phaser power starting to drop, Captain," Shabalala called out.

Gold turned to Fabian Stevens, who was operating an aft bridge console that had been reconfigured during the battle to act as an engineering station. "Shut down all nonessential functions and divert every ounce of available power to shields, weapons, and life support."

"Aye, sir," Stevens replied as he quickly got to work. "But I'm afraid that won't give those systems much more power than they already have."

Gold bit his lip. As much as this wasn't the appropriate time or circumstance, he couldn't ignore the notion that suddenly rushed to the forefront of his mind—the notion that was lurking within ever since the aftermath of Galvan VI: If only he had another ship, a bigger, stronger ship. If he commanded such a vessel, it would have undoubtedly emerged victorious by now, instead of facing annihilation by a ragtag band of terrorists.

CHAPTER 9

Corsi braced herself as the small, snub-nosed, winged spacecraft she piloted abruptly lifted off the ground and began accelerating through a dark, spacious tunnel leading to the mouth of a cave outside the city. She was certainly no stranger to being behind the controls of a ship, and was relieved to find that this vessel flew well and was not too difficult to master, despite its somewhat ramshackle appearance and a control panel that was partially built from spare parts.

Elless explained to her before she climbed into the cockpit that the Taru Bolivar "fleet," such as it was, consisted of vessels that were once shuttles, called "runners," that transported the riches mined from Phantas 61 to larger ships for distribution across space. But when Elless and his comrades formed the Taru Bolivar, they completely reconfigured the runners and outfitted them with whatever defensive and offensive ordnance they could obtain.

Pretty industrious, these Phantasians, she thought as her runner exited the long tunnel and began climbing into the gray sky. She followed Elless's ship, which was in the lead position. Behind her, six more runners headed up through the tunnel, each piloted by either a Taru Bolivar operative or a member of her own team. P8 Blue and Powers were each given a ship to fly, following Elless's pilots, one of whom was Vazga. Corsi had since learned that the tough-looking woman she had thought of as "Buzz-cut" was Elless's second-in-command.

Once all eight runners were in the sky, they accelerated together up toward the stratosphere, their sensors locked on the incoming missile. After several moments, the dart-shaped, ten-stories-tall projectile was in sight. The ships altered course to intercept it.

Corsi anxiously adjusted the controls of her runner so it would match the speed of the missile. She had to assume her fellow pilots were doing the same thing. With all communications still being jammed, there was no way for them to speak to one another directly, so all the details of Corsi's plan were worked out in advance on the fly. Taking a quick look around through the windows of her cockpit, Corsi saw the other ships getting into the agreed-upon flight formation, so she immediately followed suit. The eight runners formed two parallel lines, four ships in each line. Corsi took the lead position in one of the lines, and she could see that the ship marked as Elless's had done the same in the other. A wide opening was maintained between the two lines of runners, through which the missile could enter unimpeded.

The nose of the missile rushed through the opening. Corsi took a deep breath as she watched the nose slip past her. She waited until more of the missile's body had entered the gap between the two lines of runners. She could feel her heart pounding through her chest, the veins in her forehead pulsing madly. The missile continued to rush through the gap.

Wait for more missile . . . just a little more . . . now!

She slapped on her tractor beam, then briefly glanced at the other runners through her cockpit window. They had all activated their tractor beams too, more or less at the same time. All eight beams were now fixed on either side of the missile, from the nose to the long midsection to the base of the propulsion unit, where Corsi's ship was now located. So far, so good.

Considering the speed at which the missile had been traveling when they intercepted it, it was no surprise when the huge projectile continued its relentless descent toward the surface—or when it dragged the eight runners along with it. Corsi kept her cool and waited for any signs of a change. Slowly but surely, she began to detect a decrease in the missile's rate of descent. The tractor beams were having an effect on it, however slight. Now all the runners would have to do is gain complete control over the missile and alter its direction before it hit the surface.

The runners kept their tractor beams fixed on the missile and remained in their parallel lines on either side of it. Then they began to rise in unison and pull on the projectile through the tractor beams, trying to nudge the missile's nose up and gradually move the entire thing out of its downward trajectory.

The surface of the planet got closer and closer, but no great progress was being made.

Corsi hoped the others had come to the same conclusion as she: that it would be necessary to increase power to the tractor beams. She went with the assumption that they had, and began diverting some power from her runner's shields and weapons systems. Glancing out the window, she could see the pale blue tractor beams generated by the other runners quickly become brighter, denoting an increase in power level. Good—they were all on the same wavelength.

With the tractor-beam power levels elevated, the runners made another attempt to pull on the missile and force it up and away from its descent. But despite a slight shift, it continued unabated on its headlong path to the surface. Corsi decided it was necessary to sacrifice even more power from the shields and weapons to boost the tractor beam, and made the adjustments.

She glanced out the window as she strengthened her tractor beam again. She noticed that the ship being flown by Elless's lieutenant, Vazga, which was in the other line of runners, was the first to follow her in this—its tractor beam suddenly grew even brighter.

But Corsi's eyes widened in shock and dismay as she watched chunks of Vazga's ship start to fall away—apparently it could no longer withstand the stresses placed upon it. Vazga's runner dropped out of the formation and began gliding—then plummeting—toward the ground, like a bird suddenly stripped of its wings.

As if serving as an echo, the last ship in Corsi's own line of runners began to break apart. Corsi frantically checked the identification marker on the vessel to figure out who was piloting it. She determined that it was one of her own: Powers. His crumbling ship followed Vazga's out of the formation and into a steep downward glide toward the surface.

Corsi swallowed hard, determined not to let her concern for her subordinate be a distraction. She told herself there was a chance—however slim—that Powers and Vazga could survive their crash landings.

But as the missile continued its long plunge, and with two less ships to act against it, Domenica Corsi silently, regretfully concluded that her plan was doomed. She would go down fighting—simply giving up was not in her nature—but success was not going to be in the cards, not this time. She and the rest of her team, along with Elless and the Taru Bolivar, and every living thing on Phantas 61, would soon be dead.

And up above, in space, the *da Vinci* was fighting for survival against overwhelming odds—assuming it hadn't already been destroyed. She thought of Fabian Stevens, wishing she could have at least had the chance to see him one last time, or even say goodbye over the radio.

Damn Rod Portlyn, she cursed bitterly. *That smug, arrogant, greedy piece of slimy—*

Suddenly, Corsi noticed a runner in the other line breaking off from the formation, and starting to descend toward the missile. She checked the ID marker, and determined that this ship was the one being piloted by P8 Blue.

What in the world is Pattie up to?

As P8 Blue brought her runner closer to the missile, she hoped Corsi was not being too hard on herself over the failure of her plan. The idea of using the runners to intercept the missile and alter its course was a good one, and definitely had the *potential* to succeed. It was unfortunate that the tractor beams simply weren't strong enough to do the job, and that some of these tough little recycled ships could not hold up under the strain.

Corsi's idea did have a positive effect, though—it got the runners up in the air. Had they not gone up, there would never have been a chance for Pattie to launch her own crazy scheme. With "Plan A" having fallen through and the situation even more desperate now, the Nasat did not doubt that what she was about to do would represent the very last chance to save everyone on Phantas 61.

She pulled her ship in so close to the side of the missile that it was practically touching the deadly projectile. Setting the ship on autopilot, she popped open the canopy of her runner, stood up in her cockpit, and hurled herself onto the topside of the missile.

With each of her eight limbs struggling against the staggeringly powerful winds, Pattie managed to crawl along the length of the missile until she came upon the hatch that she knew had to house the device's computer guidance system. She devoted two of her limbs to prying off the cover of the hatch—the other six clung to anything on the missile's surface that could be tightly grasped.

Pattie tugged on the hatch cover three times, using all of her strength, before it finally popped up and revealed the guidance system. A display screen and a small keyboard were set within a gold-colored panel. Each unit had wires and cables that ran through a central matrix in the panel, and then out of sight into the missile's innards. Pattie quickly checked the coordinates that were flashing on the display as bright red numbers. She determined that the missile was programmed to strike right in the heart of the main city. Pattie looked up from the guidance system to see the surface of Phantas 61 growing closer at an ever quicker rate. They were well below the stratosphere now.

Pattie turned back to the guidance system and tapped on the keyboard, trying to change the programming, but nothing happened. The coordinates were locked in, and could not be

THE ART OF THE DEAL 253

tampered with. She examined the wires connecting the keyboard to the display screen and to the central matrix. For a moment, she was paralyzed with uncertainty—she wasn't absolutely sure that what she was about to do was the right way to go.

She then told herself, *At this point, you have absolutely nothing to lose.*

Pattie yanked out a yellow wire that had run from the keyboard into the display. She tapped the keyboard again, randomly.

The numbers on the display changed. She had removed the lock on the system.

Buoyed with excitement, Pattie did some quick mental calculations and tapped in a new sequence of numbers. Once she was done, she looked up again to see the heart of the main city rushing toward her, less than ten kilometers away now. They were fast approaching the point of no return, where even if the missile started to change direction, it would not have time or room to avoid crashing into the ground. She went ahead and pressed a tiny key marked "commit."

Pattie looked around, taking everything in, just in case these were her last few moments of life. Her runner remained at the side of the missile, its tractor beam still locked on to the projectile. She saw that the other runners continued in vain to use their own tractor beams to try to pull the missile out of its dive. She placed her head down against the metal skin of the missile, knowing she had no choice now but to await the outcome of her efforts.

Was it wishful thinking, or did she suddenly feel the missile start to push itself upward? She looked up and still saw the planet's surface looming ahead, much closer than it had been a few moments before—the tallest buildings in the main city looked as if they were rushing up to embrace her like a long-lost lover. And the other runners finally deactivated their tractor beams—there was no reason to keep them on anymore—and pulled away from the missile.

But then, slowly but surely, and there was no mistaking it, she saw that the nose of the missile was starting to rise, away from the crumbling skyscrapers.

The missile completed a midair arc that brought it frighteningly close to the roof of Phantas 61's tallest structure. It missed the building cleanly, though, and then began climbing up. But in completing the arc, too much strain was placed on the tractor beam on Pattie's runner, and the connection between the missile and the small ship was broken. The runner continued plunging toward the city before finally crashing into the side of a skyscraper. Pattie was now trapped on the missile as it headed for its new destination: the sun of the Norvel system.

Higher and higher the missile climbed, returning to the stratosphere and fast approaching the mesosphere. Soon, it would be back in outer space, with Pattie along for the ride.

But then the Nasat saw one of the other runners rise up alongside the missile and pull in closer. She recognized the ID marking on the ship: It was Corsi. Pattie could even see the security chief through the cockpit window, motioning for her to jump. She did not need any further prompting. She released the hold that each of her limbs had on the missile and allowed her insectoid body to get yanked off and into free fall.

Pattie landed roughly on the nose of Corsi's runner, her protective shell bearing the brunt of the impact. She swiftly used her limbs to grab on to the ship, which was already descending out of the stratosphere. Pattie clambered up the length of the nose to the cockpit, where Corsi raised the canopy high enough so that the Nasat could crawl in and fill the empty copilot's seat in the rear.

"Pattie," Corsi began once the canopy had closed again, her voice filled with joy, anxiety, relief, and exasperation, "that was the stupidest, bravest, most reckless, ill-conceived, wonderful display I've ever seen!"

"Thank you, Commander," Pattie replied simply.

They watched in silence as the missile headed up into space, toward the sun.

"Time for us to get back to the stars ourselves," Corsi said as she adjusted controls and the runner began climbing above the clouds. Pattie saw the other five remaining runners approaching and heading up with them.

Phantas 61 was safe, at least for the time being. Now their efforts would be devoted to helping the *da Vinci*.

Corsi was gladdened when the *da Vinci* came into view, still intact and defending itself. It was taking a pounding, to be sure, and its shields were drastically weakened, but it was still there, and still putting up a fight. In fact, it was right then ripping into one of the attacking Orion mercenary ships with a barrage of quantum torpedoes, a relentless torrent that did not end until the attacker was blown to bits. Corsi did a quick survey of the scene, noting that there had been ten mercenary ships to begin with, but now there were seven.

Way to go, Captain!

"Is the communications jamming still going on?" Pattie asked from behind her.

"It is," Corsi replied. "Thankfully, we don't seem to need communications at the moment. Elless and his people followed us up here to help the *da Vinci*, just like they agreed to before we lifted off. It seems pretty straightforward from here on in: Each of us picks an Orion ship and opens fire."

Corsi picked her target and dived in. With her tractor beam deactivated, she had transferred power back to the shields and weapons systems and got them up to full capacity again. As she swept by the Orion ship, she fired the plasma guns mounted atop the wings of her runner. The weapons were fairly easy to master, somewhat similar to the kind found on the wings of an old-style Romulan bird-of-prey.

The plasma shots were deflected by the Orion ship's shields, so Corsi came about for another attack. But the Orion fired its disruptor cannons first, catching Corsi's runner across the starboard side. The runner shuddered from the impact, but its shields held. Corsi rushed toward the Orion ship and fired the plasma guns again at her opponent, at point-blank range, which had the desired effect—the Orion's shields began to fluctuate. Corsi swiftly followed up with another bombardment of plasma energy, then switched over to phasers at full intensity. At last, the Orion's shields came down. Corsi switched back to the plasma weapon and fired. The Orion ship burst into a ball of brilliant light before quickly disintegrating to nothingness.

Corsi turned her ship around to face the main battle and chose another target. She immediately saw the *da Vinci* pummeling two Orion attackers with quantum torpedoes, while Elless's runner had gained the upper hand on another and was firing its plasma guns relentlessly.

Suddenly, without fanfare, the Orion ships began pulling away from the battle, retreating from the *da Vinci* and the runners. One by one, the Orions fled at top speed for parts unknown.

"Maybe that was their leader you destroyed," P8 Blue suggested.

"Could be—or they simply decided Portlyn isn't paying them enough for this kind of aggravation."

Checking her sensors, Corsi located the one ship that remained: the freighter in low orbit that had launched the missile at Phantas 61. That was the last target. She set a course to intercept it, and saw that Elless and the other runners were also headed in that direction.

Above Phantas 61, aboard his private ship, Gerard watched from a safe distance as the remaining Orion mercenary ships fled and the Taru Bolivar ships raced toward the remote-controlled robot freighter. Mr. Portlyn would not be happy about this unfortunate turn of events, Gerard knew. But the agent also knew that his employer would undoubtedly find a way to turn it into a victory. For that to happen, though, there could be no evidence of what had transpired here.

Gerard activated the computer console on his control panel and tied it into the systems on the robot freighter. Tapping in a numerical sequence, Gerard finished by pressing ENTER.

On his viewscreen, he watched as the robot ship obliterated itself. He smiled as the Taru Bolivar ships scrambled desperately to get out of the way of the blast—they never saw it coming. Too bad the explosion didn't take some of them, too.

Gerard then set a new course for his ship and turned away from Phantas 61. As his ship accelerated out of the region, he deactivated the communications jamming device on his control panel, took a deep breath, and prepared to transmit his status report to Mr. Portlyn.

CHAPTER 10

Corsi wasn't sure what surprised Captain Gold more—that she and P8 Blue were part of the mysterious squadron that came to the *da Vinci*'s aid, or that the squadron also consisted of the terrorists that the *da Vinci* had come to hunt down.

With communications no longer jammed, Corsi contacted Gold from her runner and gave him a brief update on what had happened on Phantas 61. She explained what "Taru Bolivar" meant and informed the captain about who had really attacked his ship. Gold ordered Corsi back to the *da Vinci*, and at Corsi's urging, the Taru Bolivar leader, Elless, followed her to the Starfleet vessel in his own runner.

Thinking ahead to the full briefing she planned to give her captain, Corsi requested that both Soloman and Bart Faulwell be on the bridge of the *da Vinci* upon her return.

Once aboard, Corsi and P8 Blue escorted Elless directly to the bridge to meet with Captain Gold. Stepping out of the turbolift and onto the command deck, Corsi was very pleased to see Fabian Stevens, and exchanged the briefest of smiles with him. She told herself they'd have to make some time to talk, as soon as possible. But Corsi quickly returned to "all business, no nonsense" mode, and approached the captain's chair.

"We picked up two distress calls from the planet," Gold told her without preamble. "Powers and someone else." The captain looked over at Elless. "One of your people, I presume?"

Elless nodded. "Vazga," he said flatly. Corsi could tell from the look on his face how concerned the Taru Bolivar leader was about the fate of his lieutenant. Clearly, he considered Vazga a trusted comrade and confidante . . . and perhaps something more.

"They crash-landed," Gold continued. "We beamed them up and Dr. Lense has them in sickbay. They both sustained some pretty extensive injuries—Powers especially. At the very least, he'll need hip replacement and some nerve regeneration in his spine. At any rate, right now, neither of them could even wrestle a tribble."

"At least they're both alive," Corsi said with a relieved sigh.

"Thank you, Captain," Elless murmured, bowing his head briefly.

Gold nodded once at Elless, grimly. He then focused on Corsi. "Hawkins is there, too. He contacted us as soon as the communications jamming ended. Just getting his arm looked at—he should be back on duty shortly." The captain then leaned back in his chair and looked squarely at his security chief and the Taru Bolivar leader. "Now how about bringing me fully up to speed?"

Gold was obviously stunned by what Corsi and Elless had to say: Rod Portlyn was behind the attack on the *da Vinci*. He was also responsible for the missile that nearly killed everyone on Phantas 61. And he intentionally ruined the soil on Vemlar to get the farmers to sell their land to him. Corsi knew all of this was hard for the captain to accept, but she also knew that she had his trust, and that meant he had to believe what she was telling him.

Gold leaned forward in the center seat and rested his chin atop his fist. "We're going to need hard proof," he mused. "Without solid evidence, there'll be no way to bring Portlyn down."

Corsi then pointed to Elless. "You said the file you stole from Portlyn has all the information we'd need."

Elless pulled the computer file out of his pocket and held it up, waving it derisively. "I also said it can only be opened on Portlyn's personal computer. Believe me, we've tried to extract the information. Several times. It's hopeless."

"Not necessarily," Corsi insisted. "Maybe we can use the *da Vinci*'s equipment, and the expertise we have aboard, to get it open. I mean, it's worth a *try*, don't you think?"

"Absolutely it is," Gold replied, holding his hand out to Elless for the file. The Taru Bolivar leader shrugged and handed the file over to the captain. Gold then turned his attention directly to the Bynar computer specialist, who had been standing quietly with Bart Faulwell near the bridge's aft stations.

"Soloman, get to work on this right away. If we're going to get something on Portlyn, we've got to do it fast."

The Bynar stepped forward and took the file.

The captain then looked over at Faulwell. "Your talents will come in handy if Soloman gets the file open and the data is in code."

"I'll be happy to help, Captain," Faulwell replied enthusiastically.

As Soloman and Faulwell entered the turbolift and left the bridge, Gold focused on Elless. Corsi noticed from the moment the captain met the Taru Bolivar leader that there was tension between them. Corsi knew Elless and his group were terrorists in Gold's eyes, just as they had been in her own. But a certain degree of trust had been established between Corsi and Elless through their shared experiences on Phantas 61 and in battle. Her view of the Taru Bolivar was no longer quite as harsh as it had been. She still did not approve of their methods, but she understood what motivated them. She wondered if Captain Gold would take a similar stance.

"We'll be getting under way shortly, Mr. Elless," the captain began. "You helped us against the Orion ships, and I appreciate that a great deal."

"Just as I am grateful for the aid your people gave us in saving all the lives on Phantas 61, Captain," Elless replied cautiously. All eyes on the bridge briefly glanced over at P8 Blue, whose singular efforts in stopping the deadly missile had been dutifully reported by Corsi once communications were reestablished.

Gold continued. "But I'm afraid you present us with a dilemma. You and your group have engaged in terrorist activities, and that cannot and will not be tolerated. Those activities have to end now."

Elless replied coldly, "This is not your jurisdiction, Captain."

"But it *is* our fight, now that Portlyn tried to wipe us out. Look, my primary focus now is to stop him. If that's what you and your Taru Bolivar want, as you claim, then you'll stay out of our way and not interfere with our efforts. No more terrorist acts, Elless. I'd hate for us to end up on opposite sides after what happened here today, and I don't want to have to split my attention between Portlyn and you. So don't give me any *tsuris,* okay?"

Corsi couldn't help but chuckle inwardly. Gold had to know that Elless probably never heard that term before. But the Taru Bolivar leader seemed to understand what it meant, and that was enough.

"All right, Captain. We won't cause you any trouble—for now. But if your efforts fail, the Taru Bolivar will act again."

"Until then, Elless, I would say our business is finished. There's just the matter of the two people from your group who are currently in our sickbay. I trust you have medical facilities on Phantas 61 to care for them?"

"Of a sort. The man you picked up from Vemlar is my brother. What is his present condition?"

Gold frowned and shook his head. "He's in bad shape, I'm afraid. Dr. Lense says there's not much hope for recovery."

Elless nodded. "I understand. I would appreciate it if your doctor would prepare him and Vazga for beamdown."

"I'll have Lense see to it," Gold assured Elless. "Commander Corsi will escort you to sickbay." The captain then turned to his helmsman. "Wong, once our guests have beamed down to the planet, set a course back to Vemlar, warp two-point-five."

Gold then stood up and headed for the turbolift. "Shabalala, I'd like you to contact Patrice Bennett at her residence on Tau Ophiucus, and have the call sent directly to my quarters, private channel."

With that, Gold left the bridge.

Corsi thought, *It's none of my business, but why does he want to talk to an ex-girlfriend at a time like this?*

"Why would the captain want to talk to an ex-girlfriend in the middle of all this?" Fabian Stevens asked Corsi as they rode together in the turbolift, on their way back to the bridge from visiting Hawkins and Powers in the sickbay. They were alone for the first time in what felt like days instead of hours.

"My, aren't *you* the curious little cat?" Corsi replied, putting a disapproving tone in her voice.

"C'mon, Dom, you're telling me that question didn't cross *your* mind?"

Her attitude became serious. "What do I look like, the ship's gossipmonger? I don't engage in that childish nonsense. It's none of my business."

Stevens stared at her blankly for a long moment before she finally broke into a grin. "Okay, you got me," she chuckled.

Stevens laughed. "You *almost* had me going there." Now it was his turn to become serious, but in his case, he wasn't play-acting. He said, "Computer, halt turbolift." The car smoothly came to a halt. "You know, Dom, at one point today it really looked like we would never get another chance to be together like this. To share a laugh . . . or anything else."

"I know," Corsi replied softly.

He continued. "Look, I've been in Starfleet long enough to know that the end can come at any time, and I accept that. But with me almost getting killed on Teneb and you not being there, and what we just went through separately at Phantas 61 . . . well, I just don't want anything left unsaid between us in the event that the worst happens, and—"

She put her finger on his lips. "You don't have to say anything, Fabe."

They stared at each other for a few moments, Stevens staring into those eyes that were ice-cold most of the time, but which were now the pleasant blue they were that first night they slept together months ago.

Finally, in a soft voice, Stevens said, "Computer, resume." The car restarted its journey up the turboshaft.

The *da Vinci* was minutes away from arriving at Vemlar when Captain Gold returned to the bridge. As he took his seat, Soloman's voice piped in over the intercom.

"*Soloman to Captain Gold.*"

"Gold here, go ahead, Soloman." The captain smiled, anxious to hear what the Bynar had to say. He was looking forward to good news, and to viewing the evidence against Portlyn.

"*Sir, I regret to report that the file has indeed proven impossible to open.*"

Gold's face fell.

"*The encryption is as intricate as Elless warned. We are unable to get around it to open the file and gain access to the data within.*"

Gold was sorely disappointed, but not overly surprised. He had, after all, been warned in advance that the file might not be penetrable. But he nonetheless allowed himself to hope that the experts aboard his ship would somehow find a way around that.

"Thank you, Soloman," he said with a sigh. "I know how hard you and Faulwell have been working on it." Gold signed off and leaned back in his chair.

Behind him, the turbolift doors slid open and Corsi and Stevens stepped out. Gold updated the security chief on the Vemlar file as she came up beside him.

"Damned frustrating," she groused.

Gold tried to come off as optimistic. "Well, we'll just have to confront Portlyn with what we know, and try to get a confession out of him."

She shot him a look that told him she was thinking the same thing he was: *Yeah, right.*

Wong then announced, "We're approaching Vemlar, Captain."

Haznedl suddenly spoke up. "Captain, I'm detecting another ship in orbit around the planet. It's one of ours, sir. *Sovereign*-class."

"Oh?" Gold was intrigued.

Haznedl adjusted the controls at her station to augment her scan of the area, and then looked up at her commanding officer. "Sir, it's the *Enterprise*."

Shabalala spoke next, and his voice sounded grim. "Captain, I'm receiving a transmission from the *Enterprise*. They're insisting that we stand down immediately."

CHAPTER 11

That is one big, beautiful ship, Gold thought upon seeing the U.S.S. *Enterprise* on the bridge's main viewscreen. The starship grew larger and larger on the screen as the *da Vinci* approached it over Vemlar.

Gold turned to Shabalala and said, "Put the transmission on screen, Lieutenant."

The image of the *Enterprise* was replaced by the familiar, but now ultraserious, face of Captain Jean-Luc Picard, seated in his command chair. Gold had known the younger man since the Academy, when Gold was in his final year and Picard his first. They'd last seen each other about six months earlier.

However, any trace of their friendship was noticeably absent from Picard's demeanor.

"Captain Gold," Picard began flatly. *"I have been ordered by Starfleet Command to take authority over this situation immediately, and to investigate the alleged illegal activities of you and your crew."*

That charge took Gold by surprise. "Captain Picard," he said, trying to maintain a pleasant, friendly tone. "I would say that's a bit of an overreaction on the part of Starfleet Command."

"I'm afraid Admiral Adair doesn't share your view, Captain. He asked me to come here, after being informed directly by Rod Portlyn that you and your crew had gone rogue and sided with the terrorists against Mr. Portlyn."

"Don't tell me Adair actually *believed* that? Or that *you* believe it?"

"I know what I'd like to believe, Captain, but that is in conflict with my orders—and what Admiral Adair and I have seen with our own eyes."

"What are you talking about?" Gold did not like the sound of this.

"Mr. Portlyn has shown the admiral and myself recorded images of the *da Vinci* aiding terrorist ships over Phantas 61, against a group of independent merchant vessels trying to help stop the terrorists' activities."

Gold had to give Portlyn credit for ingenuity, and for acting so quickly. Presenting visual recordings in a way that made a specific event seem like it happened differently—that was one of the oldest tricks in the book, and still very effective, obviously.

"Captain Picard, I can explain all of this. If you and I can just talk privately—"

"*That won't be possible, Captain Gold. I'm sorry.*"

Picard did seem sincere. Gold sighed, well aware that he had little choice in the matter. He was certainly not going to fire on the *Enterprise,* nor was he going to try to pull a fast escape.

"Very well, Captain Picard. You can send over a boarding party at your convenience."

Within moments, six shimmering images appeared on the bridge of the *da Vinci* and solidified into humanoid figures both known and unknown. Captain Picard was front and center, as would be expected. He was backed by a short woman with round blue eyes and hair styled in a pageboy cut—Gold recognized her as Lieutenant Christine Vale, the *Enterprise*'s security chief, who had spent some time on the *da Vinci* during their investigation of the *Beast*. She had three male security guards with her, all armed with phasers.

And bringing up the rear was none other than Rod Portlyn, looking around the *da Vinci* bridge with his hands clasped behind his back and a satisfied grin on his round, pale green face.

"Mr. Portlyn, I wasn't expecting to see you here," Gold said to the tycoon, barely containing his contempt.

"Oh, I insisted on coming," Portlyn replied casually. "I won't be kept on the sidelines any longer. Captain Picard understands that."

Gold looked over at Corsi to share a moment of mutual astonishment at the sheer *chutzpah* of the tycoon. But she was having a moment of her own, exchanging an uncomfortable glance with Vale. The two women had known each other a long time, Gold knew, and this was hardly the ideal circumstance for even a cordial reunion.

Picard stepped to the center of the bridge and faced Gold. "I'll start by saying that this investigation does not extend to Commander Gomez and her team on Vemlar. As far as Starfleet Command is concerned, they are in the clear, since they have been working on the construction project the whole time."

"Fair enough," Gold replied. "But before your investigation begins, Captain, there's something you should know. Before Mr. Portlyn bought up all the real estate on Vemlar, he secretly used a bioengineered viral agent to ruin the soil, in order to give the inhabitants no choice but to sell their land to him."

Portlyn let out a hearty laugh. "That is the most absurd thing I've ever heard. I'll give you credit for originality, though, Gold. Very amusing."

Picard brushed off this exchange and said, "A formal inquiry will begin shortly. Until then, Captain Gold, I'll have to ask you to confine yourself to your quarters." There was no pleasure in Picard's voice as he said it, and Gold did not bear any animosity toward the *Enterprise* captain. Still, the thought of being confined to quarters on his own ship galled him.

Picard motioned to his security chief. "Lieutenant Vale will escort you," he informed Gold. Vale and one of her security officers stepped forward toward Gold. If Vale was aware of the icy glare she was getting from Corsi, she did a good job of not letting on.

"Captain, if you'd please come with us," Vale said. She and her subordinate guided him to the turbolift. But then a strange beep sounded from the tactical station.

"The main viewscreen is being overridden," said Shabalala.

Ignoring Vale and her guard, Gold whirled toward the screen, in time to see the image of Vemlar disappear and be replaced by a large block of running text set against a plain white background, with the distinctive Portlyn logo adorning the top of the screen.

VEMLAR PROJECT, the text began. Gold didn't have time to read the whole thing, but there was enough information that could be picked out through skimming that his heart started pounding with excitement. Sections of the text were broken down under headers such as SOIL TRANSMOGRIFICATION and BIO-AGENT "V," with accompanying details, technical information, and scientific formulas. He also spotted terms such as INDUCED FAMINE, UNTRACEABLE, and, farther down, PURCHASE PLAN.

Soloman, Faulwell . . . bless you both, Gold thought, feeling a wave of relief rush through him. He turned to Picard, who was also skimming the text on the screen. "Look at the date on that file, Captain," he said to Picard. "If you check the records, you'll find that's a full year before Portlyn actually purchased Vemlar."

Picard nodded, but before he could say anything, the file on the viewscreen suddenly compressed in width and was pushed to the left half of the screen. On the right side, a series of sensor readings popped on, showing a schematic representation of a planet and the area of space around it, with a single blip identified as *U.S.S. da Vinci*. Gold didn't know what to make of this. He wasn't expecting it at all.

"That's Phantas 61," Corsi said. "Those are the sensor readings we saw at the Taru Bolivar headquarters."

Sure enough, the readings showed ten blips surrounding the one identified as the *da Vinci*, and then opening fire without provocation. Then came yet another blip, this one identified as a freighter, which went on to launch a missile at the planet. Technical data on the missile popped up on the screen and showed that it was carrying a viral agent—and the specifications showed that it was the same viral agent detailed in the Vemlar file on the left side of the screen.

Gold looked over at Portlyn, who gazed at the screen with his mouth hanging open and his scarlet eyes looking as if they were about to pop out of his head. Gold thought he heard the tycoon mutter under his breath, "How . . . how could they have gotten it open . . . ?"

"You no longer seem amused, Mr. Portlyn," Picard said.

Portlyn managed to pull his gaze away from the screen and faced Picard and Gold, who now stood side by side. Gold had to give Portlyn credit—he quickly recovered from his shock.

"All right," Portlyn said tightly. "So it's out. I can't do anything about that now. But you can't touch me. I'm not a Federation citizen and, in case you've forgotten, we're in nonaligned space. You're out of your jurisdiction."

"And you're out of your mind if you think the Federation is going to stay in business with you after this," Gold said with a great deal of satisfaction.

Portlyn frowned and nodded, not even trying to conceal his great disappointment. "Yes . . . I'll probably lose some other business, too." The tycoon then seemed to inflate himself with defiance as he continued. "But you know what? My empire still stands, and there are plenty of *other* species out there who'll continue to deal with me, with no qualms—the Ferengi, for example. Not every civilization has the same air of moral superiority as the Federation. You people seem to view the pursuit of wealth, success, and power as something evil, something to be ashamed of."

Gold shook his head, deciding that the tycoon just didn't get it. "There's nothing wrong with wanting any of those things," he told Portlyn. "It all comes down to how far you're willing to go, what actions you're capable of taking, to attain them."

Picard added, "And what you do with them once you've attained them."

"Sure, whatever," Portlyn replied, waving off the two captains. "Look, I'm ready to return to Vemlar. Where's the transporter room around here?" He headed toward the turbolift.

Just then, Shabalala called out, "Captain!"

"Yes?" replied Gold and Picard. They then looked at each other awkwardly.

"Uh, I actually meant Captain Gold," the tactical officer said, helping them out of the moment. "We're receiving a transmission from a ship now entering this sector. It's Patrice Bennett, sir."

Gold smiled, openly delighted. *Here's where the real fun begins.* "On screen."

Patrice Bennett popped onto the main viewscreen. She had a very serious expression on her face, but Gold recognized the warmth in her eyes.

"Hello, Captain Gold. Ah, I see Mr. Portlyn is with you. Good. That means I can announce right now that I'm taking control of a number of Portlyn-owned properties—including Vemlar and Phantas 61."

"Patrice, what are you babbling about?" Portlyn asked.

Patrice smiled sweetly. *"I just finished a subspace radio conference with your creditors, Roddy. You remember them, don't you? They're the ones you borrowed money from to build your 'empire.' I'm sure you're well aware that you're past due on paying off your debts to them. Well, they agreed to sell those debts to me. Which means I now have the right to take control of the properties you put up as collateral—and I'm exercising that right."*

Portlyn's face turned a darker shade of green. He started breathing faster and heavier. "This isn't over. I'll fight you, and I'll win."

"You're out in the cold, Roddy. After Captain Gold told me what you did to Vemlar, I contacted your creditors, partners, and investors, and let them know. The word of a distinguished Starfleet captain was enough to make them all decide to wash their hands of you—to be honest, they never really liked being involved with you in the first place. Now, I'd appreciate it if you would be gone from the system by the time I arrive. That'll be within the next thirty minutes or so."

Picard turned to Vale. "Lieutenant, I'd like you and your team to escort Mr. Portlyn down to Vemlar and make sure he's not delayed or distracted as he clears out his things."

"Oh, we'll make sure he maintains his focus, Captain," Vale

replied. She and the guards surrounded the flabbergasted Portlyn, giving him no choice but to leave with them. As they entered the lift, Vale turned and gave a little salute to Corsi, who nodded back at her with a small smile.

Picard turned to Gold and patted him on the shoulder. "Looks like you've gotten yourself out of a rough spot, David—and saved the day."

"I had a lot of help, Jean-Luc," Gold replied with a relieved grin. "And believe me, only *some* of it was expected."

"And what will you do with all your new properties, Ms. Bennett?" Picard asked the image on the viewscreen.

"Well, for starters, I plan to have a team of experts look for a way to counteract the effects of the viral agent. I want to restore Vemlar to its original state, if possible."

"I'm sure the Vemlarites will appreciate that, if it happens," Corsi said, stepping forward to join the two captains. "But what will they do until then? They were counting on the jobs that Portlyn promised them."

Gold nodded. "That's been taken into account. Patrice, you want to answer that?"

"Certainly. I actually like the idea of a scientific research and development center, but I don't see why it can't be built on Phantas 61 instead. That's a better use for the planet than turning it into a garbage dump. It would a big, long-term project, and if the Vemlarites and the Phantasians are willing, they can work together on building it. It'll be steady work and good pay. And if we can restore Vemlar, the Vemlarites can return and take back their land."

"Sounds like a plan," Corsi replied.

Gold added, "And if I have anything to say about it, Patrice, you can expect as much help from the Federation and Starfleet as you'll need. Of course, that's assuming I'm not getting drummed out of the fleet."

Picard chuckled. "I think it's safe to say that won't be happening. And I echo Captain Gold's sentiments, Ms. Bennett. If you need anything, let either of us know."

"Thank you both. I'll be seeing you shortly." With that, Patrice Bennett signed off.

"Very clever, bringing her into this," Picard commented.

Gold responded with a nonchalant shrug. "Just following a classic engineering maxim I picked up from Montgomery Scott: 'The right tool for the right job.'"

"Well, Captain Gold," Picard said, tugging on the bottom of his uniform jacket. "Shall we contact Admiral Adair and update him on the situation? I have a feeling my investigation won't be necessary after all."

"An excellent suggestion, Captain Picard. This is one conversation with the admiral that I'll actually be looking forward to."

EPILOGUE

Captain's Log, Stardate 53816.2:

Admiral Adair has rescinded his order for Captain Picard's investigation. Having made sure that Rod Portlyn has cleared out of Vemlar and the Norvel system, Captain Picard and the Enterprise *have departed for their next assignment. With our responsibilities at Vemlar now at an end, the* da Vinci *is departing, as well.*

Captain Gold sat behind his desk in his ready room as the *da Vinci* prepared to leave orbit. Soloman, Faulwell, and Blue had just arrived, at his request, and stood in front of the desk at attention.

"At ease," he told them. "I asked you all here because I wanted to let you know how proud I am of you. You all did remarkable work, under very difficult conditions."

Gold then focused on Pattie. "Blue, your actions were nothing short of extraordinary." The Nasat twitched her antennae gratefully.

"As for Soloman and Faulwell—well, what can I say? Thank you both for the work you did getting that file open at just the right moment."

Faulwell and Soloman looked at each other sheepishly. Modesty, no doubt.

"So tell me, how'd you two manage it? Last you told me, the situation was hopeless—there was no way to open that file."

Faulwell and Soloman glanced at each other again, unsure who should answer. Finally, Faulwell swallowed and looked up at the captain.

"Well, sir, the file really *was* impossible to open. But as we got within range of Vemlar, I, uh, suggested to Soloman the idea of tapping into the main computer at Portlyn's headquarters and hacking into his private system. I knew it wouldn't be too difficult—we helped set up that system, after all. I was thinking that once we were in Portlyn's computer, we'd be able to open the file and retrieve the information."

"I . . . see," Gold replied, motioning for the linguist to continue.

"Soloman got through, and we were able to open the file, so we downloaded the information onto our system, and sent it to the bridge's viewscreen. Then, I contacted Elless and had him transmit the Taru Bolivar's sensor readings of the Orion attack and the missile launch. So there wouldn't be any lingering doubts about Portlyn's guilt. Sir."

Gold didn't know what to say. Faulwell and Soloman shifted uncomfortably.

"Our actions were not exactly aboveboard," Soloman said.

"That's . . . one way of putting it," Gold said.

"We were worried that Portlyn would get away with what he'd done," Faulwell said. "We couldn't just do *nothing*, sir. We'll gladly accept whatever disciplinary action you decide on for us."

"That's very thoughtful of you," Gold replied wryly. He looked them over silently for a long moment before finally continuing. "I won't tell the top brass if you don't . . . but never do anything like that again."

"Yes, sir," said Soloman.

"Not without your say-so, sir," said Faulwell, with a mischievous gleam in his eye.

Gold pursed his lips, trying to hold back a smirk.

"Dismissed," he told them as he rose from his chair. He followed the trio out of the ready room and onto the bridge. Soloman, Faulwell, and Blue entered the turbolift to return to their duties as Gold sat down in his command chair.

Gomez and Corsi took up positions on either side of the captain's chair.

"Wong, take us out of orbit," Gold said.

"Aye, sir," the conn officer replied, working his fingers across his console.

Settling back into his chair, Gold took a deep breath and was silent for a short time, until he glanced up at Gomez with a grin.

"Sir?" she asked him quizzically.

"I was just thinking about my meeting with Soloman, Faulwell, and Blue . . . quite a crew we have on this ship."

Gomez smiled. "Yes indeed, Captain."

As the *da Vinci* broke out of orbit, Corsi said, "I wonder if we've seen the last of Rod Portlyn."

"We can only hope," Gomez replied.

"Well," said Gold, "hope is a pretty powerful force in the universe—maybe even as powerful as 'Big Business.'"

After watching Vemlar shrink away on the main viewscreen as the *da Vinci* began its cruise out of the "Corporate Corridor," Gold looked around at his bridge and his crew. He smiled. There was no question in his mind: This is exactly where he was meant to be. On this ship. With these people. Doing this work. He knew that this was reality as it should be.

Taru Bolivar.

SPIN

J. Steven York & Christina F. York

CHAPTER 1

Commander Sonya Gomez rolled the small, egg-shaped alien artifact in her fingers. It was copper-colored, about the size of a hen's egg, and she had only the vaguest idea what it was.

It was a puzzle, the sort she enjoyed. Alone in the hololab of the S.C.E. ship *da Vinci*—currently set up as a straightforward engineering isolation lab of the type you'd find at the Utopia Planitia Yards on Mars—she could immerse herself in the search for an explanation. So far, she hadn't found one.

Okay, they weren't really her fingers. They were plastic, mechanical digits moved with artificial muscles, and covered with tactile sensors. The sensations were so realistic, the movements so natural, sometimes she forgot.

"It's a communicator," she said to the empty lab, "or maybe a smart identity tag." Or not.

The computer's voice interrupted her thoughts, making her start. *"Incoming subspace communication for Commander Gomez from freighter* Vulpecula."

She sighed. "Oh, Wayne, give it a rest."

"*Command not understood,*" said the computer.

"Take a message."

Satisfied, the computer responded, "*Recording message.*"

She turned her attention back to the object. Two minutes passed. She tried to focus, but her concentration wouldn't return.

"Computer, replay message."

A viewing window appeared on her console, with the image of an angular male face, handsome in an unconventional way. Most notable was the color of his skin: pistachio ice-cream green.

A shock of black hair hung casually over his forehead, and his eyes were the color of emeralds. Though it was not communicated by subspace, and though the thought made her uneasy, she also knew the man smelled *good*.

He was Wayne "Pappy" Omthon, former first officer, now owner and captain, of the private freighter *Vulpecula*. Mostly human, his grandmother had been a green Orion. Other humanoids found the pheromones of green Orions to be pleasant, even intoxicating, a characteristic that had caused them to be victimized by slavers for centuries.

Unconsciously, she straightened her jacket and tucked a strand of her wavy hair behind her ear. It was very hard for her to think straight when Wayne was around. But why was she still having trouble thinking straight when he was light-years away?

"*Sonya,*" he said, "*I've been trying to contact you for weeks.*" He smiled a little. "*I'm beginning to think you're avoiding me, and that is exactly* not *my intent. I've been waiting to ask you in person, but since I just keep talking to* da Vinci's *computer and time is short, I'll ask now. You must have some leave coming, and there's a traveling exhibit of ancient Bajoran technology making the rounds. It's going to be on Galor IV for the next month. It's a long way, but I know a guy,*" he grinned and waggled his heavy eyebrows playfully, "*with a ship.*" The smile faded, his expression puppy-dog hopeful. "*Seriously, I've got some cargo to drop off there. I'd enjoy the company, and somebody to talk shop with. Uh, let me know.*"

The screen blanked.

Talking shop? Is that really what this is about? No, I think not.
"Too soon," she said to the empty room.

She looked at the alien artifact and sighed. It was late, she was getting nowhere with this, and the faint trace of ozone in the filtered air was giving her a headache. "Computer, secure and store artifact, containment level six." A shower and a soft bunk sounded good.

She stepped into the corridor, then grabbed the doorway as a wave of dizziness made her stumble. Then she spotted a tiny windmill, a replica of the kind once common on pre-twentieth-century Earth, hanging upside down from the corridor ceiling. The sight was made stranger by the gaudy tracery of tiny lights around its spinning blades, undoubtedly an anachronism.

She turned and saw Cade Bennett, one of Nancy Conlon's engineers, at the far end of the corridor with a golf club in his hand. He took three rapid steps, like a gymnast starting his routine, flipped forward into a somersault, and landed firmly on the ceiling. From his perch, he spotted Gomez and smiled sheepishly. "Evening, Commander. Working late, I see."

She nodded. "And you're standing on the ceiling, I see."

"Yes, sir. Commander Tev complained the old miniature golf course blocked the corridor, so I—made some adjustments."

She reached up and touched the spinning windmill, confirming her suspicion. It was a hologram that passed through her fingers with a flicker. Even though her feet remained planted on the deck, there was a gentle upward pull on her head and extended hand.

"You're not violating any laws of physics, are you, Cade?" She smiled. "Because I won't have that on my ship."

"No, sir! No gravity up here. An adjustment of the inertial damper force fields mimics the pull. Makes the game a special challenge, because if the ball bounces, it travels in a sawtooth pattern rather than a series of parabolas."

"I see," she said, having only a vague idea how he'd pulled it off. She would find out later though, in detail. It amazed her how often these little "engineer games" later found valuable application in their real-world problems.

The thrum of *da Vinci*'s warp drive changed pitch. Reflexively, she reached out and brushed her fingertips against one of the corridor wall's supports. It was a DX-1045 support, tied directly to the ship's main space frame, and a good conductor. She opened her senses and smiled slightly as she thought of Vulcan mind-melds. *Talk to me,* da Vinci.

She felt the faint vibrations with her fingers, heard the timing of the plasma injectors, the cycling of the warp core. It was a trick Geordi La Forge had taught her on *Enterprise* a decade ago, though she suspected she was better at it than he ever was.

The ship had increased speed, warp five, and they were coming hard about. She couldn't detect any extra load to indicate shields were up or weapons activated.

No threat, but something's up. Why wait for it?

She tapped her combadge. "Gomez to Gold."

"Gold here."

"What's the mission, Captain?"

"It took you four whole seconds to call the bridge, Gomez. In your old age, you're losing your touch?" He chuckled, then said, *"Meet me in my ready room, and I'll tell you about it."*

CHAPTER 2

"The mission is pretty routine," David Gold said from behind the desk of his ready room. Gomez sat in one of the guest chairs, nursing the Earl Grey tea the captain had offered when she came in. "We had a call from the Lokak system. They've detected a derelict ship. It's a navigation hazard and its course is headed for an inhabited world. Salvage is beyond the technical capability of the locals, so we've been asked to step in. We'll need to either alter its course or destroy it."

The intercom interrupted. *"Captain,"* said the voice of the beta-shift tactical officer, Joanne Piotrowski, *"Ambassador Goveia's standing by for you."*

Gold said to Gomez, "Goveia's our representative to the Lokra people." He looked up. "Put it through, Piotrowski."

The screen on Gold's workstation lit up to show the Starfleet Diplomatic Corps seal. The seal was in turn replaced by the image of a slender, middle-aged man. His aristocratic bearing and stiff ceremonial uniform were at odds with his full red beard and the unruly mop of red curls atop his head.

Gomez presumed he was the ambassador.

"David, good to see you again. It's been a while."

"Years, Alfredo. Not since Vulcan."

"That was a while back."

"This is my first officer, Commander Sonya Gomez."

"Ambassador," Gomez said, nodding her head.

"A pleasure, Commander."

"What's this about, Alfredo?"

"The locals detected a derelict ship headed on an impact trajectory with their planet. It seems to have drifted in from deep space. It's big enough to devastate half a continent if it lands."

"The Lokra have warp drive. Why do they need us?"

"They barely *have warp capability. Besides that, the whole system is metal poor. They have only a few ships, robot probes for prospecting and mining nearby systems. Staffed spacecraft don't go beyond the planet's moons. Without tractor beams, which they don't have, this would be a dangerous undertaking."* He grinned. *"At any rate, I'm eager to show them the Federation would be a valuable ally."*

"This was a Breen base during the war, wasn't it?"

Goveia's face hardened, and his blue eyes turned icy. *"The Breen violently occupied the planet. That was the Lokra's first contact: a military occupation. Now the Breen have withdrawn, and we're eager to establish a presence here. It could be a valuable buffer zone."*

Gomez asked, "What information do you have on the derelict?"

"Not much, Commander. Trajectory, a size estimate, some crude sensor readings. I've transmitted them to you. Lokra sensors aren't very sophisticated, I'm afraid."

"We're headed your way at high warp," Gold said. "We'll reach your derelict in about eight hours. You sit tight and let the S.C.E. handle it."

"Thanks. This isn't an imminent threat, but the Lokra government is adamant it be dealt with immediately."

"Anything for good relations. We'll get back to you as soon as we are able to assess the situation. *Da Vinci* out."

Gomez tapped her combadge. "Gomez to Saldok."

The *da Vinci*'s beta-shift ops officer said, *"Go ahead, Commander."*

"We should have just received some files from Ambassador Goveia on Lokra."

"They just came in, actually."

"Good. Transmit the files to the captain's ready room, please."

Moments later, the ambassador's files were visible on Gold's screen. Gomez peered forward and studied it intently. "Not very useful. Trajectory and velocity information. On the current heading, computers confirm planetary impact, with ninety-seven percent certainty."

There were no visuals, but she pulled up a wireframe diagram of the ship, based on the low resolution sensor data.

"It's a disk about five hundred meters in diameter. Or—" She hesitated, refining the display. Some of the readings on the center of the object didn't jibe with the rest. "It has a hole in it, or a window. There's a section transparent to their scanning beam." She pulled up an energy scan. "It's giving off some infrared, some moderate particle radiation consistent with radioactive decay, but that's it. The radiation suggests a pretty primitive power source. If I had to venture a guess, I'd say it's the product of a civilization new to space travel."

"Well, if it isn't a Lokra ship, then it's a long way from home. It's twelve light-years from the nearest class-M planet."

Convinced she'd seen all there was to see, Gomez closed the files. "Shall we gather the troops?" she asked with a smile.

Gold shook his head. "It can wait until morning. You look like you could use some rest."

"I was headed for my bunk when you called."

"Go with that, then. I intend to do the same."

On the turbolift back to her quarters, Gomez sagged against the wall, fatigue pushing down on her.

The door to her quarters slid open, and the computer greeted her. *"Incoming subspace communication."*

She groaned. No point in putting it off any longer. She *had* to talk to him. She tugged at her jacket and straightened her sagging posture, pulling her shoulders back.

"On screen."

Her small viewscreen came to life, and Wayne "Pappy" Omthon's face appeared. His face was expressionless, except for one raised eyebrow. She could see him only from the shoulders up, but she could imagine him, arms crossed over his broad chest, foot tapping impatiently. *"Sonya. Glad I could finally catch you."*

She grimaced. "I'm sorry, Wayne. I've been busy."

"Nobody calls me Wayne."

"Well, I'm not calling you 'Pappy.'"

"It's just a nickname. Everybody calls me that."

"It's a stupid nickname. Why 'Pappy'?"

"I'm younger than most of the crew under my command, so of course they started calling me 'Pappy.'"

"I'm still sticking with my stupid assessment."

"The best nicknames usually are."

Gomez refrained from pointing out that there was nothing stupid about "Sonnie," the nickname Duffy had had for her, but she really didn't wish to go there. She sat down on the edge of her bunk, leaning forward to pull off her boots. "I was just coming in."

"I know."

She glanced sharply up at the screen. "How?"

"I spent a week on the da Vinci *after that holoship business, remember? I got to know people."*

"You called Corsi?" she guessed.

He nodded. *"The security chief always can find out where people are."*

"And she ratted me out?"

"Absolutely and without hesitation. I like that lady."

"Then ask *her* out."

"She's taken."

So am I.

The thought came without warning, and her chest tightened with an ache she thought she had finally left behind. It had been months since Galvan VI. Months since Duffy proposed to her and she couldn't answer—and then never got the chance to when he, along with half the crew, were killed.

She had moved past the grief, past the discomfort, past the lethargy. True, it took a near-death experience on Teneb to give her the kick she needed, but she thought she had finally gotten on with her life.

Wayne recognized her discomfort. *"Look, this isn't a week on Risa I'm talking about, Sonya. We're friends. This is a friendly outing to a museum. We'll look at eight-hundred-year-old spaceships. We'll talk engineering shop talk—"* He frowned, reached out past the edge of the screen and slapped something, so that the image shook. *"—you can tell me how to keep this damned viewscreen from glitching."*

She chuckled.

"It'll be fun. I'm sure it will do you good to get you out of that uniform for a while." He realized what he'd said, and blinked.

She grinned. "You know, you turn kind of blue when you blush."

He grinned sheepishly. *"Aquamarine, actually."*

To her own surprise, she didn't say an immediate no. "We've got a navigation hazard to clean up in the Lokak system. It should be quick, but I don't know. Let me think about it, and I'll get back to you when I have a better idea how long our mission will take."

"You'll call back soon though? Promise?"

"We'll be there in the morning. I'll scope out the situation, then call you back as soon as I get time." She stretched, feeling the pull of tired muscles across her shoulders and down her back. "Now I'm going to sleep. Good night."

"Good night, Sonya."

The screen went blissfully blank.

She lay back in her bunk and closed her eyes. Sleep, however, was not forthcoming.

Domenica Corsi signed off her shift and headed for her quarters. She paused along the way and tapped her combadge. "Computer, locate Fabian Stevens."

"Crewperson Stevens is in the mess hall."

She turned back to the turbolift, rode up a deck, and emerged a few steps from the mess hall door.

The mess hall was deserted at this hour. No odor lingered from the evening meal, and chairs were squared neatly under the tables.

Fabian sat alone at a table near a window, his head silhouetted by the blue glow emitted by the port warp nacelle. He sat slumped in his chair, long legs stretched out and feet crossed in front of him. A half-eaten peanut butter and jelly sandwich sat neglected on his plate. His nose was buried in a padd.

He glanced up and waved at Corsi when she entered the room. She stopped at the replicator to pick up a cup of herbal tea, then strolled over and joined him. She leaned over and gave him a peck on the lips, enough to be fun, not enough to distract from his coming shift. "You're up early," she said.

"Pre-mission jitters. I'm anticipating blowing this thing up." He glanced at her. "You're working late."

She sat down and sipped her tea. It was good, but had a faint replicated aftertaste. She dumped in two sugars and made a mental note to pick up some real tea on her next shore leave. "Powers is still in sickbay after Phantas 61, so we had to juggle the shifts a bit. I *did* tell you about that."

He stared at his padd and grunted. "I suppose you did."

"Besides, I like the gamma shift when we're cruising at warp. It's usually quiet, like having the ship to yourself." She reached over and pulled down the top of his padd, so she could see the screen. "What're you reading?"

He shrugged. "A Starfleet Intelligence white paper on Breen tactical systems. Not very informative, and dry as a bone."

"I've got gossip."

He tossed the padd on the table and reached for his coffee cup. "Yeah?"

"I got a call tonight from that freighter captain. The one we rescued from the holographic ship? The green one?" She watched his face for a reaction, some trace of jealousy. She'd made no secret during his visit that she found "Pappy" Omthon very attractive.

Fabian looked at her with a perfect poker face, not rising to her tease. "He was a first officer, not a captain."

"He's a captain now. He bought the ship from his old captain."

"Well. Good for him."

She frowned. "That's not the gossip. He called to ask about Commander Gomez. He'd been calling her, and she'd been avoiding him."

"That's her right."

"With respect to a superior officer, she's an idiot. Omthon is a great guy. It's time she let herself have a life again."

Fabian looked thoughtful. He took a deep breath and let it out slowly. He nodded.

"So, I totally abused my security clearances to help him ambush her when she returned to her quarters. I probably violated about a dozen regulations. I could be court-martialed. Proud of me?"

He gave her a sidelong glance. "She's the first officer. You *could* be court-martialed."

"She'll thank me later."

"Yeah, but she'll court-martial you now. What," he said in mock horror, "were you thinking?"

She frowned and stared into the teacup cradled in her hands. "I was thinking, life is too short to waste it."

Fabian leaned forward, his face serious, his eyes troubled. "Is something bothering you?"

Corsi hesitated. It was one thing to talk about Gomez, and what she should do. Talking about herself was another matter. "I've been thinking about our little talk in the turbolift after Phantas. And I'm wondering—what would you do if you knew it was the last day of your life?"

He grinned. "Kick Bart out of the cabin, tell you to cancel your shift, and come right over."

"I'm serious." She frowned at him.

Fabian's grin faded, and he reached for her hand. "I *am* being serious."

Her hand rested lightly in his, but Fabian could feel the tension in her fingers. She looked out the window, watching the star-streaks traveling by.

"It's part of the job," he said, stroking her fingers. "We live with it." He tried another grin. "Hell, you shoot people for a living."

Her mouth twisted into an approximation of a smile, and she sighed. "I suppose you're right. I just worry that she's going to completely close herself off, like—" She cut herself off.

Fabian put his finger against her lips. "I know."

They sat in silence for a while after that.

CHAPTER 3

Gomez arrived on the bridge as they were ready to drop out of warp. Stevens was at one of the aft stations. Lieutenant Commander Tev stood next to Captain Gold's chair. "Good morning, Captain. Tev."

Tev's deep-set eyes gave her a sideways glance. His snout wrinkled slightly and the corner of his mouth twitched down a bit, all of which seemed to say, *"I've been up for hours. Where have you been?"*

She grinned slightly. She was learning to let the Tellarite's natural arrogance roll off her. He seemed oblivious. She had to admit that, as his superior officer, it helped to know she could simply *order* him to behave himself. It wasn't her style to actually do it, but knowing she could provided an escape valve.

Now, if she could just improve his relationships with the rest of the crew, she'd be getting somewhere. The only person with whom the Tellarite was in any way friendly was Bart Faulwell. Gomez wondered what the linguist's secret was.

"Wong," said Gold, "take us to impulse."

The ship dropped out of warp, and the stars on the screen changed from moving streaks to diamondlike points.

"One quarter impulse, sir."

"Haznedl, where's our derelict?"

The alpha-shift ops officer's strawberry blond hair was drawn into a tight bun, an imitation of Corsi's severe style, in an attempt to counter her youth and small stature. She tapped at her console. "I show it three hundred twenty kilometers ahead, sir."

"Visual and magnify, on screen."

"Aye."

Gomez stared. The ship wasn't a disk at all, it was a dark-colored torus. Its surface was a complex pattern of gray and black, with glinting highlights of silver, and occasional splashes of caramel brown. Small projections spaced evenly around the rim might have been thrusters or emitters of some sort, and other small projections were even less identifiable. It was hard to make sense of it all because the whole thing was spinning, and quite rapidly.

She tried to fix her eye on one of the projections and count seconds as it spun. "That's what, about eight revolutions per minute?"

Tev leaned over the ops console, studying the sensor displays. "A fraction over seven RPM, actually."

Gold grinned slightly. "It looks like a bagel."

Gomez grinned back. "A five-hundred-meter bagel."

"That," he said, "would need a lot of lox."

Tev snorted, a sound of disgust, at the casual banter between the captain and first officer.

"Captain," said Haznedl, "scanners are having a hard time reading the interior. The ionizing radiation and some exotic alloys in the hull are interfering. I'm detecting no life-forms, but there is a pressurized space occupying about thirty percent of the interior volume. Helium, argon, various trace gases, including a heavy concentration of radon." She tapped more controls. "Neither the atmosphere nor the technology matches anything in the Federation database. This is a total unknown."

"Well," said Gomez. "Looks like we have ourselves another puzzle. Tev, what's your analysis?"

"It's a ship or probe, probably unoccupied. There's no indication of warp capability. I suspect those projections on the rim are primitive impulse thrusters."

She nodded. "I'd say you were right about everything except about its being unoccupied. There, you're dead wrong."

Tev glared at her. "It doesn't have the characteristics of a ship designed to support life."

"On the contrary, it has a characteristic that leads to no other conclusion. It's spinning."

"I don't understand."

"Maybe Tellarites don't suffer ill effects from prolonged exposure to microgravity, but many other species, including humans, do. Some of our early space station and spacecraft designs used centrifugal force to simulate gravity for long space voyages."

Tev snorted. "How stunningly primitive." He considered for a moment. "Clever though."

"I suggest," said the captain, "there will be plenty of time to study this thing. What say we save a planet first? This is your show, Gomez."

She nodded. "Aye, sir."

She pulled out a padd and checked her calculations. She'd plotted an orbit that would take the spinship safely past the Lokra homeworld, having adjusted for the mass, configuration, and now the rotation of the derelict ship, based on their more refined sensor readings. After double-checking her final check, she transferred the final results to the ops console.

"Susan, lock on tractor emitters two and three. Songmin, stand by thrusters. Full astern as soon as we have lock."

Emitters two and three were among the many *da Vinci* upgrades that originated with Duffy's *"U.S.S. Roebling"* S.C.E. dream ship, made when the ship was being repaired following Galvan VI. Located at the far edges of the saucer section, the long baseline separating them allowed for precision manipulation of objects at a distance. Their locations allowed them to connect directly into the same structural spar that tied the warp nacelles to the ship, and to hook directly into the ship's main EPS power conduits.

"Aye," said Haznedl, "we've got lock."

On the main viewscreen, Gomez watched a pair of converging blue beams lock on to either side of the ring-shaped ship.

"Thrusters full astern," said Wong. Even before he finished speaking, a note of hesitation crept into his voice. He frowned at his console. "Captain, I'm getting some anomalous firing of the attitude thrusters. The automatic systems are throwing in a roll component, but our attitude is stable."

Gomez glanced at the viewscreen for the oldest kind of confirmation. The stars remained in fixed positions. *But if the roll thrusters are firing—*

Gomez reviewed her calculations. She'd compensated so there would be little or no coupling of the derelict's spin back to the *da Vinci*. Maybe there was an unrelated malfunction in the automatic stability systems.

"Captain," said Wong, tension creeping into his voice, "thruster quads one through four and eleven through fourteen are reaching maximum output. We can't maintain thrust astern."

Gomez stared at the screen. This couldn't be happening, but this wasn't the time to be guessing at what was going on. "Shut down the tractor beams! Back us away!"

Haznedl tapped the ops console, her voice thin with strain. "I've cut power, but the beams are still active."

On screen the tractor beams were clearly visible. More disturbing, the stars were rotating, like the second hand of an antique clock, and they were getting faster.

Gomez ran to the engineering station and pulled up an EPS status panel. "The plasma relays may have fused. I'm going to cut the main EPS conduits feeding the system. We'll lose phaser power too, but—"

Tev came and looked over her shoulder, staring at the master display as she located the master plasma cutouts and activated them. She glanced back at the screen. *The damned tractor beams were still active!*

"Where are they getting power?"

Wong tapped frantically at the helm. "I've lost attitude control. Thruster quads one, four, eleven, and fourteen are reaching critical overheat. I have to shut them down before they blow."

"Wait as long as you can," shouted Gomez, looking for any other way power could be reaching the tractor beams. The thrusters would slow their accelerating rotation and might buy them critical seconds to shut down the tractor beams. Plus, it was only a matter of time before the acceleration itself started to cause problems.

"Inertial dampers and structural integrity field systems are showing the strain," said Haznedl.

"Our roll rate is fourteen RPM and accelerating," Wong said. Their mass, relative to the derelict, was quickly accelerating their spin rate.

"The news just keeps getting better," muttered Gomez. She could hear the ship groaning from the strain, feel a slight lean to the deck that the inertial dampers couldn't compensate for.

She couldn't understand it. The tractor beams were isolated from any power source, yet they kept operating. She triple-checked the EPS schematic. The tractors and main phasers were isolated at the end of a major EPS feeder. There was no way they could be getting power, unless—

"It's got to be some kind of feedback loop. The beam interaction with the derelict is generating power, not dissipating it. It's feeding power back through the beams. That's what threw my calculations off!"

She was suddenly aware Captain Gold was standing next to her. "How do we turn it off?"

"We can't, unless we can get someone down to directly disable the emitters. And if we break the circuit, I don't know where the energy will go. It could kill anyone near the emitter, even make them explode."

"Roll is at twenty RPM," said Wong. The stars whirled on the viewscreen like a child's pinwheel.

"*Warning,*" said the computer, "*inertial dampers in overload. Failure imminent. Warning, structural integrity field reaching critical load.*"

"Damn, there just isn't time!"

The ship moaned and shuddered as it tried to tear itself apart.

It was a race. If the SIF failed, the ship would break up. If the inertial dampers failed, they'd all be splattered against the nearest bulkhead.

Tev blinked. "Put the main phasers in overload."

"That'll blow up the ship," said Gold.

"It'll do nothing," said Gomez. "The phasers don't have power."

"Just do it," said Tev. "It's the only way."

Stevens, holding on to the tactical station for support, had a sudden look of revelation. "Captain, he's right! It's our only hope!"

Gomez scowled at the EPS diagram. She didn't see what good it would do, but Captain Gold had once told her, *Trust your people.*

"Setting main phasers to overload." She was leaning sideways in her chair now, struggling not to slide out of it.

"Warning," said the computer, *"phaser overload requires command authorization."*

"Authorization, Gold, alpha tango one!"

There was a noise, as though the phaser banks were about to fire, which turned abruptly into a dull thud that shuddered through the ship. A flash illuminated the derelict on the screen. By the time Gomez's eyes adjusted, the tractor beams were gone.

The ship shook violently. The lights on the bridge flickered. Then things smoothed out. The rotating stars on the screen began to slow.

"Damage report," said Captain Gold.

"Minor buckling in the hull and secondary structural members," reported Anthony Shabalala from tactical. "Tractor beams and main phasers are off-line. Damage to EPS conduits ten and thirty. Minor damage to structural integrity field systems and reaction control systems. No casualties."

Gold stared at the object on the screen. "Well, *that* was exciting." He turned and made eye contact with Gomez. His look made it clear he was trying not to be judgmental, but she knew she'd better have a damned good report ready for him ASAP.

First, though, she wanted to know how Tev pulled that rabbit out of his hat, and she gave him an expectant look.

To his credit, the Tellarite spoke up immediately. "The phasers were isolated on the same branch of the EPS system as the tractor beams."

Stevens nodded. "Energy was flowing in through the emitters when it should have been going out, feeding that branch. Putting them in overload was like putting a dead short across the circuit. It shut the feedback down, and the excess energy was dissipated harmlessly through the phaser strips."

Tev nodded, obviously a little annoyed at being cut off in his moment of glory. "In far too simple terms, that's more or less what happened."

"That was a close one," said Gomez.

"Just for the record," said Gold, annoyance slipping into his voice, "I do *not* like close calls. There will be a full S.C.E. briefing at 1100 hours. I'll expect a complete report on this incident, and what we're going to do about this—" He gestured at the screen. "—thing, now that we have no tractor beams *or* phasers."

"Now, if you'll excuse me, I have to go call the ambassador and explain why there's still a killer ship heading toward his planet."

Gold stepped into his ready room and stood ramrod-straight until the doors closed behind him. Once they did, he relaxed his posture and breathed deep. That *had* been a close one.

When he'd taken this assignment, he'd imagined it would be beneficial and interesting. What he had not anticipated was that S.C.E. was perhaps the most hazardous duty he'd ever served. Not only did they face constant unknowns and first-contact situations, by definition they rolled up their sleeves and dived straight into the thick of them. Often they were deeply entangled in the guts of an alien technology or a derelict spacecraft before unknown hazards presented themselves.

As this mission showed, even the seemingly most routine missions could turn deadly. There had even been a few moments, especially following Galvan VI, when he resented that.

Yet now, even as he let his pounding heart settle down in his chest, he knew that it was necessary, it was good, it was how things were done in the S.C.E., and how they *had* to be done. Maybe that had been their mistake this time. They'd taken the situation for granted, handled it the same way as any other Federation ship would have.

In the shuttledock at S.C.E. headquarters, there was a colorful mural painted on a hangar wall. It portrayed a standard Federation Work-bee, a small yellow utility spacecraft frequently used by the S.C.E. for space construction and repair.

The little yellow spacecraft had been anthropomorphized, cartoon eyes glaring from its forward viewport, and a sneering mouth, teeth gritted in determination, on its nose. A pair of cartoon arms projected from its sides. One hand held a hammer, the other an old-fashioned open-end wrench. Below it was a simple motto: HANDS ON!

Maybe that was the problem. They had stood off at arm's length, tried to work the problem by remote control. *Have we gotten timid?* He made a mental note to have a talk with Gomez on the subject. But for now, he had other business.

He sat at his desk and punched up a subspace link to the embassy on the Lokra homeworld. It took him a few moments to be routed to Ambassador Goveia's office.

The ambassador smiled when he saw Gold, the corners of his beard lifting toward his pale eyes. *"Captain Gold. You have good news for us, I hope."*

"I thought the Lokra sensors might have already told you what happened."

The smile faded. *"Is there a problem?"*

"There have been—complications. We tried to put a tractor beam on the derelict ship, but there was a technical difficulty of some sort before we could appreciably alter its course. Our ship received minor damage. We're currently reevaluating the situation, and we hope to have a new plan shortly."

"A tractor beam?" The gravelly voice came from offscreen. *"Why didn't he destroy it? I thought your Federation ships had powerful weapons. I thought you would destroy it."*

The ambassador addressed the unseen speaker. *"These are

our finest engineers, Siletz. I'm sure they'll have the situation under control shortly."

"Let me speak to him. I want to speak to him."

The ambassador looked apologetically at Gold. "Captain, this is Siletz, First Prime of the Lokra. First Prime, this is Captain Gold of the S.C.E. starship U.S.S. da Vinci."

The view widened to include the speaker.

Siletz was a large, simian-looking humanoid. He was completely covered with bushy white hair, except for his face and hands. Gold couldn't be sure if the color was normal for the Lokra, a special badge of office, or a sign of advanced age. Siletz wore no clothing, but on his left wrist was a bulky electronic device that could be a communicator or computer access device.

"Why, Captain, did you not destroy the ship when you had the chance? I was told you would destroy it."

"Is that so, Ambassador?"

Goveia looked uncomfortable. "Not to contradict the First Prime, but I don't believe those were my exact words. I said we could destroy the derelict, if necessary."

"This is disturbing." Siletz bared his rather sizable teeth at the screen, a gesture that could have been the equivalent of anything from a smile to a threat, as far as Gold knew. "We are told the Federation has powerful weapons, and they will defend us from this threat. We have no weapons of our own. After the Breen left we hoped to develop them. We were assured it would not be necessary—the Federation would see to our security—and once we joined your Federation, technology would be shared with us. Is this a lie, Captain? When the Breen first came, they told us lies as well, so we would not resist until it was too late. Are all outworlders like this?"

"I assure you," said Gold, "that we will see that your planet remains safe."

"Then I insist you destroy the derelict at once!"

It was Gold's turn to look embarrassed. "That may be difficult. Not only were our tractor beams damaged, but our phasers as well. If necessary, we can destroy the object using torpedoes, or even demolition charges, but it will require time for study—"

Siletz seemed outraged. *"And until then, our planet must live under a death sentence? Unacceptable!"* Siletz leaped to his feet and left the room.

The ambassador watched him go. *"They're a temperamental people, Captain, and very physical. They have all manner of social mechanisms for defusing tension before it turns into a fight. Leaving the room is one of them, and it happens a lot here."* He shrugged, the exaggerated shoulders of his uniform shifting up a fraction of an inch. *"Captain, I can't stress the importance of this. These people will not feel safe until that ship is destroyed, by whatever means. They are all quite insistent about it."*

Gold took a deep breath and forced himself to remain calm. There was a reason he was a starship captain, not a diplomat. And at the moment, it felt like he and Goveia were on opposing sides. "As I said, Ambassador, that may be beyond our resources at the moment. At any rate, this spacecraft represents the work of a totally unknown species, and the technology is quite unusual. We hope to study the ship, and perhaps learn something about its point of origin."

"Captain, I appreciate that, but there is a danger of panic here." Goveia's voice was as frosty as his ice-blue eyes. *"A Galaxy-class starship, the* U.S.S. Norman Scott, *is on a mission just a dozen light-years from here. Perhaps a larger and more formidable vessel could make quick work of the problem."*

CHAPTER 4

Gomez entered the observation lounge ready to get her ass chewed. She'd screwed up and put the ship in danger, and would be lucky not to be court-martialed. She'd had only a few hours to pull her team together and set them analyzing both what happened, and the spinning derelict that still floated off their bow.

Everyone was seated around the table when she arrived. Stevens and Tev, as well as language specialist Bart Faulwell, cultural specialist Carol Abramowitz, insectoid structural specialist P8 "Pattie" Blue, and Bynar computer specialist Soloman. Dr. Lense was also present.

Several of them greeted Gomez, but the air hummed with suppressed tension.

They're all waiting for the hammer to fall.

Gomez nodded at Tev. "I didn't have a chance to thank you for what happened on the bridge. Your quick thinking saved the ship."

"It was nothing," said Tev.

"It's not like you to be modest," she said.

He looked at her blankly. "No, it was really nothing. I can

read an EPS schematic. I assumed the rest of you were simply too agitated."

Gomez nodded and turned slowly away. *Okay, I knew that was coming.* She stiffened as she heard the doors open behind her. *And this, too.*

She turned to face the music. "Captain Gold."

"Gomez, I'd like the floor for a minute."

Gold took his seat at the head of the table, Gomez sitting to his right. The derelict loomed behind her in the lounge's window, as though mocking her.

The captain cleared his throat. "This matter has gotten somewhat complicated, and not just because our initial attempt to divert the derelict failed. There are diplomatic and political issues that make it necessary for me to stand over your shoulders from here on in. I'm under pressure to solve this situation, and solve it fast."

Gomez quickly said, "That's hardly a problem, sir." Generally Gomez's autonomy over the S.C.E. team was a given, but the "separation of powers" between her and Gold was sometimes a problem, most recently on Rhaax III, where a diplomat named Gabriel Marshall had co-opted Gomez and forced her to act without informing Gold. It was not a situation that either captain or first officer was eager to repeat, and Gomez was wondering if that redheaded ambassador was going to pull something similar to what Marshall did.

Gold continued. "I can try to buy time, and I'm sure I'll need to do just that. But I need something to work with." He glanced at Gomez, one eyebrow raised. "There's also the matter of my ship very nearly being turned into cream cheese a few hours ago. I want to know what happened and what we're going to do about it."

Gomez let out a breath. "Captain, we've all been working on an analysis of the situation. The makeup of the alien ship's hull and the ionizing radiation it's emitting are interfering with our sensors. What we didn't know, when we tried to tractor the ship, was that the hull is wrapped with bands of high temperature superconducting cables. They could be some kind of EM field, a weapon, or even part of a communication device. All that matters is that they were there, and they were spinning. The fields of our tractor beams interacted with them like a generator, coils of wire moving through a field. In this case the energy fed back through the tractor beams, creating a self-powering reaction. Until Tev figured a creative way to use the phaser couplings to break the circuit, we were in real trouble."

Gold studied her. "So at the time there was no way you could have known about these cables?"

"They didn't register on our sensors until the energy from the tractor beams charged them up."

"And this wasn't caused by our new tractor array?"

"No. In fact, if the system hadn't been so robust, and if the emitters hadn't been tied in to the main spar, we likely would have had a major structural failure almost immediately."

"What *do* we know about this ship?"

"Well," said Gomez, "it has fusion impulse engines augmented with a time-space driver coil. They don't have warp drive, but were clearly close to developing it. Pattie has been studying their systems based on the limited data so far."

The Nasat waved her antennae. The attention-getting gesture was like a human making a polite cough. "This ship is most interesting in many ways. As Commander Gomez states, the people who built this appear to have advanced nearly to the point of developing warp drive. Their materials science is quite advanced, in terms of alloys and superconductors. They might possibly have a thing or two to teach us, but in other ways the ship is almost startlingly crude. To all indications, the ship was built entirely without standardized or prefabricated parts. Most of what we can see seems to have been handcrafted, with parts fabricated in position. It's more appropriate to compare it to nests made by insectoids using wax, paper, or webbing."

"Could this be a nest created by nonsentient life native to deep space?" Gold asked.

Bart Faulwell waved a hand. "I can answer that, Captain."

Pattie nodded to Faulwell, and settled back into her custom-fitted chair.

Faulwell said, "We've imaged over six hundred examples of glyphs on the hull. They appear to be warning or instruction placards. I can even make good guesses on what some of it means, based on the adjacent ports and mechanisms. Not enough to translate the language, but it's a start." He scratched his beard thoughtfully. "Every last bit of writing is oriented in one direction relative to the ring. It's as though the ring was assembled in a gravity well, lying on its side, and the writing was intended only for use in that orientation."

Gold turned to Lense. "Any signs of life?"

Lense shrugged. "Our sensors don't pick up any life-forms, or any residue consistent with bodies, though that isn't conclusive. We're not even sure we know what we're looking for. At floor level, the ship's spin is creating an artificial equivalent of approximately fourteen standard gravities. There's all kinds of radioactivity and free radon in the air, which would quickly be toxic to most carbon-based life-forms. The atmosphere is mostly inert gases at about three hundred kilopascals. It won't support any respiratory process we understand. Or maybe they didn't use it for respiration at all. It could be a fire-suppression mixture, or a coolant."

"Exotic life-forms then?"

"Very. I worked on silicon-based life-forms at the Academy, and I've studied Horta anatomy. They all seem tame compared to whatever built that ship."

Gold sighed. "I'm under a great deal of pressure to destroy this ship."

Stevens sat up in his chair, as though this was the moment he'd been waiting for all day. "I've been working on that, sir. Phasers are down for at least two days, and I doubt we can destroy it with torpedoes. In an explosion, the ring will fragment before it can vaporize, and the energy stored in the spinning makes it highly unpredictable. We'll send large chunks sailing off in random directions.

"Our best bet is multiple fusion detonation charges individually placed around the ring. To be most effective, they'll need to be placed on the outside rim—"

Gold held up a hand. He looked at his first officer. "What do you have to say about this, Gomez?"

Gomez considered for a moment before answering, licking her lips, which suddenly felt as dry as her throat. "Pattie believes the ship is undamaged and operational, or nearly so.

The crew may have died, or abandoned ship for some reason, but the ship itself seems sound." She paused, choosing her words carefully. This was her opportunity to state her case. She had considered the options, and she knew what she had to say. "There's an easy way to do this, and a right way. Blowing it up is the easy way. If we can get inside it, figure out the controls, power up the impulse engines, we can steer it away from the planet. That's the right way." She swallowed hard, her throat dry, and continued. "Then we can study it at our leisure, and it's an artifact worth studying. We can retrace its course, or maybe even access its onboard computers. It might lead us to a first-contact situation. At the very least, this thing is a treasure trove of metals that are rare in this system. The Lokra might well want an opportunity to salvage it for themselves. That's how I'd do it, sir. That's the S.C.E. way."

Gomez realized Gold was smiling at her, with that fatherly "that's my girl" smile he sometimes got when he was especially pleased.

She blinked in surprise. *What have I done now?*

She was still wondering after Gold had excused himself and left. The dressing-down she'd been expecting had never come, and she felt guilty about it. It left her even more determined to get things right this time. She focused her attention on her crew and the problem at hand.

"People, we've got a lot to do, and very little time to do it. I'm going to need two hundred percent effort. We need to board that ship, survive there, work there. We need to figure it out, fire it up, and move it. We don't have time for a fully formed plan, so I'm counting on you to work it out as we go."

"We could use the experimental gravity suits," said Stevens.

Gomez shook her head. "No. This isn't actual gravitons, it's the *illusion* of gravity created by centrifugal force."

"Vectored inertia," said Pattie, her shell making a dry rattling sound as she shifted in her specially designed chair. "We need suits with their own inertial dampers, like—" Pattie hesitated. After a moment, Gomez knew why. Duffy had gone to his death in a suit modified with—among other things—an inertial damper. It wasn't something the survivors of Galvan VI liked to talk about.

Tev, who replaced Duffy, grunted in blissful obliviousness. "There are miniature IDF generators used to stabilize antimatter containment in our photon torpedoes. They can be adapted. But the shape and interior volume of a pressure suit is in constant flux. It will be challenging."

Gomez nodded, for once grateful for Tev's obtuseness. "You're on it, Tev. We need suits for Stevens and me immediately, and a backup suit in case we get into trouble and need help."

She turned to Pattie. "I'd like you there first, but you don't have a pressure suit we can adapt. So I'm tapping Fabian," she glanced at the tactical specialist, "as your eyes, ears, and hands on the mission. Tev, you will adapt suits for team members until we have everyone over there, if necessary. The order they come over depends on who we need most."

Tev frowned. "With respect, Commander, I would be more valuable on the away team."

"I need you to modify the suits, Tev. It'll be complex and challenging, and if it isn't done right, we're going to die over there." She paused for effect. "However, if you don't think you're up to—"

Tev made a little noise of disgust. "You're right, of course."

She smiled, remembering the miniature golf course yesterday. "Tap Bennett to help you. Cade's done some creative stuff with inertial dampers. Let me know the moment those first three suits are ready. Pattie, work with Fabian. Figure out how we can safely beam on board and what we should look for when we get there. Elizabeth, Bart, Carol, we're working with limited information and secondhand data, but I'll need ongoing analysis from you all. I need to understand the ship's crew, to figure out how to tell the ship's helm controls from the captain's toilet, and decode the interface once I find it."

She smiled. The challenge, the pressure, the thrill of discovery. *This* was why she joined the S.C.E.

Captain Gold sat in his ready room studying the local planetary survey. Something about the First Prime didn't feel right.

Despite the danger, he was far too insistent the derelict ship be destroyed. Gold sensed the First Prime was hiding something, and he was determined to find out what.

Reconstructing the ship's trajectory didn't point them to any of the local stars. That meant it had maneuvered under power since leaving its origin system.

As he followed the ship's path, it was apparent it had probably braked and maneuvered after entering this system, which made its current status as a ghost ship even more mysterious. Where was the crew? Why would they abandon an undamaged ship?

He did have one useful fact, the gravity the ship's spin was designed to simulate. Their survey had turned up a close-orbiting giant with the same surface gravity. Even more interesting, it was less than two light-years away, and rich in metals. There wasn't much more in the survey. A detailed analysis of the system had never been performed.

Gold leaned back in his chair and rubbed his chin. The ambassador had been right about another thing. The *U.S.S. Norman Scott* was operating in the area, and as it happened, the captain was a big fan of his wife's cooking. "Computer, open a subspace channel to Captain Huxter on the *Norman Scott*." It was time to call in a favor.

CHAPTER 5

Gomez grunted as Pattie cinched the environmental suit tighter. "We're putting the *da Vinci* where?"

"Hold still," said Pattie, tugging at the closure on the rigid torso section until she was satisfied.

A few feet away, Transporter Chief Poynter and Stevens—who was already suited up—watched with amusement.

"As for the *da Vinci*, I think the human phrase is 'threading the needle.' We're going to take up station inside the ring. It minimizes the transporter range, and the hull is thinnest on the inside of the ring. It will simplify transporter lock and make our sensors more effective as well."

Gomez sighed. "I'm trusting you on this one, Pattie."

"Unless you'd rather we beamed you onto the hull inside the ring and let you try to phaser your way in, it seems to be the only way. The only hatches we've been able to identify are on the *outside* of the ring, don't seem to have airlocks, and open *inward*, which is just an insane way to design such a ship."

"Unless," said Gomez, "you never intended to be outside it, except in a gravity well. Most ancient spinning designs include a hub, with an airlock or docking point, at the center. These builders didn't want to experience null gravity. Pass that idea on to Elizabeth, would you?"

"Certainly," said Pattie. She made one last inspection of Fabian's suit.

The suits were an awkward-looking affair, cobbled together using a type-4M extravehicular work garment already designed for heavy gravity missions, though nothing like what they were expecting today. The type-4M incorporated linear motors that enhanced and supported the joints, normally allowing work in up to two standard gravities. To this, hung externally to the backpack, had been added a fusion power source, a polarized gravity source, and a miniature IDF generator. Tubular field-wave guides snaked across the exterior of the suit and down the arms and legs like veins. They were in constant communication with Pattie, as their controller.

Gomez raised the control panel on her left forearm to the visor of her suit, and activated the IDF system. Her head swam as the field engulfed her, but the feeling quickly passed. "Okay, how do we test these?"

"Tev didn't have time to come up with a formal diagnostic," said Pattie. "I suggest you throw yourself against a wall."

Gomez stared at her.

"I'm serious," said Pattie. "Throw your shoulder against a bulkhead, the harder the better. And be careful, your sense of balance will be thrown off by rapid movements."

Gomez took a few quick steps and staggered, tripping over her own boots. After the first step her inner ear told her she wasn't moving. Her impact with the bulkhead was accidental, and completely unavoidable. Her arm hit the wall, cushioned by the thick suit, but there was no sense of deceleration. The sensation made her stomach turn over.

Pattie looked at her. "You did take your motion sickness pills, didn't you? Human regurgitation is unpleasant enough under the best of circumstances, but in a pressure suit—"

"We took our pills," said Gomez. *And we're going to need them.*

"I'm going to go join the rest of the 'Greek chorus' in the engineering lab. Elizabeth, Bart, Carol, and I will be monitoring your communications and helmet cameras at all times. Talk to you over there." Pattie dropped from her bipedal form and scuttled out of the transporter room on all eight legs.

They stepped onto the transporter platform. Turning to Poynter, Gomez said, "Energize."

They were briefly enveloped in the blue shimmer of the transporter effect, and then darkness.

Should have expected that. She stood motionless for a moment to make sure the IDF system in her suit was functioning, then turned on her suit lights. Fabian did likewise.

"We're fine over here. Tell Tev the IDF system is working. Radiation is high, but within suit limits." She slowly turned, taking in their surroundings. The ship looked more like some kind of nest than a technological artifact, as Pattie had suggested. There were no straight lines or right angles, nor even strongly contrasting areas of color. Just light, and lots of shadow.

The interior surfaces were a slightly translucent reddish brown. The surfaces looked polished, like marble or wax. What was really interesting was the variety of textures. Every surface was veined, webbed, rippled, spiked, or textured in some way, floor to ceiling.

"Da Vinci," she said, "are the cameras working?"

"We've had to boost the receiver gain to maximum," said Bart, *"but we're getting a decent picture now. Ah, Pattie just joined us."*

"Pattie," said Gomez, "does any of this make more sense to you than it does to me?"

Gomez turned slowly, trying to take in the larger space this time, and give Pattie a good look. The interior of the tunnel was about thirty meters wide and seven meters tall at the center of the curved ceiling. It was one continuous space as far as she could see, without bulkheads, doors, or rooms. It curved up into the darkness in either direction with no indication that what lay beyond was any different.

Breaking up the space were large irregular shapes. They might be consoles, or machinery, or who-knew-what. They were all the same shade of rusty brown.

"Could somebody take readings using one of the medical tri-

corders I provided," Lense asked, "and relay them back to the ship?"

Gomez hefted the tricorder, one of two hanging from her suit. Outside the volume of the suit, it wasn't subject to the inertial damping field. The normally lightweight piece of equipment felt like it was made of lead, and took two hands to lift comfortably. She grunted as she lifted it. As she scanned the area, she said, "Elizabeth, remember how much of a pain it was to be in EVA suits for all that time on the Shmoam-ag ship? Right now, I wish I was that comfortable."

However, Lense seemed to be more interested in the scan. "This is amazing. Sonya, can you turn about ninety degrees to your left?"

Gomez turned slowly, taking small steps, until she faced the outside wall of the ring. About three meters ahead of her was a large reddish lump, about the size of a shuttlepod. It differed from its surroundings because some of its surfaces were curved panels, relatively smooth and unmarked compared to most of the rest of the ship.

She stepped toward it. Her extended foot seemed to twist to the right, pulling her off balance. She nearly stumbled, and Fabian reached out to steady her.

"Thanks," she said. "The IDF doesn't entirely compensate for the Coriolis effect. We need to be careful moving at right angles to the direction of spin. Take baby steps."

Heeding her own advice, she shuffled toward the object, but she still felt dizzy.

"These suits still need a little work, Tev," she muttered, reaching out and leaning against the object of Lense's interest. A large, tree-trunk-like projection emerged from the object, made a right angle turn, and met up with the floor. It made a convenient seat.

Fabian watched her with concern, but didn't rush to help, lest he have his own problems. Through the suit's speakers, she heard him ask, *"Are you okay?"*

"I'm fine. Just dizzy. I don't know if you've ever been sailing, but this is going to be like getting your sea legs, only worse. Okay, Elizabeth, what's so interesting?"

"The crew never left. There are bodies on the ship. I'm picking

up twenty-three, and there may be more around the ring out of tricorder range. Their construction is silicon-based, but the metabolism isn't entirely chemically-based. I'm still figuring it out."

Gomez looked around. She didn't see anything that looked like a sentient being. "Are any of these bodies close to us?"

"*I think,*" said the doctor, "*that you're sitting on one.*"

Gold watched the ambassador's face on the screen, looking for any sign of deception. "Alfredo, are you sure the Lokra are being entirely truthful about this derelict?"

"*What do you mean? How would they even know anything about it? It's an alien ship from outside their system.*"

"That's right, and we have a fair guess as to what planet it came from. The gravity and atmospheric pressure of a giant planet in a nearby system are consistent with the derelict. The *Norman Scott* scanned the planet. It's overrun with self-replicating mining machines, and those machines seem to have originated with the Lokra."

Goveia pursed his narrow lips and waved a long-fingered hand in dismissal. "*Those mining machines were launched well before the Breen occupation. They were part of a long-term plan to establish a reliable metal supply. Once they've mined enough materials and duplicated themselves, they'll build cargo ships and send the metal back to the Lokra. It will take decades for the first metal to arrive, but once the flow starts, it won't stop.*"

"Don't you find that suspicious?"

"*Did the* Norman Scott *find the civilization that sent the ship?*"

"No, nor any ruins either. We're not entirely sure what we're looking for. The derelict was built by exotic, silicon-based lifeforms of some sort."

"*Who may have originated somewhere else. Maybe they were only exploring your giant planet, and moved on to this system, experiencing some mishap on the way.*"

Gold considered Goveia's argument. He was certain it was wrong, but he didn't want to provoke a confrontation. Not until he knew more. "That's possible, I suppose, but I have to rule out all the possibilities. Ambassador, are you sure the Lokra don't have any space-based weapons? Perhaps something left by the Breen?"

Goveia laughed, a harsh, brittle sound. *"Captain, you already have the answer. The S.C.E. swept out all Breen weapons and military technology immediately after the Breen withdrew. All that's left is an orbiting subspace communications relay that we handed over to the Lokra. It has no weapons capability, and I assure you the Lokra have no weapons of their own. Whatever happened to that ship, they had nothing to do with it."*

Goveia smiled with his mouth, but not his eyes. They had last encountered each other on Vulcan when Gold was captain of the *U.S.S. Progress,* and back then he had come across to Gold as a man who was confident of his assessments, and who disliked anyone who questioned his authority. The look on his face showed that that several-year-old assessment still held true.

Gold nodded reluctantly. "I'll take your word for that at the moment, Ambassador, but our investigation of the derelict is ongoing. My crew is making progress on powering up the impulse drive. We hope to divert it to a safe course shortly."

The ambassador frowned. *"I certainly hope so. The First Prime is impatient with my assurances, and I don't blame him after what's happened so far. Don't let scientific curiosity lead to the death of millions, Captain. Goveia out."*

Gomez found the spinship a much more agreeable place to work once they installed work lights. They were set every few meters along a seventy-meter section of tube they thought to be the control room, and along another forty-meter section they guessed corresponded to engineering.

When he saw the first images of the illuminated control room, Captain Gold described it as looking like "an exhibition of abstract art staged in the Holland Tunnel."

The tunnel analogy was somewhat lost on her, though she gathered it was a New York reference. Certainly the interior did look like a tunnel, razor straight and curving upward out of sight in either direction; and there was a gallery-like feel to the objects scattered there.

They were all massive. Some of them were control interfaces, consoles of sorts. Others were display devices. Lense assured them that one five-meter-wide, dome-shaped object was a food dispenser. Many more were mysteries, and would remain so unless they proved to be necessary in maneuvering the spinship.

Even the alien corpses, too large and massive to move, had a sculptural quality to them. Their surfaces were dry and rock-hard, seemingly unaffected by decay or mummification. Gomez had no idea what one of the living creatures looked like normally, but it was possible they had not deteriorated at all.

Their headless beetle bodies were belly-down on the floor, each set of eight massive, trunklike legs arrayed at the ready. They looked to Gomez as though they might at any moment stand up and scurry away. Their deaths were as mysterious as what happened to their ship.

Despite Gold's colorful metaphor, to those actually working there it was more like some sort of giant fun house, one of those "vortex spots" that sprung up as tourist attractions on every backwater planet, where sloping land, optical illusions, and ingeniously distorted architecture made people believe the laws of physics had somehow gone haywire.

The whole team was there now except Pattie, who, much to her frustration, was stuck on the *da Vinci*, and Tev. Despite having a functional suit, he had been ordered to remain on the ship to coordinate the data and to act as their backup in case of an emergency.

They adapted quickly to working in their peculiar environment. Tiny, shuffling steps and long detours avoided the full force of the Coriolis effect. If there had been time to watch, the effect would have been comical.

Even moderate-size objects required heavy mechanical assistance to move. They'd brought along a variety of carts, jacks, and electric lifts to assist in their work, all crude but effective.

Gomez shuffled over to one of the consoles, a wedge-shaped

structure four meters long and taller than her head, where Fabian and Bart were carrying on a heated three-way conversation with Pattie back on the ship. "How's it going? Any luck with the controls?"

Stevens frowned through his faceplate. *"That's the problem. We've identified the key systems, but we can't access them in any but the crudest way. Near as Soloman can determine, there are no computers of any real sophistication on the ship, nor are there controls in the typical sense. We're manually shorting circuits to activate things."*

She pointed at the console. "Then what's this?"

"Think of it as an interface port," said Soloman. She turned to see him and Lense a few meters away, in front of the nearest alien corpse. *"To understand the ship, we have to understand the crew. They don't just* look *like part of their ship's technology, they* are *part of it. The most important part."*

Gomez shook her head in puzzlement. Alien biology wasn't her strong suit. "Explain."

Lense pointed at the front of the corpse. There was no head, but there was a flat area on the front of the body that seemed to be a face of sorts. There were three sets of eyes, stacked vertically, interspersed with pairs of translucent organs and small limbs that might have been external feeding organs, except the mouth was far below, almost on the bottom of the body.

"We've learned quite a lot about these guys. The bodies are made of silicon molecules, but it isn't a conventional silicon lifeform, if that isn't an oxymoron. The metabolism is complex, and has chemical, electrical, and nuclear-thermal components. They don't breathe, but they need some atmospheric pressure for health, and helium is circulated through the body to provide cooling. Notice the horizontal banding all through the body? I'm calling the species 'Strata,' like rock strata. The bodies are built up in layers, like sedimentary rock, or for that matter, like isolinear chips."

"The ship," interjected Soloman, *"doesn't have complex computers because the Strata are complex electrochemical computers, though of natural origin. Each Strata is easily the equal of some of your early duotronic computers."*

Lense pointed at the creature's black, lidless eyes, then the nearby console. *"These lower two sets of eyes correspond to the four windows in the front of the console unit. They're visual input ports of some kind. These six patches on the console correspond to these feeler organs above the eyes."* Lense ran her fingers over the translucent projections between the sets of eyes. *"These 'feelers' are densely connected to the nervous system. They may have evolved to allow separate Strata to interface their brains, a kind of electronic mind-meld. But in this case, they allow the Strata's nervous system to connect directly to the ship's systems."*

Gomez looked at the creature's face, then the console. Now that she knew what she was looking at, the connection was obvious. "Crud. So what you're saying is that to fly the ship, we're going to have to build an artificial Strata?"

"It's possible," said Soloman, gesturing at the computer implant grafted into the side of his bald head, *"that we could design an interface that would allow me to control the ship through my own access port. It would be a complex task, though, and might entail some risk on my part. I'm willing to attempt it."*

Gomez frowned. "I'm not so sure I am. Let's look for alternatives first." She turned to Lense. "Elizabeth, would it help if we tried beaming one of these corpses back to the ship for an autopsy?"

Lense glanced at Soloman and licked her lips. *"I'm sure I could learn a lot, but I'm reluctant to do so."*

"Why?"

"We—that is, Soloman and I—" She faltered. *"It's about what happened to them. We believe there may have been an electromagnetic pulse. It would instantly disrupt their electronic systems, the way an otherwise nonfatal electric shock can stop the human heart. They just* stopped, *you see—"*

"Their memory," said Soloman, *"is very computer-like as well, nonvolatile* computer memory.*"*

Gomez had an idea where this was going, and she wasn't sure she liked it. "You're saying their memories are intact, that we might be able to read their minds?"

"Yes," said Lense, *"I suppose that's so, but what we really mean is that—"*

"Every memory, every component of their personality, the very last thought they had before their 'death,' is in there, and presumably intact." Soloman completed her sentence. "There are no decay organisms here to degrade the bodies, and their unique metabolism doesn't cause the kind of breakdown you see in most organic species. They're absolutely, perfectly *preserved*. They're not dead so much as just—shut down."

Gomez looked at Soloman. "Go ahead. Say it."

And the little computer expert did. *"They've crashed, and we think we can reboot them."*

CHAPTER 6

Ambassador Goveia scowled, rubbing the narrow bridge of his nose. *"You're telling me, Captain, that there are* survivors *on this derelict?"*

Gold sighed. "Not survivors, precisely. Their life processes have ceased. My crew believes they can be resuscitated."

"Captain, these beings could have died years, even centuries ago. It seems unlikely even the famed S.C.E. can bring back the dead. It's not even really your area of expertise. Besides, there are how many—"

"Forty-one."

"Forty-one corpses *on that ship. That has to be weighed against the lives of* millions *of Lokra."* Goveia's voice wavered slightly, as though asking for understanding, or sympathy.

"If the crew can be revived, their ship is functional and can be flown to a safe trajectory that will bypass the planet. There's ample time."

"And if this madness fails?" There was no pleading this time.

"Then we'll be forced to consider other options."

Goveia frowned. *"I suggest you not wait that long. I'm expecting a call back at any moment from your Captain Scott at*

Starfleet Command." He somehow managed to look down his thin nose, without moving. *"If I have to go over your head to resolve this situation, Captain, I will."*

The screen on Gold's desk blanked.

Gold's jaw tightened with frustration. His instincts told him the Lokra were hiding something. They also told him Goveia was a good but stubborn man who was too close to the situation to be objective.

If he was going to uncover the truth, it would require going around the ambassador, not through him.

Almost immediately there was another incoming subspace communication. It was Captain Huxter on the *Norman Scott*.

"David, I thought you should know I just heard from Ambassador Goveia."

"As it happens, I just talked with him myself."

Huxter frowned. *"Then he told you we're on the way?"*

"No. No, he left out that piece of information."

"Sorry, David. I just ran out of excuses." Then he grinned. *"But at our current speed of warp one, we'll be there in about one and a half years."*

Gold returned his grin. "It won't take the ambassador that long to start wondering where you are."

"I'm sure. But it will buy you a little time, and I'm starting to think your suspicions are justified. My science officer found something in the sensor logs from that giant planet."

Gold instantly sobered. "Something you didn't see during your initial sweep?"

Huxter's grin faded. *"We didn't know what we were looking for. I'm sorry it took this long to find it. Those mining machines have messed up the surface pretty badly in spots. We found a planetwide network of crude roads designed for foot or possibly cart traffic, simple dwellings made of stone and metal, and what seem to be mines and quarries. Those are the sites most disturbed by the Lokra mining machines, though, so it's hard to be sure."*

"But no signs of an advanced civilization?"

"That's where it gets strange. We found exactly one site with any signs of high technology, right on the equator. The miners nearly obliterated the site. We think there's a two-kilometer radio

dish built into a natural depression, a radio telescope or a communications dish, or both. Right next to that is a large complex surrounded by primitive fortifications. There are quarries inside the fortifications; something big was built there that isn't there now. There's a ring-shaped scar about half a kilometer in diameter with radiation residue consistent with fusion rocket exhaust."

"That fits our spinship, but it doesn't make any sense."

"Yeah. How does a civilization barely out of the Stone Age build a large radio dish overnight, and then follow up with an interstellar spacecraft?"

"Perhaps," said Gold, "a better question is, why?"

Gomez monitored the exchange between Stevens and Lense from a few meters away. She wondered if she would have to step in. They had worked round the clock for two days in the grueling conditions of the spinship, and tempers were short.

Fabian waved his arms. *"You want me to start spinning the ship back up? It took Pattie and me a day and a half to figure out how to steer and fire the thruster nozzles to spin the ship down!"*

"Well," Elizabeth replied, "I'm sure you learned a great deal. We may be able to apply it elsewhere, but I'd suggest you turn them back around now, and return the ship to its original spin. The artificial gravity is down to what, twelve standard gravities? We'll hardly notice the difference."

"That's not the point."

"That's exactly the point. These are high-gravity organisms, and they need that gravity to survive. It holds the layers of their bodies together. If I resuscitate them in anything less then ten g's, the pressure of their own circulatory system will blow them apart. Anything less than a full fourteen carries risk."

Fabian looked doubtful.

"Look," said Lense, "you've checked over every inch of this ship's structure. There are no airlocks, no docking hub, no pressure suits. The Strata knew if they left their ship in flight they'd die instantly. They didn't build parts they could never use."

Sighing and turning away, Fabian said, *"You heard her, Pattie. Let's get to work. Have Laura beam me across the ship to the engineering section."*

In a moment he disappeared in a blue shimmer of lights. Moving on the ship was so difficult, it was easier to beam point to point if you were traveling more than twenty meters or so.

Gomez shuffled over and examined the Strata body Lense and Soloman were working on. It was connected to a web of cables and wires that snaked off along the floor in both directions, and injection pumps marked with radiation warning symbols hung off the body at several points.

Lense saw her dismayed expression. *"Did I give the impression that this was going to be simple?"* She grinned slightly. *"Okay, so maybe I did. A little. It isn't simple. It's not like applying a defibrillator to a humanoid heart or administering CPR. We have to restart both the body systems and the brain at the same time. I can electrically stimulate most of the body systems, and injections of radioactive isotopes will act like adrenaline in a human patient. But the brain is Soloman's bailiwick."*

Soloman stood on a low work platform where he could reach a row of electrical connections along the Strata's body. *"The Strata brain isn't centralized. It occupies a stack of sixteen thin body layers. Because it's physically distributed, it depends on timing pulses to keep the various processing and memory elements in sync. We need external pulses to restart the brain. It's a very delicate operation. If the procedure fails, this will probably be why."*

"But if it doesn't work," said Gomez, "they're no worse off than they were before, right? We can try again?"

Soloman and Dr. Lense exchanged a glance that raised the hair at the back of Gomez's neck.

"What aren't you telling me?"

Lense looked grim. *"We decided our best odds are an all-or-nothing approach. That's why the bodies are all connected with these wires. We've wired them in parallel. We plan to revive all forty-one Strata at the same time."*

Gomez blinked in surprise. "Why didn't anyone run this by me first?"

Lense shrugged. *"We've been working fast, and you've had a lot on your plate. We haven't had time until now."* Lense hurried on, before Gomez could protest. *"I know it sounds risky, but the Strata evolved to link electrically. This is our master for the circuit,"* she gestured at the elephantine body they were working on. *"If we get one brain started, it will provide the external pulses for the other forty, through the amplified connections we've made. If we bring this big guy back, the rest will follow. But if we do them individually, while we'd have forty-one chances to get it right, we'd also have forty-one chances for something to go wrong."*

Gomez looked at the cables snaking from this body to the next one, ten meters away. "And if it goes wrong?"

"Once we start the process," said Soloman, *"we won't be able to stop. If things don't go as planned, the Strata's memories will be scrambled, even erased. We might be able to bring back their bodies, but their minds would be gone."*

Gomez sighed. The first things that came into her head was that Lense had recently assured a young boy that she could provide a cure for a vicious disease that was, in fact, beyond her means, and that Soloman's consistent refrain since his bond-mate 111 had died last year was that he was in many ways inferior as a single Bynar.

But she banished those thoughts. Lense was tops in her field, and Gomez herself was the first to tell Soloman he was being silly whenever he decried his own abilities. Besides which, Soloman himself hadn't been singing that refrain very much since their mission to Venus.

Trust your people.

On the other hand, the Strata didn't quite fit in anyone's field, engineering or medical. She could only hope for the best. "How long till you can do it?"

"Within the hour. As soon as Fabian and Pattie have the spinship back up to the proper rotation, we'll be good to go."

Corsi stepped out of the security office into the corridor, and jumped as she nearly ran head-on into Fabian. He impulsively leaned over and gave her a quick kiss. She frowned and took a step back, looking around to make sure none of her security people had seen them. "Could we have a little professionalism here? I'm on duty."

He grinned. His eyes looked red, and he needed a shave and a shower. "I thought you'd be glad to see me. I've hardly been off the spinship in days." He stretched, hopped, and to her surprise, put out his arms and did a little pirouette in the hallway. "You've got no idea how good it feels to be out of that suit and back in a real gravity field, where you can *move* like a normal human being."

"I am. I just wasn't expecting you, is all. Should I see if I can get someone to cover for me for a while?"

"No time. I've got to go consult with Captain Gold. That's why I'm back. The captain requested me, and Tev was more than happy to take my place for a while. He's been dying to get over there. The captain's taken a sudden interest in electromagnetic pulse weapons, in particular how to defend an unshielded, unhardened ship against them. Something about an ionized plasma shield. I'm going to have to recite from literature I haven't even *thought* about in years." He grinned. "It'll be fun. You should come."

"Pass. There must be *something* else I have to do."

Fabian started walking away backward, still talking. "Sure you won't come with me?"

"Sure," she said. "I think I'll go work out." She wiggled her shoulders. "I've been sitting for far too long."

Tev beamed into the spinship's control room, making a point-to-point transfer from the engineering section. "We are at seven-point-one RPM," he reported, "and you have fourteen standard gravities at deck level. You may proceed when ready."

A temporary Starfleet-issue console had been set up to control and monitor the revival process. It looked incongruous, tiny next to the massive Strata devices and the inert bodies of the Strata themselves. Lense and Soloman worked intently, as Gomez looked on.

Gomez turned to Tev. *"I thought you would stay in engineering."*

"I didn't want to miss this. Besides, if the doctor succeeds, the Strata should quickly be able to tend to their own ship."

"Well," said Lense, *"here goes nothing. I'm starting the primary timing pulses—now—with a low-level current to preheat the circulatory system."*

Lense and Soloman tapped at the console. A small screen displayed a flat, wire-frame grid. The image was labeled BRAIN ACTIVITY, but the grid wasn't very active. One corner pulsed several times a second, with the timing impulse.

Then there was the smallest change. A slow rolling wave crossed the grid from one side to the other, taking several seconds in the process.

"We're committed," said Lense. *"Bringing up nervous system base current two points. Soloman, let's go for phase two."*

Fabian sat in front of the captain's desk in the ready room where he'd been for nearly an hour. Once again, the old man had surprised him, asking a series of insightful and probing questions about EMP defense strategies. Engineering might not have been Gold's specialty, but he was a quick study. The man's grandfatherly demeanor made you forget the razor-sharp mind behind it.

Gold had found a reference in the Starfleet archives to a comet that had been vaporized by phaser fire and ionized to temporarily shield a space station against an EMP attack. It was a workable solution, except for the lack of a convenient comet.

"Begging your pardon, Captain, but I assume you don't want this information just out of curiosity. Where are you expecting an EMP attack to come from?"

"I'm still trying to figure that out. I'm certain there was an intentional EMP attack on the spinship. If it happened once, it could happen again. Our shields can't protect something as large as the spinship, so I'm looking for alternatives."

The intercom beeped, followed by Shabalala's voice. *"Captain, you've got an incoming call from Ambassador Goveia."*

Gold scowled. "He's probably figured out why the *Norman Scott* has been 'delayed' and plans to give me an earful."

Stevens rose, but Gold motioned him back into his seat. "This shouldn't take too long."

He turned to face his desktop viewer. "Pipe it in here, Shabalala."

But the man on the screen didn't look angry to Fabian. He look contrite, and just a little frantic. *"Captain, I just heard from the Second Prime. He didn't support the action. There was great debate among the Lokra. I knew there was division in the government, but I assure you I had no idea—"*

Gold stood, leaning forward on his desk. "Quickly," he said. "What happened?"

"The Breen communications relay. They're going to fire an electromagnetic pulse."

"When?"

"They were already turning the array. It may have fired by now."

Gold bolted through the bridge doors, with Fabian right on his heels. "Wong, full impulse!" He glanced at Fabian. "That array is six light-minutes away," Gold said as he made for his chair. "We've got something less than that to create and deploy a plasma shield between it and the spinship. Find me the best spot, and we'll figure the rest on the way."

Lense stared so intently at the brain activity monitor display, Gomez thought it might burst into flame from the power of her attention. Other than an occasional ripple and the artificial timing pulses, there was nothing.

The doctor ventured a sidelong glance through her faceplate at Gomez. *"What's the body temperature?"*

Gomez checked the readings. "Up twenty degrees from the last reading."

Lense grunted. *"Which is either approaching normal, or a deadly fever, depending on which, if either, of my estimates of normal body temperature for the Strata is correct."*

"That's strange," said Tev.

"Please, not strange," said Gomez. "Right now almost any 'strange' is bound to be bad."

"*I suspect so,*" said Tev, who was scanning upward with his tricorder. "*The da Vinci just left the ring at maximum impulse. No voice communications. I'm getting a low-speed data stream on the tricorder, probably all they could punch through the hull once they left position. It says,*" he made an unhappy snuffle, "*prepare for EMP. Going to intercept.*"

Gomez pounded her fist against the console. "The captain was right! We were so close. We're going to bring them back just so they can be killed again."

"*Well, good news, then,*" said Lense, her voice grim, "*this doesn't seem to be working anyway.*"

CHAPTER 7

The *da Vinci* jumped to warp as soon as Stevens provided the coordinates, then dropped back to impulse after a few seconds. The bridge crew responded without question, executing the orders with precision.

"Tell me we have phasers," Gold said to Shabalala. There had been no time to check. Without the phasers, the plan wouldn't work.

"Engineering says they should be ready, but there wasn't time for diagnostics or pressure testing. We could blow an EPS manifold or the coolant system."

"No choice," said Gold. "We'll try it. Red alert."

"Aye," said Shabalala. "Red alert."

The bridge went to emergency lighting, and the warning klaxon sounded.

"I've routed the deuterium tanks and life support reserves to the Bussard intakes," said Stevens. "I'm blowing them out the purge vents. Just guessing about the mix, but—" On the main viewer, clouds of gas jetted forward from the *da Vinci*'s warp nacelles. Turning to Shabalala, Stevens said, "Tony, set phasers for widest dispersal, maximum power, and fire when ready."

"Firing."

The phasers lanced out, not in a beam, but in a broad fan that blanketed the expanding cloud of gas and caused it to explode violently outward.

Stevens watched the screen. *Faster.*

Then the failure warnings appeared on the phaser systems.

Corsi had just stepped off the turbolift on deck three when the red alert sounded. She heard the main phasers fire. She halted in her tracks, a few steps from the small bay that held the exercise equipment.

She stared up into nothingness, as though she could see through the hull and identify the unexpected threat. "What the hell is going on?"

"*Warning,*" said the computer, "*phaser coolant leak. Manifold rupture imminent. Evacuate deck three immediately.*"

T'Mandra, Makk Vinx, and Andrew Angelopoulos were on duty, and she trusted them to handle the evac.

Then she realized that the phasers were still firing. *Why don't they cease fire? That manifold is going to blow.*

In theory, the safety systems should have already shut them down, which meant someone had overridden them. Only one person knew phasers well enough to do that during a live firing.

Fabian! He'd have a damned good reason, and she knew a way to help.

At the end of the corridor was a manual override panel for the coolant system. If she could vent the coolant into space, it would buy them a few more seconds of phaser fire before thermal shutdown. It might prevent the manifold rupture.

They'd be days getting the phasers back online, but Fabian had to know that already.

She opened an emergency panel and pulled a breathing hood over her head, then charged into the corrosive clouds of phaser coolant.

* * *

Stevens studied the sensor readings. "Cloud diameter seven kilometers and expanding. Gas ionization looks good, but I don't know if the density is high enough." He shook his head. "This is all guesswork. If the phasers will just hold out a little longer."

* * *

The coolant burned Corsi's ungloved hands and made the emergency vent handle slippery. She gritted her teeth, ignoring the pain, and yanked the handle with all her strength.

There was a shriek as gas began to vent into space. The flow of gas into the corridor stopped momentarily.

Metal groaned behind the panel. The entire assembly blew off the wall, and slammed Corsi against the far side of the corridor.

She lay on the deck, stunned. Her thoughts cleared, and she realized the manifold had ruptured. With the manual vent open, pressure rapidly equalized, then reversed.

Clouds of phaser coolant were sucked out through the damaged manifold into space. *Good.*

Her ears popped, and she realized the ship's atmosphere was being sucked out as well. She struggled to move, her legs rubbery and weak.

T'Mandra appeared, grabbed her by the arm, and dragged her down the corridor. The Vulcan woman wasn't wearing a hood, but most of the coolant had been swept away already, along with much of the air.

She helped all she could, kicking her way along. They passed a corridor brace. T'Mandra pressed a button on the wall panel. An emergency force field sealed the corridor.

Corsi rolled over and struggled to her knees.

She tugged off the hood and looked up at T'Mandra. "Thanks for the assist."

* * *

On the viewscreen, the cloud of gas flared for an instant.

Gold looked at Stevens. "Was that—?"

Stevens nodded. "The EMP. We reduced the intensity, but—" He studied the panel and shook his head. "The density wasn't high enough. We didn't stop it completely."

"Let's hope it was enough," said Gold. "It was all we could do."

Lense's gloved hands clenched into fists. Gomez could see the tension in her straining muscles and hear it in her rapid breathing. Clearly, she was losing hope. *"There's nothing else we can—"*

The work lights flickered and all the displays on the console went momentarily haywire. *"Damn,"* said Lense, *"it must be the pulse."*

Tev stepped up and tapped at the console. *"Our equipment is shielded. The biosensors need a moment to reset."* The brain monitor display had gone from a gentle wave to a brief dance of static, then back to flatline. *"There,"* said Tev, *"that should do it."*

The sensor relays clicked over, and the monitor came back to life. Not with noise or the simple beat of the timing pulses, but with a clearly ordered pattern of activity.

Soloman pressed a control and a series of lights on the panel went dark. *"I'm discontinuing the external timing pulses."*

"We've got a steady rhythm! Respiration has started! Body temperature is stabilizing!" Lense's voice shook with relief.

"Timing pulses are being passed to the other Strata," said Soloman. *"They're all coming back."*

They all jumped, as a leg on the nearest Strata kicked, the torso's thick limb hammering against the deck. It was just as well helium didn't transmit sound well, or they'd all be deaf.

The six lidless eyes were already open, but the light-colored patches above each eye began to glow brightly, casting beams around the room.

"Strata," said Gomez, "have built-in spotlights."

The other legs began to move. The sound was like a slow

motion rock slide as the Strata pulled its legs under its body and scrambled to its feet, its belly abruptly rising two meters off the deck.

The huge creature loomed over them for a moment, then began to spin in place. The motion yanked free all the cables and devices attached to its body.

It stopped, all six eyes suddenly intent, studying them.

They could hear more noise in the distance. The deck vibrated like an approaching stampede, which it might well be. The nearer Strata scuttled toward them and stopped just a few meters away.

"Elizabeth," said Gomez, her heart racing, "what was your plan for dealing with forty-one multiton, radioactive rock creatures when they woke up, possibly disoriented, possibly pissed off?"

"I was going to beam us out until they had a chance to calm down and we could try to communicate."

More Strata appeared from both directions, rumbling up until the four crewpeople were surrounded by a looming wall of rock creatures.

"What," said Gomez, "was your backup plan?"

CHAPTER 8

The damage control party, dressed in full protective clothing, stepped through the force fields to repair the leak. One—Corsi recognized the chief engineer, Lieutenant Nancy Conlon, through the faceplate of her protective suit—stopped to assist the injured.

Corsi's hands were red and raw, and though her uniform had provided some protection, her whole body itched. She had a lump on the back of her head, and every muscle in her body ached, but nothing critical was damaged.

Dantas Falcão, the medical technician, approached with a tricorder, and Corsi tried to wave her away. All she wanted right now was to get back to her quarters and scrub every square inch of her skin.

Thanks to T'Mandra, today wasn't the last day of her life. But it could have been. What regrets would she have had, in the few minutes she had left? And what should she do about it?

Fabian's quick kiss outside the security office lingered in her memory. It was something she would have to think about.

*   *   *

Gomez flinched as one of the Strata trotted past her at their usual breakneck speed. It took some getting used to, but the huge beings were amazingly coordinated, and completely aware of their surroundings. They never ran into each other, never bumped a wall or a console, and they hadn't trampled any Starfleet personnel.

Yet.

Tev glanced over from the Starfleet console that still stood incongruously in the middle of the spinship's control room. *"I can't believe what they've done in six hours. The ship is fully operational, they plotted a new course, learned my language, three human languages, and Bynar code. They are the most brilliant species I've ever encountered."*

Gomez shook her head in amazement, as much at Tev's admission that someone other than himself was brilliant, as at the Strata's accomplishments. "Millennia of art, poetry, music, forms we can't even begin to understand. But no technology until the Lokra machines arrived, and they were forced to invent it."

One of the Strata charged straight at Gomez, stopping just a meter or so short of her.

"I'm sorry," Gomez said. "I haven't learned to tell individual Strata apart yet."

"I am Shipmaster Silverstreak, Commander Gomez. Our ship is now on course to fly around the Lokra sun and back into space. We have come far, but all we want is to go home."

"We could assist you, get you there more quickly. The Federation has technology . . ."

"During our long voyage, we came to understand, through thought and meditation, the mathematics of warp drive. We believe we could construct our own. But it is not necessary. Our lives are long. We do not experience time as you do. The trip back to our world will take as long as it will take." He was silent for a moment, feet moving just slightly, in a way that made the floor vibrate. "We are concerned, however. What will we find there?"

"We will remove the Lokra mining machines. But I'm afraid

everything you left there is gone. Your towns and roads are destroyed, and we find no signs of other living Strata. I'm very sorry."

"They may be hidden deep underground," he said. "If not, we carry in our minds all that is needed to rebuild the Strata. We will gladly begin again. We need only our planet back."

"You seem very calm about it all, Shipmaster."

"I have talked with your Captain Gold. He was concerned we would be filled with an emotion you call anger. It is alien to us. He is concerned about a concept called revenge as well, but that too is alien to us. What is, is. The Strata will go on. It is our wish that the Lokra go on as well. They did not know what they were doing." He turned and shuffled away.

Tev stepped up next to Gomez. *"Perhaps they didn't know in the beginning,"* said Tev, *"but when they figured it out, they didn't correct the problem. And they tried to cover up their mistakes with murder. Twice. I would not be so forgiving."*

"The Strata are good people, Tev."

He frowned at her. *"And I'm not?"*

The conference room aboard the *da Vinci* was empty of everyone but Gold and Goveia. Gold had summoned the ambassador to the ship, where they could speak privately.

Goveia was doing everything but making eye contact with Captain Gold. "Thank you for inviting me here to discuss our situation." He sat on the edge of his chair, as though ready to flee at any moment.

Gold waited. It hadn't been an invitation, but he would let that pass. For now.

"I'm deeply sorry, Captain. I wanted so badly to prepare the Lokra for Federation membership, I instilled all my hopes for the future in them. It clouded my judgment. Now it seems it will be a very long time before we're ready to consider them, if ever."

There was no arrogance in Goveia's manner, and he appeared truly contrite. Gold nodded his understanding. "You only saw the good in them, Ambassador, and I'm sure there is good. Humans have a lot to atone for in our history, too. Slavery, genocide, war, conquest. It wasn't the mistakes in their past, it was their failure to admit their mistakes and try to correct them. Instead, they compounded the errors by trying to cover them up."

Goveia shook his head. "All for nothing. The Strata just came to talk, just wanted peace and their world back. Such a waste."

"Some good may yet come of this, " said Gold. "The Lokra may not be ready for Federation membership, but what about the Strata?"

Goveia made eye contact for the first time, and smiled sadly. "I have no doubt at this point that their application to join the Federation would be accepted. But from what you've told me, the greater question is, would they have us? The good news is, we'll have the chance to ask. The Diplomatic Corps has transferred me from Lokra, effective immediately, and assigned me to talk to the Strata. And nobody's scheduled to take my place here."

Gomez shuffled into her quarters, aching from days in an inertia suit, bone-tired. She wanted nothing more than to climb into her bunk and sleep for a week. *"You have one recorded message waiting,"* said the computer.

She groaned, made a right angle away from her bunk, and slumped into her desk chair. "Play message."

Wayne Omthon's face appeared on the viewer, but he didn't look happy. *"Look, Sonya, you don't have to answer this. I knew you'd be busy. Maybe that's why I called, knowing I could get away with a recording."* He smiled slightly. *"I'm a terrible coward about rejection."* He glanced down and paused for a moment, apparently searching for words. *"I just wanted to apologize. I've been coming across like some kind of space stalker, and I've put pressure on you. That was rude."* He looked back up, his pistachio-green face pale. *"You'll do things at your own pace, and I've got no right to have any expectations. But let me explain, and then I'll give this up and move on."*

"Humans have this thing when somebody they love passes away. It creates issues. People talk about 'getting over them,' about 'letting go.' A new partner may resent the former relationship, even be jealous, while the survivor feels guilt for seeking a new relationship. These are aspects of my human heritage I don't much care for. Green Orions have a philosophy I like better. They feel that true love, whether between friends or partners or life-mates—that's forever. It doesn't end because one partner dies. It doesn't end because another partner comes along. It's something to be respected and honored. And when a friend loves someone, and they die—to carry on those feelings, as lovers, or life-mates, or just as friends, is to honor their memory. You're my friend, Sonya. Kieran was my friend, too. I want you to know that my feelings are honest, and everything I've done was with the greatest respect for both of you, and what you will always share." He shrugged. *"That's all. I won't expect a reply, and I won't intrude again. But I hope that sometime, when you're ready, you'll give an old friend a call."*

She stared at the blank viewer for a while. Suddenly she wasn't sleepy anymore. Almost of their own volition, her fingers called up a subspace link.

Wayne's face appeared on the screen, genuinely surprised. She smiled. It wasn't often she had him at a disadvantage.

"Hey, green guy," she said. "We've been busy saving the galaxy, and I've got some sleep to catch up on. But I just wanted you to know." She smiled. "You, me, someplace in the galaxy, real soon."

CREATIVE COUPLINGS

Glenn Hauman & Aaron Rosenberg

ACKNOWLEDGMENTS

Special thanks to Rabbi David Honigsberg, for keeping the ceremony Kosher.

CHAPTER 1

"*W*arning. *Warp core failure imminent.*"

The four engineers in the room glanced up from their routine tasks, startled. For an instant, no one moved as they stared at the flashing lights atop each console. Then they leapt into action.

"Taking the warp core off-line," one of them shouted, fingers dancing across the keyboard.

"Venting antimatter," a second announced, activating a manual release lever and tugging it down.

"Running diagnostics on warp core," the third called out, not even glancing up from his screen.

"Pulling the plug," the fourth declared, tapping in a quick series of commands. When one of the others glanced at him, he grinned. "I mean, switching to backup power." The lights flickered for an instant, then stabilized. "And killing the alarm." The sirens and lights suddenly ended, restoring the previous quiet bustle.

"Not bad," a fifth voice announced. It seemed to emanate from the warp core itself, as if that item had somehow developed sentience. "Good response time, reasonable reactions, though the diagnostics shouldn't have been run until after the backup power took over. That way you can make sure a power spike won't skew your results."

"So we passed?" the third engineer asked, looking up at last.

The disembodied voice chuckled. "Passed? Hey kids, we're just getting started—consider this a warm-up. Computer, continue program."

The voice fell silent, and the four engineers glanced at one another.

"This could be tough," one of them said, leaning back in her chair.

"Sure," one of her colleagues said, "but isn't that the point?"

The others nodded, and they all returned to their work, chatting occasionally without pausing in their tasks.

"So, what do you think?"

Fabian Stevens glanced up from his padd, just in time to see one of the four engineers heading right toward him. He flinched involuntarily even as she unconsciously detoured around him. Grimacing at his own foolishness, he looked up at the man standing beside him. He hadn't met Alex Sparks before yesterday, but the man certainly seemed competent, friendly—and almost as humorless as a Vulcan. He also seemed committed to his students, something Fabian wished his own teachers had felt toward him, all those years ago.

"Too early to tell much, really," he replied finally. "The girl, what's her name?"

"That's Tanya, Tanya Sturtze."

"Right, Tanya. She was the first to react, and taking the core off-line was definitely the right move."

"Tanya's very focused," Alex agreed.

"The other three did fine, though," Fabian went on, continuing to type notes as he spoke. "The Vulcan—?"

"Santar."

"Santar, he saw that the core was already being handled and went for the next item, the antimatter. The other two, the tiny blond girl and the tall young man—"

"Zoe and Malcolm."

"—they took a second longer to react, but they still got the job done. Malcolm's a little flippant, but as long as he does the work and his superiors don't mind, it's no big deal." Fabian grinned. "I've been known to flip ants myself, from time to time." His companion didn't even crack a smile. *Tough room*, Fabian thought. He looked around again, watching the four students as they roamed engineering, or more accurately, the part of the holosuite that had been set aside as the engine room. They were oblivious to his and Alex's presence, of course, and would be for the duration of the exam; the holodeck had been told to keep them invisible unless they specifically wanted to appear, and would reroute people and objects around them to maintain that illusion.

What are the others up to right now? Fabe found himself wondering. He thought about the rest of the crew, Gomez and Pattie and Soloman up on the *da Vinci*, and envied them a little. This was a lot of fun, but the three of them were just kicking back and relaxing while the ship was in port.

Then he thought about what the captain was doing, and grinned. Anything was better than dealing with *that*.

CHAPTER 2

Captain Gold contemplated the phaser.

A marvelous invention, the handheld phaser. What sort of engineering wizardry could produce an item that could generate a nonthermal stunner that worked on almost any life-form with no major aftereffects *and* a thermal beam, useful for heating up rocks or cups of coffee when set on low and hot enough to cut through starship hulls on high *and* a deathray, leaving an unscorched corpse for relatives to weep over *and* a no-mess no-fuss hygieno-disintegrator, causing its victims to glow red and simply vanish, leaving behind no searing-hot clouds of remains, organic or otherwise?

He supposed that it had been created for occurrences just like this, when he had to efficiently deal with multiple annoyances in a variety of ways. His only question was whether he was going to be able to adjust settings fast enough before he was overcome.

First, there was the Klingon behind the wooden desk that sat at the center of the large room on the top floor of the Klingon embassy on Earth: Ambassador Lantar, charming as a shaved *targ*, and not all that dissimilar in appearance. He was not so much pushy as most Klingons were, but more oily, more solicitous. For some reason, this got under Gold's skin more. He was going on about the proper forms of protocol involved for a Klingon wedding, and how it was particularly crucial to follow all the parts of the ceremony, especially with such important people involved.

Gold was wondering how Lantar came to all his good press as a diplomat. He had come to the conclusion that all of his so-called confidence and firm hand in negotiations was actually pomposity; he simply expected to be heeded without question. How the Klingon Empire chose someone with an ego like a black hole to be ambassador to the Federation was beyond him. Gold desperately wanted to put the phaser on disintegrate for him, but he'd content himself with the scorchless corpse option, so there'd be a proper death ritual scream.

Standing to Lantar's left behind the desk was his son Khor. He was looking even more uncomfortable than usual for someone who was about to be married. He spent at least half of his time looking at his father, hoping to get some form of response out of him. Lantar studiously avoided looking at him, an act wholly in keeping with a diplomat trying to avoid any show of favoritism and completely wrong for a caring father. Gold thought that stunning him would be a mercy, but then he remembered that it was Khor's suggestion that a military wedding would satisfy the necessary honor involved, and that Captain Gold should perform it. He'd use the heat setting on him, make him suffer a bit.

Khor was spending much of the rest of his time trying to catch the eye of Esther Silver, his intended and Captain Gold's granddaughter, seated on the other side of Lantar's desk on Gold's right. Esther was having no part of Khor's ocular pleading. She was being the most argumentative with Lantar, compensating for her small stature with enough volume to be heard from orbit, astroacoustics be damned. She was insisting that she have a nice Jewish wedding. Moreover, that the wedding would be performed by Captain Gold's wife, Rabbi Rachel Gilman. Stun setting for her.

And then, seated to Gold's left, there was Rachel. Love of his life, fire of his loins, meaning of his very existence, quietly and firmly insisting that if she was going to be involved with the ceremony, the canons of Jewish law had to be followed to the letter. Stun setting for her. Maybe. Then he'd have to change settings to fight his way out of the Klingon embassy, and then the court-martial for attacking Federation allies, and then—

"Captain Gold, are we boring you?"

The direct address snapped him out of his reverie. "No, Ambassador. I'm sorry—I was thinking on a matter of weaponry that's been giving me *agita* for some time, and I suddenly had an inspiration on how to deal with the problem, but it probably won't work." Using the heat setting to cut a hole in the floor to escape wasn't going to work either, if Lantar had already noticed his attention wandering a bit.

"Captain, I must insist that you take this matter seriously! After all, you are being honored by Khor's request that you perform this ceremony, but you must perform the appropriate rituals to properly—"

"Just a moment, Lantar," Esther said. "I keep telling you that some of the elements of a traditional Klingon wedding conflict with Jewish law—"

Khor snorted at just the wrong time.

"And what are you sniffing at, you big lummox?" Esther fixed him with a stare that could shut down a warp core.

"How dare you speak to my son that way?"

"Father! I can—"

"Can what?" Lantar, Rachel, and Esther spoke almost simultaneously, and glared at one another even more viciously.

Oy, Gold thought. If they knocked heads any harder, the resulting implosion would suck all the air out of the room.

"The dignity of my House and the honor of the Klingon Empire must be maintained!" Lantar's skin was beginning to darken.

"I still don't see how having ice sculptures at the reception is a violation of your dignity," Rachel said.

Lantar glared at Rachel. "If you think such frivolity has a place in a wedding, then clearly you do not understand the Klingon heart."

"She understands the Klingon heart, Father. At least, she understands mine."

Esther, in turn, glared at her fiancé. "Khor, if you think that trying to sweet-talk me is going to get me to reduce the number of bridesmaids I'm bringing, it's not going to work."

No, I'm just not as fast as I used to be. He'd never be able to switch settings fast enough. He supposed he could try stunning them all, then disintegrate as needed.

He remembered that one could also set a hand phaser to overload, which would cause it to explode in about ten seconds, killing everybody within a few meters. He was concerned about leaving the *da Vinci* without a captain, then realized that Starfleet could do far worse than to leave the ship in the hands of Sonya Gomez, and was comforted.

CHAPTER 3

"Knock knock."

Sonya Gomez looked up from her book at the entryway to the mess hall and laughed. "You don't have to knock, Pattie. Door's open."

"I know," her Nasat teammate replied, "but you were lost in your book, and it was either that or throw something at you."

"Sorry." Sonya set the book down. "I've been meaning to read it since my mom gave it to me, last time we were back, and just never had the time. Figured I might as well start it now."

"Is it any good?"

"It is, actually. It's all about this group that meets for lunch once a week, and the silly things that happen to them. It's fluff but fun—just what I need."

"What you need is to get off this ship," Pattie corrected her, antennae twitching. "Even I'm starting to go a little nuts here, and I'm used to being trapped in a shell." She tapped her own exoskeleton as proof. "Beam down with me. We'll get some food, shop a bit, and just enjoy walking on solid ground again."

"Thanks for the invite, but I think I'll just stay here." Sonya frowned. "To be honest, what with Risa, Vemlar, and the Strata, I've been off-ship so much lately I've forgotten what the *da Vinci* looks like. I don't mind being onboard, especially with everyone else gone—tons of elbow room." She waved her arms around to demonstrate. "Besides, Soloman and I are going to take advantage of the downtime. He's got those new diagnostics he wants to run, and I've got a list of repairs the ship needs from the damage we took at Lokra."

Pattie peered at her. "Is that the real reason?"

Sonya laughed. "Remind me not to play poker with you. Okay, the real reason is—I feel like being lazy, holing up here, and ignoring the outside world for a bit."

Pattie's antennae waved in her equivalent of a laugh. "Now *that* I can appreciate. Okay, have fun." She walked back out of the mess hall, leaving Sonya alone with her book.

Sonya watched her go, feeling a little bad even though she knew Pattie hadn't taken it personally. That last answer had been the truth, though. She just didn't feel like going anywhere. She looked around, stretched her arms out, then tilted her chair back and swung her legs up so that both feet rested on the table. *Ah, much better.* She picked up the book again and flipped it to the page she'd been reading. *This is the life.*

CHAPTER 4

"Computer, display response times of students thus far."

Alex and Fabian both watched as a square pane materialized in front of them, numbers listed across its translucent surface. Fabian read the numbers, made sure they were copied to his padd, and sighed. These kids were sharp, no question, which meant that he'd have to revise the tests to make them a bit harder. And that meant more work on his part. *How did I get myself into this?* he wondered. *Ah, yes, that's right—it's all Kendra's fault.*

He remembered how, a week ago, Gold had announced that they were heading back to Earth.

"I have a family matter to handle," the captain had told them, "and I've arranged for the *da Vinci* to dock at Starfleet Headquarters. You'll all have the week off—I trust you'll all be sober again by the time we head back out?"

After the meeting, Fabian had called one of the only people he still knew on Earth, his old friend Kendra Dolby. He and Kendra had gone to the Rigel Polytechnic Institute—*"Go, Dominars!"*—together, and had stayed in touch ever since. She still looked the same when she answered his call, though her hair was a bit shorter than it had been last time, and was that a silver hair he saw along one temple?

"*Fabe!*" Kendra's dark eyes had lit up when she saw his face on her viewscreen. "*How are you?*"

"I'm good, how are you? And, more important, what are you going to be doing next week?"

"*Are you coming to visit? That's great!*" She grimaced. "*I'm not sure I'll be much company, though. Not at the rate things are going.*"

"Problems in R&D?" Kendra had landed a dream job with Starfleet's Research and Development unit. But right now she looked anything but thrilled.

"*Yeah, you could say that. I finished the* Hyperion."

"Ken, that's great!" She'd told him about it in previous conversations, of course. The *Hyperion* was meant to be a new class of Starfleet vessel—larger than a scoutship, smaller than a *Saber*- or *Defiant*-class ship, but with full warp capability and an impressive weapons system. The ship was meant to be both a fighter and a courier, and made for speed and maneuverability. Starfleet had actually wanted something like it for a while now, as the next step after the *Defiant,* but no one had been able to create something strong enough to travel dangerous areas alone but small enough to slip through security nets undetected. Kendra had been wrestling with it for over a year, and if Starfleet approved her design it would make her career. "So why don't you look happy about it?"

She shook her head. "*Because Felder'nar waited until yesterday to tell me that he hadn't submitted the testing request—'I couldn't in good conscience file the paperwork until I knew the schematics would be completed on time'—which means it goes to the back of the line. And since he filed the request for his own design a week ago, the wait's up to two years now.*"

"Wow. That bites."

She sighed. "*Tell me about it. I wouldn't mind so much if it wasn't such a blatant attempt to cut me out of the running— and if his* Rover *design wasn't such junk.*"

"Isn't there some other way to test the design?" Fabian

thought about it for a minute. "Wait, couldn't you input the schematics into a holodeck and test it out there?"

Kendra smiled. *"Still got it, Fabe—took you a minute to figure out what I needed two hours to stumble upon. Yes, a holodeck can do it, if it's got enough memory to handle that much complexity and run full diagnostics at the same time. The only place around here that fits the bill is—"*

"Starfleet Academy."

"Right. I talked to them about it, and they love the idea. Their holodecks can handle the load without a problem, and they want to use it as a final exam—take the top students of the current engineering class and have them test everything out, including simulated crises. Remember Crawford Pressman?"

"Old Crawfish?" They both laughed as they thought about the classmate they had teased so many times.

"Well, he's a senior instructor at the Academy now—I know, I know, but he loved the idea, and helped champion it to the board. So they've agreed to do it. And Starfleet likes the idea, because it lets us run a full test on the ship without draining any of our own resources. They've agreed to let a full-fledged holosuite test stand in for the normal testing procedure."

"Great, so what's the problem?"

She sighed. *"Politics, what else? The Academy insists that they be the ones to run the test—their students, their suite. Starfleet says it has to be one of us, since it's our ship design. And the only time the Academy can do it is next week, because it needs to be during their exam period, which is right when we've got our annual presentation to the budget oversight committee. I can't get out of that, which means I can't be there for the exam, and I don't trust anyone at the Academy or elsewhere in Starfleet to handle it without me."* Then she paused and looked at Fabian with that slow smile he'd learned to fear years ago. *"Wait, when did you say you were visiting?"*

"Next week. Why—? Wait a second!"

Kendra, damn her, pulled her winsome look on him, knowing full well that it was unfair. *"Please, Fabe? I trust you completely, you know that. And you'll understand the design better than anyone else could—hell, half of it came out of those late-night doughnut runs we used to make, when we'd blue-sky ship* designs. Plus you're Starfleet, so I'm sure they'd be fine with you stepping in—if R&D can't run an engineering simulation, S.C.E. would be the other logical choice. And you'd be doing me a huge favor. What do you say?"

He'd pretended to think it over, but actually he'd loved the idea. It was a chance for him to teach the next generation of Starfleet engineers, some of whom might even join S.C.E. someday. And it helped Kendra out. Plus it looked like fun.

Kendra had called him back the next day.

"*Starfleet loves it,*" she told him. "*They're thrilled with the idea of S.C.E. testing both the ship and the graduating class. And the Academy is happy about it, because they want to see if their kids can handle whatever the S.C.E. throws at them. The one catch is, they insist that one of their own faculty supervise and assist.*"

"Not Crawfish," Fabian said, but she was already shaking her head.

"*Fabe, would I do that to you? Actually, he didn't even ask for it—probably afraid to be in a room with you again. No, it's going to be one of their other instructors, an Alex Sparks. I've met him once or twice, and he seems pretty decent.*"

"Well, that's fine, then." Then Fabian had another thought. "Hey, do you need anyone else involved? Like a second S.C.E. officer?"

His old friend shrugged. "*If you want to bring in one of the others, I'm sure it'd be okay.*"

"Good, because I think it'll make things easier—he can stay onstage while Sparks and I work behind the scenes." They'd made the final arrangements, and Fabian had talked to Tev later that day. He'd known exactly which buttons to push, and the Tellarite had agreed immediately to assist in the exam. *Which is why,* Fabian thought, *I'm now babysitting a bunch of kids in a holodeck when I could be out partying. Kendra owes me for this.*

CHAPTER 5

"No self-respecting Klingon would allow such a thing! It would be a disgrace!" Lantar cried.

"So would looking like you've never even heard of a bath, much less taken one," Rachel shot back. Then she smiled at him—the smile Gold knew meant to stand well clear, and to hide any edged weapons. "You have heard of baths, haven't you?"

"Are you disputing the honor of my House?" Lantar thundered. His face was darkening with rage, which, unfortunately, Esther seemed to find funny. She was fighting a losing battle not to giggle.

Captain Gold quietly placed his thumb on his phaser and changed the settings.

"Stop laughing, human! If you were Klingon, I would teach you the meaning of respect!" Lantar raised his voice even more. It was almost pure melodrama, of course, but that didn't make it any quieter.

"Father, calm down," Khor said in an almost-hiss. "You are making a fool of yourself!"

Captain Gold, very calmly, pulled out his phaser. He aimed vaguely upward.

"I'd like to see you try and earn respect, you swaggering—"
"How dare—"
"Don't you—"
"Get your—"
BZZZZZZZOUNT!

The ceiling light exploded. Captain Gold lowered his phaser, idly thumbing the setting to stun. The room fell silent for just a moment, then the doors flew open and two Klingon guards burst into the room, disruptors drawn and pointed at the Gold family.

"Ambassador, is everything all right?"

"Not a problem," Captain Gold started, before Lantar could speak. "Looks like the overhead lighting suffered some kind of overload, and chose an—interesting time to let go. Wouldn't you say that, Lantar?"

The guards kept their phasers on the humans, and looked to Lantar. Lantar looked at Captain Gold, then up at the damaged light, and finally back at the guards with a big smile on his face. "Yes, I suspect things got a bit overheated in here. No serious harm done. Go back to your posts, and notify maintenance that I'll want this repaired before the end of the day."

The guards looked a bit disappointed that they didn't get to shoot anything, but quickly replied, "Yes, Ambassador," and left the room.

When the doors slid shut, Lantar turned to Gold. "I defer to your direct—if somewhat destructive—solution."

"I apologize for the damages caused. Please feel free to bill Starfleet."

"No need, Captain. We realize that occasionally negotiations can get heated." He spoke with such a tone in his voice that Gold thought Lantar should have become a used-hovercraft salesman.

Gold turned to address everybody else in the room. "Now then. We are going to handle this in a calm, orderly fashion. Esther, Khor, Lantar, and Rachel. I want each of you to go into separate rooms and write down the ten things you most want in this ceremony. Now. This minute. Without talking to one another."

"Wait a minute," Esther said. "What about—?"

Gold stared at his granddaughter, and she closed her mouth and made a little "hmph" noise. *Thank God*, he thought, *it worked. I'm going to have to remember this for the next time she comes over for the High Holy Days.*

"When you're done, I'll look your lists over and see what I can do about reconciling them."

"And what about your list?" asked Khor.

"I'm not making a list. Starfleet weddings have a lot of leeway, so I'm not really invested in any one method—which is why I'm playing mediator." Everyone looked thoughtful, but no one immediately spoke up, so Gold took that as assent and went on before anyone could find a reason to object. "Lantar, could I impose upon you for a few unoccupied rooms here in the embassy, so everyone can retire to neutral corners?"

"That could be arranged. In fact, why don't you stay here in my office? I'd like someplace quiet to gather my own thoughts, and someone should stay here while the repairs take place."

"That sounds quite reasonable."

"Then let me show the rest of your family to separate quarters. Khor, you can find your own way out. There is still enough Klingon in you to find your way to the mess hall, I hope. Ladies?" Lantar exited the room, trying to ooze charm all the way. Rachel and Esther followed him.

Khor walked over to the debris of the light fixture that had fallen to the floor. He bent over and picked up a piece of metal about the size of his fist, then stood up. And stayed there silently. After ten seconds, Gold was about to say something when Khor suddenly threw the remnant straight up into the hole, causing another small explosion. When Gold looked back at Khor, he was already storming out the door.

Maybe I can just pronounce them married and be done with this mishegoss, Gold thought. *No, to do that I'd have to get everybody back to the* da Vinci. *Property damage is one thing, kidnapping is quite another. Khor owes me for this. For that matter, so do Esther and Rachel.*

CHAPTER 6

Fabian's reverie was broken by a high-pitched siren somewhere nearby.

"That's the *Hyperion*'s warning klaxon," Sparks said. "Something's wrong with the ship."

"I certainly hope so," Fabian said. "After all the trouble I went through programming glitches into its systems, and crises for the holosuite, if nothing was wrong we'd have a problem." Still not the slightest smile from Sparks—maybe he was a robot? Fabian remembered a few professors who, based upon their lecturing style, would have qualified as such. "Well, let's go take a look."

They stepped out of the area they'd marked off as their office—a small space that did not appear on the *Hyperion* and contained only a pair of desks and a pair of chairs—and passed through a wall and into the simulated spaceship. Alarms were still blaring throughout the corridors, and the two men walked quickly down one hallway, searching for any hint of trouble. When they turned a corner, they found it.

"Whoa!" Fabian windmilled his arms, trying to regain his

balance, but it was Alex's hand on his shoulder that pulled him back from the brink. Literally, since he found himself staring down at an irregular hole in the floor, and into the deck below. *What the hell?*

Crouching down, he saw that the edges of the hole weren't burnt, nor had they been cut. Instead, the ceramic alloy sagged around the edges, in much the way that hot wax dripped around the sides of a candle.

"I don't understand," Alex said, running one hand along a wall and then inspecting the thin film that now coated his palm and fingers. "The walls are—melting?"

"Looks that way." Fabian rose to his feet again. "Come on, let's see what the kids make of all this."

Not surprisingly, they found the students clustered in engineering again, all except the one assigned to the bridge. The rest were stationed at the consoles around the room, or using padds they had plugged into ports along the walls.

"I'm reading a marked increase in ferric acids across the entire ship," one of them called out. He was short and slight, with a shock of brown hair over pinched features, and Sparks supplied the name "Ben Martin" when Fabian turned toward him.

"Shields are at one hundred percent," the tiny blond girl Fabian recognized as Zoe Wilson added from a console.

"Is it just me, or are these kids getting younger every year? She looks too young to be in the Academy," he said, and Alex nodded.

"That's because she's thirteen."

"Thirteen?"

"Yes—she's a prodigy."

"She'd have to be," Fabian muttered, turning back to watch them again.

"No spatial anomalies," someone else, Tanya, was commenting. "We're all alone out here, and the space around us reads as normal."

"Okay, so it's not coming from without—it must be from

within," a slender Bajoran woman mused out loud. "Anybody picking up anything strange?"

"You mean, besides the fact that the floors look like ice cream at a picnic?" Malcolm asked. "Nothing."

"Ferric acid would indicate corrosion," Santar said. "We are dealing with corrosive acids, and they are eating through the ship."

"But where did they start?" a stocky, olive-skinned man demanded. "It had to start somewhere, right?"

Sparks whispered, "Tomas delFuego," even though the students couldn't hear him.

"Sensors show the corrosion is consistent all around the outside," a tall, stocky young man said.

"That's Ian Gymis," Alex said.

"The next layer has its own level," Gymis continued, "and it's got less corrosion, but what it has is uniform throughout the level."

"So it began from the outside, and is working its way in," the Bajoran, Latha Meru, mused. "And it hit every side at once."

"But the shields should have—the shields!" Tanya turned back to her panel and rapidly typed several commands. "Got it! The shields are the problem! Something's altered their composition, so they're producing ferric acids. They're corroding the ship!"

"Killing the shields," Malcolm called out, and suited his action to the statement.

"Corrosion no longer spreading," Ben said a few seconds later.

"I've got emergency force fields around the bulkhead," Zoe said. "So we've still got hull integrity—for now."

"We've got to repair the damage," Tomas said, and looked around. "Any ideas?"

"Computer," Santar called out, "reverse gravity field throughout the ship." Several other students looked confused, but a few nodded. So did both Fabian and Alex. "The corroded material was essentially liquefied, and falling inward," he explained in the way that so many Vulcans did, assuming that everyone else was kindergarten age. "With the gravity reversed, any remaining liquid material should flow back out."

Tanya took the lead next. "Computer, purge all air in the rooms along the outer bulkhead, unless a room is occupied. Drop temperature in those same rooms to minus ten degrees."

"Purging, temperature approaching requested level," the computer reported an instant later. Tanya waited almost a full minute before telling it to pump fresh air into the rooms again.

"Nice," Sparks said, and Fabian nodded his agreement. Corrosion involved ferrous oxide, or rust, and its reaction to open air. Oxygen fed the reaction, just as it fed the flames of a fire. By removing the air from those rooms, Tanya had halted the process, making sure nothing else would melt. The cold also slowed chemical processes, and between that and the lack of air, the acid would have become inert. Now it was just a matter of repairing the damage that had already occurred.

"Cute," Tomas muttered, spinning in a circle. "Professor Sparks, Mr. Stevens, can you hear me? That was cute—making the shields corrosive."

"Oh yeah," Malcolm added, nodding. "The ship was eating itself, man. Get it? The ship was eating itself!"

"That was a nice idea," Sparks said as he and Fabian stepped back out into the hall. "I'm surprised they figured it out so quickly."

"So am I," Fabian said. "We're so used to thinking that shields are always our best defense, and this turned that notion on its ear. Their inexperience was actually an advantage this time—they haven't been conditioned to always trust their ship's shields, so they actually checked on the shields first, and really looked at the data on them." He glanced around. "There's one problem, though."

"What's that?"

Fabian frowned. "I didn't come up with that one, and I sure as hell didn't program it in." He eyed his companion. "What about you?"

But Alex held both hands up in surrender. "Don't look at me," he replied. "I'm here to make sure everything runs smoothly—you're the man with the tests. I've left you to come up with details on what we should do to them, and to the ship." He gestured behind him as they reached their office and sank into the two desk chairs.

Fabian leaned back, the back of his head brushing the wall. "Well, if I didn't program that one, and you didn't . . ."

"The students?" Alex asked, and Fabian nodded.

"It's got to be. Nobody else has such immediate access, besides us. And this sounds like a typical prank." He saw that Alex was frowning, and waved a hand at him. "Don't worry about it. Most engineers play pranks on each other or on the rest of the crew as a way to pass the time. And this one didn't really put anybody at risk. Sure, someone could have fallen through the floor into the rooms below, but that was the only real danger. The holosuite safeties would kick in anyhow."

"So what do we do now?"

Fabian shrugged. "Same thing we'd do if it had been one of ours, I guess. We log it in, and score everyone on how they handled it." He scratched his temple absently. "Actually, we can do that later. Maybe we should stop by and see the captain first, check in with him." His companion nodded, and together they set out for the bridge.

CHAPTER 7

"Cadet, what is our present speed?"

"Warp one-point-five, Captain."

"Very good. Continue at present speed and course."

"Aye, sir."

Tev leaned back in his chair, hands resting comfortably on the armrests, and cast a proprietary eye over the bridge. *His* bridge. The room had been designed to maximize its small space, and felt far larger than it was, despite the consoles arranged around it and the crew members stationed at each one. The floor was clean, the walls spotless, and the instrument panels practically sparkled. And his crew was obedient, well-mannered, and quiet. All was right with the world.

"Having fun?"

The voice belonged to Specialist Stevens, who materialized right next to the captain's chair. This wasn't a transporter beam, however—Stevens simply winked into existence. Standing slightly behind him and to one side was that instructor, Sparks, who was idly stroking his beard with one hand.

"Actually, yes," Tev admitted. "Leadership suits me, and I'm sure it comes as no surprise that I am very good at it."

His colleague grinned at him, and Tev reminded himself that, after all, Stevens was the one who had gotten him involved in this project. That had come as a bit of a surprise, actually. The two of them had settled their differences, based primarily on Stevens's inappropriate friendship with Tev's predecessor, and they now made a fairly good team—with Tev taking the lead, of course—but they were hardly friends. So he had been unprepared when Stevens had caught up with him outside the engine room on the *da Vinci*, thirty-four hours after Captain Gold's announcement of their impending leave.

"Tev, what are you going to do when we're on Earth?" Stevens had asked him. For a moment Tev had considered saying that it was none of the specialist's business, but his time on the *da Vinci* had taught him that such a reaction was unnecessary, and counterproductive. The question was most likely an innocent one, and answering it so tersely was an overreaction.

Instead, he told the truth. "I had planned to visit several former colleagues, and make sure I was current on the latest engineering techniques and discoveries."

"Well, how would you like to do something else instead?"

Tev sighed. "I just told you what I was planning to do. Since obviously I am the one who selected that activity, it must be exactly what I wanted to do."

"Ah, but that's because you haven't had a better offer." Stevens grinned. He leaned in more closely. "How would you like to captain a starship?"

That had piqued his interest. After all, Tev knew himself to be extremely capable, and fully intended to become a captain someday. But these things normally took time—years or even decades of proving oneself. Stevens was suggesting that he could help circumvent that delay.

"I'm listening," Tev had said, crossing his arms.

"Okay, there's this friend of mine, and she's designed this ship. . . ." Tev had listened, and then considered. It was not a real ship, of course. But it would seem like a real one, and that meant that being its captain would also seem real. If nothing else, it would give him some idea of what sitting in that captain's chair would feel like someday.

"What about crew?" he'd asked. "I will need a bridge crew."

"We'll rotate which student handles the operations console," Stevens had assured him. "The rest will be holograms, but they'll act like a real crew."

That had made Tev realize something else. "I assume, since these are merely holograms, that we can program the crew to be anyone we want?" Now he looked past his S.C.E. teammate's shoulder, watching as his detested third cousin Renn and his tiresome primary education provider, Strenya, handled the monotonous tasks of maintaining proper air mixtures throughout the ship and monitoring their immediate area for any signs of radio chatter or subspace communication. Oh yes, he was definitely enjoying this.

"The students are doing a fine job," Sparks commented from the side. "They've been responding quickly to each new situation, and handling it with maximum efficiency and minimal damage or personal risk."

"We do have a small glitch, though," Stevens said. "Looks like one of the students has hacked the holosuite and inserted a few pranks of his own." The specialist filled him in on the recent crisis.

"An excellent jest," Tev said after he had heard the details. "We were informed of the change in structural integrity, of course, but I have not yet received a proper status report from engineering. In fact—" he held up one hand, then stabbed a button on the chair's left arm. "Engineering, this is the captain."

"Engineering here," came the reply. Whoever was speaking was young, female, and, judging from the tone, irritable.

"I have not yet received a status report on the ship's recent difficulty. I will expect one within the hour."

The girl on the other end made a rude noise. *"Sir, all due respect but we're a bit busy here. We've got to reconstitute those hull portions that melted completely, and we still need to—"*

Tev cut her off. "Cadet, this is not a request. You will follow proper procedure, and submit a full report of the incident."

"Why should we?" A different voice—a male one—spoke. *"Professor Sparks and Mr. Stevens probably saw what happened. Just ask them."*

Tev repressed a growl. "Cadet, because you are new I will explain this to you this one time. I already know what happened. That is not the point. Starfleet continues to exist because it has rules and regulations, and because every Starfleet member follows those codes. One such stricture states that, when an incident occurs on a starship, those responsible for identifying and handling the matter file a full report with their commanding officer, who then enters it into the ship's log. This is part of your duty. If you are incapable of handling the report, you will never rise above the level of third technician, no matter how brilliant your deductions or how clever your repairs. And while you are taking part in this exercise, you will behave as a full Starfleet engineer aboard a true Starfleet vessel. Which means that you will have that incident report to me within the hour. Have I made myself clear?"

"*Very clear, sir,*" came a third voice, this one also female. "*We'll have that report to you within the hour, sir.*"

"Very good. Captain out." Tev turned back to Stevens and Sparks, noting that the specialist was trying to hide a smile. "Sometimes it is necessary to remind them of their place."

"Actually, you made a good point." Stevens looked as surprised as Tev felt at that admission. "They've got to learn that, no matter how smart they are, they still have to follow the rules. Even the dumb ones, like filing an incident report."

"Precisely." Tev leaned back in his chair again. Haranguing that cadet had been a great deal of fun, and he was debating the merit of making a surprise inspection of engineering at some point, and verbally dressing down the students for anything he found amiss. But perhaps later. Work came first.

"The ship itself is handling well," he informed Stevens. "All systems are performing at well above adequate levels. We have noticed a few small flaws in the shipboard systems, primarily in navigation and internal security, and I have already designed and applied corrective measures in those areas. But overall, the *Hyperion* is handling quite well. It is more maneuverable than any other vessel this size, and has more acceleration than most larger ships, plus its shielding has proven more than sufficient for the spatial anomalies we've encountered thus far. Of course, we have yet to test its weapons capabilities, but I have every confidence that it can hold its own against anything short of a full warship."

"Thanks for the update." Stevens looked genuinely grateful. Tev reminded himself that the ship designer was a friend of the human's. During this experiment, Stevens's primary responsibility was to supervise the students, to see how they handled themselves during each crisis. Tev was in charge of monitoring the ship and analyzing its design. That made far more sense than having one person handle both tasks simultaneously, of course, and it was why Stevens had asked him to participate in the first place. For his part, Tev had agreed because it gave him the chance to try his hand as captain, he got to be the first person to test a new class of ship, and he approved of the logic of having two S.C.E. members conducting the exercise.

The fact that it was so much fun was simply an added bonus.

T'nok watched from the operations console as the Tellarite S.C.E. officer conducted his one-sided conversation. Judging from his mannerisms, he was speaking with two others, which suggested that both Mr. Stevens and Professor Sparks were present on the bridge. Clearly, however, they had instructed the holosuite computer to maintain their cloak except in regard to their fellow supervisor, and so she could neither see nor hear them.

Not that it mattered. T'nok maintained her casual inspection of the console, assuring herself that the ship was rapidly returning to pristine order. As the student currently assigned to the bridge, her job was merely to monitor the instrumentation, and to alert the captain of any problems. She did not need to know what the other instructors were telling him. Of course, that did not mean she could not listen to his half of the conversation—indeed, on such a small bridge it was difficult not to overhear everything—or try to guess at what the others were saying in response. T'nok saw nothing wrong with such behavior—she was determined to do the best job possible on this examination, and that meant acquiring as much information as she could, from every available source. Just now, for example, "Captain" Tev's pause after stating that it was necessary to remind people of their place suggested that he might be considering additional opportunities to rebuke her and her fellow students for some perceived lack of discipline. Perhaps a surprise inspection. T'nok would simply make sure that her workspace was kept spotless, and that all of her notes and files were in proper order. She also saw no reason to inform the others of this possibility—let them discover it on their own.

Her musings were cut short by a strange fluctuation on one of the monitors. It vanished almost immediately, but she was sure she had seen it, and focused on tracking down the cause. Then the captain's combadge beeped, and T'nok listened intently, already sure that the incoming hail would somehow connect to that same reading.

"*Captain,*" Ian called over the comlink, distracting Alex from the conversation with Tev and Fabian, "*we've got a problem with the galley.*"

"What sort of problem, Cadet?" Tev said, and Alex had to admit that he looked every bit the starship captain—completely at ease in his command chair, and more than a little bit arrogant about it. The arrogance was replaced by confusion a second later, however, when Ian replied.

"*It—it's missing, sir.*"

"What?"

"*Yeah, we lost the cafeteria,*" Tomas chimed in. "*Guess we should have brought our own lunches, huh?*"

Tev was already glancing at T'nok, who shook her head. As always, Alex admired her calm—she was Vulcan through and through, with all of their usual logic and composure, tempered by personal ambition and a desire for knowledge that matched anything the other students could muster. She had apparently been listening to the calls, and had already guessed Tev's question.

"I'm not showing anything wrong with the galley, Captain," she said. "The ship's structure is unaltered. I did, however, detect a brief pulse of energy in that vicinity, just seconds before the first call."

As Tev gave T'nok instructions on rescanning the area, Fabian turned to Alex. "Come on, let's take a look at this wandering café."

Alex shook his head but followed Fabian off the bridge anyway. What was it with most engineers that they needed to handle every situation by joking about it? He'd never understood that attitude, even back in school. Which could have been the reason why he'd wound up as an instructor rather than serving on a starship himself—perhaps you were supposed to make jokes when things looked bad. He just didn't have that knack, though, and he generally didn't find such jokes amusing.

Still, Fabian wasn't a bad fellow, Alex mused as they took the lift down. He certainly knew his job, and he was doing a very good job of creating obstacles for the students. *He'd have made a fine instructor,* Alex thought. *And, with his casual attitude and his constant quips, the students would probably like him a good deal more than they do me. At least they'd feel more comfortable with him.*

The lift doors opened, and the two of them stepped out into the hall, almost running into Ian, Tomas, and Ben. Several more of the students were milling about in the hallway, and Alex was glad that the computer made them swerve around him automatically—otherwise he and Fabian would have had a tough time squeezing past. As it was, they navigated a path down to the point where the corridor turned right toward the galley or ran straight toward storage, and headed right—only to find themselves at the storeroom instead.

"That's strange," Fabian muttered, and turned back toward the galley. Alex mimicked him, and an instant later they both found themselves facing the storeroom again.

While Fabian studied the storeroom door in case it was somehow masking the galley entrance, Alex turned to his left, to glance down the corridor again. The students were still there, and were also acting strange. Even as he watched, he saw Latha Meru turn away from him, apparently retreating to the lift—but wind up facing him again anyway, as if she had done a full circle rather than a simple quarter-turn. And Ian, who had his back against the right side wall, turned his head to continue speaking to Meru, but wound up looking at the lift instead.

"No right turns," Alex whispered, and repeated himself when Fabian glanced up at him. "There are no right turns! That's why we can't get to the galley—it's a right turn down the corridor, and we can only turn left!"

Even he thought it sounded insane, but Fabian straightened up and considered it. Alex also told him what he'd seen the students do, and his companion finally nodded.

"Let's test it," he said. "I've got my back to the storage room now, right?" He grinned. "I mean, correct?" Alex nodded. "Okay, I'm going to turn to the right so that I'm facing it again." And then Fabian turned left, looking down the corridor toward the lift. "Hm. I told my body 'right' and it went 'left' instead. Interesting." He turned left again, and said, "Aha! And here's the galley! From this end of the corridor we need to turn left to get to it, so we can actually reach it."

Even as they watched, the students came to the same conclusion. They had been going around in circles near the middle of the corridor, but Meru finally walked down to their end, and by turning left several times, wound up facing the right-hand side, and the galley door. She called out to her classmates, and they all repeated her trick. But that told them why they hadn't been able to locate the galley—it didn't explain why they couldn't turn right.

"Clever," Fabian admitted to Alex as they watched the students struggle with it. "The ship's untouched, which is why T'nok's scans didn't show any problems. It's messing with the people directly instead." He tapped his combadge. "Computer, has anyone accessed the program today besides myself, Lieutenant Commander Tev, and Professor Sparks?"

"*Negative,*" the computer replied, and Fabian shrugged. But Alex had a question of his own.

"Computer, has anyone replicated hallucinogenic gas within the ship?" Again the reply was negative, but Fabian nodded.

"Nice. You're right—whoever did this could have done it by using the ship's own replicators, without ever touching the main program. And gas would certainly make us see things, though to make everyone have exactly the same problem might be too sophisticated. But what do I know—I'm an engineer, not an alchemist."

Alex didn't bother to respond to that. Instead he turned to see what his students were up to now.

"—nothing wrong with the ship itself," Santar was reporting, "so something is affecting our perceptions instead. Convincing us that we cannot turn to the right."

"Gas?" Ian asked, but Meru shook her head.

"Too specific for a gas," she pointed out, and Alex nodded. *Good girl.* But then, Meru had always been clever. Perhaps too clever—she never seemed to struggle with anything, or even to work too hard, and he suspected her classmates resented that.

"Well, what could make us all lose a direction?" Malcolm demanded.

"T'nok," Zoe called over her combadge, "can you turn to the right?"

"Excuse me?" T'nok replied. *"Are you requesting that the* Hyperion *make a course change?"*

"No, I'm asking you to turn to your right and tell me what you see."

"Very well." T'nok sounded confused by this request but apparently complied, because a moment later she stated, *"I am facing Captain Tev."*

The other students nodded—given the layout of the bridge, if T'nok was at the operations console the captain's chair would be on her right side.

"Okay, so it's not affecting the bridge," Tomas said. "T'nok, are you picking up anything strange on this level?"

"Negative," she replied, *"but I did notice a brief signal burst a moment before your first call to the captain. I am rescanning now, trying to pinpoint its origin."*

"Great, let us know when you do," Tomas told her. Alex noted that he had once again taken charge of the group—Tanya's frown showed that she had noticed it as well, but most of the others were willing to follow Tomas's lead. "So we're dealing with some kind of signal," he repeated to the others. "What signal could make us lose all sense of 'left'?"

"The brain stores such information as electrical impulses," Santar said. "Perhaps something is blocking that particular signal?"

"A scrambler!" Malcolm exclaimed. "It's frying our direction senses, so that every time we want to turn left we go right instead!"

"No way!" Ian said. "It would have to figure out what each person's brain signals were for 'right' and 'left,' and then swap them. Without studying us beforehand, it'd have no way to know those, and no system could handle maintaining that for all of us at once."

"Don't be an idiot," Tanya snapped at him, and Ian turned red. "If a device were scanning your brain when you went to turn right, all it'd have to do is isolate that signal. Then it could reverse it, and that would probably be 'left.' And once it had the signal for a particular person, it could just automatically replace it with the reversed signal each time."

Ian wasn't too happy at being shown up, Alex noticed, particularly by Tanya. But then, Ian often assumed he knew more than he really did, or could do less work than required, and got belligerent when he was proven wrong.

"T'nok," Meru called into her combadge, "have you isolated that location yet?"

"*Affirmative,*" their Vulcan classmate replied. "*It originated at the galley door.*"

Zoe, Meru, and Santar had started walking in that direction even before T'nok's reply came—obviously they had already figured it out, and had simply wanted confirmation from her. The others followed behind them. Fabian had been studying the door frame himself, and Alex knew from the look on his face that the S.C.E. technician had also guessed the device's location.

"I don't see anything," Zoe remarked as they all clustered around the door.

"Me either," Ben agreed, studying his tricorder, "but there's a small hologram field right above the center of the door."

Ian, who was the tallest, reached up and the others watched

as his hand seemed to pass through the wall. He grimaced and yanked his arm back, and a small metal box came with it, trailing several wires.

Tomas then turned in a circle—starting to his right. "That was it," he reported. "I'll bet one of those wires tapped into the ship's power, and when Ian pulled it loose he disconnected it."

"All I care about," Malcolm announced, "is that we can get into the galley without going the long way around. Let's eat!"

Alex waited until the students had all shuffled into the cafeteria, then turned to Fabian.

"So, was that one of yours?"

Fabian grimaced at him. "Nope. I wouldn't mess with their minds like that—this is a test of their engineering abilities, not their willpower or their senses. Another prank."

"Well, at least that one wasn't dangerous."

"We could have starved to death." Fabian grinned, and Alex stopped just short of rolling his eyes.

CHAPTER 8

Captain Gold was getting very, very hungry.

He couldn't help it. He'd been here for much longer than he had expected, and, try as he might, he just didn't like Klingon food. He wasn't a stickler for kosher meals, but he did prefer that his meat actually be dead before he ate it. And of course he couldn't exactly snub his hosts by calling out for a delivery of human food.

He tried very hard to ignore his rumbling stomach and the ruckus that was coming from the two repairmen fixing the overhead light, and endeavored to give all of his attention to the list Khor had given him. Khor looked at him with the expression of one eager to please, one who expected a pat on the back for a job well done.

And for the most part, it was a job well done.

"This list is exceedingly reasonable, Khor. Thank you."

"No, thank you, Captain. I appreciate all the work that you have done."

"Although, to be honest, the last item is just a bit over the top."

"It is a point I don't expect to compromise on, sir."

"Yes, but saying 'to be marrying a wonderful woman' just sounds like you're trying to butter up your grandfather-to-be."

Khor simply smiled.

"The diplomacy of my father is not a style I'm accustomed to, Captain. I'm trying to shift paradigms here, but I'm a few cents short."

Captain Gold looked at Khor with a bit of puzzlement on his face.

"Did I get the translation of that idiom wrong?"

"No, I don't think so. I think it was just a weak joke in the first place. Don't worry about it."

"I don't worry about anything," Khor said, just as something came down from the ceiling, making him jump a bit.

"We lost our grip on the overhead panel," one of the technicians said.

"No problem," Gold said.

"There is no need to inform the ambassador of our—clumsiness," the other technician said slowly.

"Absolutely not," Gold replied with a smile.

"No, why should he hear anything that conflicts with his view of the universe?" Khor muttered.

Gold paused. "Is there something you wish to add to the list, Khor? Something you aren't telling me about?"

"Not at all."

"Khor, we don't know each other really well yet. But I think I've gotten enough from the three or four times we've been together that I know when something is bothering you."

"I am merely irritated that I have to be going through all of this. I had made compromises, and I expected that it would be the end of the matter. But no." He stood up abruptly. "I am done with being diplomatic. You have my list of demands."

"Demands?"

Khor considered. "Requests, then. I expect them to be included. Now if you will pardon me, I have other preparations to attend to." Khor turned and left, nearly colliding with the technicians bringing in a new light fixture.

Gold exhaled. The hell of it was, there really wasn't anything here that seemed that unreasonable; in fact, Khor had probably been the most reasonable one so far. Esther had always wanted her dream wedding, and her visions never included being attacked by the ushers at the conclusion of it, like in a Klingon wedding. Khor had had the inspiration of having a military wedding performed by Esther's grandfather in the first place, which he thought would satisfy his father's side of the equation. There was a tacit agreement to the entire arrangement in principle weeks ago. So why was everybody yelling at each other now?

"Hello, dear one. Having a problem?" Rachel said as she entered.

Gold put his fingers to his temples. "I just finished talking with Khor."

"Yes, I know. I heard the door slam."

Gold looked up. "How do you hear an automatic sliding door slam?"

"I hear these things. It didn't go well?"

"As well as can be expected. He's irritated as hell, a condition that seems to be going around. There's an undercurrent of something going on here, but I don't know what—" Gold stopped, and sniffed the air. "What is that wonderful smell?"

"Guess." She presented a small plate covered with a cloth napkin over it, hiding the contents—but Gold knew that smell.

"You made *latkes*? For me?"

"Well, I was feeling a bit fidgety. And there's fresh applesauce too, with just the right amount of cinnamon." She placed the plate down in front of him, and pulled off the napkin with a flourish. "Ta-dah!" She produced some cutlery out of nowhere, and laid it next to the napkin.

"Glory be! A feast for the senses!" He reached for the fork and knife, mouth watering as if a bell had been rung, and began to cut off a mouthful of the nearest *latke*. "What did I ever do to deserve such a . . ." Captain Gold's voice trailed off. He eyed his blushing bride, the light of his life, who gazed at him with the sweet adoration that he had seen many times before. He placed the fork down and started to drum his fingers on the tabletop.

"What?" she asked. "What is it?"

"You're playing me."

"What do you mean?" She just looked more adorable. If he didn't know better, he'd swear she was manipulating the lighting in the room to make her look saintly.

"Don't try that little routine with me, Atalanta, it's not gonna work. This is a bribe." He picked up the fork and waved it at her for emphasis.

"What, this?" She had stiffened for a moment at the mention of that nickname, but covered it very smoothly. No one else would have noticed it. Of course, no one else would have used that nickname.

"Yes, this. You sure didn't make these here; you must have gone home to make these."

"So maybe I did. What would I be trying to bribe you for?"

"I don't know yet, but I have a suspicion. Why don't you tell me?"

"Well, it's just that Jessica—"

"Jessica. Naturally." Of course she would want a say in her daughter's wedding. He marveled how someone who could be such a pain in the posterior could also be at least fifty percent responsible for such a delightful granddaughter. *Must be excellent genetics showing through*, he thought, though he wondered from which of her parents Esther got the stubbornness chromosome.

He heard Rachel go on, despite his closed eyes and the beginning of his headache. "She's hurt that you're not considering her feelings."

"Rachel, what does she have to do with this?"

"She's Esther's mother! She should be involved with her daughter's wedding."

"Oh yes, silly me. I remember how much your mother was involved in ours."

"That's not fair."

"She can learn to deal with that in this case. Lord knows I certainly indulge her in just about everything else."

"Were you not strapped in during warp drive or something on your way back to Earth? Your body is here but your heart seems to be orbiting Bajor."

"This is a wedding between two people. She can't—"

"She can."

"Pardon me. I meant to say that she *shouldn't* have a say in this."

"Khor's father has a say."

"That's different."

"Well, that's nice, but Jessica doesn't see it that way."

"Khor's father is the Klingon ambassador, for crying out loud! His feelings have to be considered in this matter."

"Oh, really?"

"Yes. He is representing the Klingon side, just as you are representing the Jewish side. You want Jessica to have a say? Fine—then you don't get one."

"Then who do you think is going to perform the wedding?"

"I'm performing the wedding, not you—" As soon as the words were out of his mouth, he knew that he had said something very, very wrong. Rachel said nothing, and merely looked at him. It was a look that told him he was going to be sleeping on the *da Vinci* tonight, and yet a part of him was determined to press on, hoping to salvage something from this.

"Rachel, having Jessica involved in the planning of this thing adds yet another layer of complexity to something that's taking as long to resolve as the Sheliak peace treaty."

"Don't get pompous with me."

"I'm not pompous, I'm pedantic. There's a difference. Speaking of which, where's your list of items?"

"I don't have a list."

"No list." Gold quietly counted to ten in Yiddish, and then said, "I can't tell if you have an ace up your sleeve or if it's missing from your deck altogether. Why didn't you make up a list, dear?"

"Because all my items are nonnegotiable."

"Could you have done me the favor of writing them down, at least?"

"I'm willing to be incredibly flexible on most matters. My few points you should already know."

Gold probably did know them, or he thought he could make a few reasonable guesses. But if he didn't match precisely what she was thinking, she'd blame him for not being telepathic. "Honey, of course I know them. But I'm juggling the demands of multiple parties here, and I want to make sure I don't forget any of them in the commotion. And in addition, I'll want to make sure that I have them if anybody else would like to see them."

"All right. I'll write them up and send them to you."

He sighed quietly. He was *definitely* going to be sleeping on the *da Vinci* tonight.

"Yes. Because I'm convinced that in your rush to get back here to Earth, you left your heart orbiting Andor. Which is a shame for you."

"Oh? Why?"

Rachel stood up. "Samuel 13:14. 'But now thy kingdom shall not continue: the Lord hath sought him a man after his own heart, and the Lord hath commanded him to be captain over his people, because thou hast not kept that which the Lord commanded thee.'" She turned on her heel and headed out the door so quickly that he was amazed it slid open in time.

One of the technicians looked up from what he was doing—or rather looked down from the ladder. "She's magnificent." The other one was muttering something in Klingon that sounded like poetry, and they both laughed.

He hated it when she quoted Scripture. The devil wasn't the only one who could quote Scripture to suit his own purposes. Resignedly, he pulled the plate of *latkes* to him.

"Captain?"

Gold looked up from his plate. Lantar was standing in the doorway. Gold stood up. "Ambassador. I didn't hear the door chime."

"It was open."

"Probably isn't going to close right after being slammed."

"How can an auto—"

"Never mind." He pushed the plate of *latkes* aside. He knew that they'd be cold by the time he got back to them. "Please come in." Gold swore that he could hear the door sigh as it closed.

"How are the repairs going?" Lantar said to the technicians.

"We are done, Excellency. We merely have to pack up our—"

"Surely you can do that later, after I am done speaking with the captain?" The tone was smooth, but the undercurrent was unmistakably *"Here's your hat, what's your hurry? Don't let the door nip you on the way out."* The technicians picked up on it and left, not even stopping to grab their tools.

When the door had closed behind the exiting Klingons, Lantar spread his arms wide. "Captain, before we start, I would like to register my regrets at the acrimonious tone that these negotiations have taken."

"As would I. I'm hoping we can come to an amicable resolution."

"Indeed?"

"Yes."

"I will be pleased if we can do so. I am always happy to engage in a productive dialogue that will increase the understanding and warm friendship between our two cultures. I know you share the same concerns as all decent and hardworking Klingons. You want to achieve the best possible outcome, just like I do."

Ambassador, Gold thought, *your words could be used as a renewable energy source for dirigibles.*

"Lantar, level with me. How did you ever become an ambassador in the first place?"

The ambassador pursed his lips, then said, "Good manners." After a moment's pause, he added, "For a Klingon."

"What does that mean?"

"Good manners is the art of pretending one is not superior."

"Ah. And what about cases where you are not superior?"

"There is no such occurrence."

"Don't be so sure."

Lantar made no visible reaction. "Really?"

"Really."

"And why should I brook this new insult to me?"

"Because you've been trying to use indignation as a debating point, instead of actually having any substantive points you might have to concede." Gold expected an additional outburst or retort, but Lantar merely sat back in his chair, his face calm and impassive. Gold took the silence as a good sign and went on. "In this world, you have to be oh-so-smart or oh-so-pleasant. I've spent years being smart. I highly recommend pleasant."

"Indeed you do, Captain. Are you familiar with the concept of *QIp'ong*?"

"Can't say that I know it under that name."

"It would probably translate as 'stupid-cunning' or 'stupid-smart.' It refers to the concept of one who plays the fool but hides great subtlety and facility."

"Ah, I see." Gold thought for a moment. "There is an old Earth word that describes a similar sort of person—*dummschlau*, I believe. That is applied to someone who is not all that smart but possesses animal cunning. A very dangerous sort of person."

Then Lantar smiled—or rather, Gold hoped it was a smile, because otherwise Lantar was baring his teeth at him. "I'm glad to see that you are not without wit," Lantar said. "It shows me that you are amenable to reason."

"I'm always open to hearing what other cultures have to say. It's important to keep an open mind."

"Indeed, but not so open your brains fall out."

"Do you anticipate that being a problem, Ambassador?"

"It has already happened to people close to me in the past."

"I see." Gold steepled his fingers, then pointed forward. "Someone very close to you?"

"Unquestionably."

Gold picked up his padd. "You know, Khor was in here earlier. His list seems quite reasonable—there are enough points of congruence that we should be able to find common ground."

"Sadly, I doubt it, Captain. Khor has let the heat of his blood affect his reason. He is thinking with his heart, not his head. As such, my son has lost sight of the duties he must perform in his marriage ceremony. Therefore, it is my duty to remind him."

"Lantar, can Khor pick up a blade?"

"Of course he can."

"And he has gone through an Age of Ascension ritual?"

"Certainly."

"Got poked with painstiks? Traveled the River of Blood?"

"Captain, is there a point you are trying to make?"

"Is your son not a warrior, capable of making his own decisions?"

"It is not merely his decision."

"Granted. There's his *par'machkai* to consi—"

"Captain, you make me tired. You are playing an endgame with a king and no other pieces."

"All things considered, that's okay, Ambassador. I'm not looking to win—I'm looking to reach a draw among all parties. You don't need to bring your adversaries to their knees, just to their senses."

"There will be no compromise on the part of the empire, Captain."

"The empire? With all respect, what do they have to do with it?"

"The wedding will take place, and it will take place in accordance with Klingon customs. If it does not, we will take it as an insult to the Klingon Empire, and we will be forced to sever our ties with you."

Gold sat upright. "Ambassador, I believe you're taking this a bit too far."

"Make no mistake, Captain. I will not brook an insult to my House or my empire. Do not take advantage of my kindness, and never mistake it for weakness." He stood up abruptly. "Here is my list. Now I must go and remind my son of his obligations. I expect that you will accommodate all of my concerns, for I am sure you are cognizant of what will occur if you don't. Feel free to use my office for the remainder of the day." And with that he left.

Gold sat there, trying to resolve what had just been thrust in front of him. His position had become even more intractable since the earlier discussions, and he didn't think that was possible. The list included a full Klingon wedding, right down to the preliminary evaluations and tests of strength for the bride. No mention was to be made of the bride's religion—in fact, no human religious component at all. He wanted Rachel out entirely. And Gold himself would also have to undergo the full *Kal'hayh* rituals—including the trials of fasting, blood, pain, sacrifice, anguish, and death.

Perfect. Maybe he could get the death thing out of the way early.

The door chimed. Of course. "Come in, Esther. Abandon all hope, ye who enter here."

The technicians stood at the door, slightly puzzled. "May we retrieve our tools now?"

"Oh. Sure." Gold quietly considered how Starfleet would take the news that the Klingons were willing to break treaties over a wedding he was supposed to perform. Something less drastic than the punishment for visiting Talos IV, but not by much . . .

Esther poked her head inside the door. "Grandpa Gold?"

"There you are. I was hoping you'd eloped."

"Uhh, is this a bad time?"

"No, come in. This is as good a time as any."

"Oh, good. I came up with the list you wanted, but I wasn't able to keep it under ten items."

He rubbed the bridge of his nose. "How many?"

"Twenty-seven."

"*Twenty-seven?*"

"If I combine a few of them, I can probably get it down to eighteen or nineteen, depending on how you—"

Gold held up a hand. "Esther, I am having a very hard day here. People are bringing me grief upon grief. Your fiancé is frustrated, your grandmother is furious, and your father-in-law is ready to tear up treaties, and for all I know is willing to go to war over all this. My headache can probably be heard from orbit. And my food is getting cold."

"Wow." She paused. "I've heard of women that empires go to war over, but I never thought I'd be one. My shoulder blades are too bony."

"Look, Esther. You have always tried to be a delight to your old grandpa. Please, give me some good news. A bright side to all of this. Anything."

"Anything?"

"Yes, anything."

"Well . . ." Her voice trailed off. "You're going to be a great-grandfather again."

Captain Gold looked at Esther. She nodded.

"Esther, that wasn't quite the good news I had in mind."

CHAPTER 9

"All done on my end," Alex called from his desk. "They're locked out for good this time. What about yours?"

"Nearly there," Fabian said, typing into his console. "A few of the safety protocols were off—nothing major, probably just a holdover from a previous exercise in here. I'm resetting them now." He clicked off a few more of the protocols, then started the testing sequence to make sure they would be back at normal levels when switched back on. But both he and Alex glanced up when they heard what sounded like screaming.

"Something's wrong!" Alex was already out of his chair and racing back to the public part of the ship, and Fabian had to sprint to catch up. A minute later they were back on the *Hyperion*, where sirens were already blaring again.

"Tev, what's going on?" Fabian demanded over his comlink. Fortunately, his teammate showed his usual efficiency in responding.

"The lift is malfunctioning," was his reply. *"I believe Cadet Martin is still inside."*

"Crap." This time Fabian led the way, with Sparks right behind him. They barreled down the hall to the lift doors and ordered the computer to open them.

"*This turbolift is presently out of service,*" the computer replied in that calm voice that always made Fabian want to reprogram it with an ax. "*It has been quarantined, and is about to undergo emergency decontamination.*"

"Damn!" Fabian bashed his hand against the door, but of course that didn't help. "We've got to get that kid out of there!"

"What's wrong?" Alex asked, following Fabian as he turned back down the hallway, heading for the nearest access panel. "Decontamination?"

"Somebody's tricked the lift into thinking it's contaminated." Fabian removed the panel and crouched down to crawl inside. Fortunately, Kendra had clearly remembered one of their old gripes about early ship designs—"only a mouse could fit back behind those walls, and mice can't repair wiring!"—and the *Hyperion* was riddled with access ports and panels.

"So it'll shut down until cleaned?"

"Worse." The word came out as more of a grunt, but that couldn't be helped, since he was currently crawling around a corner and back toward the lift tube. "The lift cleans itself. It releases nitrogen into the compartment, to kill any bacteria, then uses microwaves to make sure nothing's left."

"They'll be killed!"

"That's the idea. Freeze or cook any potential dangers. Of course, there are about half a dozen blocks to keep the lift from doing that without express authorization and with a live body in the lift, but clearly someone's bypassed those." He did actually growl this time, as he stepped out into the wider space before the emergency lift access door and straightened up. "When I get my hands on whoever did this—"

"It's not a problem, Fabian," Alex said with that annoying calm, "and you're wasting your time. Computer, are safety protocols engaged?"

Fabian stopped in mid-crawl. *I'm an idiot,* he thought. *This is a holosuite. It'll keep everyone safe. And if that doesn't work, we'll just turn it off. No problem.*

Then the computer said the last thing Fabian wanted to hear. "*Safety protocols disengaged.*"

Quickly, Alex said, "Computer, reengage safety protocols, authorization Sparks alpha-three-bravo."

"*Access denied.*"

"This is very not good," Fabian muttered. "Computer, shut down *Hyperion* program."

"*Access denied.*"

He tapped his combadge. "Stevens to Tev."

"*This is—*"

"Shut down the holosuite, now."

"*Why should I—?*"

Fabian didn't have time for Tev's arrogance. "If you don't, Ben will die!"

That got Tev's attention. "*Computer, shut down Hyperion program.*"

"*Access denied.*"

"*I beg your pardon? Computer, don't you know who I am?*"

Now Fabian had even less time for Tev's arrogance. "We've got to shut this thing down the hard way. I need to get to the lift capsule and manually override the process," Fabian explained, tugging on the manual release lever. "Let's hope the computer will still talk to me about routine stuff. Computer, what is the lift capsule's present location, relative to my own?"

"*The lift capsule is twenty-point-four-five meters below and one-point-three-one meters ahead of your present location,*" the computer replied immediately, to Fabian's relief.

"Okay, it's below us," Alex said to Fabian. "Which is good."

"Quite a ways below," Fabian said. "At least one level down. And there's no time to climb down and then back around to the lift tube again. The problem is, I'm going to need to keep hold of the ladder, which means basically tapping the system one-handed."

"Why can't we use those?" Alex pointed, and Fabian almost laughed when he looked. *Kendra, you think of everything*, he thought, admiring the safety harnesses hanging just inside the door. The two of them quickly slid harnesses on and connected their safety lines to anchor points set in the wall. Then they pulled the door open and peered inside. Sure enough, the lift was visible below them. A good ways below them. Fabian made sure the tether was secure, since he no longer could depend on the holosuite's safety protocols to protect him, played out what he thought would be enough line, took a deep breath, and jumped.

"Oof!" Fabian hit the lift and remembered to bend his knees, for all the good that did. His legs were going to burn tomorrow. He'd guessed right with the line, though, and had just enough slack to move around comfortably. Almost immediately after he landed, he heard pounding from inside the lift.

"Somebody, help!" It was Ben.

"Hang on!" Fabe called back, then cursed as he realized the boy couldn't hear him. "Computer, deactivate cloaking on myself and Professor Sparks," he said instinctively.

"Cloaking deactivated," the computer replied.

"Will wonders never cease. Ben, can you hear me?"

"Yes! Help!"

"Hang on!" Fabian jumped a little when Alex landed on the roof behind him, then turned back to locating the release lever for the lift's access panel.

"What can I do?" Alex asked him, and Fabian gestured him back so that the instructor wasn't standing on the panel itself.

"Give me a hand here," he replied, wrestling with the lever. "Once we get this open, I'll drag him out and hand him to you, then try to shut down the sequence." But the lever wasn't budging.

"I think it's locked," Alex said, gesturing at the small red light at the lever's base.

"Damn!" It made sense, of course. With a possible contaminant inside, the lift had been locked down—including the emergency hatch. He should have realized that. "Okay, change of plans. You find the lift computer access port, which should be over there somewhere." He gestured toward the far corner. "Tap into it and shut down the process. I'll try to short out this circuit here, see if I can disconnect this lock and get the panel open. Whoever gets the door open first, wins."

They set to work, both trying to ignore Ben's pounding and shouting from inside. Fabian had the easier task in that the lever's locking mechanism was right at hand. But the lock was supposed to be foolproof—the idea was that the computer wouldn't lock down unless absolutely necessary, so if it did the lock should stay closed—and Kendra had done everything she could to make it that way. Severing its connection to the computer didn't work, because it had several backup switches that ran through the lift structure itself. Removing its power supply wasn't an option, because doing that would have required cutting out a section of the lift, and if he'd had that option he simply would have cut a hole and been done with it. For once, Fabian wished Kendra wasn't so damned thorough.

Alex kept him posted on his progress, which wasn't much better. He'd gotten into the access port, and was trying to reprogram the lift system, overriding its current initiative. But Kendra had set up the code to prevent unauthorized alteration, and she knew enough about illegal programming to cover most of the obvious entry points. *There's never a Bynar around when you need one,* Fabian thought dolefully.

Meanwhile, Ben was still hollering from inside, and the computer was counting down. *"Forty-five seconds to decontamination."*

Then something occurred to Fabian. "I'm an idiot," he muttered, "again." He settled back on his haunches for a second. There was no way he was going to break the locking code in time. And the lift walls were too strong and too thick for him to cut through. But what about the lock itself? The actual physical latching mechanism was only a few inches wide, and he could clearly see where it hooked into the door frame.

"Computer, give me a phaser," he demanded, and a phaser materialized in his hand. Again, Fabian cursed the luck that allowed him to do pretty much whatever he wanted inside the holosuite—except turn it off.

He set the phaser to a narrow, high-intensity beam, full disintegrate, and aimed at the lock. It took two seconds to cut through the tough material, but finally there was a clank as the lock flange fell to the roof, and a faint pop as the lock released its hold, reducing some of the pressure on the access panel.

"Got it!" Fabian shouted, setting down the phaser and yanking on the lever. "How's your end?"

"I've gotten past the first levels," Alex called back. "The computer's recognizing my authorization, finally. Now I've just got to track down the decon activation code, halt the process, and prevent it from resending. Give me a minute."

Fabian listened for a second, and heard the faint computerized voice counting down. *"Twenty seconds to decontamination."*

"We haven't got a minute," he called, and slammed the lever down. "I'm going in!" Hauling up on the panel, he pulled it aside, revealing the lift compartment below. There was Ben, his face pale and shiny with sweat, one hand raised as if about to bang on the wall again.

"Thank God!" the student said as he looked up at Fabian.

"Later," Fabian said. "Grab my hand!" But Ben was short and skinny, and couldn't jump high enough to reach him. After two tries, Fabian growled and lowered himself into the compartment.

"Okay, give me your foot," he told the terrified youth, and boosted him up toward the access panel. "Now grab the edge and haul yourself up." Ben did as he was told, though his arms shook so much he could barely lever himself out of the lift. "Good, now move aside." Fabian leaped up, and caught the edge of the opening with one hand. "Damn, I need to stop snacking," he muttered as he grabbed on with his other hand and started pulling himself up. Around him, he could hear the computer still.

"Now starting decontamination process."

Suddenly the lift compartment was filled with a hissing sound, and Fabian felt cold wash over him. Fear gave him added strength, and he swung one leg out of the lift, then the other, and collapsed, panting, on its roof.

"Damn, that was close," he muttered to himself, ignoring the boy who stood quaking nearby. Too close. In fact, he realized as he caught his breath, he couldn't feel his left leg.

"Got it!" Alex called out, and below them Fabian heard the hissing stop. A moment later the instructor appeared beside him. "Are you okay?"

"I'll live," Fabian admitted, sitting up, "but I think I've got some frostbite, and possibly some nerve damage in one leg." He glanced over at Ben. "You okay?"

The boy nodded. "Yeah, thanks. I wouldn't have been, though. What the hell happened?"

"I don't know," Fabian admitted, accepting Alex's hand and hauling himself to his feet. "But we're going to find out. This is way beyond a prank, and I'm sure as hell not laughing."

An hour later, however, the two of them were still stumped. They had helped Ben get back out of the lift tube, and then had returned to their office to look into the matter, switching back to "ghost mode" in order to step outside the *Hyperion* and across the holosuite. Alex had used the holosuite's emergency medkit to patch Fabian up, but it was only a quick fix—he was going to need to see a real doctor soon to avoid permanent damage to that leg. But for now he was more concerned with finding out who had done this, and how—and why they couldn't turn the holosuite off or reengage the safety protocols.

"It can't be one of the students," Alex insisted. "I'd locked them all out just before the lift malfunctioned. They've got no access to the system."

"Sure, but what if one of them had programmed it in advance?" Fabian said. "They modified the codes before the lockout, so it was already in place. They can't do anything else, maybe, but that one slipped past."

But Alex shook his head. "When I locked them out, I also ordered the computer to kill any pending processes they'd started." He half-grinned, the first sign of amusement Fabian had seen on him. "Trust me, I know how students think, and how to get around them."

"Okay, fair enough." Fabian absently massaged his left leg, which was still numb. "But if it didn't come from them, and we know it wasn't one of us, that only leaves one option."

They both nodded. If the reprogramming hadn't been done from inside, it could only have come from outside. Which meant that someone was actively trying to sabotage the exercise.

"Whoever it is, they've done a pretty good job so far."

"Much as I hate to admit it, we'd better bring Tev in on this. Let's head upstairs."

Together they walked back to the ship and up to the bridge, Fabian limping a little. They found Tev pacing in front of the captain's chair, while one of the students—the girl, Zoe—and the hologram crew looked on.

"Where are they?" Tev was saying as Fabian and Alex entered. "This is typical of Stevens."

"Computer," Fabian said, "remove cloaking for Captain Tev only, please." He waited, but got no response. "Computer, make me visible to Captain Tev, please." Still nothing. "Computer, acknowledge."

"Acknowledged," came the reply.

"Computer, deactivate cloaking on myself and Professor Sparks."

"Access denied."

"What?" That was Alex. "Computer, I am Professor Alex Sparks, deactivate my cloaking immediately."

"Access denied."

Alex looked at Fabian, who stared back at him. Then both of them looked at Tev, who was pacing mere feet from them but completely unaware of their presence.

"This time the joke's on us," Alex whispered, and Fabian couldn't help but agree. Obviously whoever had been pulling these pranks had decided to pull one on them. They were locked in ghost mode, and until they figured out how to get around that, they couldn't talk to anyone. They were stuck in here, while whoever had trapped them continued to play games that could get them all killed.

CHAPTER 10

"Typical."

Tev glanced again at the door, but it remained closed. Where was he? Not that Stevens would use the door, necessarily, but it provided a good focal point. Stevens should have reported in, to let Tev know what had happened. Especially since Martin had mentioned that Stevens had been injured.

"Computer," Tev called out, "Locate Specialist Stevens."

"*Access denied.*"

Damn and blast! Of course, he'd tried locating Stevens several times already, and that had been the response each time. For most requests, the computer still recognized his authority and complied, but when it came to shutting down the program, exiting the suite, or locating Stevens and Sparks, it refused. Tev dearly wished he had access to the holosuite's programming panels—then he would teach it to respect him properly. Unfortunately, revealing those was another thing it refused to do.

He glanced around the captain's quarters—his quarters—again. The *Hyperion* was not a large ship by any stretch, but the rooms were well arranged and certainly this was larger than his cabin on the *da Vinci*. It was actually larger than Captain Gold's rooms there—Tev knew this because he had memorized the measurements of every room on the ship before he had gone on board. It would be hard to give this up, once the exams were over.

Next to his bed was a small nightstand, a flask, and a book sitting atop it. Tev frowned. The flask was his, a present from his granduncle upon finishing first in his scholastic exit exams, but the book did not belong there. He walked over and picked it up. It was a handsome volume, leather-bound with gilt edges, and had a certain comforting heft to it. Then the title caught his eye:

The Plight of the Hyperion.

Intrigued, Tev flipped the book open to the first page and read:

> *Tev, it's Stevens. The computer's locked us out, and we're stuck in ghost mode. I tried sending you a direct message through the communicators, but it was blocked. Looks like someone's programmed the computer to cut us off from everyone else, in every way possible. Then I thought of this. The computer is still letting us alter things, as long as it doesn't lead to anyone stopping the program. So I created this book.*
>
> *Alex and I think tha*

The text ended abruptly there, and began again a page later with some drivel about a kidnapped spaceship and a band of blue-haired teen rescuers. Stevens clearly had not written that. Tev tossed the book onto his bed and began pacing. The computer was locking them in, as Stevens had called it, ghost mode? That would explain why he'd been unable to—

He lost his train of thought when something moved off to the side, at the edge of his peripheral vision. Turning, Tev found himself facing his bathroom mirror, and his own reflection—which was frantically gesturing to him. Approaching the mirror, Tev saw that his reflection was holding its hands oddly.

"What exactly are you doing to my image?" he demanded of

the mirror. "That posture is unbecoming of a Starfleet officer, much less a starship captain. I demand that you straighten up at once!"

The reflection started banging its head against the glass. Then it raised one hand and thumbed its nose at him.

"How dare you! If you were a real person, instead of my own reflection, I would have you brought up on charges of insubordination! You're worse than Stevens!"

At that, the reflection nodded. And Tev understood.

"Stevens? What do you mean, hijacking my reflection? Ah, wait—the computer caught on to your book idea, and so you switched over to here. Fine. Who is behind this?"

The reflection shrugged.

"No idea? Is it someone within the holosuite?"

The reflection nodded but then shrugged again.

"You think so, but are not certain?" Another nod. "Is Sparks with you?" Nod. "Is he injured?" A shake of the head. "Are you injured?" Nod. "Badly?" Nod and shake. "Moderately?" Nod. "Do you require medical attention?" Nod. "Is your life at risk?" Shrug. "I see."

Tev idly stroked his chin, but the reflection did not move. "I will monitor the students, and watch for any signs of complicity. Since the two of you are trapped in this intangible state, you'd best spend your time studying the matter. Perhaps you can deduce who is behind this. Communicate with me when you have any new information, via any method necessary."

The reflection nodded, then mimed writing something and shrugged again.

"The exams?" Nod. "Of course they should continue. The students are trapped here as well, and they should put that time to good use. Keeping them focused on their testing should help quell any panic. I will simply remind them that this is Starfleet, and thus anything could happen."

The reflection nodded again, and waved.

"Yes yes. Stop making me slouch and get back to work." His reflection shifted, straightening up and moving its hands to match his own. Stevens had gone.

Tev sighed. Leave it to Stevens to get locked out of a holographic program. With anyone else he would think it was bad luck, but Stevens had a way of finding difficulties. Or vice versa. He was almost as bad as Gomez herself. Of course, the S.C.E. commander was supposedly relaxing on board the *da Vinci* during this trip, but Tev had a suspicion that wasn't the case. If anyone could walk into trouble on a regular basis, it was his superior officer.

CHAPTER 11

Captain Gold had never felt like a bigger screwup in his life. He wondered if they'd ever find him if he moved to an island in the South Pacific, just him and a replicator.

He was sitting behind Lanter's desk. The décor was not conducive to calm, rational thinking. He thought that if Klingons had just used a few more windows and a few less torches and things with antlers on the walls, the galaxy might have known peace a century ago.

He sighed. Back to the task at hand. It was time for Gold to sit down and make a list of his own. He'd asked everyone else to make one; it seemed only fair. And Gold found it soothing to go through the list of problems in front of him. He found that by doing so, it allowed him the time to breathe and calm his mind.

He looked around the desk for a pen and paper—the pen was easy enough, but there didn't seem to be any paper, and he didn't want to rummage through Lantar's desk. He was reasonably sure that looking through the desk of the Klingon ambassador to the Federation was tantamount to spying, and could get him shot on sight.

He considered it for a second. Tempting. Instead, he flipped over the list from Khor and began to write on the back.

First, a list of what had happened to date.

He had come back to Earth to perform the wedding of his granddaughter, Esther.

Gold had expected the planning of the wedding to go incredibly smoothly—Lantar had insisted on being involved both as the father of the groom and as a representative of the Klingons but he was an experienced diplomat, Rachel was an exceedingly reasonable person who had conducted hundreds of weddings in her day, and Khor and Esther were two young people very much in love.

What went wrong?

He couldn't put his finger on the exact moment things had begun to turn sour; it was simply a bunch of people being stubborn. And strong-willed. And boneheaded to the point of ridiculousness.

Gevalt and *geshryin.*

Somewhere in here, there was a solution. That was, after all, what the S.C.E. did—found solutions to the insoluble problems. What was going to be required, though, was more diplomacy than had been in evidence so far. How was he going to get everything to work together smoothly?

Clearly, he was going to have to get one of them on his side and then try to build the coalition from there.

He looked at the list again. Who was going to be the person who was going to cause him the greatest amount of trouble if he didn't resolve things well? And who was he going to want on his side backing his play?

Only one person fit both criteria . . . and boy, he was not looking forward to the groveling.

Maybe he should open Lantar's desk after all and take the easy way out.

CHAPTER 12

Sonya Gomez paced the *da Vinci* bridge.

"Anything on the comm channels?" she demanded.

"No, sir," Shabalala replied. "Just routine dock chatter and standard requests. Nothing for us."

"Damn. Where's a nice catastrophe when you need one?" She ignored the tactical officer's puzzled glance and continued pacing. If only something turned up, no matter how small. Something for her to do.

Because, face facts, she was bored. Severely bored. Unbelievably bored.

All of the repairs from the damage they'd taken at Phantas 61 and in the Lokak system had been taken care of. The *da Vinci* was as good as new—better, actually. Soloman had finished his diagnostics, and had already corrected the few minor glitches he'd discovered in the ship's systems. He'd even started building a complete computer model of the ship, so that in future they would be able to examine possible alterations ahead of time, in holographic form. And she'd finished her book. There was another in that series—apparently about the same group having lunch at the same place over and over again—in the ship's library, but she didn't feel like downloading it. The first book had been cute, but she wasn't sure she could handle reading more of the same.

Maybe one of her crew would have a problem for her to handle. Of course, Pattie was still out shopping—no help necessary there. Abramowitz and Hawkins were off somewhere, Bart was spending some much-overdue time with Anthony, and Lense had simply vanished. She knew better than to interrupt Gold, and Fabian and Tev were doing that holosuite thing at the Academy. So what did that leave?

She sank down into the captain's chair. Not a thing.

Just then, the comm panel beeped. "Incoming voice signal," Shabalala said. "From Stevens."

"On audio," Sonya said quickly. Fabian probably just wanted to tell her how much fun they were having, and to share a joke at Tev's expense, but it was better than nothing. "Fabian, that you?"

"Commander, thank God!" His tone made her sit up straight. *"Are you busy?"*

"Not even a little," she said. "What's up?"

"We've got a situation down here. I hate to ask, but do you think you—?"

"Absolutely!" She leaped to her feet. "What do you need?"

Fabian gave her a quick rundown of the situation, and Sonya whistled. "Nasty."

"I'm actually surprised the computer let me contact you, but I guess it just doesn't want us talking to anyone else inside. It did block Sparks when he tried contacting his dean, but it must not consider the da Vinci *a direct threat."*

"And Tev and the students are trapped with you? Are they safe?"

"That'd be a big yes to the first question, and a resounding no to the second. The safety protocols are off, and it won't give us access to turn them back on. So all the threats are real now. Tev's warned the students, but that may not be enough. Especially since somebody else has added situations to my setup, and a lot of them are designed to cause maximum damage."

"Okay, first things first. You need someone to look at that leg, which means getting you out of there. Let's see if we can beam you up here—that'd be easiest." She tapped her combadge. "Gomez to Poynter. Lock on to Fabian down at the Academy holosuite and beam him directly to sickbay."

After a pause, Laura Poynter's voice sounded over the intercom. *"I can't get a lock on anyone in the holosuite, Commander. I just tried Tev as well, but something's blocking the beam."*

"Well, it was worth a try." She sighed and sat back down. "Okay, I can't get in and you can't get out. But I'll do what I can to help you from up here."

"Thanks, Commander," he replied. *"I get the feeling we're gonna need all the help we can get."*

CHAPTER 13

Gold walked down the hall of the embassy, stopping in front of the room his wife was supposed to be in. The door beeped. "Who is it?" he heard his wife call from inside.

"It's me."

"*nuqneH*," she said.

"It's me, David."

"I know who it is. *nuqneH*!"

Uh-oh. She was using the traditional Klingon greeting not because she didn't know who it was, but because she *did* know. And since the door wasn't opening, and since the literal translation of the phrase *nuqneH* was *What do you want?* Gold wasn't getting off to a good start.

"Honey, I would like to start off by saying I was a jerk."

"No, you really weren't." It was not said in a tone of reconciliation.

"No, I really was."

"No. Think bigger."

Gold winced. "I was a fool?"

"Wrong direction."

He sighed. "I was a *momzer*?"

The door opened, and Rachel was standing there. "*That's* the one. I'm glad that we agree."

"Fine. May I come in now?"

"Be my guest." She stood aside. He entered, and the door closed with a sigh. Like it knew.

"To be fair, you were trying to manipulate me, Atalanta."

"Stop calling me that. I just thought making *latke*s was a nice thing to do for you. I shouldn't have had to manipulate you."

"I beg your pardon?"

"You should have just gone along with me."

Sigh. "Dear one, you know that I love you. But you also know that I can't blindly ally myself with you in this case. Doing so wouldn't have solved anything—it would still be several sides attacking one another. Someone has to mediate, and I had no stake in this beyond a successful wedding for my granddaughter."

"Are you saying I was letting—"

"Yes. And you know it."

She was blessedly silent to that. Gold drummed his fingers for a moment. "Look, I'm going to assume that you and I are going to work together to get Esther married and to avoid sundering an alliance while we're at it. Am I wrong in this assumption?"

"No, you're not wrong."

"Fine. Now that that's settled, what do you think are the important things that need to be dealt with in the ceremony, and what has to be included?"

"Well, honestly, as long as they sign the *ketubah* and put everything in writing, and they exchange rings, I'm okay with whatever pomp and circumstance needs to be put in."

Gold blinked in surprise. "What about breaking the glass? Having a *chuppah*? Doing the blessings? These are important aspects of a Jewish wedding."

"Of course they're important. But it's like the conversation between Hillel and the Convert." Rachel leaned forward, getting into full professorial mode, which made Gold smile. This was a side of his wife he rarely got to see. She went on:

"The Convert asked to be taught the entire Torah while standing on one leg. Hillel told the Convert, 'What is hateful to you do not do to your friend. The rest of the Torah is an explanation of that concept. Go and study.' Similarly, the glass is a tribute, the *chuppah* is a reminder, and the blessings are a send-off. To make it a Jewish wedding, the bare essentials are the contract and the rings. Everything else is ceremony."

"That's all?"

"That's it. The Klingon gods are dead, they—"

"We've been having a huge fight over *this*?"

"No, we've been having a fight over you not knowing what I want and not knowing your own religious background. Will you get that through your head?"

Gold smirked. "I always had you to keep that stuff straight."

"If you're going to have someone else attend to your religious faith, perhaps you also should have someone else run your ship."

"That was low."

Rachel glared at him. "That's my point."

"All right. I'm sorry. But I wish you had just handed me the list, so that I didn't have to keep it in my skull. I had enough other things on my mind, and I am not a mind reader. Saying 'you should just know' doesn't cut it."

"I am not one of your subordinates on your ship. I am your wife."

"Wife, I refer you to Genesis, chapter 3, verse 16. 'Unto Eve the Lord said thy desire shall be to thy husband, and he shall rule over thee.'"

She shook her head. "Damn. You were almost paying attention."

"Almost?"

"In the same verse, the Lord also said unto the woman, 'I will greatly multiply thy sorrow.'"

"My dear," and here the captain got down on one knee and took her hand, "I apologize for any multiplication of sorrow on my behalf. It won't happen again. Atalanta shall always be my equal."

"You big *momzer*. Apology accepted, provisionally." She pulled him back up to standing. Gold was thankful for that—he really wasn't as young as he used to be. "As I was saying; the Klingon gods are dead, they happily admit it, so there's no conflict with the Commandments. If we have to do everything with a heavy Klingon flavor, then so be it—although I have had some thoughts on combining the two. I think there're enough spaces in the respective traditions that are complementary, without any contradictions as to how the relevant cosmologies play off each other."

"You've been waiting your entire academic career to do something like this, haven't you?"

For the first time since Gold walked in the door, Rachel smiled. "Is it that obvious?"

"Yes—and it also goes a bit to explaining."

"How so?"

"It was a perfectly lovely idea right up until you had to use it with actual Klingons."

"No, dear, it worked fine when I suggested it to actual Klingons. It's when I brought it up to *Lantar* that I started to have problems."

"Point conceded. Do you think we can get Lantar to go for it now?"

"I don't know."

"Shall we take it to him and try it out?"

"Are you planning on shooting any more poor, defenseless, innocent light fixtures?"

"No." Gold looked thoughtful. "And to sweeten the deal, I think I'll give him an additional platform where he can showcase Klingon grandeur."

"Really? What did you have in mind?"

"You'll see. And with any luck, it'll also solve a little problem that I hadn't quite gotten around to dealing with."

Her eyes narrowed. "What sort of problem, dear?"

"I'll tell you later, I promise. For now, let's go and find the ambassador. Oh, and while we're on the way, would you take a look at these lists and see if there's anything in here that gets in the way of what you have in mind?"

"Certainly." She took the lists from him, and expressed a low whistle. "Esther wants ice sculptures?"

"Oh, that's not the least of it. Keep reading."

Pause. "You know, suddenly I'm glad we're not trying to accommodate Jessica's wishes, too. I don't think there's a chapel big enough."

CHAPTER 14

Sparks shook his head. "It'll never work."

Fabian grinned at him. "You never know. And if it doesn't, I'll try something else." They both watched as a small horde of tiny black ants raced across the bridge and stopped just to the left of the command chair, immediately catching Tev's attention. Not to mention frightened looks from Latha Meru, who was currently on bridge duty. Apparently she had a problem with small insects.

"Computer," Fabian said, "have the ants disperse themselves to match these patterns," and he wrote several words on his padd. Hopefully, the computer would treat them as patterns instead of words, as instructed, and would allow it.

It worked, and the ants spelled out the following message: CHECKED ACTIVITY LOGS. EXAM CLEAN. NO OUTSIDE INTERFERENCE.

The letters dissolved quickly, but not before Tev had read them and nodded. "I concur," he said to the air in front of him. "I performed my own inspection, and found nothing to indicate inappropriate entry. There is no one interfering from outside this suite, which means the culprit is on the *Hyperion* itself."

Fabian rubbed absently at his left leg. It was still numb—he needed a real doctor, and soon, or the damage might become permanent. "Damn," he muttered to Sparks. "I was hoping he'd found something we hadn't."

Sparks nodded. "But how can it be an inside job? We locked the students out of the program, just before that problem with the lift. And we're not doing it. Could Tev be responsible?"

Fabian laughed. "You clearly don't know him. He'd never do anything inappropriate—oh, he'll make a cutting comment or two, but that's it, and he'd never let it interfere with his work. He wouldn't do this sort of thing."

Sparks sighed. "I didn't think so, but I had to ask. But what does that leave?"

Fabian shook his head. "I don't know. You're sure the computer shut down anything pending?"

"Absolutely. Anything the students had set into motion at that point, it removed."

Stevens shook his head. "Which means it had to start before then, and finish as well." Sparks looked confused. "Think about it. You told the computer to find anything that was in the works and shut that down. But if they'd programmed something in, and it had already done its damage, the computer wouldn't have noticed that—the program was no longer active."

Alex nodded. "Makes sense. But I didn't find anything in the system except your tests. If someone had added some mishaps of their own, I'd have seen them."

"Yeah, you're right." Fabian frowned. He'd seen enough of Alex's work these last two days to know that he was a good engineer, and a thorough one. He wouldn't have missed something like that.

Fabian sighed. "Well, we might as well go back to our office for now. At least there we can sit down. Maybe Commander Gomez will come up with something on her end." He hoped so. As he limped off the bridge, he realized that things were getting worse. The students had already dealt with two new problems this morning—a short circuit in one of the bridge consoles and a faulty replicator that added poisons to everything it created. Both situations could have had lethal results, but the students had handled them fine. The question was, how much longer could they keep this up?

Unfortunately, Gomez wasn't having much luck herself. Her first idea had been to contact Starfleet Academy and have them shut down the holosuite. But the suite had been designed to be self-sufficient—it had its own internal power supply, and while it was running no one without the proper codes could access its systems. And since Fabian had been given the codes before the exam had begun, she was betting the computer wouldn't let anyone shut it down, inside or out. So calling the Academy would only make a lot of people very nervous, which wouldn't solve anything.

Her next thought was to contact Fabian's friend Kendra Dolby. The *Hyperion* was her design, and this entire test had been her idea. Unfortunately, she and the rest of Starfleet R&D were making their annual presentation to the oversight committee. It had taken several hours before she'd been able to respond to Sonya's page.

"*Dolby here,*" the attractive blond on-screen announced. "*You're Commander Gomez?*"

"That's right," Sonya replied. "You can call me Sonya. I'm Fabian's CO."

"*Oh, call me Kendra.*" Kendra grinned. "*Fabe's CO, hm? I bet you've got some stories to tell.*"

"A few." Sonya grinned right back. "But Fabe's a good guy, and a great engineer. I'm happy to have him on the team."

"*Yeah, he's the best.*" Kendra frowned. "*But if this wasn't to trade Fabe stories, why did you call?*"

Sonya had been dreading this part. "Actually, it's about your *Hyperion* project; more specifically, the test at the Academy. There's been a problem." She told Kendra what had happened, and watched the other woman's face pale.

"*Is Fabe okay?*" was her first question, and Sonya was quick to reassure her.

"He's got some nerve damage in one leg, but otherwise he's fine."

"Nerve damage?"

"Don't worry, a doctor will fix it right up," Sonya said quickly. She didn't point out that they'd have to shut down the program before that could happen, but she could tell that Kendra had already figured that out for herself.

"And the rest? The students?"

"Everyone else is fine—so far. But that may not last."

"What can I do to help?"

"Can you get back to the Academy?" Kendra's grimace told her the answer even before the other woman replied.

"The committee's taking a short break for dinner, then we're doing the next portion of our presentation. I've got about ten minutes before I'm called back in. And the presentation's going to take at least another day, if not more. I'm sorry."

"Okay, we'll just have to do this by remote." Sonya tapped one hand on the arm of her chair. "First off, who's got access to the *Hyperion* program?"

"Only a few people, actually. I do, of course. So do Fabian, Professor Sparks, and Lieutenant Commander Tev—at least, they did. My boss, Felder'nar, has access, though he hasn't bothered to use it and he's stuck at the presentation same as I am. The review board has access, and so does the dean of the Academy. Actually, I think all of the engineering instructors were given access, in case Sparks couldn't make it and one of them had to fill in. That's everybody."

"Okay." Gomez tapped some more. "So far, the dangers have been directed at the students—Fabe got injured pulling one of them out of the turbolift. But why would anybody want to hurt a student? Particularly the top students in engineering?"

"A class grudge, maybe?" Kendra chuckled. *"Back in the day, there were at least three fellow classmates I'd have happily murdered."*

"Could be, I guess. I wasn't that bloodthirsty, myself, but I did hate a few of them. Maybe someone saw this as the perfect opportunity." She sighed. "Can you get me access to the students' files?"

Kendra frowned. *"Depends. The ones taking the test, sure—the Academy sent me their files, and I've got them here on my padd. I don't have any others, though."*

"That should be fine to start with," Sonya said. "If I were actually trying to off a class rival, I'd want to watch it happen. Send me the files, and take a look at them yourself. Between us, maybe we'll find something Fabian and Sparks can look into."

She signed off, then leaned back in her chair. It was pretty sad when she found herself hoping that one of Starfleet's brightest potential engineers was a homicidal fiend.

CHAPTER 15

Esther was sitting on a sofa in her assigned room in the Klingon embassy, going over her list for the eighth time, playing with a Klingon knife she had taken off the wall. Grandpa Gold was clearly upset at her inability to trim her list down, and she was determined to have another go at it.

But really, is that fair? I already cut it down from thirty-five, and now he wants more? Whose wedding is this, anyway?

Her lips pursed. Khor obviously was beginning to think it was his father's wedding. She would have been quite happy with something quick and quiet, like a bridal package on Risa, just to get it out of the way. But no. Khor kept going on and on about how it was important to his dad for political reasons, that this entire wedding should be a showcase for his friends and his ambitions. He didn't come right out and say that, of course—he said that it should be a ceremony worthy for one entering the House of Lantar—but she could tell what he Really Meant.

And what he Really Meant was to make her life as difficult as possible, and to prevent her from having any enjoyment of her own wedding. Instead, she was going to be the centerpiece of a giant ceremony that had nothing to do with her. The figurine on her wedding cake was going to be more involved than she was—no, wait, she wasn't even sure if Klingon ceremonies had wedding cakes. Well, the heck with that. She was going to get the kind of wedding that she always wanted. And nothing—not wind, water, or warp core breach—was going to get in the way of what she . . .

She shook her head. She wondered if she would be having such extreme mood swings if she was marrying a nice Jewish boy. She chalked it up as one of the great mysteries, since there was no way *that* was going to happen.

The door chimed. "Who is it?"

"It's me, Esther."

"Go away, Khor."

"No. Now open this door."

"Forget it." The door slid open anyway. Esther turned to see Khor standing in the doorway. Her surprise must have shown on her face.

"Come on, Esther. This is the Klingon embassy and my father is the ambassador. You think I can't enter any room in the compound at my whim?"

"Ooooh. Big man."

Khor exhaled and counted quietly to five. "Esther, would you care to tell me what's irritating you?"

"Are you sure we can talk freely? There's no bugs or anything in the room?"

"The room is free of any insects."

"Listening devices, you clod."

"There are none of those either."

"Oh, really? I'm not in here as a prisoner?"

"Esther, I don't know what you're talking about or what your grievances are—"

"Fine, let me go through the list. One: Your father is a stubborn idiot. Two: You inherited it from him."

"I—"

"I'm not done yet!" She moved closer to him. "Three: For reasons known only to God and Kahless, you still want your father's approval. Four—"

"*Enough!* I came here to tell you something."

Her eyes narrowed. "What, then? Out with it."

Khor began to walk around the room, as if he were hunting something. "I—am intoxicated by you, as by the finest wines and spirits. The memory of you sings in my blood."

Esther looked around. She considered the plate in front of her, but was looking for something easier to hold in her hand.

"As my pulse thunders, I come to you, guided by a flame that burns in my heart, a fire taken from the heart of a star." Esther reached for a flower vase.

"And as I reach for you . . ."

She picked up the vase and threw it at him.

CHAPTER 16

Fabian nodded. "Okay, got it. We'll check it out. Thanks." He started to tap his combadge, then paused. "Wow, I'm an idiot."

"No argument there," Sonya's voice replied. *"But what was it this time?"*

"I was about to go let Tev know what you just told me, by having one of the bridge viewscreens display an array of shooting stars whose trails formed letters."

"Clever."

"Maybe, if the computer would let me pull that whole 'letters as shapes' trick twice. But then it occurred to me—I was able to call you just fine, and vice versa."

"Sure. So? Oh."

"Right." Fabian rubbed at his leg. "If you can call me, you can probably call Tev, which saves me from having to orchestrate this whole elaborate light show just to create a terse sentence or two. But it took me this long to realize that. Hence, idiot."

"I'll call him now," Sonya told him. He heard her tell Shabalala to connect to Tev, but then lost the connection. Apparently the holosuite would let her talk to either of them, but not

at the same time because that would mean he could talk to Tev through the shared link. Smart program.

A minute later, Sonya called back. *"I told him, and he said he'll speak to her."*

"Great. Thanks, Commander. Alex and I'll tail Tev, and I'll let you know what happens." He signed off, and hopped off the desk, gesturing to Sparks where he sat nearby. "Come on, Alex. Time to go haunt some corridors."

Tev heard the door chime and automatically straightened, running one hand absently down his chest to make sure his shirtfront was perfectly smooth. "Enter," he called out, and the door slid open. The young woman stepped inside, and blinked uncertainly until she spotted him. Tev knew that many people felt interrogations were best performed under bright light, to make the suspect squirm and have problems focusing, but he preferred the opposite. With the lights in his rooms set low, the cadet would have a hard time seeing him, and that would make her uncomfortable and keep her off balance.

"You wanted to see me, Captain?" She stepped a little closer, but Tev gestured for her to stop where she was. No sense in letting her get close enough to focus her eyes again.

"That is correct, Cadet Sturtze. It has been brought to my attention that you may be responsible for the *Hyperion*'s recent difficulties, and for the dangers you and your classmates have faced."

"M-me?" The girl—Tev remembered that her first name was Tanya, though of course he would not use it—looked surprised, but she also looked scared. And a little guilty. One thing Tev loved about humans was that their faces were so easy to read.

"Yes, you. Did you not file a complaint one month ago, accusing your classmate Ian Gymis of stealing your thesis notion?"

"He did steal it," she snapped, anger overcoming fear for a moment. "He claimed it was just parallel development, but that's a load of crap! Ian's a damn freeloader, doing as little work as possible and stealing anything that isn't nailed down. He's been ripping off classmates for years. But this time he tried it with me."

Tev frowned at her. "These are serious accusations, Cadet. Yet the review board cleared Mr. Gymis of all charges."

She shook her head. "Sure they did. Ian's a slouch, but he's not completely stupid. He'd change just enough details to make it look like he could have come up with it on his own, and they bought it. He doesn't even understand half of what his so-called thesis says, but he stood there and told them it was really his and they went for it."

"You must have been livid when you discovered that he had also been chosen to participate in this exam."

"What, you mean because he's a slouch and a thief but conned his way into a test meant only for the best in the class?" Her lips peeled back in what, in a feline of any sort, would have been a definite snarl. "You're damn right I was mad."

"And so you rigged the exam, hoping he would be injured during these exercises." But Tanya was shaking her head.

"I'd love to see Ian fail, sure, but I wouldn't hurt anybody. Not even him."

"So you did not tamper with the program?" Tev watched her closely as he asked this, and could see the guilt. If she claimed that she had never touched the systems, she would be lying.

But Tanya apparently knew that she'd been caught, and her shoulders slumped. "Okay, yes, I tinkered a bit. But nothing drastic. I bumped up the risk factors a little, and told the computer to add random twists here and there. Ian doesn't think well on his feet—he only understands half of the stuff he's stolen from other students. So when there's a crisis and he has to have all of the knowledge on hand, he chokes. I wanted everyone to see that. And I did set up one prank."

"Which was?"

She actually grinned up at him. "The synaptic scrambler. I knew Ian wouldn't have a clue what to do about it, and I wanted to see him walking in circles and bumping into walls." Then she sobered. "But that was the only thing I added. Honest."

Tev grimaced at her, and leaned forward—it was an old trick to make him look bigger and more threatening, and it apparently worked, because Tanya curled in on herself and took a hasty step back. Then he straightened and nodded.

"Very well. Professor Sparks will deal with your interference after the test has ended. Now return to your duties."

"Yes, sir." She turned and walked away, and back out the door. Tev waited until she had gone before speaking to the apparently empty room.

"She was telling the truth," he informed the air. "She is not the one responsible."

The lamp near the couch blinked on once. Then it flickered, and a thick stream of smoke rose from it. The smoke had twists of dark gray among the light, and the dark twists slowly formed words:

WILL CALL GOMEZ. KEEP LOOKING. THIRD PARTY?

Tev nodded. "Clearly, if not the students it *must* be a third party. But no one from outside the suite has had access since we started the exam. It is a conundrum. Now go away—I wish to sleep, and I have no desire to share my room with a pair of invisible observers."

The smoke puffed once and then faded, and Tev washed up. They were no closer to finding out who was behind the recent problems, or figuring out how to get everyone back out safely. Still, he had used his temporary rank and position to bully a cadet, so the day hadn't been a total loss.

"Thanks for the update, Fabian. Hang in there—we'll figure it out."

Sonya signed off, shaking her head. The girl, Tanya, was clean—well, not guilty of rigging the recent death traps or locking Fabian out, anyway. And none of the other students had anything else on file that would give them reason to hurt one of their classmates. But if they weren't behind all this, who was?

One of her first suspects had been the only nonstudent non-S.C.E. inside the suite: Professor Sparks. But Fabian had assured her that he had nothing to do with it, and he'd been working closely with the man for the past two days, so she believed him. Which meant yet another dead end. Besides, why would a Starfleet instructor want to hurt his students?

She paced as much as she could within the narrow confines of her room, tossing the question back and forth. Why would anyone want to hurt a student? Then she stopped midstride. What if nobody had?

What if hurting the students hadn't been the goal at all? She'd assumed it was, because the threats seemed to be targeting them, but the only other people inside were Fabian, Tev, and Sparks. The students outnumbered them, so by statistics alone they'd be the victims more often. What if that was a mere coincidence? Perhaps whoever had set all this up hadn't wanted to seriously hurt anyone—so far the only real injury was Fabian's, and there was no way anyone could have planned that one.

Then she took it one step further. What if the point wasn't injury at all? What if that was merely a bonus—or an unexpected side effect?

The door chime interrupted her musings.

"Come."

The door opened, and Soloman stood there. "Commander, I have finished the security upgrades to the *da Vinci*. Would you like a detailed list of the changes I have made?"

"Yes, please." Then, when he opened his mouth, she hastily added, "Write it up and send it over, okay? That way I can add it to the ship's maintenance records."

Soloman nodded, though she thought he looked a little disappointed. "Of course. If I may say so, I'm quite pleased with the changes. In particular, I was able to tighten our access protocols."

"Oh?"

"Yes, during the diagnostics I discovered that anyone with a sufficient Starfleet clearance could gain access to our entire system. While I realize this is a Starfleet vessel, the likelihood of anyone needing to effect repairs without at least one of us present is extremely low. So I installed a subroutine, preventing Starfleet personnel from gaining access to the higher functions without at least one member of the crew tapped in as well. And then I set up safeguards to prevent anyone from entering the lower-priority system branches and then sneaking through into the more restricted sections."

Sonya managed to fight back the smile when she saw how serious he was, and how proud. "Do you really think," she said finally, "that Starfleet officials are going to try tapping into our systems and modifying our ship's programming without our permission or assistance?"

Soloman shrugged. "I would not expect it, no. But I have seen many strange things in my life, and irrational behavior is one of the most common. It seemed better to eliminate the chance, especially since, if someone had gained such access, it would have been easy for them to then alter the code so that they could regain that access at any time, no matter what new security measures we added."

"Right." Sonya nodded. "A back door. Thanks, Soloman."

He nodded and turned back toward the door. "I will have the report within the hour. I have also completed most of my work on that holographic model, and should be done with that shortly as well." But she was no longer listening.

"Could someone have been aiming for one of you?"

Fabian glanced at Sparks. They were back in their office again, and Commander Gomez had just contacted them. Kendra was already connected to her—the presentation was done for the night, though she did have to go over tomorrow's with her colleagues in a few minutes. Fabian had finally convinced his old friend that he'd live and that he didn't hate her forever, at which point Gomez had asked the question that had prompted her call.

"Aiming in what way?" he asked her. "I got hurt getting one of the students out of the turbolift—nobody attacked me directly, and he was in more danger than I was."

"Yet you're the one who got hurt," she replied. *"That's not what I meant, though. It's not physical. Forget about the specifics of each problem, and pretend that the students aren't*

behind it, but they aren't the targets either. Could anyone want one of you to fail?"

"I don't see why," Sparks commented. "What would anyone gain from this test's failure?"

"*Well—*" Kendra sounded a little guilty, almost. "*I suppose some of my coworkers might gain a little. I mean, if the* Hyperion *fails, that's one less design for Starfleet to consider, which improves the chances for the competing designs. The only problem is, nobody else has a pet project for this slot. Oh, we've got a few other designs in the works, but none as far along and none more than a few tweaks on existing ship patterns. Even Felder'nar's not that hooked on his own design—he entered it, but I doubt he seriously expects it to be approved. I actually think he only did it so that he could show he was working on viable projects instead of goofing off and watching those horrible docudramas all day. So taking mine out of the running might not help anybody.*"

"Anyone at work have any personal grudges against you?" Fabian asked.

"*No, I get along pretty well with my coworkers.*"

He believed it—she'd always been good at that, even back in school. Most of their classmates had envied her ability, but no one had hated her for it, and everyone she'd worked with on a group project had been thrilled to have her on the team.

"*Okay. Professor Sparks? What about you?*"

"Call me Alex, please." He waved one hand as if brushing away the formality. "I don't really have any enemies, I'm afraid. I get along well with the other instructors, and with the dean."

"*Do you have tenure?*"

"Yes, I got it several years ago. I'm still one of the junior faculty members, though. Most of my peers have seniority on me."

"*Okay, so no professional reasons for anyone to go after you. Personal ones?*"

He frowned. "No, as I said, I get along fine with the other instructors."

"*Fabian, what about you?*"

He shrugged, even though Gomez couldn't see it. "I don't see how. I haven't been back here since our last trip home, and

I was only on Earth for a few days. And before that it was the previous downtime, and the same before that—I've spent maybe a month here in the past three years. Who'd even know me to hate me?"

"*You're sure there isn't anyone? It could be work-related or a private matter. An old grudge, perhaps?*"

Fabian started to shake his head, then stopped. "Wait a second."

Alex leaned forward, and Fabian could almost hear the other two doing the same. "What? Did you remember something?"

He nodded slowly. "Yeah. I do still know one other person here, and he's not too fond of me."

"*Crawfish,*" Kendra replied, and they both laughed. It was still funny, even now.

Of course, Gomez and Alex had no idea what they were talking about.

"Crawford Pressman," Fabian explained after he'd calmed down. "He and Kendra and I all went to Rigel for engineering."

"You called him 'crawfish,'" Alex said.

"Yeah, well, that was his nickname." Fabian chuckled a bit, thinking back. So did Kendra. "He was long and disjointed and a bit sticky. Plus his whole face turns bright red any time he lies or fails. Or gets annoyed. Or seriously embarrassed. Ken and I used to torment him constantly."

"*He was an easy target,*" Kendra said. "*And now he's one of the senior instructors here. He helped me get this whole test set up.*"

"Which meant he had access the entire time."

"*Sure, but so did the rest of the instructors. Maybe one of them did it.*"

"Well, let's check." Alex pulled up the suite's activity logs—the computer was allowing them passive access to the programming levels, so they could look, they just couldn't touch. "Aha."

"What aha?" Fabian limped over to peer over his shoulder.

"Right there." Alex pointed at a spot in the records, and Fabian nodded.

"Crawfish accessed the program, all right," he told Gomez and Kendra. "About an hour before the exam started. And it looks like he added some new code. We can't tell what, though."

"*That bastard!*" Kendra snapped. "*Sure, we picked on him, but that was harmless, and it was years ago! And now he's trying to kill you, and everyone else in there, because we made fun of him? I'll bite his head off, just like a real crawfish!*"

Fortunately, Gomez was able to stay calm. "*Let's talk to him before we start plotting revenge. For all we know, he added some safety measures, or a test of his own, or simply a monitoring program so he could see how the students were doing.*"

"The commander's right," Fabian said. "Crawfish was a pathetic little twerp, but I don't remember him getting nasty. We'll—" he paused as the *Hyperion*'s alarms sounded. "Whoops, got another crisis here. Alex and I'll check it out. You two go ahead and check in with Crawfish. Just ask him what code he inserted, and see what he says. Don't bite his head off just yet." He signed off and headed out of the office, but not before he heard Kendra muttering something about hot sauce.

CHAPTER 17

"Ambassador, this is unprecedented," Gold said.

Lantar merely sat at his desk, facing Gold and his wife, his fingers interlaced together at the first knuckle, and saying nothing—as he had for most of the conversation. Behind him, the same workmen who had repaired the lights earlier were busy polishing the wood and checking for any other imperfections in the office.

The captain went on. "Centuries ago, the ceremonies of the Klingons were much more fluid, tailored to each individual. So creating a ceremony that's specific to Khor and Esther is traditional."

Lantar raised an eyebrow. "It is traditional to forgo tradition?"

"It is traditional for nothing to stand in the way of two Klingon hearts who have chosen to join," Gold replied.

"Go on."

"And the old ceremonies honored family, faith, and strength. Our family is Jewish, and ours do the same thing."

"I am confused about one thing, Captain. I had always believed your people not to have any spiritual traditions."

Gold managed to restrain himself from saying, *Some ambassador* you *are*. "Not at all—it's just that there's no one faith. Some have plenty, some have none, and regardless, it's up to each individual. We recognize the equality of all religions, and welcome them all. In the case of our family, it's Judaism. If you ask ten other humans, you'd probably get ten other answers."

"If not more," Rachel added.

"I understand," Lantar said, though Gold wasn't entirely sure he did.

"Then you understand that we value and honor the same traits that you do. And that incorporating some of the elements of a traditional Jewish ceremony shows respect to another ancient tradition, to those who have gone before."

"Which in no way belittles the honor she gains by joining the house of Lantar," Rachel added. *Nicely timed*, Gold thought.

"Yes, there is merit to your words."

"I have asked Rachel to plan out a ceremony that honors both worlds, and would like to present the first draft for your consideration." He produced a padd and handed it to Lantar.

Rachel piped up. "I think you'll really appreciate the *Haray Aht*—that's the exchange of the rings, which symbolizes the exchange of each other's hearts. I believe this ties in very closely with the beating of two Klingon hearts from the traditional Klingon ceremony."

Lantar looked it over. "I am pleased that you understand the values of the Klingon ceremony, for one so new in the field."

Rachel smiled sweetly and nodded her head respectfully. If she opened her mouth, she would have told Lantar that she had studied the Klingon culture longer than his son had been alive, in very colorful language. But she was quite happy to take the quick shot for now. Gold knew it, so he tried to get things moving along quickly. "So, does all this work for you?"

"I believe that this is acceptable. It is respectful of our tenets. It seems to be heading in the right direction. Of course, I will want to see the final draft."

"Oh, certainly." Gold put Khor's and Esther's lists on the

desk. "Is there anything on these lists that you object to, anything that you believe is contrary to the ceremony you have in mind?"

Lantar studied the pieces of paper in front of him—for longer than he needed to, Gold suspected, but he probably wanted to make the humans in front of him squirm. Lantar's forehead wrinkled at various points (rather, it wrinkled more) and at other points he shook his head. At last, after what seemed like a short stay in purgatory, Lantar said, "There is nothing on his list that is objectionable—and although her list is somewhat frivolous, I am willing to be somewhat indulgent to my future daughter-in-law."

"Good!" Gold gathered up the lists. "Then we can—"

"However," and here Lantar stood up and began to pace around the room, as if he were striding to a podium, "the frivolity unsettles me." He stood facing a window, his back to the two of them. "The ceremony . . . it still seems . . . too bland. And yet, too unconventional. A certain decorum must be observed for a man in my position, certainly you understand."

Gold smiled. "I certainly do understand, and I agree. The Klingon Empire should have a showcase, to proclaim its might to the galaxy. In fact . . ." his voiced trailed off.

"Yes?"

"Lantar, why don't we hold the reception for the wedding here, at the embassy?"

The ambassador looked genuinely surprised at the suggestion. "Here?"

Rachel jumped in. "Of course! It's brilliant! How else would you show the true meaning of the Klingon heart? What better way could there be?"

"No, honey, that's unreasonable. There's no way we could possibly expect Lantar to put together the equivalent of a full state dinner in just a few days—"

"Think nothing of it!" Lantar boomed. "The embassy staff thrives on such challenges!"

There was a quiet snort from one of the workmen, but nothing more.

"We will have a chance to show you true honor, passion,

and romance." Lantar paused. "Do you think Esther will be amenable to this plan?"

"Why don't you let us discuss it with them?" Gold said. "You obviously have much to do—"

"Yes! My son is getting married! And we shall make it an event that shall not soon be forgotten!"

Gold and Rachel both got up. "We'll let you get to it then," said Rachel.

"Yes, yes—" Lantar waved his hand. "I'll have to contact musicians. Songs are going to have to be written about this day!"

"Shall we, dear?" Gold offered his arm.

"Surely."

"Let's." And they strolled out of Lantar's office together. After the door had shut and they were halfway down the hall, Gold turned to his wife. "So, what do you think?"

"I think that you were very lucky that we were in an embassy where you could get away with belittling me to make a point. It was a cheap way to score points."

"Yes, I know. I'm sorry. Again."

"Oh, I understand why you did it, as long as you now know that I know. Now—"

"Did that make sense to you as you were saying it?"

"Knowing what I now know, did I know now? I knew. *Nu?*"

Gold shook his head. "You're too old for these word games. What do you think of the deal we got out of Lantar?"

"Seemed pretty well-handled. Now what was that problem that you said you had to deal with?"

He smiled. "Already dealt with it."

Rachel was silent for the next ten paces, thinking. "You forgot about the reception, didn't you?"

He mock winced. "I didn't really forget—I just didn't really have any place to put it on the ship. We're not equipped to handle dinner for three hundred."

"So you fobbed the job off on him, and made it look like a privilege. You played off his vanity and patriotism."

"Yep. Let him do some of the hard work. I see no reason the Klingon government can't absorb some of the costs of this *megillah.*"

"What will the kids think of all of this?"

"Khor and Esther? They're young, they're in love. They'll be fine. They're probably a bit jumpy right now, but that'll—" and then Gold stopped, because he heard a crash come from Esther's guest room. Then another. "Come on!"

They stopped at the door to the room, and they heard the door chime, followed by another crash. "What is going on in there?"

Rachel pressed her ear to the door. "I don't know, hush for a bit."

"Forget it, I'm—"

"*Quiet!*" Rachel could hear a loud male voice through the door, she was pretty sure it was Khor, saying something in Klingon—very, very impassioned. And then a very loud crash.

And then she heard Esther screaming, "You come to me, begging like a *human*?" Another crash. And then something like a snarl . . .

Gold started, "I'm getting a guard to open this up n—"

"No," Rachel said, standing up. "I don't think we are." She quickly grabbed Gold's arm and started leading him back from where they had come.

"What are you doing? Esther is in real trouble back—"

"No, dear, she isn't. And we have a wedding ceremony to write."

"But—"

"It's best that you don't think about it, because if you do your brain will probably melt and dribble out your ears. Come along, dear."

CHAPTER 18

Sonya let Kendra do the honors, but she stayed online and even split her viewscreen so she could see both of them. She'd never met Pressman, but when his face appeared she had to smother a laugh. It was a long, narrow face, with a small sharp nose, a tiny pointed chin, and large, slightly bulging eyes. His hair was dark brown, receding, and thin, and pointed off his forehead in several places so much so that, if she squinted a little, it looked like he had antennae waving over his temples. Crawfish indeed.

Right now he wasn't red, though. And his expression was anything but angry or embarrassed. In fact, when he saw Kendra on his screen, he didn't even give her a chance to speak.

"Ah, Kendra," he said, deliberately dragging out her name. He was at his desk in the Academy, and leaned back a little. *"I've been expecting your call."* He smiled at her—it wasn't a friendly smile, or a pleasant one. *"I've finally gotten even with you and Stevens for that thing you did with the fire hose. I expect you're regretting that now, hm? And Fabian is as well—of course, not that he can tell anyone that."*

Sonya had spent several minutes before the call calming Kendra down, but Pressman's smug manner and callous remarks undid that in an instant. *"You insufferable little bastard!"* Kendra snarled. *"You pathetic, no-talent git! You endangered the entire graduating class—your own students—just so you could get even over a little—"*

She didn't get the chance to finish—Pressman, who had turned a vivid red (very crawfishlike, Sonya couldn't help but notice) during her rant, interrupted her. *"Wait, what are you talking about? What danger? What's happened?"*

Kendra was fuming too much to speak without cursing, so Sonya stepped in. "Professor Pressman, I'm Sonya Gomez, commander of the *da Vinci*'s S.C.E. crew. I'm Mr. Stevens's CO. The reason we're calling is that someone has sabotaged the *Hyperion* test."

She now had Pressman's full attention. *"Sabotaged? In what way?"*

"Well, Fabian had programmed in several tests, simulated crises for the students to deal with."

"Yes, yes." Pressman waved a hand. *"I looked over the list. He was always a good engineer—much as I'd like to believe otherwise."*

"Yes, well, someone decided to add additional tests. And they deactivated the safety protocols, so the students—and Fabian, Lieutenant Commander Tev, who's helping out with the test, and Professor Sparks—are all at real risk. Fabian's already been injured saving one student's life, and he needs immediate medical attention."

"What?" Pressman had gone from red to white. *"We need to get them out of there!"*

"I agree," Sonya told him. "Unfortunately, the suite seems to have locked itself—no one in or out. And we can't shut it off."

"Oh, no." Pressman turned toward Kendra now. *"Kendra, you have to believe me—I didn't do that. I wouldn't endanger my students, not ever. Or Alex, or that lieutenant commander. Or even Fabian himself—scare him, yes, but not actually hurt him. I didn't do that."*

"We found evidence that you inserted new code into the program," Kendra said curtly. *"What did you do?"*

Now he regained a little of that smug expression, though only a little. *"I set it up so that, at a certain point in the program, once Fabian went into intangible mode he would be stuck there. I set Alex up the same way, mainly so that he couldn't act as a go-between for Fabian and Commander Tev. I just wanted Fabian unable to talk to anyone else or to make himself seen or felt. I figured, with how much he loves to get into everything, it would seriously get on his nerves."*

Sonya nodded. That was a fair assessment of Fabian—he preferred things he could touch, and he was always the first to want to get his hands dirty. Being unable to do that would be driving him nuts.

"What were the actual lines of code you added?" Kendra asked.

Pressman nodded and typed in a few keys, then sat back again while Kendra and Sonya both read the lines he'd sent them.

"The ghost-mode trick itself is clean," Sonya pointed out, but Kendra had already read past that, and then doubled back.

"Sure," she said, *"but that's not the problem. Crawfish, you're an idiot—don't you bother to check your code before you implement it?"*

He turned red again. *"What are you saying? It's fine!"* He gestured toward Sonya with his chin. *"She just said so!"*

"Yes, the trick itself. But you used your instructor privileges to access the system so you could make those changes." Kendra highlighted the relevant portion of his code so that all three of them could see it. *"And then you never closed back out afterward."*

Pressman shrugged. *"So? I left it open, in case I wanted to monitor it—and so that I could switch Fabian back out if I needed to."*

Now Sonya saw what Kendra had meant. "But you left the door open, Professor Pressman. Anyone who found your code in the program could tap into it and add extra lines branching from there, and the computer would treat them as if they had instructor privileges as well. In other words, you gave anyone who wanted it free access to every level of the test program."

He had turned pale again as he'd realized what she was going to say before she had finished. Now he slumped back against his chair. *"Oh. I didn't think that—no one else would have reason to—"*

"You thought that you'd be the only one who wanted access, so it was fine to leave it open," Sonya stated, and he nodded. "And if you'd been right, this *would* have been fine. Fabian and Alex would be stuck in ghost-mode and seriously annoyed, but no one would have gotten hurt. Unfortunately, someone else did want access, and you gave them that opportunity." She paused then, because an idea had just popped into her head.

"Okay, so now we know this idiot is responsible for letting someone in," Kendra said, gesturing toward Pressman. *"But we still don't know who, or exactly what, they did. And we still don't have any way to stop it."*

"That last part may not be true," Sonya replied, still thinking. "In fact, I think Professor Pressman's mistake might actually help us fix things." She held up a hand to forestall the questions she could already see Kendra forming. "Hang on, I need to check on something first. But if I'm right, Crawfish may have just given us a way out—or, in this case, a way in." She turned away from the viewscreen, and tapped her combadge. "Gomez to Soloman."

Meanwhile, in the engine room of the *Hyperion*, the students had their hands full.

"Everything's shutting down!" Ian shouted. "I don't know what to do!" He was frantically punching buttons on his console, to little or no effect.

"We've lost main engines." Santar was reporting to Tev on the bridge. *"Impulse drives at twenty percent and failing. Life support also at twenty percent. Backup generators offline. Emergency beacons—"*

"Dammit!" Tanya stepped back, shaking her hand, as sparks flew from the open panel where she'd been working. "We just lost the—"

"*—offline,*" Santar continued, updating his information. "*Predicting complete shutdown in fifteen minutes.*"

"Engineering, shunt all available power to life support," Tev said. "*Jettison warp core immediately, and prepare to abandon ship.*"

"Abandon ship?" Malcolm asked, glancing up from his console. "Where does he expect us to go?"

"Hull doors and airlocks not responding," Ben reported from another console. "We'll have to open them manually."

Latha started to say something, but was interrupted by a klaxon. "Proximity alert," she said after a glance at her console. "Another ship just appeared, and it's approaching fast. Thank the stars we still have sensors working."

"*All hands, this is your captain speaking,*" Tev said a moment later. "*A ship has been spotted nearby, and is rapidly approaching. Long-range scans indicate—*" A groan from Latha told the others that this was not going to be good news. "*—that it is a Jem'Hadar warship. Prepare for possible combat.*"

"With what?" Tanya asked. "We've got no shields, no phasers, no torpedoes! We're sitting ducks!"

"We might be able to modify one of the lifepods," Zoe suggested, "transform it into a guided missile and fire that at the warship."

"That is a worthwhile notion," T'nok said. "If we can create the illusion of life-forms on board, the Jem'Hadar will seek to capture it rather than destroy it. And that will put it inside their hull when it explodes."

"It's the only shot we've got," Tomas said. "Zoe, start prepping one of the pods. Trick its systems into thinking there are three people aboard. Ian, set the engines to overload in ten minutes. Malcolm, find some way to boost that explosion when it happens. Everybody else, keep salvaging what you can here. See if we can draw power from anywhere to get our shields back up, otherwise we're goners with the first hit. Let's move, people!"

"Not bad," Fabian said. He and Alex stood off to one side, watching as the students scrambled from console to console.

Right now Zoe, Ian, and Malcolm were leaving the engine room at a run—a few of the others glared at Tomas, but they all did what he'd suggested. "I'd probably want to use the warp core itself as a weapon—prime it to overload, then jettison it directly at that warship—but the lifepod's a nice idea. And Tomas did a good job of assigning tasks."

"Yes, he's a born leader," Alex agreed. "Much to Tanya, T'nok, and Latha's chagrin. The four of them often compete for control, which is why I don't normally assign them to the same groups." He glanced around him. "Things seem to be building to a head here."

"That they do," Fabian said. "One way or another, the next few minutes are going to get pretty interesting. I just wish there was something we could do." But the computer had caught on to most of their communications tricks by now, and they were left with no way to contact Tev or the students. Not that they had much to share about the current situation. All they could do was stand there and watch, and hope that these youngsters were as smart as they appeared to be.

"Warp core shutdown in progress," T'nok reported a few minutes later. "It will be completed in one-point-three-five minutes. But it will need to be jettisoned manually—the regular systems are not acknowledging me."

"Life support is good for another minute, two at most," Ben said. "I shunted some of its power over to the shields, so we might survive the first hit, but I doubt we can take a second."

"We've lost impulse drive," Latha said. "I managed to get us maximum inertia, so we won't be at a full stop for several more minutes, and we can even execute minor course changes—nothing preprogrammed, but navigation might be able to dodge an attack if they're careful. And I shunted what was left of the power into the lifepod, to fully charge its engines."

"I've—" Tomas started, but then paused as his console beeped. "Hang on, we've got a second ship incoming! Just off our starboard bow, and coming right for us!" His fingers moved rapidly across the controls, and then a grin split his face. "It's a Starfleet ship!"

The others cheered and hollered. "*Sovereign*-class? *Defiant*-class? *Galaxy*-class?" Ben asked eagerly. But Tomas shook his head.

"No, *Saber*-class. Definitely too small to take on that warship." He glanced around. "Still, it can probably get us out of here."

As if on cue, a voice spoke over their communicators. "*Hyperion, this is Commander Gomez of the* U.S.S. da Vinci. *I'm beaming all of you across in ten seconds.*"

Several of the students cheered again, but T'nok tapped her own communicator. "Negative, Commander," she replied. "I will need one-point-two-three more minutes here."

Ben and Zoe stared at her, but Tomas and then Latha and Tanya all nodded. And then Tomas tapped his communicator as well. "Commander, this is Tomas del Fuego in engineering," he said. "We need at least one more minute to properly shut down the *Hyperion*'s systems. Otherwise, this ship could pose a threat to other starships."

"*Fabian?*"

He reflexively tapped his combadge, still staring at Tomas and the others. "Commander? How'd you—"

"*I'm still locked out,*" Gomez told him quickly. "*The* da Vinci *is another hologram, and I've got a holographic version of myself captaining it, though I'm inputting my responses as we go. What do you want me to do about this request?*"

"This is just a hologram," Fabian said. "Once we shut it down, this version of the *Hyperion* will be gone for good, so it's not like it could really hurt anyone."

But Alex, standing next to him, shook his head. "That's not the point though, is it? They're willing to risk their own lives to do their job properly, and to prevent others from being put at risk. Isn't that exactly the sort of person Starfleet wants on its ships?"

Fabian nodded. "Yeah, you're right. They're good kids, and they're doing the right thing. So let's reward them for that. Give them the extra minute."

"*You got it,*" Gomez said. "*But I'm beaming you and Alex across right now—I've reset the codes so that, when you hit the* da Vinci, *you'll no longer be ghosted. And you, Mr. Stevens, are going to land in sickbay, where my hologram Lense can take a look at that leg.*"

"Great," Fabian muttered as he and Alex dematerialized, "because Lense in the flesh isn't stiff enough."

"*Engineering, you have eighty seconds,*" Commander Gomez informed them. "*I am beaming your captain and bridge crew away now, however.*"

The students didn't bother to acknowledge her message. Instead, they all got to work. Zoe, Malcolm, and Ian launched the lifepod—now that it had been turned into a makeshift bomb it could not be safely left on the *Hyperion*—while T'nok and Ben jettisoned the warp core. Then Tomas, Latha, and Tanya made sure the ship was safely shut down, and that the computer had been purged of any important Starfleet files. They had just typed in the last command when Gomez announced, "*Beaming up, on my mark,*" and they all vanished from the *Hyperion*—

—to find themselves standing on the bridge of the *da Vinci*. Tev was there, and Santar, and so was Professor Sparks, who greeted them all with a smile. "Well done, class," he informed them. "You've handled yourselves very well indeed."

"And that should do it," Sonya muttered, typing one last command into her own console on board the real *da Vinci*. "Fabian, why don't you do the honors?"

"*Happy to,*" he replied, fresh from his bed in the holographic sickbay. "*Computer,*" he called out, "*end* Hyperion *program.*"

Instantly the *da Vinci* disappeared, leaving the students, Fabian, Tev, and Sparks standing in the empty holosuite.

"Everybody out," Fabian announced, gesturing toward the open door, and the students quickly filed through it. Even as they did, Sonya tapped her combadge. "Gomez to Poynter. Laura, can you lock on Fabian now?"

"*Yes, sir, him and Tev both. Want me to beam them up?*"

"No—but beam me down to their location."

A moment later, she materialized outside the holosuite, where Fabian, Alex, Tev, and the students were milling about—as was Kendra. She too had beamed over.

"Are you okay?" Sonya asked Fabian, and he nodded over Kendra's shoulder—she'd wrapped him in a hug the instant he'd cleared the door.

"That hologram of Lense knows her stuff," he said, gesturing at the bandages on his left leg. "She got me patched up right away, and I should be fine."

"We'll have the real Elizabeth take a look once she gets back," Sonya said with a smile. Then she nodded at Tev, who nodded back, and turned to Sparks. "Professor Sparks, I'm Sonya Gomez. Nice to meet you in person."

They shook hands, and Sparks smiled. "Likewise, Commander. Thank you for the timely rescue. But if you don't mind my asking, how did you manage it?"

She smiled. "Actually, you have Professor Pressman to thank for it, at least in part." She nodded to Fabian. "Yes, we talked to him, and he did have something to do with this. But by no means all of it." She explained what he'd told them. "So he'd allowed someone else to gain access, but he hadn't set any of that up himself."

"And since the door was still open, you could slip in yourself."

"Soloman had just built a holographic model of the *da Vinci* for diagnostic purposes, so I tapped into the hololab and then downloaded the *da Vinci*. Pressman's lock on you was specific to the *Hyperion*—he hadn't counted on another ship being in here."

"There was no reason he should," Tev said. "It would take most engineers at least a week to build a passable ship model."

"Good thing we have a Bynar on staff," Sonya said. "Soloman managed it in two days flat. I was hoping that all the other traps and flaws were also centered on the *Hyperion,* and that once everyone was off it the computer would respond properly again."

"Which it did." Fabian shook his head. "And not a moment too soon."

They all nodded. Even if the *Hyperion* had been fully functional, it might not have survived against a Jem'Hadar warship. And with the *Hyperion* barely afloat, the *da Vinci* wouldn't have stood a chance.

Tev glanced over at the students, who were standing nearby but just far enough for the adults to converse in private. "It has been a pleasure to serve as your captain," he said. "You have all demonstrated the skills Starfleet looks for in its officers, and I would be proud to have any of you under my command again." He glanced from face to face, then frowned. "But I count eight of you. One of you is missing."

Fabian and Alex looked up, then quickly scanned the faces themselves. "Where's Malcolm?" Alex demanded.

The other students glanced around, but no one seemed to know. "Leave it to him to screw this up," Ben muttered, but not quietly enough.

"Yeah," Ian agreed softly. "I don't know why he was here in the first place."

"What do you mean?" Sonya asked them. "Why shouldn't he have been?" None of the students replied, so she glanced at Alex.

"Malcolm is a solid student," he explained, "but he spends far too much time playing jokes to earn top grades." Alex frowned. "To be honest, I was a little surprised when I saw his name on the list. But I wasn't privy to the final selections, so I assumed some other factor merited his participation."

"So the class clown took part in an honors exam, and now he's missing?" Kendra asked. "Why does this sound fishy to me?"

Fabian stepped back over to the computer panel beside the holosuite door. "Computer," he said, "how many students were on the *Hyperion*?"

"*Eight students were present,*" it replied. Fabian glanced around, and assumed that his face had the same surprised look as Tev's, Kendra's, Sonya's, and Alex's did.

"Computer, display student files from that exercise," he requested, and it promptly displayed a list of files. He tapped in a few commands, and scrolled through several screens before stopping. "Aha." He gestured, and the others crowded closer. "Right here."

"Clever," Kendra said, nodding. "He reprogrammed it to include his name."

"But the computer said we had only eight students," Alex pointed out. "Yet Malcolm was there the whole time."

"There, yes," Tev agreed. "But I did not notice him once we'd beamed onto the *da Vinci*. And he did not exit with us."

"So he was confined to the *Hyperion*," Kendra said. "Just like the traps." She reached over Fabian and tapped a few commands of her own, shunting the display to a different screen. "Right there." She tapped a line. "He pulled one from your book," she told Sonya. "But he did it first."

"He was a hologram?"

"Not just any hologram," Fabian commented, reading the rest of the associated code. "He programmed himself in with an AI, so that his hologram could react with autonomy. Most of the pranks were his." And as he glanced around, Fabian had the feeling the final piece of the puzzle had just slid into place.

"It all makes sense," Fabian told the others. They were sitting in Kendra's office—her group's presentations had finished just before she'd met Sonya at the Academy, so they'd been free to move here after sending the students home for some well-earned rest. "It wasn't anybody's fault—well, no one person alone."

"Malcolm inserted an AI to play pranks on the other students," Alex said. "It should have been on the surface of the program, and only able to cause harmless problems. He didn't intend to hurt anyone."

"But Crawfish left the door open," Sonya added, "so the AI moved itself up to the command level, where it could rewrite aspects of the program itself."

"Cadet Sturtze increased the risk factors," Tev noted. "That would have allowed the AI to create more dangerous pranks with impunity."

"And we had just switched off the safety protocols when Crawfish's little prank kicked in," Fabian mentioned. "We were about to turn them back on at the default levels, but we were stuck in ghost-mode and the computer wouldn't allow us to change anything."

"So suddenly," Kendra picked up, "we had an AI designed to play pranks, inserted at command level, with encouragement to increase risks and no safety protocols restricting its actions. No wonder things went haywire."

"It's a good thing you beamed everyone over to the *da Vinci*," Fabian told Sonya. "Malcolm's AI was stuck on the *Hyperion*, so it couldn't cause any more trouble after that."

"What happens now?" Sonya asked, and everyone else turned to Alex. He squirmed a little—Fabe had noticed that the instructor didn't like being the center of attention, except with his students.

"Malcolm will be disciplined," Alex said, "but not severely. His was meant to be a harmless prank, and it wasn't his fault that it got out of hand. Actually, the programming he did was far above his usual work, so he'll have a reprimand, but I've also given him credit for the actual design. Tanya won't have anything appear on her record—Tev already spoke to her during the test, and I'll speak to her again in a day or so. I think she's already learned, however, not to bring her personal issues into the workplace."

"And what about Crawfish?" Kendra demanded. "This *was* all his fault."

Fabian surprised even himself by shaking his head. "It really wasn't, Ken. Sure, he set up a prank for me and Alex—but I can't really blame him for that, not considering all the pranks we pulled on him over the years. And it wouldn't have hurt anything. Oh, sure, I'd have been a little annoyed, but that would've been it. He made a stupid mistake and left his code open, that's all. And Tanya and Malcolm both took advantage of it, without realizing it. It happens."

"So you're saying he's going to get off scot-free?" she asked.

He grinned at her. "Oh, I wouldn't say that."

CHAPTER 19

Captain's Log: First Officer Sonya Gomez reporting. Eight bells and all is well.

Captain's Log: First Officer Sonya Gomez reporting. Nine bells and all is well.

Captain's Log: First Officer Sonya Gomez reporting. Ten bells. See previous entry.

Captain's Log: First Officer Sonya Gomez reporting. Eleven hundred hours. Ditto.

Sonya Gomez looked around at the bridge and drummed her fingers on the command chair.

Well, that was exciting, she thought. Now that the *Hyperion* situation had been straightened out, it was back to the humdrum, monotonous, workaday grind that she had established for herself and the crew of the *da Vinci* while Captain Gold was busy with wedding preparations.

The ship was running fine. Just about every conceivable diagnostic test had been run, with the exception of running diagnostics on the diagnostic equipment itself. They were on the verge of polishing the chrome.

She was bored bored *bored* out of her skull.

But you know, boring occasionally is nice. Peaceful. Quiet. Nobody shooting at you. She sighed. *Maybe I can catch up on my reading of technical manuals. No, wait, I can't do that, I'm on duty. Well, I probably could, but I don't want to now. Maybe I can—*

"Excuse me, Commander." Gomez looked up, startled. Soloman was next to her chair. "May I speak with you for a moment?"

"I'm a tad busy, Soloman."

"Clearly. I will be brief. May I speak with you?"

"Certainly. What is it?"

"Privately, please?" His eyes looked over at the turbolift—the doors had just opened and Tev had come out.

She was curious. What could Soloman have to say that he couldn't say in front of Tev? "Okay. Tev, you have the chair."

"Aye, sir." She noted a bit of a spring in Tev's step when she handed him command. She went to join Soloman, who had already walked to the turbolift. She entered and the doors closed behind her.

"Yes, Soloman, what is it?"

"Deck four, please."

"Are we going somewhere?"

"Yes."

She was expecting more. Soloman stayed quiet. "Where are we going?"

"To the shuttlebay."

"Oh, no—what's wrong? Is it going to mess up the wedding?"

"Nothing is wrong. We are going to the wedding."

"Turbolift, halt." The turbolift obliged. She counted to ten. "We are not going to the wedding. First off, there is no 'we' to go to the wedding."

"We are not going as a 'we.' I am escorting you."

"I beg your pardon?"

"I thought that you would not want to escort me, so I am escorting you."

"Soloman—"

"Commander Gomez. From my observations, you are in a

closed programming loop. It is a loop I have found myself in from time to time."

"Soloman, I thank you for your observation, and I don't mean to invalidate it, but—"

"I was the same way when 111 died."

Sonya was taken aback by the starkness of what Soloman said, but she tried to respond. Soloman held up a hand and said, "Tev is perfectly capable of taking the center chair himself. In fact, I'm sure he is even more enthusiastic about it after his recent experience at the Academy."

"That's what worries me. His little taste of power—"

"—is a concern for another day. You are making an excuse to avoid a social occasion that you would have attended with Lieutenant Commander Duffy. As such, I offer my own services as escort."

She stood there, stunned for a moment. Then she tapped her combadge. "Gomez to Tev."

"Tev here."

She took a deep breath. "I'm going to be taking a few hours here. I hope you don't mind. I'll rearrange your duty schedule later."

"Understood. Oh, and Commander? Thank you for taking my place. I find Klingon weddings to be tedious, overblown, and irritating."

It took most of Gomez's willpower to avoid making the obvious retort to that remark. Instead, she simply said, "You're quite welcome, Tev." She sighed. "Turbolift, resume." The gentle movement started up again. "Thank you," she said to Soloman.

"I just hate going to bonding ceremonies alone. Hopefully, Pattie has saved us seats."

CHAPTER 20

Sonya was convinced it was the first time the shuttlebay had been cleaned since the *da Vinci* had been relaunched.

The ceremony had required the shuttlebay—the number of guests couldn't be fit into any other single space on the ship. However, it did mean that a lot of the equipment had to be moved, along with the shuttlecraft themselves. The crew, quite logically, solved both problems at the same time by shoving all the clutter into the shuttlecrafts and then shoving them out into space.

An innovative solution, though she had to wonder once she got the ships back how long it would take for them to actually empty out the shuttle and put everything back—if not to where the items might actually belong, then at least to their previous piles.

Sonya did have to wonder if they got everything, though—there seemed to be a sort of sickly sweet smell, some sort of chemical she couldn't quite identify. She sniffed.

Pattie, who was sitting next to her, said, "Is there something wrong?"

"I don't know. There's a scent of— I don't know what it is, precisely."

"Oh, I'm sorry. That would be me."

"You?"

"I always secrete at weddings."

"Oh." Sonya didn't really know how to respond to that—she certainly wasn't going to offer Pattie a handkerchief—so she just looked around the room.

The captain and the rabbi were standing in front of the airlock, which was open to space with standard force fields keeping the air and guests in. The captain had given specific instructions to the helm, in order to give the best backdrop possible—the sun was just becoming visible over the earth, with the orbit maintaining that view. The crew was especially proud of the polarizing they were doing with the shields to keep everybody from being blinded.

Many of the crew were there. The invitation had been optional for most of them, as space was limited and there were ship duties to take care of, and Captain Gold clearly didn't want to make it mandatory for his crew to show up at a wedding where they didn't know the couple getting hitched. But let's face it, if your ship's captain is performing a wedding, you tend to show up anyway. Sonya was sitting on the groom's side, as the bride's side was already full.

Sonya heard a deep female voice whispering from her side of the aisle. "Real *var'Hama* candles. That takes class—nobody takes the time to do that anymore."

And then the strains of Mendelssohn started up. That was Rachel's extra touch—she couldn't stand Wagner, and tried to make sure it was in as few weddings as possible.

Esther's bridesmaids, Audrey, Nikki, and Elaine, entered. As was traditional, one was tall and dark, the other short and blond, one red-headed and a bit chubby, and the dresses looked amazingly wrong on all of them. Three Klingons accompanied them, each with a *mastaka* in his free hand.

Then Khor's *DawI'yan* (loosely translated as "sword bearer," Sonya recalled) walked in. He was a stout fellow named Timrek. It looked like the deprivation of *kal'Hyah* had been a bit wearing on him, although he probably could have stood to lose the weight. He carried four *bat'leth*s instead of the traditional two. Timrek was accompanied by Esther's sister, Leah, who was the matron of honor. And the two of them were followed by Khor himself, escorting Lantar and Jessica down the aisle.

Finally, Esther entered. She wore a gown that gave off a faint pearly glow. She was on the arm of her father, Daniel, who looked uncomfortable with all the attention.

Sonya heard another whisper from the groom's side. "She wore white to the wedding? How improper . . ."

While Khor removed the veil from Esther's face, Timrek handed out *bat'leth*s to the groomsmen. Together, they placed the tips of them at the four corners of the *chuppah*, and raised them over the heads of the officiators.

Gold smiled and began to speak. "Since the days of the first wooden sailing ships, captains have enjoyed the happy privilege of joining two people in the bonds of matrimony. And so now it is my honor to unite you, Esther, daughter of Daniel and Jessica—my granddaughter—and Khor, son of Lantar, together in marriage here in the sight of your friends and family."

Rabbi Gilman gestured behind her at the open airlock. "We hold this most sacred of ceremonies under the stars, as a sign of the blessing given by God to the patriarch Abraham, that his children shall be 'as numerous as the stars of the heavens.'"

Gold continued, "In Starfleet, our mission is to explore strange new worlds, to seek out new life and new civilizations." Someone in the room coughed; Sonya couldn't tell who.

Gilman took up the thread. "But the two of you are about to create a new world together, a world filled with new life of your own."

Gold read from his notes. "With fire and steel did the gods forge the Klingon heart. So fiercely did it beat, so loud was the sound, that the Klingon gods cried out, 'On this day we have brought forth the strongest heart in all the heavens. None can stand before it without trembling at its strength.' But then the Klingon heart weakened, its steady rhythm faltered . . . and the gods said, 'Why do you weaken so? We have made you the strongest in all of creation!' And the heart said . . ."

Khor stepped under the *chuppah* and said, "I . . . am alone."

Gold acknowledged him with a nod of his head and continued. "And the gods knew that they had erred. So they went back to their forge and brought forth another heart." And Esther came forward, resplendent in her gown. This was her moment, and she knew it. She walked under the *chuppah*, and began to circle Khor while her grandfather continued. "But the second heart beat stronger than the first, and the first was jealous of its power. Fortunately, the second heart was tempered by wisdom, and said . . ."

Esther said, "If we join together, no force can stop us."

"And when the two hearts began to beat together, they filled the heavens with a terrible sound. To this day, no one can oppose the beating of two Klingon hearts." Gold cast a brief look at Lantar, who didn't quite seem to get what he was implying.

Gilman then brought forth a glass goblet filled with a nice Chateau Picard '53. "We now recite the blessings over the wine."

Sonya heard grumbling from the groom's side of the aisle when the rabbi began her benediction.

When she was done with that, she said, "You may now drink of the wine." She handed the glass to Esther, who took a sip, and then to Khor, who drank the remainder. Gilman smiled and took the glass back, wrapping it in cloth while her husband began to speak again.

Gold turned to his granddaughter. "Esther, daughter of Daniel—does your heart beat only for this man? And will you swear to join with him and stand with him against all who oppose you? For richer, for poorer, in sickness and in health?"

She smiled. "I do."

"And Khor, son of Lantar—does your heart beat only for this woman? And will you swear to join with her and stand with her against all who oppose you? For richer, for poorer, in sickness and in health?"

Khor looked at the captain blankly . . . and said nothing.

And continued to say nothing for a whole second.

His face was expressionless, but Gold saw the flickering in Khor's eyes—the same flicker he was sure he'd had in his own eyes on his wedding day, the knowledge that his life was going to change forever, that he could no longer go back to being who he was before.

Two seconds now. If Khor didn't say something soon—

"It's an easy question, Khor," Esther said very quietly, her lips unmoving. "The answer is 'Yes' or you die where you stand."

Khor turned and gazed at his bride, a huge smile on his face. "Now that," he replied softly, "is a Klingon response." Then, loudly, "I swear."

"The ring, then, if you please," said Gold.

Khor turned to Timrek and cleared his throat. Timrek leaned in and looked confused about where to put his sword while he dug out the rings. Finally, he handed the *bat'leth* to the groomsman on his right, and handed the rings to the captain, who then handed them to his wife. She said, "Khor, place this ring on Esther's finger and say, 'Be sanctified to me with this ring in accordance with the law of Moses and Israel.'"

"Be sanctified to me with this ring in accordance with the law of Moses and Israel."

"Esther, place this ring on Khor's finger and say, 'Be sanctified to me with this ring in accordance with the law of Moses and Israel.'"

"Be sanctified to me with this ring in accordance with the law of Moses and Israel."

Rachel smiled. "May the Lord bless you and protect you. May the Lord show you favor and be gracious to you. May the Lord turn in loving kindness to you and grant you peace . . . and let us all say Amen."

And the congregation said, "Amen."

Gold brought the wrapped glass forward as the rabbi continued speaking. "There is a tradition of our people of the breaking of the glass, to symbolize that in celebration there should always be awe and trembling, as well. And that even in the height of their joy, the couple must pause in remembrance of sad events of the past. The shattered glass is a reminder to all in attendance that the world is replete with imperfection and it is an imperative to all to partake in the mending of the universe. Khor and Esther, you should consider these marriage vows as an irrevocable act—just as permanent and final as the breaking of this glass is unchangeable."

As Gold placed the glass down on the floor, a few Klingons started to sing—a deep, throaty rumble of a dirge. Sonya thought of Kieran Duffy, and her lip quivered. After the first verse, Khor joined in to the end of the second, then exhaled, and smashed the glass with his foot. Cries of *"Mazel tov!"* came from the bride's side of the aisle, with more inarticulate grunts that the translators couldn't handle from the groom's side.

"Well," came a comment from in front of Sonya, "that's the last time he gets to put his foot down in the marriage."

The rabbi smiled. "Then let it be known to all here that this male and female are married."

And then the groomsmen attacked. And a wonderful time was had by all.

CHAPTER 21

"That is a wonderful tradition you have, Rabbi, the breaking of the glass at the end of the cermony."

"Thank you, Lantar," Rachel said with a bow of respect to the ambassador. "That's very kind of you to say."

"I do have a question, though. Does the groom always wear footwear during it? It seems most . . . restrained."

Rachel got the impression that the sudden elevation in status for her people had just dropped a bit and could plummet quickly based on her answer, so she simply shrugged and said, "It's a Reform thing."

Lantar seemed satisfied by that, so he went on. "How do you like the reception so far?"

"I'm truly stunned." That was putting it both politely and mildly. Rachel had never seen a spread quite like this before. The Klingon embassy was going all out, as they would for a full state dinner—but without any of the polish that they might put on for a diplomatic affair. This was all Klingon.

"Rabbi!" She looked around, and saw that some people over at the buffet were waving for her attention. "Could you come here, please?"

"Would you excuse me, please, Lantar?"

"Of course, go ahead."

She went over to the buffet table, a traditional gathering place for Jews at a wedding reception—except the ones here were just standing in front of the spread with suspicious looks on their faces. "Yes, how can I help, folks?"

"This stuff here—what is it called?"

"It is called *gagh*," Rachel replied.

"Yes, *gagh*. Um, Rabbi . . ." The woman lowered her voice to an exaggerated whisper. "Is this kosher?"

"Sadly, no. They crawl upon the ground."

"Oh, okay. Sorry, sir. What else can you recommend?"

"Well, we have this . . ."

"Rabbi, is replicated food kosher?"

"Of course. What do you think gefilte fish is?"

"How are you doing, Captain?"

"Fine, thank you, Hawkins."

"That was a lovely ceremony. A truly fascinating hybrid of cultures."

"Thank you very much, Abramowitz." He continued to nurse his drink.

"Sir, are you okay?" Vance Hawkins said. "You look like you're having a bit of a stress headache. You can relax now, your job is done."

"I know—I'm just having a very hard time getting used to a small Klingon orchestra trying to play klezmer music."

"Really?" said Carol Abramowitz. "I like it."

"Of course you would," said Gold.

Hawkins rolled his eyes, hoping he wouldn't get dragged into this.

"Hawkins, what do you think?"

The deputy security chief's luck was running true to form. He looked at the glass in Gold's hand. "You know, I don't think I've ever seen you hold on so tightly to a drink before, sir. Are you sure you're okay?"

"In a manner of—"

"*Daaaaaavid!*" It was said from only halfway across the room, but there was a good chance it could have been heard from orbit. Hawkins, out of reflex, moved to interpose himself between the sound and the captain. Abramowitz saw a very large woman heading toward them—not so much large as wide, but—

"David, that was a very, very lovely ceremony."

"Hello, Mother Gilman." He turned back toward Carol. "Chief Vance Hawkins, Dr. Carol Abramowitz, I'd like you to meet Eva Gilman, my mother-in-law."

"Oh, a doctor? How lovely!" Eva said. "Maybe you can help me, I've been trying to find someone to help me with my knees, I've been told I have to have them replaced, you know, at my age, it's a horrible thing, and I can't find anybody on the West Coast that I like, they're all these technicians, no bedside manner at all, it's like they don't even want to talk to you as a real person, so do you know anybody?"

"I'm sorry, Ms. Gilman—"

"Eva, darling, it's Eva."

Abramowitz smiled. "Eva, I'm sorry, I don't think I can help."

"Oh, you must know somebody on Earth, I know that you must spend a lot of time in space with David, but there must be someone."

"No, it's not that. My field of study is cultural anthropology."

"Oh, so you're not a real doctor, Carol?"

Abramowitz smiled even more. Hawkins knew that look and was suddenly worried for Eva Gilman's safety. Captain Gold rubbed his temple with his thumb.

"Wasn't that a lovely ceremony?" Bart said to Anthony. The two of them were tucked away at a quiet table, each nursing a drink.

"That's all you can think to talk about, how the wedding looked? Nothing about how good I look in a tuxedo?"

"I never thought you could get away with wearing leather to a wedding."

"Only after the summer."

"Well, of course. Heatstroke."

Anthony looked over at the bride and groom, who were going from table to table doing the meet and greet, yet another tradition that transcended cultures. "It really was lovely . . . I bet we'd look good in those outfits."

Bart arched an eybrow. "Which of us wears the leather instead of the dress?"

"Me."

"No."

"Vain."

"Beast."

"Stereotype."

"Stereotype? *Moi*?" Bart put his hand to his chest and fluttered. "You're the one trying to put me in taffeta."

Anthony rolled his eyes. "Seriously, Bart."

"Seriously? Here we were, having a nice time at a wedding, and you ruin it by talking about getting married." He swallowed the rest of his drink. "I'm empty. Can I get you a refill?"

"Sure. Whatever."

"Proprioception? What is that?"

"It's a rare offshoot of my Betazed heritage," Rennan Konya said. "Rather than having empathy or telepathy, I have proprioception."

"Yes," Dantas Falcão said, "but what is it? I don't think I've come across it in the medical books."

"Oh. It allows me to tap into other people's motor cortexes, specifically. I can sense what an opponent will do in hand-to-hand combat before it happens. It gives me a great advantage in martial arts fighting."

"Rrrrreally. Can I test it?"

"Sure. Come at me. I'll even close my eyes, make it easy on you."

Dantas looked at him, then lunged straight at him. He blocked her easily, grabbing her by her shoulders and stopping her a few inches from his face. Quickly, she leaned forward and kissed him.

He opened his eyes, surprised. "Well, I didn't expect you to do *that*."

"Can it be used for anything else? Such as . . . dancing?"

"What kind of dancing?"

"Let's get on the floor and see what happens." She smiled wolfishly. As he knew she would.

"Once upon a time, not long ago," Rachel said to the assembled crowd, "there lived a princess named Atalanta, who could run as fast as the wind. She was so bright, and so clever, and could build things and fix things so wonderfully that many young men wished to marry her."

"This is the Atalanta of Greek mythology?" Abramowitz asked.

"More or less, but that's not how I heard the story, and that's not how I explained it to Rachel," Gold said.

"Oh, a later reinterpretation?"

"Yes," Rachel said, "and if you'd let me finish telling the story, you'd see how."

"Sorry, Rabbi."

"Where was I? Oh yes. Everyone wanted to marry her, which was vexing to Atalanta's father, who was a powerful king. 'So many want to marry you, and I don't know how to choose.'

"'You don't have to choose, Father,' said Atalanta. 'I will choose. And I'm not sure that I will choose to marry anyone at all. I intend to go out and see the world. When I come home, perhaps I will marry, and perhaps I will not.' The king, of course, did not like this at all. He was an ordinary king: powerful, and used to having his way." Lantar cleared his throat. Rached smiled, ignored it magnificently, and went on. "He told Atalanta, 'I have decided how to choose whom you will marry. I will hold a great race, and the winner, the swiftest and fleetest of them all, will win the right to marry you.'

"Now, you must know that Atalanta was as clever as she was swift. She told her father, 'Very well then, let there be a race. But you must let me run in it, too. And if I am not the winner, I will accept the wishes of the one who is. If I am the winner, I will choose for myself what I will do.' The king agreed to this. He would have his way, marry off his daughter, and enjoy a fine day of racing as well."

"The king agreed to let his daughter race?" Khor said. Esther shushed him, a rapt expression on her face.

"He felt he had naught to fear from her actually winning—it was unheard of. But Atalanta was preparing for the race. Each day at dawn, she went to the field in secret, until she could run the course in just three minutes—more quickly than anyone had ever run it before."

"Captain," Hawkins whispered into his ear, "isn't this your story? Shouldn't you be the one telling it?"

"She's made it her own. And besides, I'm not going to interrupt a storyteller in front of her audience. Look." He indicated the growing crowd, with a number of Gold grandchildren and great-grandchildren sitting and looking on, as well as a number of Klingons who were curious at this new story. Even Esther—this was one of her favorite stories from childhood.

"As the day of the race grew nearer and nearer, suitors for the hand of the fair princess began to crowd into the town. Each was sure he could win the prize, except for one. That was young John, who lived in the town. Young John saw the princess only from a distance, but he understood how bright and clever she was. He wished very much to race with her, to win and earn the right to talk with her, and to become her friend. 'For surely,' he said to himself, 'it is not right for Atalanta's father to give her away to the winner of the race. One so alive and filled with life must choose for herself whom she wants to marry, or whether she wishes to marry at all. Still, if I could only win the race, I would be free to speak to her, and to ask for her friendship!' And so, each evening, after his studies of the stars and the seas, John went to the field in secret and practiced running across it. Night after night, he raced as fast as the wind across the twilight field, until he could cross it in three minutes, more quickly, he thought, than anyone had run it before.

"Finally, the day of the race came. The young men gathered at the edge of the field, along with Atalanta herself, the prize that they sought. Then a bugle sounded—" She mimicked a bugle cry, which got laughter from the children. "—and the runners were off!" And now she started to move in a small circle, playing to the kids.

"The crowds cheered as the young men and Atalanta began to race across the field. At first, they ran as a group, but Atalanta soon pulled ahead, with three close behind her. As they neared the halfway point, one of them put on a great burst of speed and seemed to pull ahead for an instant, but then gasped, and fell back. Atalanta shot on!" The kids squealed.

"Then another drew near to Atalanta, reached out as if to touch her sleeve, stumbled for an instant, and lost speed. Atalanta smiled as she ran on. 'I have almost won!' she thought.

"Just then another man drew near to her. This was young John, running like the wind, as steadily and as swiftly as Atalanta herself." At this, Gold came up next to his wife. "Atalanta felt how close he was, and in a sudden burst, she dashed ahead." She took a step forward and continued. "But John didn't give up."

"'Nothing at all,'" said Gold, "'will keep me from winning my chance to speak with Atalanta.'" And he took a step, to be side by side with her. The children stared, enraptured.

Rachel continued. "Atalanta was aware of him, and she raced even faster. But John was a strong match for her. And smiling, Atalanta and John reached the finish line together!"

"A tie!" Esther said, and led the young children in a cheer as they shouted and leaped about.

Rachel affected a stern king voice, and addressed David. "'Young John,' said the king, as John and Atalanta stood before him, 'you have not won the race, but you have come closer to winning than any man here. And so I give you the prize that was promised: the right to marry my daughter.'"

And here Gold took up the story. "Young John smiled at Atalanta, and she smiled back. They had found their match in each other. 'Thank you, sir,' said John to the king, 'but I did not win this race, and could not possibly marry your daughter unless she wished to marry me. I have run this race for the chance to talk with Atalanta.'"

Rachel laughed. "'And I would like nothing better than to spend the afternoon with you.' And she held out her hand to young John, who took it." And so did Rachel and Gold. "Then the two of them sat and talked on the grassy field. Atalanta told John about her books and her studies, and John told Atalanta about his globes and his star charts. At the end of the day, they were friends.

"The next day, John set off by ship to discover new lands, and Atalanta set off on horseback to visit great cities. Perhaps someday they'll be together for the rest of their days, and perhaps they will not.

"In any case," they finished in unison, "it is certain they are both living happily ever after."

Rachel grimaced. "To this day, he calls me Atalanta whenever he thinks I'm being too much of a princess."

"But what does it mean?" said a young Klingon to his mother.

"It's a silly human story," she said as she led him away from the gathered people.

"But I thought she was brave...."

"Look, fuzzy—"

"My name is ge'Nilet, madam."

"Ge'Nilet, all I want is a tequila. Is that so much to ask?"

"I'm sorry, we don't have any of this—what did you call it?"

"Tequila." Domenica Corsi spoke very slowly and deliberately. "I could have sworn you would have it. It's an alcoholic beverage with a worm in the bottle. Klingons should love it."

"Oh! You want *gaghtlhutlh*. Just a moment." The al'Hmatti bartender reached under the bar and pulled out a black bottle.

Corsi looked at the bottle dubiously. "I assume the skulls painted on the side are just for decoration?"

"Oh, it's quite mild." He poured out a small amount. It had a reddish tint and seemed a bit oily.

Oh, what the hell. "To your health," she said, and sipped at the rim of the glass. *Spicyspicyhothothotwow!*

"Do you like it?"

"I'll take the bottle," she gasped. "I have phaser rifles I can clean with this stuff."

"Happy to oblige."

Corsi eyed the oversized, bearlike bartender. "What are you doing here? I would have thought that everyone working this event would be a Klingon."

"Oh, I've been with Lantar's House for a long time. So long, in fact, that I'm first in line to be the al'Hmatti ambassador to the Federation, when that day happens."

"God willing, then, and praise the al'Hmatti." Corsi toasted the bartender.

"Captain, although that was a lovely story, it's not quite in line with the traditional version in mythology."

"Oh? How so, Abramowitz?"

"Well, in the traditional myth the suitor won, not tied. And he won only by tricking her along the way. And those who lost the race were put to death."

"Hmmm." He stroked his chin in exaggerated thoughtfulness. "How about we don't tell her about that version, then?"

"Of course, sir."

"Good."

"*Daaaaavid!*" The captain winced again.

"Would you excuse me for a moment?" Gold asked.

"Are you sure you don't want us to keep you here for a while?" asked Hawkins.

"Thank you for the offer, but no. I better go deal with her, lest she undo the last ten years of treaty negotiations." He moved off quickly on an intercept course between Eva and Lantar.

Hawkins watched his captain go to face a peril worse than death. "Well, I guess I know why now."

"Why what?"

"Why young John is still off sailing the seas."

Carol looked up at him for a second. Then she stepped on his toes. Slowly.

* * *

Anthony continued to sit in the corner, silently observing the ebb and flow of people around him. Over there, a couple was beginning to dance.

"Hiya, Anthony. Do you mind if I join you?"

He looked up, surprised. "Dr. Lense?"

"Please, it's Elizabeth." She sat down next to him, a bit ungracefully.

"Why come over here? I thought you'd be the belle of the ball."

"Nah. The Klingons want no part of me whatsoever. They heard I was the savior of Sherman's Planet. Apparently, it's still a sore spot in their history. Something about the great tribble hunt of eleventy-seven or something." She gestured over to the gathering of humans. "And the bride's family wants to ask me about all their little aches and pains." She looked at the glass in her hand. "And I am also, I suspect, a little bit drunk."

"Ah."

"And what about you? What are you doing here?"

"Waiting for Bart, I suppose."

"Bart? Last I saw, he was in line at the bar, chatting with Fabian and being a general social butterfly."

He looked over at her. "Let me ask you a question."

"As long as it doesn't require a physical exam, shoot."

"Why do most relationships break up?"

"You are asking the wro-o-ng person, Anthony." She looked up at the ceiling. "I don't think I've ever had a successful romantic relationship in my life."

"Do you think these two will make it?"

She sighed. "I don't know. The odds are good in so many ways—but there's a lot against them, too. They come from different cultures—"

"Don't we all, when you get down to it?"

"Point."

Anthony leaned forward, looking more intent. "Really, what do you think makes one coupling work over another?"

Lense pondered that for a bit, and then said, "Po."

"I beg your pardon?"

Lense leaned forward, and spoke very slowly. "Po."

"Doctor, maybe it's time that you switch to drinking synthehol."

"No, no, no . . ." she waved her hand, as if swatting at flies—or for all Anthony could tell, green fairies. "*Po*. One word. Two letters. *P-O*. Concept described by de Bono." No sign of recognition of the name came to Anthony's face, so she continued. "Edward de Bono was born in Malta on Earth in the twentieth century. He attended St. Edward's College during World War II and then the University of Malta, where he qualified in medicine. He proceeded, as a Rhodes Scholar, to Christ Church, Oxford, where he gained an honors degree in psychology and physiology and then a D.Phil. in medicine. He also held a Ph.D. from Cambridge and an M.D. from the University of Malta, and held appointments at the universities of Oxford, London, Cambridge, and Harvard. Brilliant, brilliant man." She rattled off the credentials as if she'd just finished writing her college thesis on the man.

"I've never heard of him."

"And this is what passes for a Federation education these days? De Bono's special contribution was to take creativity and, for the first time in history, put the subject on a solid basis. He showed that creativity was a necessary behavior in a self-organizing information system, and how the nerve networks in the brain formed asymmetric patterns as the basis of perception. He was ten years ahead of contemporary mathematicians dealing with chaos theory, nonlinear and self-organizing systems." Still nothing. "He invented the term 'lateral thinking.'"

"Okay, *that* I've heard of."

"Oh goody." She was beginning to warm to the topic. "He showed that the logical alternatives are easily explored in most situations—either 'yes, it is,' or 'no, it isn't.' But logic isn't effective in coping with open-ended problems. It takes a long time before an unjustified step is taken, because no one feels justified in taking it. Yet only unjustified steps are likely to open up new patterns of thought."

"So what does Po have to do with this?"

"Well, de Bono suggested that to solve a problem, the thinker should relate the problem at hand to a random input, such as a word chosen by chance in a dictionary, and then see if he can, by connecting the two, open up a new approach to the situation. And the word he created to couple the two concepts was . . ." Here she paused.

After a second, Anthony realized she was waiting for him to reply. "Po?"

"Gold star! Head of the class! I have competition!" She raised her glass to him, took another sip—a big sip—and went on. "So you use it to combine concepts and see where it takes you. Like diamond *po* spaceships."

"Or rabbits *po* flight."

"Kidneys *po* electricity."

"Marbles *po* frontier."

"Holodeck *po* headgear."

"Klingons *po* Judaism."

"Yes! That's it exactly. Maybe it'll work, maybe it won't. But if a coupling of complete non sequiturs can be made and held together, even for a little while, something new and exciting can come out of it. And that's what a marriage needs. Creativity. Being in an ongoing relationship means that things always have to be kept new and interesting, yet at the same time secure and stable. People love nothing more than to be pleasantly surprised—even by the familiar and the comforting."

"You have to give the other what they want and need, but not always what they expect?"

"Exactly." She leaned even closer to him, putting a hand on his shoulder. "That's exactly what I mean. Sometimes you have to look in strange places to get something new, and sometimes it's right there all the time, you just have to find a new way of looking at it."

"You're right. Thank you." And he kissed her on the lips, a kiss that lingered. After a second or two, he pulled back. "I'm going to go find Bart and talk with him. See you soon."

Elizabeth sat there, not moving at all except for blinking.

"Yes," she said at last. "Exactly like that."

"Nice ceremony," Kendra commented, handing Fabian a glass of champagne.

"Yeah, it was," he agreed. "Though I think I'll stick with the old 'I do's.'"

She nudged him, smiling. "Got someone in mind there, mister?"

He laughed. "You never know, Ken. You never know."

Just then Kendra's padd beeped.

"Trouble at work?" Fabian joked, but stopped when he saw the look on her face. "Ken, is everything okay?"

She had turned completely pale, and looked a bit stunned. "Fabe, I—"

Quickly he pulled the padd from her hand and read the message. Then he glanced up at her.

"Ken, they approved the *Hyperion*! That's fantastic!"

She still looked shocked. "But—I don't understand. It failed."

"Not at all," he assured her, and she looked at him, then looked again. He was trying to hide the smile, but knew he wasn't succeeding.

"What did you do, Fabe?"

"Me?" He laughed. "Nothing. Well, okay, I did point out to Starfleet that none of the problems were with your design—they were all from outside sources. And I also mentioned that no existing ship design could have handled so much damage for that long. I guess they agreed."

"But—" She was still at a loss for words, and Fabian hugged her.

"Ken, relax. You did it. The *Hyperion*'s a great design—trust me, I spent two days going over every inch of it. You did a great job, and Starfleet saw that. They do occasionally notice such things, you know." He held up his glass, and she finally raised hers.

"Here's to good friends," Kendra managed, smiling at him. "I couldn't have done this without you, Fabe."

"Maybe you could have," he replied, "but it probably wouldn't have been such a mess." Then he clinked her glass. "To old friends. And to the *Hyperion*."

"To the *Hyperion*." She started to move her glass, but paused as she saw the look in his eye. Sure enough, Fabian clinked his glass against hers again.

"And to a good prank," he toasted, and she laughed.

"Always," she said. "To a good prank." She sipped her champagne, then grinned at him. "So what did you do to Crawfish?"

Fabian grinned back. "Oh, just a little of his own medicine. But I'm not the one who did it."

"Computer, open this door!"

"Access denied," the computer replied.

Crawford Pressman banged on his door again, but to no avail. Somehow the computer was refusing to recognize his voice or his password. Which meant that, since his door had inexplicably locked itself, he couldn't open it. And he'd been stuck in here for hours now!

"Computer," he shouted again, "this is Professor Crawford Pressman. I demand that you open this door!"

"Access denied," the computer replied again. And was it his imagination, or did it sound a little smug?

"Dammit!" Pressman pounded on the door again. "Someone, help me!" He was starting to feel faint from hunger. And he desperately needed a bathroom. "Anyone!"

Outside his office, several students glanced at the door on their way past, and laughed but kept on walking. Alex Sparks watched it all from where he leaned, directly across from Pressman's door. He had to admit, imagining the look on his colleague's face was entertaining. And the looks from the students were priceless. Perhaps there was something to this whole prank thing, after all.

"Help!" Pressman called again, though Alex could barely hear him through the door. Chuckling a little, he levered himself away from the wall and walked off down the hall, whistling softly to himself.

SMALL WORLD

David Mack

CHAPTER 1

Flames licked at Araneus's abdomen as another disruptor blast pummeled his tiny ship. One of his long, sinewy pedipalps shot down from his cephalothorax and silenced the shrilling alert signal on his wraparound helm console. Another tentacle-like appendage keyed the transmitter switch again. "Repeat," he said, trying to speak slowly and clearly. "This is the transport *Lycosa*, requesting assistance. Do you read me?" A squall of static rasped from the speaker.

The metallic, pyramid-shaped container tucked between his back legs seemed more fragile than it really was. *It is probably faring better than I am,* Araneus mused glumly.

The wheel-shaped space station was barely visible beyond his cockpit windshield. It was silhouetted against the sunset-red surface of the gas giant behind it. Though it was a mere few hundred *toscam*s away, he despaired of reaching it.

Another cacophonous boom rattled his ship's critically weakened hull. Araneus scuttled sideways against the bulkhead, away from the tongues of fire snaking through fractures in the gray deck beneath his legs. The acrid odor of burned hair and scorched flesh crept into his spiracles. Another alarm confirmed that the Silgov had locked their weapons onto his engines.

It was all over. The greatest journey in Koas history was about to end in tragedy.

With a sound like crumbling *lerfo* bark, a reply to his S.O.S. spat in disjointed bursts from the console speaker and echoed around him in the cramped, circular cockpit. "Lycosa . . . *is Varkala Station . . . course one-four-four mark six* . . ." A brief silence was followed by " . . . *unidenti . . . stand down or we—*"

The Silgov ship broke its weapons lock on the *Lycosa* and unleashed a volley of plasma fire at the space station. The barrage impacted on the facility's energy shield, which flickered like an ephemeral golden cocoon.

Then came the station's response—a quartet of fiery red projectiles that screamed past Araneus's ship toward the Silgov scout, which peeled away into an evasive maneuver. Unlike Koas weapons, which were extremely limited, the crimson missiles pursued the sleek, dartlike Silgov vessel relentlessly and eventually overtook it. Four brutal explosions hammered its shields, which collapsed. Without further delay, the ship broke off its attack and engaged its stardrive in retreat.

Araneus was about to thank his rescuers when his main console went dark. From the bowels of his ship came an ominous rumble, followed by the low, hungry roar of fire racing forward from the engines, looking for fuel to feed its wrath.

The station was still too far away. He would never reach it in time. With four legs he clutched the pyramid against his abdomen and prayed to the Architect of Time for forgiveness.

Varkala Station commander Cody Mui watched with mounting anxiety as the unidentified vessel fractured on the main viewer. Most of the staff in the station's drab, utilitarian command center worked in tense silence. Eric Theriault, his operations foreman, slammed his fist against his console. "They're breaking up. I can't tractor 'em in without ripping 'em apart."

Mui turned toward his station manager, Kari Spada. The blond young woman answered before he gave the order. "Boosting transporters to quantum resolution."

Wiping the sweat from his palms, Mui asked, "How long?"

"Ten more seconds," she said.

"Eric, can you get a lock on the crew?"

The beefy foreman punched in a new set of commands. "One life sign," he said. "Locked."

On the viewer, a bright orange flare pulsed in the rear third of the tiny ship, which resembled a spiny sea urchin. Mui had never seen a vessel like it before. He had no idea whether its origin lay within Thallonian space or if it had simply passed through it. The only thing he knew about it for certain was that, in a few more seconds, it would explode.

"Transporters ready," Spada said.

Mui nodded. "Energize." He opened a channel to the infirmary. "Doc, it's Cody. You got a patient comin' in."

"He better have an appointment," Dr. Safford grumbled over the comm, sounding like someone who'd been woken from a very nice dream and wasn't at all happy about it.

Spada initiated the transport sequence. She was still completing it as the vessel erupted and vanished in a rapidly dispersed cloud of atomized particles. Looking up from her console, she reassured Mui, "It's okay. Transport complete."

The commander heaved a relieved sigh, then said, "Nice work. I'll head down to meet our guest." Walking toward the turbolift, he felt an extra spring in his step; apparently, the diet his wife had inflicted on him by reprogramming his replicator was working after all. He made a mental note to thank her later.

Spada called after him. "Should we call this in?"

Stepping into the turbolift, he said, "Let's wait until we know what to call it in *as*."

Inside the battered Silgov scout ship *Starlit Wing*, the temperature was falling rapidly. Maleiras, the chief scout, supervised the repair of the damage inflicted by the alien space station. "Never mind the weapons," she said softly. "Focus on restoring communications. We have to alert the fleet."

Sesslom, the ship's soldier-mechanic, shimmied out from under the main control panel. The honey-hued skin of his delicately symmetrical face was marred by irregular smears of smoky black filth, and his silvery hair—normally coiffed into a bold vertical crest down the middle of his head—was as tangled as a *thokka* nest. "Communications will take at least two *shav*s to restore, my lady," he said.

"I understand," she said. "Work as quickly as you can."

"As you command," Sesslom said.

Maleiras turned aft and kneeled down to look through the hatchway into the ship's lower compartment. Coleef, the pale and slender young pilot-engineer, had so far avoided soiling her pristine garments and her mane of metallic-violet hair. The chief scout called down to her. "Do you require my help to restore defense screens?"

"They are irreparable, my lady," Coleef said. "I can reroute their power to long-range sensors in an *oloshav*."

"Well done," Maleiras said, then returned to her post.

Without shields, her ship would be no match for the alien space station. The *Starlit Wing*'s sensors had detected a matter-transference beam removing the pilot and the Koas's mysterious artifact from the courier's ship before it exploded. Now both were aboard the enemy stronghold, temporarily out of reach.

The artifact had eluded her for now . . . but not for long.

Dr. Bob Safford was no expert in arachnid psychology, but the giant black spider in his infirmary seemed a tad agitated.

Its voice sounded like a guttural rasp. "No time to wait," it said, frantically waving the six tentacles that dangled from its octopoid head. It rambled on without waiting for Safford to attempt a reply. "Where is my ship? Must finish journey. Need to reach Starfleet. How did I get here?"

Mui entered like a man in a hurry, then came to a quick stop as the mammoth arachnid pivoted swiftly toward him. The commander recoiled, a reaction that Safford presumed was mostly instinctual. He certainly wouldn't fault his boss for cowering a bit; watching the creature take shape in the middle of the dingy, decades-out-of-date infirmary—smack dab between himself and the exit—had ranked very high on the middle-aged physician's list of all-time moments of gut-twisting terror.

"My name is Cody Mui," the commander said. "I'm in charge of this station. We rescued you from your ship."

"I am Araneus," it said. "You are Starfleet?"

"No," Mui said. "We're civilians. Mining survey."

Araneus waggled its pedipalps at the profusely sweating young commander. "But this is Federation?"

"Um, not exactly." Mui shot a tense look at Safford, who shrugged, unsure of what the commander wanted him to say. Mui pressed on. "We're just outside the Federation border, on the edge of the former Thallonian Empire."

With a sharp hiss, Araneus pivoted first clockwise, then back again. "Thallonians are gone," it said, moving forward.

"Yeah," Mui said, his voice a fearful tremolo. "We know."

Safford pointed at the pyramid-shaped box on the floor.

Mui followed Safford's gesture, then looked back at Araneus. Nodding toward it with his chin, he asked, "What's in the container?"

"The future of my people," Araneus said. Leaning back on its hind four legs, Araneus lifted the pyramid delicately with its four forelimbs. It brushed a symbol near the base of the object with one of its pedipalps, then held out the box toward Mui. Safford leaned cautiously forward to get a better look.

The pyramid's sides folded outward to reveal what looked like a planet the size of a large melon, encased in a shimmering, pale-orange sphere of energy.

Mui looked up inquisitively at Araneus. "A hologram?"

The spider made a gurgling sound. "Koa. My homeworld."

The doctor was surprised to see Mui absorb that bit of news with perfect sangfroid.

"I see," Mui said. Seconds later he shook his head. "Actually, I don't see. If that's . . . your homeworld . . . why do you have it in a box?"

"Star went supernova," Araneus said. "Must move world to new star." It scuttled over to a companel along the wall and, despite the apparent unwieldiness of its appendages and extremities, deftly manipulated the panel interface. An image of a star system appeared on the monitor display.

Mui joined Araneus at the screen. "Mu Arae," the commander said. "Eighteen light-years away. That's not so bad."

"My ship," Araneus said. "You can fix?"

Safford knew from the pained expression on Mui's face that bad news was just around the corner. "I'm sorry," Mui said. "We couldn't save your ship. It . . . well, it exploded."

The doctor was glad he wasn't the one staring into the beast's unreadable, huge, faceted eyes right now. After a tense pause, Araneus seemed to deflate. Its abdomen sagged to the deck and its legs crumpled and splayed around it like fractured black bamboo. Bowing its bulbous head, it muttered, "All is lost."

"Maybe not," Mui said, trying to sound encouraging. "We don't have a ship, but we can get one in no time." He used the companel to hail the command center. "Kari, get Starfleet on the horn, tell them we need a ship here, pronto."

"You got it, boss."

"Thanks." Mui closed the channel. Looking down at the ostensibly despondent arachnid, he said, "Don't worry, we'll get you to Mu Arae in a couple weeks."

Araneus groaned. "All for naught," it said again. "Journey has ended."

"No, you don't understand—we can get you there."

"My world is trapped," the creature said. "Key is lost."

Safford had a bad feeling brewing in his gut. He sat down at his desk, opened the bottom drawer, and took out a tall bottle of cheap vodka and two short glasses.

Mui asked the obvious follow-up question. "What key?"

"Key that releases my world," Araneus said. "On my ship."

"Could we make another key?"

"Ancient," Araneus said. "Unique. A code. Lost." It curled

its legs beneath its abdomen and ducked its head, clearly withdrawing from further conversation.

Mui reopened the channel to the command center. "Kari, tell Starfleet we need tech-heads, good ones. . . . We've got a planet stuck in a box."

Safford poured stiff drinks for himself and the commander, certain this would be only the first round of many.

CHAPTER 2

Captain Montgomery Scott's order, delivered with a broad grin, had been simple enough: "Jump in and see how far it goes."

Four mornings later, as Captain David Gold stepped from the turbolift onto the bridge and watched stars streak across the *da Vinci*'s main viewer, he adopted Scotty's smile for himself.

His blissful moment was short-lived.

Lieutenant Songmin Wong stood next to the conn station, where Ensign Martina Barre sat, her hands planted firmly on the console. "Get up," he said to her. "It's my shift."

"Just a few more seconds," she said.

The captain shook his head; for the past three days, each shift change on the bridge had resulted in the same contest of wills between the pilots. Every morning, Wong wrested control from Barre, only to resist handing it over to Rusconi for beta shift eight hours later. Rusconi had proved equally possessive.

"Solve this in the next three seconds," Gold said to the quibbling pair, "or else I'll take both your next shifts."

Barre huffed softly, her shoulders sagging as she grudgingly pushed aside the conn panel and stood up. She and Wong locked eyes for a moment of half-joking challenge. Then Barre stepped aside and Wong took his post with a grin.

Gold didn't blame them for being eager; it wasn't every day that a Starfleet pilot was able to fly a ship at a steady warp 9.99 without risking calamity. As part of a classified research project, the *da Vinci* was charting a recently discovered, shifting subspace "slipstream" that could be entered by making the proper adjustments to the ship's warp field. Once inside, the phenomenon greatly accelerated warp-speed travel across vast distances. The *da Vinci* had traveled at high warp for three days to cross the twelve light-years from Earth to the nearest terminus of the slipstream; it had taken less than four days since then to traverse more than seventy light-years, out to the edge of Federation territory.

Ensign Susan Haznedl settled in at ops. Behind Gold, Ensign Winn Mara stepped gracefully aside as Lieutenant Anthony Shabalala took her place at tactical. Lieutenant Commander Mor glasch Tev, the *da Vinci*'s Tellarite second officer, stood at attention next to the center seat as Gold approached.

"Status," Gold said as he settled into his chair.

"We've just passed Theta Indii," Tev said. "ETA at the Typhon Expanse is five hours. Long-range scans suggest the slipstream extends well past the other side of the expanse."

Tev handed Gold a padd. The captain reviewed the data. "Any sign of an end at all?"

"None yet, sir."

"Then I guess we're in for a long ride," Gold said.

"It is not an unpleasant proposition," Tev said. For the past few days, the Tellarite engineer's tireless work ethic had kept him on the bridge longer than anyone else. He had filled the hours by collecting raw data on the slipstream, running analyses, and charting projections. What had lately impressed Gold, however, was not Tev's indefatigable labors, but his complete lack of boasting about them. Tev gestured to the aft science console. "With your permission, Captain?"

"Of course," Gold said. Tev nodded politely, then moved quietly to the science station and resumed his research.

Gold decided to retire to his ready room and enjoy a cup of coffee while recording a mission update for Captain Scott. As he stood up, an innocuous-sounding chirp emanated from the tactical console and hushed the already muted chatter on the bridge. Everyone stopped and turned to look at Shabalala while he reviewed the incoming transmission. "Priority signal from Starfleet Command, Captain."

The captain's mouth tightened into a frown. "I'll take it in my ready room." Quick-stepping across the bridge, Gold mused darkly, *I knew this assignment was too good to last.*

Commander Sonya Gomez stood next to Captain Gold in the transporter room. Like a study in contrast, Chief of Security Domenica Corsi (slender, pale, and blond) and Deputy Chief of Security Vance Hawkins (broad-shouldered, ebony-skinned, with a shaved head) flanked the two command officers. Behind them, Ensign McAvennie stood by to assist Transporter Chief Laura Poynter, who was completing the beaming sequence.

A large, languid cyclone of shimmering matter coalesced above the transporter pad with a singsong hum. Both the glow and the sound faded as the energizer coils powered down, and a massive black arachnid with a head like that of an octopus was revealed. An odor of burned hair, mild at first, quickly grew stronger. Clutched in the pedipalps that extended from either side of the creature's mandibles was a metallic, equilateral pyramid on a base approximately forty centimeters wide.

"Mr. Araneus," the captain said, sounding not the least bit unnerved to be addressing a gargantuan arachnid, "I'm Captain David Gold. Welcome aboard the *da Vinci.*"

Araneus skittered forward, its eight legs rising and falling like gears in a dark machine. Poynter and McAvennie recoiled. Corsi and Hawkins held their ground without blinking. Gomez's jaw clenched with the effort of keeping her feet still. The captain, for his part, seemed perfectly relaxed.

"Thank you, Captain," Araneus said.

"This is my first officer, Commander Sonya Gomez," Gold continued. "Security Chief Domenica—"

"No time, Captain," Araneus interrupted. The lumbering alien scrambled down from the transporter pad. Everyone took two steps back to avoid being trampled. "Koa is in danger; we must reach Mu Arae as fast as your ship goes." It pushed the pyramid toward Gold. "We must find the key. No time!"

Glancing sideways, Gomez caught the subtle nod from Gold that meant he was handing off the conversation to her.

"Mr. Araneus," Gomez said, "we're aware of the rather . . . *unique* predicament your world is in. I assure you, after we collect some basic information from you, we'll be proceeding to Mu Arae at our best possible—"

The arachnid reared up on his hind legs and adopted a pose that reminded Gomez, in an unsettling way, of the Federation-standard "biohazard" icon. The creature let out a series of clicks, grunts, and hisses. Either the universal translator was unable to decipher the sounds, or they were never intended as anything other than an inchoate expression of frustration. After several seconds, with a voice like a breath from the grave, Araneus groaned, "No time!"

Then the giant spider collapsed on the deck.

A sickly gurgle escaped its maw as a viscous gray-white fluid oozed out of its mouth. As its legs splayed limply between the *da Vinci* personnel's feet, its pedipalps gently stroked the base of the pyramid, whose four sides unfolded to reveal the shrunken orb of Koa, imprisoned in its glowing energy shell.

Corsi and Hawkins pulled tricorders from their belts and sprang forward to kneel at Araneus's side.

"Poynter," Corsi said, "relay Araneus's transport bioscan to my tricorder."

"Aye, sir," Poynter said, keying in the commands.

Hawkins devoted his attention to scanning the open pyramid.

Gomez furrowed her brow. "Someone report, please."

Corsi replied, "Best guess? I think he had a heart attack."

"Well," Gomez said. "We're off to a great start. As usual."

Gold massaged his wrinkled brow with the fingers of his right hand. *"Oy vey."* He ran his hand through his sparse white hair. "Gomez, get your people working on that pyramid contraption. Poynter, beam our guest to sickbay—and warn Dr. Lense first, please." The captain turned away from the group as he tapped his combadge. "Gold to bridge."

"Tev here, sir."

"Set course for Mu Arae, maximum warp."

The transmission from Viceroy Narjam was frazzled but growing stronger by the moment. *"You're sure they removed the artifact from the station?"*

"Yes, my lord," Maleiras said, maintaining eye contact with Narjam on the small screen attached to the arm of her chair. "With a matter-transference beam, to one of their vessels." In the front of the cockpit, Coleef was completing the preflight systems check. Down below, Sesslom was hard at work keeping the comm system functioning. "They have just departed," the chief scout continued, "following the Koas ship's original course."

"What is their velocity?"

"Factor five-point-two-three."

Narjam tilted his chin upward, clearly pleased at the news. *"Very good."* He looked down and checked his console. *"We will reach you in less than a* shav," he said. *"Will you be ready to rejoin the fleet?"*

"Yes, my lord." Coleef swiveled her seat toward Maleiras and gestured that the *Starlit Wing* was ready for flight. Though the frigid temperature inside the ship was betrayed by the wispy clouds of vapor produced by her exhaled breath, Maleiras suppressed her body's urge to shiver. She was determined to retain her dignity before her superior. "Shall we relay our tactical scans of the alien space station?"

The viceroy dismissed the query with a twitch of his delicate hand. *"Unnecessary,"* he said. *"The artifact has left their possession. They no longer concern us. Maintain sensor lock on the alien vessel."*

"As you command, my lord. May I make a request?"

"Speak."

"My vessel requires a replacement for its defense-screen regulator," Maleiras said. Sesslom looked up through the aft hatch from the lower deck, eager to hear the viceroy's answer.

"I will see it done," Narjam said. *"My engineer will transfer the component to your vessel after we arrive."*

"Thank you, my lord. Most gracious."

"You've served well today, Maleiras," he said. *"And the day is only just begun. We'll be with you shortly. Narjam out."* Maleiras bowed her head, then the channel flickered off.

Turning fully to face Sesslom, Maleiras said, "Make as many other repairs as are possible. I want defensive screens restored before we overtake the alien vessel." Sesslom acknowledged the order with a half bow, then returned to his calm but tireless work. On the tactical display, an icon representing the alien ship crept slowly toward an unremarkable star.

Soon, the Koas technology will be ours, she told herself. Imagining the power that the mysterious, planet-shrinking pyramid must contain . . . trying to conceive of the energies it would have to harness to pluck a world, intact, from its orbit and hold it in stasis . . . such thoughts terrified Maleiras to the depths of her being. The only thing that terrified her more was the idea of being returned to bondage. *When the pyramid is ours,* she reminded herself, *we will finally set our people free.*

A fearful silence lingered in the *da Vinci* sickbay. The unconscious, mammoth arachnid lay sprawled across two biobeds and two gurneys placed between them. Dr. Elizabeth Lense shook her head. "I don't even know where to start," the curly-haired physician said.

Behind her, Medical Technician Dantas Falcão and Nurse Sandy Wetzel peeked over Lense's shoulders. "The biobed's readouts are completely messed up," Falcão said, her pretty face twisted into a mask of frightened apprehension.

Wetzel, her arms folded across her chest like a shield, reluctantly said, "We have to do *something*."

Lense picked up her medical tricorder and trained its sensors on her patient. "Dantas, download comparative anatomy data on all known arthropod species and try to recalibrate biobed two. Sandy, take a sample of that discharge from its maw and run a full chemical analysis—enzymes, molecular structure, trace elements, everything."

Moving closer to Araneus, Lense tried to locate the center of its circulatory system—assuming that it even had one.

Wetzel collected a sample of the substance that was rapidly congealing inside the patient's mouth. She paused. "Should we try to clear its mouth, Doctor?"

"No," Lense said, shaking her head. "Don't stick your hands in there." Brushing her fingertips lightly across the arachnid's carapace, she said, "It appears to breathe through a network of large spiracles. Don't worry about clearing an airway." She looked up. "Computer, activate Emergency Medical Hologram." Overhead holoprojectors awoke with a quickly rising hum. The holographic doctor took shape in front of her.

"Please state the nature of the—" The EMH eyed Araneus with an expression of clinical curiosity. "I see. How may I assist you, Doctor?"

Handing a large and, ironically, spider-shaped mechanical device to the EMH, Lense said, "I need to place a cardiopulmonary contact monitor on the patient, but I can't reach the center of its torso."

"Understood," he replied. Without a moment's hesitation, he lifted the CPCM over his head and strolled toward the center of Araneus's body. Adjusting his holographic matrix to make himself noncorporeal from the chest down, he passed like a ghost through the patient. He placed the monitor near the forward curve of Araneus's prodigious abdomen. No sooner did the device's radial extensions clamp down on Araneus's body than its six largest limbs snapped inward, stingers extended. Lense gasped at the swift, lethal, and obviously involuntary reflexive action, then heaved a relieved sigh as she remembered that the EMH was just a photonic construct, impervious to harm.

Striding back through the clenched tangle of dark limbs to rejoin Lense, the EMH said, "I await further instruction."

"Please assist Nurse Wetzel with her analysis."

The EMH acknowledged Lense's order with a brief nod, then walked away quickly to join Wetzel in the adjacent biolab.

A rattling groan from Araneus drew Lense's attention back to her patient. Fixating on its huge, dangerous limbs, she was grateful that she hadn't tried to place the cardio monitor herself. She had no interest in being on the receiving end of a giant spider's fight-or-flight reflex. Recalling her semesters of xenophysiology at Starfleet Medical all those years ago, she vaguely remembered learning about the medical advances that had been made by studying the synaptic development and seemingly precognitive reflexes of arachnids. That gave her an idea.

She tapped her combadge. "Rennan Konya, please report to sickbay."

The turbolift thrummed along, quickly traversing the length of the *da Vinci*—but not quickly enough for Bart Faulwell.

"So what I'm thinking," Carol Abramowitz said, continuing a monologue that already had persisted all through their shared lunch, "is that his birthday is next week and I want to get him something nice. You know, something he wouldn't get for himself, but that he can use, or that he and I can use together."

Faulwell wanted to tell her to shut up, to stop talking, to keep her newfound romantic euphoria to herself, to stop being so damned happy when he was anything but. Instead, the middle-aged cryptography and linguistics expert smiled through his salt-and-pepper beard and nodded and made vague noises of acknowledgment.

He really didn't resent Abramowitz for her recently ignited romance with Vance Hawkins. When he'd first heard the news, he'd been elated for her. Ever since she had revealed to him during the Galvan VI disaster that she had never truly been in love, he had been worried about her. Emotional openness had never been her strong suit, in Faulwell's opinion; sarcasm impelled by a mordant wit had always been the petite cultural specialist's forte. That shortcoming had almost led to her death on Vrinda, and he was glad that she was emerging from that particular shell.

The turbolift stopped and the doors parted to reveal the starboard corridor of deck five. Faulwell followed Abramowitz as they stepped briskly toward the science lab. She was still talking, staging a one-woman debate over what she ought to give Hawkins. Tuning her out, Faulwell reflected on the real reason for his black-dog mood. Only about a week had passed since the wedding of Captain Gold's granddaughter, Esther. During a lighthearted aside, Faulwell's longtime partner, Anthony Mark, had made a good-natured remark to him, suggesting that maybe the two of them ought to get married. It had been so casual, so off-the-cuff, that Faulwell had simply brushed it aside with a bon mot and forgotten about it.

But now the moment—and the suggestion—weighed on his mind.

He snapped out of his reverie as they reached the lab door. "Anyway," Abramowitz finished, "we can finish this later."

Faulwell stifled a derisive snort. *Yes, I'm sure "we" will.*

He followed her into the lab, which was abuzz with excited voices that concealed the humming of its walls of computers. Gathered around a large worktable were Gomez and Tev; tactical systems specialist Fabian Stevens, who was engaged in a spirited but hushed debate with the chief engineer, Lieutenant Nancy Conlon; and Haznedl, who was showing her tricorder's display to Tev and Gomez while talking a rapid string of jargon that meant little or nothing to Faulwell.

It wasn't difficult to understand what the excitement was about. On the table, hovering above a small metallic square whose four triangular side pieces were open and folded flat, was a planet that had been compressed to the size of a human head and cocooned in a flickering, golden stasis field. Turning toward Abramowitz, Faulwell muttered, "There's something you don't see every day."

Gomez stuck her thumb and forefinger between her teeth and let loose a shrill, piercing whistle. The room fell quiet. "All right," she said. "We're all here, let's get started." Tilting her head toward the miniature planet, she said, "Our mission is to figure out how to get this box to release this planet, and to determine where and when we need to do so."

Tev keyed a command sequence into his padd. A holographic star map appeared above the worktable. "The planet's guardian has indicated that its destination is Mu Arae. A yellow-orange dwarf, spectral and luminosity type G3. Its high metallicity has resulted in an abundance of exploitable mineral resources in its asteroid belt. Because of the erratic orbit of one of its gaseous supergiants, no Class-M planets are known to exist in this system's habitable zone."

Before the deactivated holographic star map faded away, Conlon spoke up. "Multiple scans of the pyramid have proved inconclusive. Its metal—or whatever it is—is impervious to physical damage, so we've been unable to take samples or run tests. I can't tell you much about the device itself except that its plates appear to be exactly three centimeters thick at their widest points, beveled on their edges, and covered on their exterior surface with raised markings."

Gomez nodded to Faulwell and Abramowitz. "That's where you two come in. While we tinker with the hardware, we need you two to try and make heads or tails of those symbols." She handed her tricorder to Faulwell. On its screen was a visual recording of the device in its closed configuration. Pointing to a marking near the object's base, she said, "Araneus pressed this symbol to open the pyramid. We don't know if the same one closes it. In fact, we don't know what *any* of them do, and we can't risk touching them until we know what they mean."

Faulwell frowned. "Do we have any records of Araneus's language, either spoken or written?"

Haznedl shook her head. "His ship exploded shortly after he was rescued by the crew of Varkala Station. The universal translator only picked up a smattering of his language so far. He spent most of his time on Varkala repeating himself."

Leaning in for a close-up look, Stevens all but pressed his nose to one of the pyramid's open sides. "No hinges or seams. Probably some kind of mnemonic polymer."

Conlon nodded. "Remarkable, isn't it? Better than ours, that's for—"

"Let's move on," Gomez interrupted. "What about this stasis field? How's it holding this planet in suspended animation? And how the hell do you compress an entire planet, anyway?"

"The shrinking part I can guess at," Stevens said. "The *Defiant* ran into something like this a couple years ago—a subspace compression anomaly. Shrank a runabout down to the size of my finger."

"I read about that," Haznedl said. "But that was a natural phenomenon—this was done artificially."

"Yeah," Stevens said, dragging his fingers through his dark hair. "Gotta say, I've never seen anything like this—any of it."

Strolling around the table, Conlon said, "As for the stasis field, Commander, the question isn't so much, how did the Koas get their planet in there? It's, how do they plan to get it out? There are so many values that would have to be restored: orbital distance and velocity, rotation and angular momentum, not to mention the quantum states of every living thing on the planet itself."

"And all with no moving parts," Stevens quipped.

An arrogant *harrumph* preceded Tev's retort. "Are you certain, Specialist? Can your eyes penetrate the box's shell and confirm that its workings are entirely nonmoving? Or are you merely wasting our time with glib remarks?"

Before Faulwell could point out that Tev's unnecessary rebuke was four times longer than Stevens's remark—certainly a more egregious waste of time by any measure—Gomez said sharply, "That's enough, Tev." Glancing at Stevens, she added, in a gentler tone of voice, "Fabian, try to stay focused." Faulwell suspected that Gomez had chided Stevens merely for the sake of preserving the dignity of her fellow officer.

Within minutes, the conversation devolved into a verbal maelstrom of technical jargon. All of it was far outside Faulwell's area of expertise. Standing mutely beside him, Abramowitz seemed equally nonplussed by the engineers' technobabble. He tapped her shoulder. "Want to get out of here?"

She rolled her eyes. "Please."

Faulwell stepped beside Commander Gomez. "Commander,

with your permission, Carol and I would like to continue our research elsewhere."

Gomez nodded her approval. "Let me know the moment you find something." He assured her that he would, then led Abramowitz back out into the corridor. For a few blissful moments, the only sound in the corridor was their footsteps.

As they reached the turbolift, Abramowitz spoke.

"Maybe I should give Vance something homemade," she said as the doors swished open.

Stepping into the turbolift, Faulwell valiantly resisted the urge to suggest that she give her lover the gift of silence.

Unlike the serene slipstream voyage out from Arcturus, the high-warp voyage to Mu Arae was giving the *da Vinci* a thorough shaking. Captain Gold was in the midst of a double shift on the bridge while Gomez and Tev searched for the key to unlock the Koas homeworld from its . . .

He found himself at a loss for words when trying to describe the pyramid. Was it a vessel? A shelter? A disguise? Whatever its original designation might have been, without the key that would free Koa and restore it to new life in orbit around Mu Arae, only one descriptor now seemed appropriate: prison.

At least the conn officers' tug-of-war is over, Gold mused. Ensign Rusconi had relieved Wong without a word passing between them, and the young woman now held the *da Vinci* steady as it hurtled back through Federation space at warp 9.6. While she worked, she chatted amiably with Ensign Saldok, an occasionally overeager but very reliable young Benzite man. He had just joined the *da Vinci*'s crew as its beta-shift operations officer during the ship's recent stopover on Earth.

Gold was about to summon Corsi to the bridge, to take over command while he took a break for dinner, when a chirping alert sounded on the tactical console. "Captain," said Ensign Joanne Piotrowski, "incoming signal from Varkala Station, priority one."

"On-screen."

The image of station commander Cody Mui appeared on the main viewer. He looked alarmed. *"Captain Gold, the ship that attacked us has friends—big ones—and they're moving fast, on a pursuit course for your ship."*

"Are your people all right?"

"We're fine, sir. They went right past us." He nodded to someone off-screen. *"We're sending you all the sensor data we could collect before they moved out of range."*

The captain's posture stiffened. "Out of range? How long ago did you detect them?"

"Less than half an hour," Mui said. *"Like I said, they're really moving. Had to be at least warp nine-point-ninety-nine."*

Piotrowski chimed in, "Sir, I'm tracking forty-one unidentified vessels, on the farthest edge of sensor range. Closing at warp nine-point-nine-nine-four. They'll overtake us in less than one hour." A new signal beeped from her console. "Another incoming transmission, sir—from the pursuing fleet."

Gold nodded to Mui. "Thanks for the heads-up, Commander. Gold out."

As the screen blinked back to the warp-distorted starfield, the captain nodded to Piotrowski to patch in the next signal. He turned back toward the main viewer to see the image of a delicately featured humanoid man, attired in ornately tailored robes and sporting a meticulously coiffed crown of multichromatic hair. *"Attention, alien vessel* da Vinci," he said. *"I am Viceroy Narjam of the Silgov. Your vessel is carrying an artifact stolen from my people. We demand its immediate return."*

Narjam's imperious demeanor rankled Gold. Even more important, something about his claim of ownership of the pyramid struck the captain as inherently suspect.

Hunching his shoulders and feigning ignorance, Gold replied, "An artifact? Like a crystal vase? Or a stone tablet?"

The viceroy bristled at the query. *"It is a metal pyramid."*

"A solid metal pyramid?"

Despite all Narjam's delicately symmetrical beauty, from his enormous almond-shaped eyes to his nigh-imperceptible nose, he looked ready to fracture from the stress of hiding his anger. *"No,"* he said. *"It contains precious cargo."*

"Spice?" Gold taunted. "Frankincense? Myrrh?"

"*A planet,*" Narjam all but growled.

"Could you *describe* the planet?"

Narjam closed his eyes briefly, then opened them. They had changed color and were now a radiant crimson. *"I will not discuss this with you further,"* he said. *"Halt your vessel and surrender the artifact to us—or we will take it from you by force."*

The channel blinked off, returning the elongated stars to the main viewer. Gold sighed and looked back at Piotrowski. "You know what to do."

With a knowing grimace, she sounded the red-alert klaxon.

CHAPTER 3

Never one to sugarcoat her opinions, Corsi struggled to tread the very fine line between conscientious objection and outright insubordination. "Captain, we don't even know which side is telling the truth," the statuesque blond security chief said, pacing back and forth in front of Gold's ready room desk. "Taking sides before we know what we're getting into—"

"—is the hand we've been dealt," Gold said. "We embarked on a humanitarian mission, and I intend to finish it."

She stopped pacing. "But what if the Silgov are telling the truth? They claim the artifact is stolen property."

The captain shook his head. "I gave them a chance to state their case. They responded with threats."

Planting her fists accusingly on her hips like a scolding parent, she said, "The way I hear it, you provoked their viceroy pretty openly."

Gold shrugged. "What can I say? I don't care for people who begin a conversation with demands and threats."

"All the same, sir, we might have just landed on the wrong side of a criminal matter." She was briefly distracted by the tantalizing aroma of the mug of sweet-smelling java on the captain's desk. Refocusing, she said, "In less than an hour, the Silgov fleet will be looking to force the issue. We need to know who's lying to us *before* they get here."

Nodding slowly, the captain said, "All right. Those are your orders, then."

"Sir?"

"Find out which side we should believe."

Frustration and annoyance flushed Corsi's face with warmth. "Aye, sir. . . . I presume we'll continue to advance Araneus's side of the matter until then?"

"Call it a hunch," Gold said. "Given a choice between siding with a big fleet of pushy *shlubs* who snap orders at me, or a lone traveler who just lost his ship and is now entirely at our mercy . . ." He let his statement trail off, apparently confident that his meaning was clear.

Resisting the urge to roll her eyes, Corsi said, "Point taken, Captain."

He picked up his mug of steaming-hot coffee. "Dismissed."

Rennan Konya found the sensations he detected in Araneus's motor cortex fascinating, to say the least. Using a finely honed psionic talent known as proprioception, the trim, angular-featured Betazoid security guard tapped into the unconscious mind of the semiconscious Koas. Subtle pulses of pain mingled with fleeting flashes of reflex reaction to heat or contact. Despite the exotic origin of the enormous creature, Konya found its nervous system less alien to his telepathic sense than its physical appearance was to his eyes.

He sensed Dr. Lense much more easily, as she tried to step up quietly behind him. Compared to the delicate, hard-to-reach synaptic web of Araneus's mind, Lense's mind was like a clarion. "No change, Doctor," Konya said, anticipating her question.

"So far, so good," she said. "Let—"

"—you know if I detect any change," he interrupted. "Will do." He could feel the curt nod of her head even though he couldn't see her. Proprioception was not nearly the same as having eyes in the back of one's head, but for a trained practitioner it came very close. In hand-to-hand combat it gave him an almost imperceptible edge. However, as he had been more than happy to demonstrate to Dantas Falcão the past few nights, it was a skill that also could be put to more *pleasurable* uses.

Ire and aggression flooded Konya's senses, affording him several seconds' warning of Lieutenant Commander Corsi's arrival. The doors parted with a soft pneumatic gasp, and the chief of security strode into sickbay with a look on her face that made clear she was in no mood to be trifled with. She stepped briskly between Konya and Araneus, then snapped at Lense, "Wake up your patient, Doctor. Now."

Konya silently noted a tiny twitch in Araneus's pincers.

Showing an inner fortitude that Konya couldn't help but admire, Lense calmly looked back at Corsi and said, "No."

Her answer brought Corsi up short. Corsi took a moment to recompose herself. "Doctor, this isn't the time for an ethical debate. Your patient has information we need if we're going to get out of this mess alive."

"Forget it," Lense said. "We've served together how long?"

"Awhile," Corsi said.

"Right, awhile. And have I ever just ignored my professional ethics and done whatever you told me to do, just because you said it was an emergency?"

Corsi wore a glum expression. "Most of the time, actually."

Even from across the room, Konya felt that Corsi had struck a nerve with her roommate the doctor, who waved her hands in a defensive, crossing gesture. "Well, not today," she said. "I'm sick of it. Cite your emergencies, your regulations, your orders—I don't care. I'm not reviving my patient prematurely just so you can harass him."

Sickbay lay gripped in a tense hush. Konya sensed Dantas and Nurse Wetzel lurking in the adjacent lab, cramped together, anxious to stay clear of the two officers' conversation. Empathy was not one of Konya's principal talents, but the two women were broadcasting their shared emotion in powerful waves.

Tapping her foot, Corsi eyed the doctor suspiciously.

"You have no idea how to revive that thing, do you?"

"Not a clue," Lense admitted, shoulders slumping.

"Tell me you're kidding," Corsi said, pacing inside a small zone of personal space. "How hard is it to diagnose a spider?"

"Corsi, the only thing Araneus has in common with spiders is general body shape and the number of limbs. Until I see its gene sequence, I'm not putting any meds into it."

"Fair enough," Corsi said. The security chief turned toward Konya. "Rennan, that thing you do—"

"You mean proprio—"

"Yeah, that," she said. "Can you send as well as receive?"

"I'm not sure," Konya said. "I have trouble sensing Araneus as it is. Sending a complex message would—"

"Nothing complex," Corsi said. "Just wake him up."

Shrugging his shoulders, he said, "Hang on. I'll try."

Reaching out with his psionic abilities, Konya projected a basic waking impulse into Araneus's nervous system.

A piercing shriek, like the amplified cry of a wounded eagle, split the quiet hum of sickbay. Konya, Corsi, and Lense all reflexively covered their ears with their hands. Araneus thrashed across the biobeds, its multiple limbs extending and retracting, its head tentacles flailing. One leg cracked a computer display screen, while another flung a rolling cart of surgical tools across sickbay with a deafening crash.

Fighting to concentrate and focus his thoughts through the din, Konya pushed more thoughts into the mind of the frightened Koas: *Calm . . . Safe . . . Calm . . .*

Araneus's panic subsided. Its enormous faceted eyes swiveled slightly. Certain that the Koas was awake and alert, Konya nodded slowly to Corsi.

She leaned carefully over Konya's shoulder. Her tightly wound bun of hair was mere centimeters from his face. Speaking softly, she said, "Araneus, my name is Domenica Corsi. I'm the chief of security on this ship. I need to ask you some questions."

Gurgling noises rattled deep inside the creature's throat. Konya remained alert for any sign of renewed anxiety, but for now the Koas seemed at ease. "Ask," it said, drawing out the word in a long breathy rasp.

"Did your people build the pyramid?"

A very long pause followed. Then the weak Koas said in a thin whisper, "Old ones."

Corsi arched an eyebrow at Konya, as if she expected him to elaborate on Araneus's cryptic answer. The Betazoid guard shrugged and shook his head.

Clearly frustrated, Corsi soldiered on. "The Silgov accuse you of stealing the pyramid from them. They claim it's their artifact."

This time Araneus tensed. Its pedipalps quivered. Drawing its huge limbs inward, it raised its body off the biobeds and the supplemental gurneys toward the ceiling of sickbay, all the while emitting an angry growl that rose steadily in volume.

Konya felt the crash coming. "Doctor! It's suffering some kind of seizure!"

Lense rushed forward, and Falcão and Wetzel entered swiftly from the lab to assist her. All three women froze as they watched Araneus's limbs tremble and give out. Its dense, ponderous bulk slammed back down onto the biobeds. As the echo of the impact faded, Konya heard a distinct cracking of polymer from one of the beds' foundations.

Singsong oscillations from overlapping medical tricorders filled sickbay. The sound was almost enough to drown out Corsi's darkly resigned sigh.

"Well," Konya said. "That was fun."

"I'll go see if the engineers learned anything from the pyramid," Corsi said, then turned toward the door. "If you need me, I'll be in the lab."

Tev took an apple rancher candy from his pants pocket and untwisted the coiled ends of its wrapper. The brittle crinkle of the unfolding paper was all but inaudible in the busy lab. No one seemed to be paying attention as he placed the tart, hard confection inside his mouth, but when he glanced to his right, he noticed Fabian Stevens looking askance at him.

In a conspiratorial tone, Stevens said, "Whatcha got there?"

"An apple rancher candy," Tev said.

"Where'd you get it?"

Irritated at being interrogated by an enlisted man, Tev said simply, "From Bartholomew."

The engineer made a small sound of acknowledgment, gave a small nod, then continued, "Got any more?"

"Yes," Tev said. "I do." He hoped that the human would not ask for one of his candies. Refusing such a request would likely be perceived by Stevens as a slight.

Stevens stared at Tev for several seconds, as if expecting some further statement. His suspicious manner verged on the impertinent, in Tev's opinion. Finally, he broke eye contact without saying anything more.

Thank goodness he did not ask for a candy, Tev thought with relief. *That might have become awkward.*

Tuning out the chatter of his colleagues in the close quarters of the lab, Tev studied the readings from his tricorder. He was convinced that the Koas pyramid had compressed the planet by enveloping it in a complex series of nested subspace shells. Though the energy fields that surrounded the shrunken planet had showed no signs of instability in repeated scans, Tev was curious to see whether he could cause a controlled disruption of the containment mechanism. *If the code to deactivate the device eludes Bartholomew,* he reasoned, *it would be wise to have another means of releasing the planet from its confinement. At the very least, it would provide me with data to measure against the baseline.*

He stepped over to a companel on the wall and began to initiate a low-power bombardment of tetryons toward the Koas containment shell. While he worked, Gomez and Conlon cycled through another series of passive scans that he had already told them would be ineffectual in discerning the device's true workings. The first officer's unwillingness to accept his professional expertise—to say nothing of Conlon's outright hostility to his recommendations for improving the efficiency of the warp and impulse systems she maintained—baffled him. It was as if they *preferred* to settle for inferior results.

Seeing that the tetryon pulse was charged, he primed an

array of active sensors to probe the inner subspace shells. Satisfied that all was ready, he triggered the tetryon pulse. Instantly, the data from the compression fields changed.

From behind him, Conlon yelled, "The planet's expanding!"

Tev turned and saw that the shimmering cocoon of energy around the planet now swirled with activity. Conlon, Gomez, Stevens, and Haznedl all took half a step back from the planet while keeping their attention on their tricorder screens. "It just enlarged by .0014 percent," Gomez said.

Haznedl added, "Current rate of expansion, if steady, will be sixteen percent per hour." Tev turned back to his companel and decided that he had collected enough data. As he terminated the tetryon pulse, Haznedl continued, "If we don't contain it—" She looked down at her tricorder, her face a portrait of confusion. "It stopped. The compression field is reasserting itself."

"Confirmed," Conlon said. "The planet is returning to its fully compressed state."

Gomez flipped the cover of her tricorder closed. "Okay, folks, I want to know what the hell just happened." Pointing at Stevens, she said, "Get me sensor logs, see if the ship encountered anyth—"

"The expansion was caused by a tetryon pulse," Tev interrupted. Four angry faces looked back at him. "There is no cause for alarm. My experiment confirmed that the compression geometry is fractal in nature, and that the critical threshold for—"

Her eyes shining with fury, Gomez cut in, "Everyone who isn't Tev, get out."

A deadly chill filled the room as Stevens, Haznedl, and Conlon hurried out of the lab to the corridor. Gomez waited in silence while they exited and fixed her enraged glare on Tev.

The door swished shut, and Gomez snapped.

"Does the word 'insubordination' mean anything to you, Tev? How about the phrase 'chain of command'? Or 'standard procedure'?"

"It was a simple experiment," Tev protested. "I assessed the properties of the—"

"That's just it," she said. "You assessed the risks of your little stunt, but you didn't confer with the group, or with me, your *commanding officer.* You can't just—"

"My efforts were successful," he said. "We learned more about its—"

"What part of what I'm saying are you not hearing? I don't give a damn if your test revealed the meaning of life—you ran a potentially disastrous experiment without telling the rest of us what the hell you were doing. Didn't you think we might have been able to help?" Sarcasm crept swiftly into her voice. "Or were you afraid we'd just slow you down? Maybe you think the *da Vinci* crew is just so much dead weight, a millstone Starfleet put around your neck to keep your brilliance in check."

"Quite the contrary," Tev said. "You're all exceptionally competent."

"Well, thank you so much for your stamp of approval," she retorted. "'Exceptionally competent.' That ranks right up there with 'superbly adequate' and 'remarkably acceptable' in the backhanded compliment hall of fame." In two quick steps she put herself nose-to-snout with Tev, thoroughly encroaching on his personal space. "You do *not* work in a vacuum aboard this ship. I know you've made efforts to ingratiate yourself with the crew—"

"As long as I have their respect," Tev cut in, "I don't require their friendship."

"Let me give you the same advice. The next time you step out of line with me, I'll have your ass in front of a court-martial at warp ten. Do you get me?"

Tev was shocked by Gomez's assertion of her absolute authority over him. When he had first come aboard the *da Vinci*, she had seemed indecisive, hesitant, gun-shy after the death of her lover—who also happened to be Tev's immediate predecessor as second officer. But now she was brash, aggressive, confident . . . and, apparently, openly hostile to him.

He tried to suppress a grin, but the more his façade cracked, the angrier Gomez became. Every uptick in her fury widened his smirk and deepened his pity for her, because he knew he could never requite the rawness or intensity of her passion.

Poor, deluded woman, he mused. *She obviously wants me.*

Rounding the corner into the lower-deck corridor, Corsi was surprised to see Stevens, Haznedl, and Conlon loitering several meters away from the lab door. The trio conferred in hushed tones and halted their discussion when they noticed Corsi.

She joined their huddle. "Do I want to know?"

"Gomez is tearing Tev a new orifice," Conlon said.

"Maybe two," Haznedl added.

About time, Corsi decided. Looking at Stevens, she said, "Details?"

"It's been getting worse by the minute."

Straining to hear Gomez's shouts through the acoustically insulated bulkhead, Corsi nodded. "Sounds like she's having fun. What did he do?"

Conlon raised her eyebrow and shook her head in dismay. "You don't want to know."

"That bad, huh?" Noticing the padd in Stevens's hand, she asked, "Unlocked the pyramid's mysteries yet?"

Stevens shook his head. "We don't even know what it's made of."

Corsi had hoped that the research team would have found at least a modicum of physical evidence that she could analyze. In the absence of anything that even remotely resembled proof, she was at a loss for how to carry out her orders to determine whether Araneus or his foes—or both—were lying to the captain.

She was turning back toward the turbolift when the lab door opened. Gomez stepped halfway out and said, "You can come back in now." The foursome in the corridor traded brief expressions of reluctance, then ambled back toward the lab.

Before Corsi had taken more than a few following steps, she heard the swish of turbolift doors opening around the corner, followed by the frantic patter of running footsteps.

Faulwell turned the corner at a fast jog. He waved the padd in his hand toward the group. "Stop! Don't touch the pyramid!"

Gomez moved quickly out into the corridor and intercepted the lumbering cryptographer. "Bart, what's going on?"

"I might know how to find its key code," he said, speaking quickly. "But you have to stop messing with that thing, and we need to brief the captain. Now."

Although the commander was fairly informal in her dealings with her S.C.E. team, she seemed to bristle at the tone Faulwell had just taken with her. "This had better be good, Bart."

"I know who made the pyramid," Faulwell said excitedly. "Trust me, Commander—we're *way* out of our league."

CHAPTER 4

Captain Gold settled in behind his ready-room desk as Gomez and Faulwell walked in behind him. The first officer moved off to one side, giving Faulwell center stage. Uploading data from his padd to the station on Gold's desk, Faulwell said, "The Starfleet historical database was able to match the symbols on the pyramid."

Symbols filled the screen, which was split into two parallel images. On the left was a detail from the pyramid that Araneus had brought aboard. On the right was an image from the archives. Even a cursory examination confirmed their similarity.

"This is from an artifact, an obelisk, that was found by the crew of the Starship *Enterprise* in 2268 on planet FGC-351772 III."

Gomez looked simultaneously amused and skeptical. "That's the planet's name? Bit of a mouthful, isn't it?"

Faulwell shrugged. "Apparently, its official name is still pending. Prime Directive issues." He switched to a wider image of the obelisk. "The device protected the planet from asteroid impacts. The *Enterprise*'s science officer deduced that the symbols on the structure's exterior were from a complex tonal alphabet and served as instructions for using and repairing the device."

Gomez held up a hand to interrupt. "Hold on—*whose* alphabet? You said you knew who built the pyramid."

"I do," Faulwell said. Gesturing toward the screen, he continued, "That's the language of the Preservers."

Gold let out a long, low groan. As far as he was concerned, the Preservers were the working antithesis of the Prime Directive. Though no one knew who they were, where they had come from, or even whether they were even a race unto themselves or some kind of multispecies coalition, the fruits of their labors were well known to Starfleet. In a word, they were meddlers.

Just like that, Gold had a headache.

"Tell me one thing, Faulwell—can you make heads or tails out of those squiggles?"

"Yes, Captain. It'll take a few hours, but—"

Pointing to the door, Gold said, "Get to it." As Faulwell stepped quickly out to the bridge, the captain turned his attention to Gomez. "The Silgov are going to catch up to us any minute, and they don't seem inclined to talk this out."

She thought for a moment. "How do you want to handle it? Run or fight?"

Rising from his chair, he said, "Whichever one gets us to Mu Arae in one piece."

At Narjam's bidding, Maleiras entered the viceroy's inner sanctum aboard the Silgov flagship *Justice Maker*. She stepped cautiously, as if fearful of despoiling hallowed ground. After months confined in the cramped quarters of the *Starlit Wing*, Maleiras felt strangely vulnerable in such wide-open spaces.

Space-time twisted past the wide, wraparound windows on either side of Narjam's home-in-exile. His desk had reconfigured its normally blank surface into a detailed report from Silgos Prime. Judging from his expression, Maleiras concluded that the already bleak situation back home must be growing worse.

"Bad tidings, my lord?"

"Sadly, yes." With a wave of his hand he blanked the desktop and looked up at her, his expression serene once more. "Your message sounded urgent."

"Yes, my lord."

Emerging from behind his desk, he said, "Speak."

"I humbly request your permission to be candid, lord."

Shooting her a wary look, he said, "Granted."

"Forgive my impertinence, lord, but I think we might be pursuing the wrong strategy with regard to the Federation."

His mood quickly grew defensive. "In what way?"

"Rather than make a foe of the Federation, could we not court them as allies instead?"

"Preposterous!" Narjam circled her like a predator. "Their ships are bulky and slow, at least a century behind ours. Such a backward civilization is of no use to us."

Maleiras replied hotly, "I disagree, my liege." She took a moment to rein in her temper. "Their propulsion is unrefined, but their weaponry is formidable. Even a remote civilian outpost was able to overpower my vessel with a single volley. Such armaments would strike terror into the Vekhal."

Passing behind the anxious woman, Narjam asked, "What are you proposing?"

"A trade, my lord. Our propulsion secrets for their armory knowledge. And perhaps an alliance."

"Entrust our fates to an unknown interstellar power? Are you quite mad?"

"The Koas have sought them out in a time of distress—a telling detail. They did not seek refuge with the Danteri, or the Breen, or the Romulans. Why travel so much farther to reach the Federation?"

Halting in his circuit of the room, Narjam seemed to consider that for a moment. Then he shook off the notion like a winter chill. "When we disable the Federation vessel, its weapons will be as available to us as the pyramid." He returned to his desk and sat down. "Our mobility is the only thing that has kept our rebellion from being crushed by the Vekhal. I won't give away our most precious tactical asset to strangers." Calling up a map of Silgos Prime on his desktop, he added, "Once the pyramid is ours, no weapon in the galaxy will be able to stand against us. And our people will be free."

Armed with the complete Koas gene-sequence, Dr. Lense had just finished administering a series of stabilizing agents, painkillers, and tissue-regenerative compounds into Araneus's battered body. Only after she'd determined what its outer carapace was supposed to look like was she able to see that Araneus had, in fact, been terribly burned. Why the stubborn Koas hadn't shared this information with Dr. Safford after being transported aboard Varkala Station, she hadn't a clue.

Through all of her labors, Rennan Konya had sat quietly with Araneus, projecting soothing moods into the patient's central nervous system and alerting Lense when her treatments provoked distress. *Amazing,* she thought. *All these gadgets, and not one as sensitive or as accurate as this security guard.*

The doors swished open and Captain Gold entered sickbay, followed closely by Corsi. The two officers split up and took positions facing each other from either side of Araneus's octopus-like cephalothorax. Gesturing toward the dazed Koas, Gold asked Lense, "He's stable, you said?"

"For the moment," Lense said.

"Wake him up, Doctor," Gold said. "It's life or death for us *and* him, and we're out of time."

Nodding to Konya, Lense instructed, "Carefully, Rennan."

Concentrating behind closed eyes, Konya reached out and placed his fingertips gently against Araneus's head. Seconds later, the Koas's faceted eyes swiveled a small bit, then its voice ushered from its maw like a note from a whispering bassoon. "Captain . . ."

"Araneus," Gold said. "Can you speak?"

Groaning with the effort, Araneus said, "Yes."

Gold nodded to Corsi, who took over the questioning. "We're being pursued by the Silgov," she said. "They claim the pyramid belongs to them."

"Lies," Araneus said.

Lense noted the mutual eye-rolling between the captain and the security chief. Corsi continued, "We think we've identified the writing on the pyramid. Where did your people get it?"

Araneus hesitated. Its eyes shifted from one person in the sickbay to another. Konya, apparently sensing that Corsi was becoming suspicious of the Koas's reluctance, gestured subtly for her to be at ease. The Koas spoke at last. "A visitor. Looked like one of us. An alien, from another star and ages past."

Gold jumped back in. "Who was this alien?"

"Preserver," Araneus said. "Called his people Preservers."

Knowing glances and satisfied nods passed between Gold and Corsi. Meanwhile, Araneus continued. "Said his people made a vow to the Koas six million years ago. Their kind . . . almost gone. But honored their pledge. Kept their promise. Saved my people."

Corsi leaned closer to Araneus. "The Silgov think they can make the pyramid into a weapon."

"No," Araneus said, drawing out the word for several seconds. "Works only once. Pyramid gone when my world is free."

Gold straightened and motioned for Corsi to follow him out of sickbay. Lense watched the pair hurry out, then looked to Konya for a report on Araneus's condition. Before she even had to ask, he reassured her with a careful thumbs-up.

Friendlier than my tricorder, that's for sure, the doctor mused—while wondering if there was any way she could convince Konya to study medicine.

Gold and Corsi exited the turbolift onto the bridge, which was awash in the crimson glow of battle-stations lighting. Moving to his chair, he relieved Piotrowski, who resumed her post at tactical. Corsi situated herself behind the captain's right shoulder. Typically, that would be the first officer's post, but with Gomez and Tev both belowdecks leading the effort to thwart the Silgov attack, Gold was happy to have Corsi there in their stead.

Leaning forward with a cold gleam in his eye, Gold commanded, "Hail the Silgov flagship."

Piotrowski keyed in the transmission and was answered seconds later by a beeping signal on her console. "Viceroy Narjam responding, Captain."

"On-screen."

The delicate features of Narjam appeared on the main viewer. *"You wish to surrender, Captain?"*

"Not quite," Gold said. "But I see now that I might have been hasty in not acknowledging the possibility that your claim of ownership is genuine."

"I see. How do you propose to remedy this slight?"

Denying himself the pleasure of sarcasm or the catharsis of harsh language, Gold said, "A simple parley, Viceroy. To avert unnecessary violence."

"Most sensible, Captain," Narjam said, his smug pretension galling to Gold even from several light-years away.

"If your lordship would be so kind as to indulge my explorer's curiosity," Gold said, "could you share with me the significance of the markings on the pyramid?"

Despite the fact that Narjam had rebuffed a similar request less than an hour ago, Gold hoped that by adopting a more subordinate tone he might induce the Silgov leader to elaborate on his assertion of proprietorship.

The viceroy did not disappoint him.

"Those symbols are part of the Silgov language, Captain," Narjam said. *"Read in sequence, they tell the history of my people."*

Wrinkling his brow in mock confusion, Gold countered, "You told your people's entire history in just twenty-one symbols?" As trick questions went, it wasn't a subtle one. Even a fleeting examination of the pyramid had made it obvious to Gold that there were many dozens of symbols on the pyramid, and he was fairly certain that no two were alike. *Time to see if Narjam can call my bluff,* he thought.

Narjam neither hemmed nor hawed; he simply kept the same vacant look of drab politeness plastered onto his bland, soft-featured face. *"Silgov is a subtle language, Captain. Though it might look to you as if there are only twenty-one symbols, they contain myriad subtle differences, which, read together, lend nuance to the overall inscription."*

Gold turned to Piotrowski and symbolically slashed his fingertips in front of his throat. The dark-haired young woman muted the ship-to-ship channel. Looking at Corsi, Gold saw that she had recognized Narjam's lie, just as he had. "He's never even *seen* that box," he said to her.

"Permission to kick his ass?"

"Granted."

"Think faster, folks," Gomez said to the *da Vinci* personnel who were gathered in the main shuttlebay while donning their specialized environment suits for damage-control duty. "The Silgov are going to start shooting any second now."

"We know their shields are subpar," Stevens said, shimmying into his gear. "If we hit them hard enough—"

"There's too many of them," Hawkins interrupted. "We'd get flanked, then fried."

Powering up her suit, engineer Brenda Phelps said, "Let's just ditch 'em, then."

Security Guard Madeleine Robins shot back, "How? We're in deep space, there's nowhere to hide."

Engineer Chris Turpin piped up. "Maybe we could jury-rig a cloaking device."

Winn Mara laughed out loud. "Sure, and while we're at it, let's reinvent the Tholian Web."

Stevens inspected everyone's suits and repair kits as the debate continued. Lauoc and T'Mandra argued over whether the *da Vinci*'s shields could be reconfigured for metaphasic operation, enabling them to take cover inside a solar mass—until Gomez pointed out that there wasn't a star close enough for the ship to reach before the Silgov would surround them. Rizz and T'Nel from engineering, meanwhile, vetoed several outrageous ideas in a row by security guard Makk Vinx, who then vexed the Bolian man and Vulcan woman by implying that a "tommy gun" was somehow the solution to every problem. Gomez resolved to find out one of these days what a tommy gun was.

Shabalala was growing frustrated. "Can't we spoof their

sensors? Make them think we've got heavy reinforcements?"

"We don't have the faintest idea what their sensor protocols are," Haznedl said. "Unless we learn all about their technology in the next five minutes, I'd say forget about it."

Ken Caitano from security grinned at Gomez. "Guess it's a bit late to say we're sorry, huh?"

Gomez smiled good-naturedly at him. "A diplomatic solution is probably off the table, yes." Looking around at the rest of the damage-control team, she said, "Three minutes, people. We need an idea now."

"Too bad we're not running the other way," Wong said. "They're fast, but in the slipstream we were faster."

Engineer Cade Bennett's face lit up. "Hang on—could we make our own artificial slipstream?"

"Sure," Martina Barre said. "We probably have a few spares in the cargo bay."

From across the shuttlebay came Tev's exasperated sigh. All conversation ceased. The crew turned in unison toward the grouchy Tellarite. Gomez felt her ire rise as if by instinct. Facing him with a withering glare, she said, "Yes, Tev?"

He droned as if he were being asked to address a class of unruly children. "If the Silgov fleet pursues us into the slipstream," Tev said, "the phenomenon's peculiar subspace physics would make their ships exponentially faster than ours."

"We already know they're faster than us," Gomez said. "That isn't helping."

Tev grimaced as a condescending, petulant whimper of annoyance issued from the deepest reaches of his sinus cavity. "Grease under their wheels, Commander," he said. "Lure them into the slipstream at maximum velocity, then collapse our own warp field and let them race past us. They will be several dozen light-years away before they can correct their error."

"Hang on," said gamma-shift operations officer Alexandre Lambdin. "We had to modulate our subspace field harmonics to within a picocochrane to get inside the slipstream. How are we supposed to lure them in unless their warp-field harmonics match up?"

"A trap door," Tev said. "We use our own warp field to create a zone of instability in the slipstream's threshold, fracture it for a split second with a modified phaser discharge, then collapse our warp field before we enter the slipstream."

Transporter Chief Laura Poynter looked dumbfounded by the suggestion. "Would that work?"

"Of course it will work," Tev said. "Provided the rest of you pay attention while I explain . . ."

Listening to Tev hand out duty assignments with arrogant surety, Gomez stifled her surging desire to throw him into the brig. Issuing orders and taking action without obtaining her approval was the very thing for which she had just excoriated him, and now, mere minutes later, he was doing it again.

The fact that Tev could be so casually brilliant irritated Gomez as much as everything else about him. She waited while the Tellarite taskmaster finished giving the crew instructions. When he got to her, he seemed on the verge of delivering another order. No doubt reading her mood from the scowl on her face, he paused, then said in a less confident voice, "With your permission, of course, Commander."

Swallowing her anger, she said calmly, "Sounds like a plan. Let's get to work." She put on her helmet, and the rest of the damage-control team followed suit. Leading them out of the shuttlebay, she silently lamented that fixing Tev's defective understanding of the chain of command was far more complicated than any engineering task for which she had been trained. The brash second officer shouldered past her into the narrow corridor. Watching him move away toward main engineering, she realized that correcting his major mental malfunctions very well might be a task best left to someone else.

A professional.

CHAPTER 5

Alone in the lab, Faulwell compared the symbols on the pyramid in front of him to the ones found more than a century ago on a massive obelisk on a planet dozens of light-years away. He shook his head in frustration. *For all their technological prowess,* he wondered, *why couldn't the Preservers have simplified their system interfaces?* He rotated the pyramid—whose instructions he had deciphered enough to close the artifact, for easier inspection—and followed a string of text that wrapped around its middle section. Its metal surfaces were cold in his hands.

Scribbling on a sheaf of linen-textured paper (which he normally reserved for his letters to Anthony on Starbase 92), he rendered a translation of what he suspected was a formula for calculating the correct time and place at which to deploy the pyramid around Mu Arae. As far as he could tell, the device had only two innate functions—one to put the planet in the box, and another to remove it. Once the pyramid was safely in position, he reasoned, the planet's release would be as easy as entering the expansion sequence.

He was about to conduct a test of his hurried translation,

then stopped himself as his fingertip hovered over the first symbol. *Probably not a good idea to expand this thing inside the ship,* he realized. Then a troubling notion occurred to him. *This has to be deployed in space. Which means I have to be out there to manually enter the code. But what'll happen to* me?

Realizing that his entire plan had just acquired a potentially fatal complication, he gathered up his notes and sprinted out of the lab. Less than a minute later, he was scrambling into sickbay, where the still incapacitated Araneus lay sprawled over most of the main room. Konya, who had seemed asleep, looked up at Faulwell with an alert expression. Sighing, he reached out toward Araneus. "Hang on," Konya said to Faulwell. "I'll try to wake him gently."

Araneus shuddered horribly, and its legs twitched as if they possessed a grotesque life of their own. In a thin and hollow voice, it said, "Who are you?"

"My name is Bart Faulwell. I'm the one trying to decipher the code on the pyramid."

"You can . . . save my people?"

The sad desperation of Araneus's query tugged at Faulwell's sympathies. "I'm trying," he said. "But I need an answer to a question."

"Ask."

"Where and when were you told to unlock the pyramid?"

"Space," Araneus said. "Orbit."

"You'd manually enter the key code while spacewalking?"

"Yes."

Though he dreaded the answer, he asked anyway. "What were you told would happen to you when the planet expanded?"

Long, rasping sounds from inside Araneus's throat preceded his reply. "Did not ask. Not important."

Faulwell's shoulders sagged. Though it was possible that the Preservers had designed the pyramid to expand the planet without harming its courier, it was just as possible that the ancient, inscrutable beings had decided that one casualty was an acceptable collateral loss in exchange for saving a world. It was entirely possible that whoever was sent into orbit to enter the code would not come back.

Before he could brood too long on that bad news, a muffled blast shook the *da Vinci* from the outside, and Piotrowski's voice sounded over the intraship comm: *"All hands to battle stations!"*

Captain Gold shouted to be heard above the rapid sequence of exploding enemy ordnance that hammered the *da Vinci*'s shields. "Tactical! Report!"

"They're too fast, Captain," Piotrowski said. "Our torpedoes can't get a lock!"

"Target an area of effect," Gold ordered. "Spread pattern Echo." Another barrage from the Silgov fleet rattled the ship and dimmed the overhead lights. "Rusconi, drop to impulse!"

Entering the command into the helm, Rusconi confirmed, "Aye, sir. Full impulse." The *da Vinci* lurched out of warp.

Gold felt the wave of apprehension sweep the bridge. "Let's see if the Silgov are as nimble at impulse as they are at warp. Helm, full evasive. Alter course and speed at will."

"Aye, sir," Rusconi said.

As the ship's inertial dampers strained to compensate for its chaotic pitching and rolling, Gold tightened his already white-knuckle grip on the arms of his chair. It amused him to note that his artificial left hand imitated the cosmetic effects of stress perfectly. *Whoever made it thought of everything,* he thought with a wry chuckle.

"Saldok," Gold said to the Benzite ensign seated at ops. "How're we doing with Tev's trapdoor modifications?"

Reviewing the status reports on his console, Saldok said, "Modifications to the forward deflector dish are hampered by the need to keep our shields raised, sir. But Lieutenant Conlon reports we should be ready within a minute or two."

More muffled blasts hit the ship. An alert shrilled from the tactical console. "They're flanking us," Piotrowski said. "Six marks, coming in fast from starboard!"

"Got 'em," Rusconi said as she accelerated into a dizzying corkscrew maneuver that doubled them back toward the majority of their pursuers. She deftly tapped her little finger on a blinking control pad, and the stars blurred on the main viewer. The image sharpened back to normal, and Gold noted that his tactical display showed the Silgov fleet behind them and scrambling to reverse course. *A half-second warp-jump,* Gold noted as Rusconi plotted her next maneuver. Though she couldn't see him, he smiled at her with proud approval. *She's good.*

His moment of elation was short-lived.

"Multiple incoming," Piotrowski declared.

Saldok's webbed fingers slapped commands into his console. "Routing secondary power to shields."

Rusconi piloted the ship through a trifecta of warp jumps, each time evading the brunt of a Silgov barrage by a swiftly decreasing margin. Gold recognized the Silgov's tactic—the *da Vinci* was being herded into a crossfire. It would take the Silgov several minutes to close this noose, but with their superior numbers and greater speed, the capture of the *da Vinci* would be inevitable. Even now, the Silgov's relentless assault was rapidly weakening the shields, one blast at a time.

"Rusconi, Piotrowski, use every dirty trick in the book," Gold said. "Every second counts."

Returning to his chair, Gold listened as the two women plotted their next roll-and-fire counterattack. As Saldok warned of another impending Silgov fusillade, the captain steeled his nerves and waited for the blow to fall.

A conduit exploded in a bulkhead just as Stevens ran past it. Stumbling, he nearly fell, but Ken Caitano reached out and steadied him.

"Easy," Caitano said. "You all right?"

"Fine," Stevens said. "Thanks."

Caitano jogged down the corridor to start repairs on the conduit. Stevens continued toward his own assignment, decoupling the phaser generators and linking the weapons to the warp nacelles' EPS system. Using the phasers as a pinpoint warp-field disruptor was far-fetched, possibly disastrous if the system overloaded, and undeniably ingenious. It sickened Stevens to have to give Tev credit for it.

Inside his pressure suit, the reek of sweat grew stale as he struggled to make minute adjustments in the high-energy system without the benefit of fine motor controls. The gloves of the pressure suit were okay for heavy labor but unsuited to precision work. Tiny wires slipped repeatedly from his grasp.

He was cursing bitterly under his breath as his suit's helmet comm warbled. *"Gomez to Stevens, report."*

"Primary generators decoupled," he said, partly distracted by the fact that he was trying to work and talk at the same time. "Load-balancing the EPS tap now."

Gomez sounded worried. *"How long?"*

"A few more minutes." He swallowed a litany of vulgarities as his gloved finger proved too fat to reach an isolinear chip in a rear control bus.

"We're losing shields," Gomez said. *"Tev's standing by at the warp core. We need that phaser link online now."*

"Working as fast as I can, Commander. Just let me—"

Feedback howled over Stevens's suit's comm as another brutal explosion rocked the *da Vinci*. Inertial dampers overloaded, and he tumbled chaotically and hit the wall. A bulkhead-gray blur of motion rushed toward him, then a dull crush pushed him past his already blurred edge of consciousness.

Ricocheting off the corridor wall, Caitano saw the forward bulkhead of the phaser control bay break loose and pummel Stevens, who collapsed to the deck, pinned beneath the massive chunk of duranium.

Turning toward his Nasat damage-control partner, the young security guard shouted, "Pattie!"

Clicking and whistling in bright, excited tones, P8 Blue scrambled over a tangled mass of ceiling struts that had collapsed into the corridor between them.

Caitano pointed to Stevens. "He's in trouble! Come on!" He sprinted ahead through a growing wall of flames that blocked the door of the phaser control bay. P8 followed close behind him, curling herself and her custom-made pressure suit into a ball as she bounced over the half-blocked threshold. Caitano had found P8's use of pressure gear odd until the Nasat reminded him that her carapace offered her no protection from fire, charged plasma, or radiation. Grabbing the edges of the bulkhead plate, the duo strained together to lift it off Stevens.

At first the ponderous slab refused to budge, then it rose a few centimeters. Burning pain surged deep inside Caitano's trembling arm muscles as he used his foot to slide a loose piece of equipment under the bulkhead, wedging it into place. P8 grabbed Stevens's arms and began pulling him clear.

"Get him to sickbay," Caitano said as he hurdled over the fallen wall section to the open panel where Stevens had been working. "And seal the door on your way out."

P8 started to protest, "Don't be—"

"That's an order."

"I outrank you," P8 said, just before a surge of plasma-fueled fire tumbled her out of the bay, back into the corridor. Apparently no longer interested in arguing with him, P8 sealed the door. Satisfied that this fire would now be contained, Caitano set to work.

Reaching through the narrow panel, he found that his gloved hands were unable to reach the back of the control board to make the final adjustments. He turned away to remove his gloves. A gust of heated air blasted greasy black smoke and aerosolized particles into his faceplate, coating it with an opaque layer of greasy filth. Attempts to wipe it clean proved fruitless. *Great,* he mused sarcastically. *Now I can't even see the things that I can't reach.*

Captain Gold's voice squawked inside his helmet. *"Caitano, Blue says you've taken over for Stevens."*

"Affirmative, sir," he replied while unfastening the seal on his helmet.

"We're about to lose shields and main power, son. It's now or never."

"Hang on, Captain." He pulled off his gloves and felt the

searing heat that now filled the room. "Bringing the link online now." Flinging aside his helmet, the hissing crackle of flames assaulted his eardrums. He pushed his hands back inside the machinery and squinted through the stinging shroud of thickening smoke. His every gasp for breath scorched his throat. Working by touch, he shuffled isolinear chips, removed safety lockouts, and opened the power conduit that would turn the phasers into an extension of the *da Vinci*'s warp-drive system.

The new link throbbed to life.

Caitano pulled his hands free and sealed the maintenance panel. Slapping the comm switch on the wall with his palm, he said, "Caitano to—" A hacking cough interrupted him. "Caitano to bridge! Link online!"

Garbled and muffled by the rising roar of the fire, the captain's reply was inaudible. Caitano turned to try and stumble toward the exit, but a new avalanche of broken deck plating and sparking cables blocked his path. Flames stabbed mercilessly at him from every side. He spun toward the collapsed forward section, hoping to spy a way out, but tripped over Stevens's tool kit. Landing face-first, his chin struck something hard. He gagged as the acrid stench of burning hair filled his nostrils. Panic set in when he realized it was his own hair that was starting to singe.

As the blaze encircled him, he hoped that his efforts had not been in vain.

Their tenacity is remarkable, Maleiras reflected as she watched Coleef pilot the *Starlit Wing* through its frantic pursuit of the Federation vessel *da Vinci*. The small starship lacked the velocity to outrun the Silgov fleet, and despite the power of its weapons it was no match for an entire armada. She had half-expected its commander to surrender once his ship had been overtaken—and she was secretly pleased to have been wrong.

Sesslom—the grime of his repair efforts now scrubbed away, returning him to his normally immaculate self—monitored the primary sensors, as well as the tactical feed from the *Justice Maker*. Looking up from his console, he reported, "The *da Vinci*'s shields are collapsing, my lady."

Alas, all your valiance has been for naught. She acknowledged the report with a nod, then turned toward Coleef. "Bring us about, and fall back half a *tolloc*, in case the *da Vinci* doubles back on its current heading."

"As you command, my lady," Coleef said as she altered course.

Maleiras pondered what attitude Viceroy Narjam might effect when demanding the *da Vinci*'s surrender in a few moments.

Then the diminutive vessel looped around and charged through the center of the Silgov fleet's battle formation. The tactic surprised her. *A suicide run?* Such an end for the *da Vinci* and its crew struck Maleiras as senseless and tragic. Bitter sadness coursed through her. *Have we become the fiends from whom we fled? Are we no better than the Vekhal? Taking what we want and leaving only death in our wake?*

The *da Vinci* fired a burst of its beam weapons, hitting nothing, then leaped into subspace at its best possible speed. *A final, futile gesture,* Maleiras thought. A comm from Narjam on the *Justice Maker* commanded all vessels to pursue and overtake, at maximum velocity. "Engage stardrive," Maleiras said.

The petite, violet-haired pilot keyed in the command.

Space-time itself disintegrated around the *Starlit Wing*.

Coleef clung to her helm console. "Subspatial disruption!"

The sensor station strobed, sparked, then went dark. Sesslom tumbled gracefully from his seat and dove headfirst through the aft hatch to the engineering deck below, no doubt moving to the auxiliary sensor console.

All around the *Starlit Wing*, the rest of the Silgov fleet tumbled erratically, struggling to regain navigational control. Equilibrium stole away from Maleiras as the normal streak of stars in subspace melted into a muddy blur of light.

Realizing that it would take her less time to do what needed to be done than it would to verbalize the orders to Coleef, Maleiras sprang from her seat and reached past the pilot. The chief scout disengaged the stardrive and initiated an energy pulse that was the inverse of the one that had snared them moments earlier.

With a gut-wrenching sensation of arrested motion, the *Starlit Wing* dropped out of subspace. The blur outside the cockpit window vanished and was replaced by a placid vista of stars. Coleef stared ahead, petrified and likely not yet aware that the crisis had passed.

Poking his head up through the aft hatch, an unusually frazzled-looking Sesslom said, "All systems nominal, my lady."

Maleiras moved back to her seat. "Do we have a reading on the rest of the fleet?"

"Negative," Sesslom said. "I believe they are still caught in the disruption. We lost contact with them when we returned to normal space-time."

"Helm, position report."

Coleef blinked a few times, regained her presence of mind, and checked her console. "Coordinates one-eleven-point-seventeen, two twenty-three-point-six, eighty-four-point-zero-one-five." Then she blinked again, in disbelief. "Nine-point-six light-*nokoshav*s from the *da Vinci*, my lady."

Checking the readings herself, Maleiras was stunned to see that they were correct. *Most ingenious,* she mused. Though she had no idea how the *da Vinci* could have hurled her vessel—not to mention the rest of the Silgov fleet—so far from the battle, she had no doubt that the Federation vessel was responsible for their displacement. Both impressed and amused, she couldn't help but smile. *Narjam is wrong to disregard the Federation,* she decided. *They are more powerful and more clever than he realized. Only a fool would make foes of such people.*

Interrupting the chief scout's musings, Coleef asked, "Orders, my lady?" Maleiras looked at the pilot, but did not respond immediately. Coleef added, "Shall I plot a course to regroup with the fleet on its last known heading?"

Maleiras considered that suggestion. She imagined that Viceroy Narjam would be livid. Judging from the distance her own vessel had been thrown, she suspected that the rest of the fleet would likely find itself dozens of light-*nokoshav*s away before it escaped the disruption. There was no longer any chance that it would intercept the Koas pyramid before its deployment inside Federation space.

The *Starlit Wing*, however, was still close enough to try.

"Resume pursuit course," Maleiras said. "Maximum speed."

CHAPTER 6

Corsi watched with a knot in her stomach as Vinx and Lauoc forced open the door to the phaser control bay. The portal slid open slowly, one grinding centimeter at a time. A stench of scorched polymers and pungent smoke reached her nose. She dreaded to look. Ken Caitano had been with her security detail less than a week, having just replaced Frank Powers during the *da Vinci*'s recent visit to Earth. Now she would have to face Agosto Caitano, her most respected mentor at Starfleet Academy, and break the news to him that his daring, bright-eyed son had perished under her supervision.

Vinx scanned the charred compartment with his tricorder. "Nothin' in there but ashes," he said with his trademark nasal accent. Looking back at the unapologetically distraught Corsi, he added softly, "Sorry, doll." Though she had told the Iotian security guard a dozen times to address her as "sir" or "Commander," she was in no mood to mete out a reprimand just now. She stepped into the middle of the blackened room and idly kicked aside a chunk of burned debris.

Never any guarantees in this job, she brooded. She had felt an almost sisterly sense of duty to Caitano when he came aboard, but she had shown him no favoritism. Now she wished she had.

From beneath her feet came an insistent tapping.

"Vinx! Lauoc! Get in here and lift this plate!"

The two guards scrambled into the room and searched for purchase with their fingertips around the sides of the deck panel. It came free with a dry scrape. Chilly gray mist mushroomed out of the space below. Coughing at the bitter, bile-inducing fumes, Corsi took a step back. The plume evaporated to reveal Ken Caitano, smiling from inside his soot-stained damage-control gear. Still clutching a plasma cutter in his hand, he was snuggled against a neatly perforated phaser-coolant intake pipe that had flooded his cramped nook under the floor with frigid coolant fluid.

Chuckling, Corsi flashed the pretzel-posed security guard a relieved grin. "Lying down on the job, Caitano?"

Keying his suit's external comm—which buzzed and crackled badly from the extremes of thermal abuse it had just suffered—he said, "Nice to see you too Commander."

No doubt about it, she thought, *he's Agosto's boy, all right.*

Bart Faulwell drifted in space, his breath close and warm inside his EVA suit, the Koas pyramid clutched in his hands. Several minutes had passed since Poynter had beamed him off the *da Vinci*. He enjoyed the quiet, but the weightlessness was making him queasy, and he felt impotently small floating alone amid the infinite reach of the universe.

The ship had made excellent time to Mu Arae, leaving him barely enough time to decipher the remaining marks on the artifact. As he had suspected, they were instructions, but they had proved so vague as to be all but useless. About the only thing he knew for certain that it said was that it should be deployed in space, within ten light-minutes of the star. Beyond that there was nothing—no formulae to calculate, no cryptic patterns to parse. Just a blessing from the Preservers, and a notation that the pyramid itself would be consumed in the process of releasing Koa.

That last fact provoked a deep pang of regret in Faulwell. He had hoped to study the device afterward, perhaps team up with Abramowitz and write a paper on it for the Daystrom Institute . . . but once the S.C.E.'s good deed for today was complete, this priceless piece of the elusive and enigmatic Preserver culture would be lost forever.

Of course, so might I be, he knew. One detail he'd been unable to glean from repeated readings of the pyramid's symbols was what would happen to the device's courier as the planet expanded.

"*Gold to Faulwell,*" the captain said over the comm. "*The da Vinci has reached station. Proceed when ready.*"

"Aye, Captain." Captain Gold had been concerned that the Silgov might catch up to the ship sooner rather than later, but Araneus was still in no condition to make the spacewalk. Consequently, the decision was made to initiate the release as soon as possible. There had been no shortage of volunteers for the mission—Pattie, Tev, Gomez, Corsi, and most of the ship's security detail had offered to make the spacewalk and enter the commands as given by Faulwell.

Then he had pointed out to the captain that the symbols on the pyramid couldn't be easily described; they had no analogs in any of the crew's native tongues. Admirable though the team's offers were, Faulwell made it clear that he was the only one qualified to enter the code. Of course, he could have recorded a visual guide for someone else, or even observed through a secure visual uplink. For whatever reason, however, no one had chosen to point out those alternatives at the time. Standing in the shuttlebay minutes later, Gold had shaken Faulwell's heavily gloved hand, patted his shoulder, and bid him a simple farewell with the words "Good luck."

Now the heavens yawned around him, endless and cold.

Turning the device slowly in his hands, Faulwell looked for the first symbols of the release sequence. The Preservers had designed their artifact to be triggered by a Koas, whose multilimbed physiology would have made it easy to hold the object while pressing symbols on opposite sides simultaneously. Because he needed both his hands to enter the code sequence, Faulwell held the pyramid steady by tucking it between his knees and doubling over it, into an almost fetal curl.

His fingers hovered unsteadily over the first two symbols. Swallowing nervously, he found his mouth was dry and sour with fear. Straining to sharpen his focus, his eyes felt incapable of blinking and were opened as wide as they could go.

"Faulwell to *da Vinci*. I'm about to begin the sequence."

Committing his hands to the task, he touched the first two symbols and pressed gently down. The two raised markings receded into the metal surface of the pyramid and vanished. Pair upon pair of symbols were reclaimed by the lustrous artifact, until only a final pair of activation markings remained. Faulwell hesitated for only the briefest moment, then finished the sequence. Stillness enveloped him.

Then he began moving.

Stars streaked past, becoming circles. Light and darkness pinwheeled around him, and he was held motionless. Zero gravity gave way to a crushing press of acceleration.

Light flared through the edges of the pyramid. Faulwell let go of it, and it drifted away in what seemed like slow time.

The sides fell open.

Koa began to swell, towering above him, dwarfing him, humbling him as its majesty was resurrected all but beneath his feet. Still the stars spun, and Koa grew, all in eerie silence.

The planet's gravity tugged at him as together they hurtled madly through the void. A whooping holler fountained up from inside his chest, not out of fear, but from sheer exhilaration. Watching the continents resume their shapes on the rapidly turning sphere below, seeing the clouds reborn from a slumbering memory, his prolonged shout of excited alarm matured into gales of joyous laughter.

* * *

It was the most amazing thing Sonya Gomez had ever seen.

One moment, the main viewer had shown only the speckling of stars. Then a planet had appeared, like a suddenly inflated balloon, and sped away.

"Report!" Gomez said. At ops, Saldok checked his readings, but Gomez could tell even from across the bridge that there was more data pouring in than he could possibly be expected to process at once. "Saldok," she added, "track the planet's movement. Joanne, keep a lock on Bart. Tev, monitor—"

Eyes fixed on the aft science station, Tev interrupted, "The gas giants are moving!"

Captain Gold turned toward the main viewer. "On-screen!"

Saldok switched the image on the forward screen while Tev narrated more of his sensor readings. "The erratic orbit of the outer gas giant is changing," Tev said. "Orbital forces are being equalized into a stable ellipse." He adjusted his settings. "The inner gas giant's orbit is shifting outward, to a distance of approximately two AUs." He peeled himself away from the sensor display. Gomez was vaguely amused by the stunned look on his face. "The artifact is completely reshaping this star system," he said in a dazed monotone.

"Saldok," Gold said, "what's Koa doing?"

"Establishing a stable elliptical orbit at a distance of one-point-two AUs, Captain. Orbital velocity slowing . . . planetary rotation stabilizing." The Benzite was trembling—with excitement, Gomez figured, judging from the pitch of his voice—as he tapped in more commands on the ops console. "The gas giants are stabilizing into their new orbits, as well, sir. Orbital profiles normalizing."

For a moment, no one said anything. Around the bridge, faces stared in wonderment at a unique technological marvel. Orbs that normally appeared static in space were being visibly and effortlessly rearranged while the crew watched.

Gomez noticed the dark look that crossed Gold's face. The captain turned slowly toward the tactical officer.

"Piotrowski," he said. "Where's Faulwell?"

* * *

High above Koa, Bart Faulwell glided, arms wide, tears of joy in his eyes. A world, a civilization, had teetered on the precipice of oblivion, and he had helped pull it back from the edge. He knew that the Preservers were the true authors of the miracle, but he couldn't stop looking at his hands.

If I do nothing else with my life, he told himself, *this I can be proud of. This is what being in Starfleet is all about.*

Sweetest of all would be putting these moments into words, inscribing them on paper for Anthony's eyes, sharing them with the one man who knew his soul, in all its imperfection.

Regardless, doubts lingered in his heart.

How can married life be more liberating than this?

Floating in solitude, Faulwell savored the privacy, the breathing room of his life aboard the *da Vinci*. It seemed almost like a paradox—the notion that committing oneself to a single other individual could somehow impart a sense of freedom. When Anthony had made his wink-nudge suggestion of matrimony last week, Faulwell had thought such a notion absurd. Now he wondered whether any of this would seem so grand, so noble, if he didn't have Anthony to share it with.

Envisioning such an empty life filled him with despair.

Before melancholy could close its grip on his heart, he caught sight of a familiar shape: The *da Vinci* cruised gracefully into orbit above him.

Captain Gold's voice was a welcome presence inside the suddenly lonely confines of his pressure suit. *"Faulwell, this is da Vinci, are you all right?"*

"Affirmative, *da Vinci*. I'm okay." He cast one more look down at the planet, then returned his gaze to the ship overhead. "And I'm ready to come home."

Captain Gold waited patiently for the bridge crew—minus Tev, of course—to cease patting Bart Faulwell's shoulders and slapping his back, in gestures that he could tell were equal parts congratulation and relief at Faulwell's safe return. When the cryptographer finally joined him in the center of the bridge, he said, "Sorry to keep you waiting, Captain." Smiling at the beaming faces around him, he added, "I was delayed."

"No need to apologize to me, Faulwell. I just hope Caliph Sicarios hasn't taken umbrage at being left on hold."

Faulwell stumbled over the honorific alone. "Caliph—?"

Gold knew that he shouldn't enjoy watching the man squirm like this, but it was all in good fun. Turning to Piotrowski, he said, "Open the channel."

The image of a sepia-hued Koas appeared on the main viewer. Though it was adorned by a few bejeweled ceremonial vestments, Gold saw that the caliph's true badge of office was its throne. The round, concave perch sat atop an obsidian pillar many meters above a sprawling, web-patterned grid of walkways and gathering areas, within which bustled more than a thousand Koas VIPs.

"Caliph Sicarios, I am Captain David Gold of the Federation Starship *da Vinci*. It has been our pleasure to assist your people in reaching our space. On behalf of the United Federation of Planets, I welcome you in peace."

"Please accept our deepest thanks, Captain," Sicarios said. *"I have already spoken with Science Minister Araneus, and he has told me of the great personal risk you took in coming to our aid. You have honored us with your bravery."*

Gesturing to Faulwell to step forward next to him, Gold said, "Caliph, please permit me to introduce to you Bart Faulwell."

Faulwell made a small bow toward the screen. "Greetings, Caliph Sicarios."

"You are the one who recovered the lost Preserver key."

"Yes, Caliph."

"Koa owes its life to you," Sicarios said. *"My people are forever in your debt."*

"Please, Caliph," Faulwell said. "There is no debt. It was my duty to serve you in your hour of need. Because that is what friends do for one another."

A gentle murmur wound its way through the assembly of Koas dignitaries beneath Sicarios, who waggled its tentacles at them, apparently signaling for silence. *"We are pleased to find that the tales we have heard of the Federation have not been exaggerated."*

That attracted Gold's curiosity. "Tales, Caliph?"

"Yes, Captain," Sicarios said. *"Though your Federation has only begun to reach out into the galaxy, your reputation far precedes you. Travelers speak of an egalitarian meritocracy, a coalition of worlds and peoples who band together by choice rather than by coercion. Some call it a utopian fantasy. Some see it as a threat to old ways and old ideas. But to some, the idea of your Federation . . . is the beginning of hope.*

"No doubt you will find foes aplenty as you push deeper into the galaxy," Sicarios added, *"but I suspect that you also will find more friends and allies than you expect."*

"I hope you're right, Caliph," Gold said.

"Bart Faulwell, please accept our invitation to visit Koa as an honored guest. It is our wish to present you with our world's written petition for membership in your Federation, so that you may carry it in person to your government."

Looking embarrassed, Faulwell said, "I would be honored, Caliph, but such a task should belong to my captain."

Gold placed a hand on Faulwell's shoulder. "Faulwell, I think we can dispense with protocol in this case." Turning toward the screen, he added, "He'll beam down to join you shortly, Caliph."

"Thank you, Captain. Bart Faulwell, we look forward to meeting you."

"Likewise, Caliph."

The channel blinked off, returning the broad, gray-green curve of the planet to the main viewer.

Now it was Gold's turn to slap Faulwell's shoulder. "Well done, Faulwell."

"Thank you, Captain. Permission to go ashore, sir?"

"Granted. Report to the transporter room. Piotrowski—inform Chief Poynter that Faulwell will be beaming down to the Koas capital." Faulwell walked quickly to the turbolift as Piotrowski relayed the order. Gold settled back into his chair and admired Faulwell's handiwork on the main viewer.

A proximity alert chirped on the tactical console.

"Report," Gold said, swiveling his chair.

"One ship," Piotrowski said. "Silgov design, small. Looks like a long-range scout."

Gomez moved to the tactical station and looked over Piotrowski's shoulder. "Any sign of its friends?"

"Negative. It's—" Piotrowski looked up. "It's hailing us."

Gold turned back toward the main viewer. *This should be interesting.* "On-screen."

The Silgov woman was, by almost any human standard, eerily beautiful. Her rich, golden-brown skin was offset by a blue-black mane of intricately coiffed luxurious hair, which swept around her head like a swirling wave. Enormous, almond-shaped, jade-green eyes looked back at Gold with an expression that seemed almost innocent. If he didn't know better, he would have thought she was literally glowing with vitality.

He remembered one of his first lessons from the Academy: *Appearances can be deceiving.*

"*Hail to you, da Vinci. I am Lady Maleiras, of the Silgov scout vessel* Starlit Wing."

"Captain David Gold." After a moment of no one saying anything, he added, "What can I do for you?"

"*I am here unofficially,*" she said. "*My lord viceroy has not authorized the deal I am about to propose.*"

"Excuse me," Gold said, unable to restrain his ire. "Did you just say 'deal'? Weren't your people just shooting at me?"

Frustration tainted Maleiras's expression. "*Please forgive us, Captain. Our fleet represents the last free members of our species. Our homeworld is enslaved, and Viceroy Narjam had hoped that the Koas's pyramid could be made into a weapon— one that we could use to free our people.*"

"It's not that I'm unsympathetic," Gold said, "but I think you can understand why I'm reluctant to trust you."

"*Of course,*" Maleiras said. "*Trust must be earned.*"

"That we can agree on," Gold said.

"*My people must take the first step, but Viceroy Narjam will resist. Now that the Koas pyramid is no more, he will likely lead* our fleet back toward home—to endless futile skirmishes and battles of attrition . . . unless I can convince him to ask the Federation for help."

"We still haven't solved our trust issue, Lady Maleiras. I don't think we're quite ready to discuss foreign aid."

"I'm certain you've noticed the speed of our vessels, Captain. Though our respective technologies might prove incompatible, I would be willing to permit your engineers to study my vessel while we meet in person—if you will permit my vessel to come aboard your own."

"You would let us study your ship? Without restriction?"

"That's what friends would do . . . is it not, Captain?"

Gold lifted an eyebrow. *She monitored our conversation with the Koas,* he realized. *Maybe our reputation has preceded us once again.* "And what do you ask in return?"

"A fresh start," she said. *"And a chance to take the first step toward friendship, on behalf of my people. I believe that we can help each other, Captain. We might be able to aid your mission of exploration. And you could help set my people free."*

Rubbing his chin thoughtfully, Gold said, "If we take this first step together, will Viceroy Narjam follow?"

Maleiras considered that for several long moments. *"I will show him the way,"* she said finally. *"And if he will not listen, I am certain the rest of my people will."*

Gold weighed her words cautiously, balancing the risks against the rewards. Forging an alliance with a civilization in bondage could mire the Federation in a foreign conflict in which it didn't belong, but turning the Silgov away might be the same as imposing a death sentence on an innocent people.

He recalled Sicarios's words: *To some, the idea of your Federation . . . is the beginning of hope.*

"Lady Maleiras, we look forward to welcoming you aboard the *da Vinci*. Signal us for instructions when you're ready to land."

"Thank you, Captain. I look forward to our next step. Maleiras out."

The captain shushed his second-guessing inner voice. Certainly, he might be taking an unadvisable risk. Perhaps this "first step" would lead the Federation into a dead-end diplomatic fiasco, or into a prolonged and bloody quagmire. But Gold chose to be optimistic: If all went well, he would forge two new alliances for the Federation today.

That would be a good day's work, indeed.

ABOUT THE AUTHORS

For more than eight years, **KEVIN DILMORE** was a contributing writer to *Star Trek Communicator*, penning news stories and personality profiles for the bimonthly publication of the Official *Star Trek* Fan Club. On the fiction side of things, his story "The Road to Edos" was published as part of the *Star Trek: New Frontier* anthology *No Limits*. With Dayton Ward, his work includes stories for the *Star Trek: Tales of the Dominion War* and *Star Trek: Constellations* anthologies, the *Star Trek: The Next Generation* novels *A Time to Sow* and *A Time to Harvest*, ten installments of the original eBook series *Star Trek: S.C.E.* and *Star Trek: Corps of Engineers*, the first installment of the *Star Trek: Mere Anarchy* miniseries, and the *Star Trek: Vanguard* novel *Summon the Thunder*. With Mike Sussman, Kevin and Dayton wrote *Age of the Empress: The Rise of Sato I*, a *Star Trek: Enterprise* novel published as part of *Star Trek: Mirror Universe* Volume 1: *Glass Empires*. A graduate of the University of Kansas, Kevin lives in Prairie Village, Kansas, with his wife, Michelle, and their three daughters, and works as a senior writer for Hallmark Cards in Kansas City, Missouri.

ABOUT THE AUTHORS

JOHN S. DREW can now say he's written stories in the worlds of *Star Trek*, *Doctor Who*, and Spider-Man and not just be talking to himself. He is also an audio dramatist, whose works include *Meltdown*, *Star Traders*, *The Justin Case Mysteries*, and his most recent, *The Dome*. You can learn even more about the man than this simple squib offers by directing your browser to www.drewshi.com.

GLENN GREENBERG is an award-winning editor and writer whose work has appeared in numerous fiction anthologies, comic books, lifestyle and news magazines, and on several websites. *The Art of the Deal* marked his return to the *Star Trek* universe after a long absence—he previously developed and wrote the five-issue *Star Trek: Untold Voyages* limited series for Marvel Comics, which chronicled adventures from the second five-year mission of Captain James T. Kirk and his crew aboard the *U.S.S. Enterprise*. Glenn's writing work for Marvel also included stints on such world-famous characters as Spider-Man, the Hulk, Dracula, and the Silver Surfer. As a Marvel editor, he was proudest of having developed the *Star-Lord* limited series written by bestselling science-fiction author Timothy Zahn, as well as the intercompany crossover project, *The Incredible Hulk vs. Superman*. The latter project made Glenn one of the very few Marvel editors in history to edit a project featuring DC Comics's flagship character, Superman. More recently, Glenn has done freelance writing for DC Comics and such magazines as *Smoke* and *Time Out New York*. He currently serves as editor and head writer for *Scholastic News*, a weekly newsmagazine for kids. In 2002, his work on that magazine earned him the prestigious Distinguished Achievement Award from the Association of Educational Publishers. Glenn's sequel to *The Art of the Deal*, titled *The Art of the Comeback*, was published as an eBook in 2007.

GLENN HAUMAN has missed out on being an internet millionaire five times and counting. Some people would have taken a lesson from this. He has fifteen years of experience in publishing, including work for Random House, Simon & Schuster, DC Comics, and Apple Comics, and has also worked as a graphic designer, editor, photo retoucher, CD-ROM producer, story consultant for films, and radio show co-host of *Destinies: The Voice of Science Fiction* on WUSB 90.1 FM at SUNY/Stony Brook. Currently, he's the VP of production at ComicMix, as well as managing the websites GrimJack.com, JonSable.com, MundensBar.com, PeterDavid.net, and BobGreenberger.com, and is the color artist on Mike Grell's *Jon Sable Freelance*. He's also involved in some super-secret schemes at the time of this writing, which by the time you read this will have changed the world, mwah-hah-hah. You can find out more about this and other plans to crush his enemies at www.glennhauman.com and www.comicmix.com.

DAVID MACK is the author of numerous *Star Trek* novels, including the *USA Today* bestseller *A Time to Heal* and its companion volume, *A Time to Kill*. He developed the *Star Trek Vanguard* series with editor Marco Palmieri and wrote its first volume, *Harbinger*, and its third installment, *Reap the Whirlwind*. Mack's other *Star Trek* novels include *Warpath*, *Wildfire*, and *The Sorrows of Empire*. His first non-*Star Trek* book is the *Wolverine* novel *Road of Bones*. Before writing books, Mack cowrote with John J. Ordover the fourth-season *Star Trek: Deep Space Nine* episode "Starship Down" and the story treatment for the series' seventh-season episode "It's Only a Paper Moon." An avid fan of the Canadian progressive-rock trio Rush, Mack has been to all of the band's concert tours since 1982. Mack currently resides in New York City with his wife, Kara. Learn more about him and his work on his official website, www.infinitydog.com.

AARON ROSENBERG is originally from New Jersey and New York. He returned to New York City eight years ago, after stints in New Orleans and Kansas. He has taught college-level English and worked in corporate graphics and book publishing. Aaron has written novels for *StarCraft*, *World of Warcraft*, *Star Trek: Corps of Engineers*, *Exalted*, and *Warhammer*. He also writes educational books and role-playing games. Aaron lives in New York with his wife, their two children, and their cat, all of whom enjoy pestering him while he's writing. He can be found online at www.arosenberg.com.

DAYTON WARD is a software developer, having become a slave to Corporate America after spending eleven years in the U.S. Marine Corps. When asked, he'll tell you that he joined the military soon after high school because he'd grown tired of people telling him what to do all the time. Ask him sometime how well that worked out. In addition to the numerous credits he shares with friend and cowriter Kevin Dilmore, he is the author of the *Star Trek* novel *In the Name of Honor* and the science fiction novels *The Last World War* and *The Genesis Protocol* as well as short stories that have appeared in the first three *Star Trek: Strange New Worlds* anthologies; the Yard Dog Press anthology *Houston, We've Got Bubbas*; *Kansas City Voices* Magazine; and the *Star Trek: New Frontier* anthology *No Limits*. Though he currently lives in Kansas City with wife Michi and daughter Addison, Dayton is a Florida native and still maintains a torrid long-distance romance with his beloved Tampa Bay Buccaneers. Visit him on the web at www.daytonward.com.

CHRISTINA F. YORK keeps her fingers in a lot of pies. She has written SF, fantasy, romance, young adult, and action-adventure, as well as things she wouldn't tell her grandmother about. Besides her own work, she likes playing in other people's sandboxes, as evidenced by her two *Alias* novels, and assorted short fiction, in addition to her forays into the world of

Star Trek. She lives on the Oregon coast with her husband and sometime-collaborator, J. Steven York, where they serve two feline overlords.

J. STEVEN YORK has now officially written enough books and stories that even he's forgotten half of them. There are fuzzy mental references to *Conan, MechWarrior,* and of course, *Star Trek,* plus many others. But he's really sure of nothing except that he lives on the Oregon coast with a small herd of cats and his wife, fellow author Christina F. York. Steve produces a weekly web-comic called "Minions at Work," which can be reached through the web page he shares with Chris, www.yorkwriters.com.